THE
ASTRONOMER
WHO HATED A GOD

For Dee

THE
ASTRONOMER
WHO HATED A GOD

Book Six of the Endurian Universe

JOE BERGERON

Endurian Press

The Astronomer Who Hated a God is a work of fiction. Names, places, and incidents either are products of the author's imagination or are used fictitiously.

Previous Title: *Return of Ronar*

Copyright © 2023 by Joe Bergeron

Cover illustration by Joe Bergeron.

Published by The Endurian Press

www.joebergeron.com

Part One
Asterope

Chapter 1

Flight

Hooves clopped and wheels creaked somewhere in the darkness. Asterope halted, peering along the road where it receded into the starlit night.

A flicker of yellow lamplight bobbed into view around a bend. Asterope padded lightly off the road and concealed herself in an olive grove, looking out from behind a tree, close enough to the road to observe the oxcart as it approached.

Two men rode the cart, both looking stolidly ahead. Their lantern was almost in their faces, dangling from a pole at the front of the cart.

Seeing that, Asterope stepped quietly out from behind the tree, standing in full view as the cart passed her by. Her boldness was inspired by her awareness that the lamp's glare would blind the men to anything more distant than the weak puddle of light it cast on the road. Fearing the darkness, they fought it with a weapon so feeble it could do nothing but hide anything that might actually menace them.

Asterope returned to the road, her bare feet pattering on the paving stones. She turned her back to the retreating wagon and stood waiting for her night vision to recover.

The lamplight had not hampered her vision so much that she lost sight of the spangled light-fog of the Whirlpool. It hung there in the southern sky, enigmatic as ever. The rest of the sky was dotted with a few hundred yellowish stars in familiar patterns.

It had always puzzled her how something that looked as turbulent and dynamic as the Whirlpool could be so static. The spiral arms that swirled out of its soft central bar of light were so kinked and twisted that they should be writhing like the tresses of a Gorgon. Yet they were frozen, changeless and motionless, for all she could tell.

Once, when Asterope was younger, she had found a ring of moonstone and silver lying on the street. Knowing she'd never be allowed to keep and wear such a thing, she'd decided to make another use of it. She pounded the moonstone into a powder, then filed particles of silver into the little glittering pile. These she mixed with goat's milk and egg yolk, brushing the mixture onto a bit of parchment which she'd blackened with lamp soot. Thus had she tried to imitate the organic glow of the Whirlpool, but her painting was only partly successful, and she'd had to discard it, lest it be discovered by her masters.

Asterope was slight and thin, her dark gold hair cropped short by her own hand just hours before. She wore a boy's chiton, a simple piece of cloth wrapped around her torso, concealing little. Her body was straight, even a little angular, though lately her legs and hips had acquired a fullness that she disliked. Her boy disguise was still convincing, or so she hoped.

Of course, even a boy walking abroad at this hour would not necessarily be ignored by anyone who happened to notice him. Although her disguise would not save her from the eyes of men, it might keep her from being recognized as Asterope the runaway slave girl, should her absence be known by now.

The night was completely silent. Even nocturnal insects were subdued in these first cool days of Autumn. She looked over her shoulder. The oxcart had passed from view. The lights of Pantheos were only a weak scattering of yellow points, not unlike the stars in appearance, but far less appealing to her eyes.

The looming black triangle of Olympos, silhouetted against the sky, rose up beyond the city. The starlit snows of the mountain's shoulders ran down its wild flanks in zigzags and broken streaks. A few sparks of red marked the campfires of the pilgrims who were braving the ascent. This was the tail end of the season of pilgrimage; already the heights of the god-mountain were so inhospitable that only the most obsessed dared try the path. Normally the summit was hidden by clouds and mists, but this was one of those rare nights when it stood naked to the heavens. Now the gentle cloak of the night-goddess Nyx was all that hid the secrets of the gods.

Asterope turned her back on the City of All the Gods and walked on, her steps brisk yet wary, her blood burning with the thrill of freedom. With the city's gates behind her, escape was practically assured, barring some phenomenally bad luck.

Her destination was not so assured. She hoped to make her way to Mersinea's wild northlands, a barren, mysterious area oppressed by the nearness of Darteharn, which lay still farther to the north. That part of Mersinea was at or beyond the limits of any real knowledge she had. She had heard that in the haunted, rocky north lived witches and hermitic wizards who might be convinced to take her in as a student or apprentice. It was a land where heroes made their reputations, aided or opposed by the many Gorgons, Cyclopses, and other monsters who were said to infest it.

Whatever else it might be, it was a land sparsely inhabited, which meant that she might be able to live there free of pursuit or persecution, free of drudgery—free, above all, of ignorance, and worse still, of ignorance under the guise of learning.

She reached a fork in the road, the parting marked by a pillar bearing a statue of Hermes, to judge by its silhouette with winged helmet and caduceus. Asterope turned toward the west, avoiding the south branch of the road which led to the port. The fastest, surest escape from Mersinea was by sea, but she had no money to pay the fare, no excuse to be traveling alone, nor any desire to put herself at the mercy of seamen. Lacking a winged horse or flying sandals, she must make her way on foot and in secret. It was well known that the gods bestowed such magical favors on men alone, and then only rarely.

Asterope knew little of other lands. She had once glimpsed visitors from the country called Thunderbird— rough-talking men dressed in trousers like Persians, speaking her language with a laughably barbaric accent. Their country lay to the south, across the waves of Aegeos. If populated solely by such strutting, unshaven oafs as she had seen, it might well be worse than Mersinea's northern wastes.

Asterope stole along the road, glancing up at the stars from time to time, alert to any sound or movement. She found herself thinking of the gods, reviewing the stories she had heard, searching for one in which a god or goddess had actually helped any female, as opposed to punishing or pursuing her. She could think of no such example. Arachne was now a spider. Atalanta had been outdone by a man given the gift of golden apples. Even Persephone, daughter of a goddess, had been carried off and raped by a god. No mortal woman had ever been equipped with magical weapons, nor whisked from danger by divine intervention, except perhaps as Callisto had been: turned into a beast and flung into the heavens, where she was said to glitter in the sky of Gaia, of Earth, a sky far removed from this sky of Colibdis.

Her whisper was a hiss in the night. "Why can't you gods respect my search for freedom? Why can't you look upon me as a hero too? But I don't expect so much of you. Can't you at least show me which road I must take?"

The night remained silent. Olympos, now on her right, towered in the darkness, mute as ever.

The road grew pale before her. Now she could make out pebbles in addition to the larger stones. A light was rising behind her...not the flickering light of torches or lamps, but a steady, creamy glow. Her shadow stretched over the dusty road before her.

Could it be...?

Her breath caught in her throat as she spun around, heart pounding.

But all she saw was the Greater Moon, shield of Selene, lifting itself over the horizon.

Asterope contracted her face into a frown. She was angry—angry that the gods should trick her this way, contriving to produce the Greater Moon just as she'd been awaiting (for she had been awaiting it, despite everything she'd told herself to the contrary) the appearance of a god.

But if she'd been thinking, she would have anticipated moonrise at about this time. She'd long since learned the ways of the Greater Moon's movements and phases through observation, though they seemed divinely unpredictable to everyone else she knew.

Tonight the ivory-colored disk appeared lopsided, not perfectly round as it had a few nights before. Each night hence it would appear even more distorted, until at last it shrank again to a crescent, disappeared, and was reborn in the evening sky, thin as a nail-paring.

A simple cycle. She failed to understand why everyone else insisted on investing it with such obscure significance. Often she'd had to suppress her disdain when men made snickering references to the phases of the Greater Moon as though they were some goddess-driven phenomenon which ruled their lives.

The moon rose higher, gradually shedding its superficial look of warmth and assuming its natural silvery hue.

Asterope turned away and could not restrain a gasp of dismay at the sight of the figure approaching her. When she saw it was a woman, if a remarkably tall one, Asterope felt slightly relieved, but was still not at ease. The woman had dark hair, coils of which escaped from beneath a tall hat— no, it was a war helmet, of all things. The folds of her stately garments hardly stirred as she floated along. Her face, pale and stern, was fixed on Asterope's.

Asterope's knees began to quake. Was this Selene? Artemis? She forced herself to look into the eyes of the goddess, and gasped again. Asterope's eyes were also grey, but surely they lacked the celestial depth and luminosity of these dusk-grey jewels which regarded her with such gravity.

"Athene!" breathed Asterope, unable to say more.

A haze of unreality stole over her as the goddess glided up, towering over her, her head seemingly set among the stars. Athene's arm came down to rest upon Asterope's shoulders, gently turning her to face back the way she had come. The touch of the goddess did nothing to dispel the dreamlike nature of the encounter.

Asterope found herself half walking, half stumbling, back up the road. Her heart soared, ablaze with hope. Somehow, despite her doubts and her insolence, she had earned, or at least received, the patronage of this great goddess. A huge smile lit her face. She glanced up at Athene. Never before had she seen a female face which was so fully informed with dignity, with confidence, with strength.

They approached the pillar, with Hermes perched atop it, which marked the fork in the road. Evidently the goddess meant her to travel by sea after all, to go down to the docks and somehow win passage to a distant land. Asterope squared her jaw. The prospect of the sea voyage was still unappealing, but with the help of Athene she had no doubt that she could accomplish it.

Yet when they came to the fork, they turned not right, but left, back toward the city. Asterope's confidence fled at once, replaced by puzzlement and consternation. Could there be some secret side-path by which Athene meant to lead her? Could she intend to bring her to the summit of Olympos, perhaps to confer with the gods? In any event, she must not reenter the walls of Pantheos! That would mean her end.

Yet as they went along the way, Athene's eyes remained locked straight ahead. Asterope became convinced that the goddess did indeed mean to return her to the city. To betray her!

Asterope drew a breath to speak, but it caught in her throat, and she remained silent. But that was not acceptable. She must not allow herself to be led back passively as a lamb. Gathering all her wits and courage, she tried again, managing to speak in a husky voice. "Goddess. Mistress Athene. Please, don't take me back to captivity."

The answer sighed into her ear from some remote place. "Hush, child. Do not dispute the wisdom of the gods."

Do not dispute the wisdom of the gods. Asterope found herself reviewing all she knew of divine folly, and it was quite a lot. Athene herself, her vanity offended by her own puckered cheeks as she played a flute…Athene, reacting with petulant retribution when a mortal dared best her at embroidery…the wisdom of the gods! It was all she could do not to burst out in hysterical laughter.

What could be behind this? The free men of Pantheos believed that some people were slaves by birth and by nature, unfit to live any other life. Could this also be the view of Athene?

With that thought, Asterope began to struggle. The arm which had guided her so gently became, suddenly, an inexorable restraint, a force she could never hope to shrug off. It was a near-weightless yoke, but one which nevertheless swept her along like a tide.

Still she struggled, flinging herself about, trying to drop down, twisting, jerking. In her growing anger and desperation she even dared conceive that she should pinch Pallas Athene. Her fingers found the flesh of Athene's arm, but found no purchase. The flesh of the goddess did not yield to her attack, being cool and firm as marble. Athene

9

glanced at her, but made no other response to this provocation.

The walls of the city loomed larger. A noisy group of torch-bearing sailors walked through the gate, coming their way. When they were closer Asterope redoubled her efforts to escape, writhing in that relentless grip. "Help me!" she shouted, her eyes wide with terror.

The sailors looked at her with consternation. "What's wrong with that child?" said one.

"She's possessed by the gods. See how she jerks and twitches. We'd best pass her by."

They sidled past her, not resuming their raucous talk until they were well down the road.

The men could not see the goddess! While she was digesting this, she also realized, to her chagrin, that her boy disguise had not been as effective as she'd hoped.

The city gate stood open, unguarded as usual. Asterope staggered through and was forced along the near-empty streets. The Agora stood deserted. The houses in the residential districts presented only blank, windowless walls to the street. Except around the temples of certain gods, the streets were almost deserted after dark. In her struggles to escape, Asterope barely noticed the few people who lurked in alleys or conversed in small furtive groups. These seemed happy enough to keep their distance from her.

"Let me go! Let me go! You witch, let me go! Crawl back into your father's head, you horrible cow!" Her cries and curses emerged of their own volition now, unconsidered and vehement. She was wild, her chiton soaked with sweat, as she spat, bit, and scratched at those unyielding limbs. She kicked at the greaves on the goddess's shins, and jabbed her elbow into a cuirass that would no doubt turn anything less than a thunderbolt of Zeus. Her mind flailed as desperately as her body, searching for some escape, trying to interpret this as something other than a betrayal. Perhaps Athene was bringing her to some secret place within the city, someplace where runaway slaves were sheltered and given guidance! Perhaps she meant to grant her sanctuary within the inviolable inner sanctum of her own temple! But no—the farther they went, the more certain she was that the great goddess was doing nothing more than dragging her back to the house of her master.

All too soon that house loomed before her. Catlike screeches of rage erupted from her throat. She struggled as though she might leave her severed hands bleeding in the goddess's grip if only she could pull away and run free.

The door swung open. Asterope was thrust in. The door slammed shut. Asterope turned at once to claw at the door, but was interrupted by a strident cry from behind her. She looked back wildly over her shoulder. There at the end of the entry hall stood Euratia, her mistress, staring at her in astonishment.

"Asterope! Where have you been! What are you doing?" she shrieked, stalking toward her like some great minatory bird. "Your hair! Child, what have you done to your hair! Little fool, don't you know your hair was the best thing about you?"

Euratia's hand lashed out and smacked Asterope's cheek, an act so natural and unconsidered that Asterope had seen no hint of warning on her mistress's face. The hand snaked out again and caught her by the elbow, dragging her down the corridor and into the courtyard. Euratia's grip was not so strong as Athene's, but it was more cruel, for Athene did not keep her nails so long and sharp.

Now the voice was lower, more venomous. "I don't know what you've been about tonight, girl. But you'll learn once again that this household is not run to suit your desires. First I'll get you out of those ridiculous boy's clothes, and then—"

A male voice interrupted, crying peremptorily from the *andron*, the main dining hall at the other end of the courtyard.

"Euratia! My guests and I need some attention in here. Send in that girl! You have found her by now, haven't you?"

Euratia's grip grew still tighter. She swung Asterope around to face her, staring down into her eyes. "Get in there and serve your master. Wear the clothing of a boy; go in dirty and wild as a little maenad. Perhaps you'll add to the entertainment. But don't think this is forgotten. You'll get your lesson later."

Asterope returned the woman's gaze with as much insolence as she could muster, though she knew it would only worsen her plight. In truth, she only managed to summon up a fraction of her usual level of rebellion. The abuses of Euratia were old and familiar, running down the same paths day after day, turn after turn. But to be abused and betrayed by Pallas Athene...that was something new, something that must be absorbed, pondered, evaluated.

Euratia released her grip. Asterope found herself standing free for what seemed like the first time in weeks. Rubbing her arm, she turned and ran into the dining hall.

Chapter 2

Symposium

Asterope stepped through the portal, entering a lamp-lit world of laughter and talk suffused with the odor of food. A professional flute-girl and a harp-girl sat in a corner, reeling out a meandering thread of melody that did not threaten to take up too much of anyone's attention.

A dozen or so men—no women, of course—sprawled on couches around the room. Most were the merchants who were her master's usual cronies, along with a scattering of savants and philosophers to provide some basis for calling such a party a "symposium". The merchants were well-fed men wrapped in their finest chitons, their bodies washed and perfumed, garlands of flowers around their necks and atop their heads. The savants affected a more ascetic mien, but they ate at least as heartily as anyone else.

Each man was attended by his own body-slave. The household slaves, at least another dozen, moved about as unobtrusively as possible, lading the small tables beside each couch with plates of fish, bread and soups, shellfish, figs, olive oil, and other dishes more elaborate and abundant than the family's daily fare. Asterope noticed shining, greasy coils of the sea medusa, that maritime monstrosity which was the current gustatory rage of the people of Pantheos, and something more surprising: large platters of a heavier, red meat—beef, probably, something not often seen in Mersinea.

Two of the guests were of a different mold than the rest. Their odd dress was literally outlandish, consisting of blue trousers, carefully tailored shirts, high leather boots, and vests studded with silver ornaments. Even more odd, inexplicably so for men who were indoors, both wore wide-brimmed felt hats with tall crowns. They were so heavily dressed that their only exposed skin was that of their hands and faces. One man, the darker of the two, wore a sweeping, unforgettable mustache, while the other, a light-haired, blue-eyed man, simply hadn't shaved as recently as he should have. Though both wore affable expressions, Asterope detected a hint of uncertainty or bemusement on their faces. They clung to their couches as though they expected to be flipped off, and ate awkwardly from the little tables. Their eyes met hers, showing puzzlement, but none of the automatic dismissal she expected from free men.

"I say, Heraminus!" cried one of the guests at the sight of her. It was Pedemus, the parasite. "Weren't you expecting a *female* slave?"

Heraminus, her master, glanced at her, looked away, then snapped back his gaze to stare at her in confusion and uncertainty.

"Why, so I was," he said slowly. "But you know, the girl's parentage is uncertain. Perhaps she bears the blood of Hermaphroditus."

The others roared in laughter at this, except for the two oddly dressed strangers, who didn't appear to understand the reference.

Asterope returned her master's quizzical gaze with level calm. Her sense of identity was certainly not based on her sex. If he hoped to sting her, he'd have to find some dearer topic.

Not that he was incapable of finding one.

"Asterope has always been a little uncertain about who she is. Girl or boy. Master or slave. She's even been known to attempt to read and write, as though she has accounts to keep or philosophies to pen."

Now Asterope's cheeks did redden a shade. She endured more laughter, except again from the two men dressed in heavy dark clothing, who actually seemed to have the grace to be uncomfortable at this mockery.

"Of course, we soon put a stop to that," said Heraminus.

Or so you think, dear master, thought Asterope.

The head steward—another slave of course—sidled up to her and whispered, "Well, girl, get to work. You were not summoned here to stand staring like some strengthless shade."

Asterope started forward, her servant's instincts taking over. She hesitated for one last hiss from the steward: "And don't think I missed what you tried to do tonight—although I don't know what could have brought you back. Not fear, certainly; I know you too well for that."

Asterope kept her face impassive as she made herself useful among the guests. Curious, she gravitated toward the two foreigners (who oddly seemed to be without their personal slaves), performing all the little tasks that made their feasting as effortless as possible. She tended their plates, adding to those dishes they seemed to find most palatable, mainly the beef, and brought basins of water in which she washed their hands. The foreigners blushed at these personal attentions, and seemed almost abashed.

Asterope found this hugely amusing, though she refrained from smiling. She had found the only two men in the room likely to notice her efforts on their behalf, and she did not wish to embarrass them.

She broke off large pieces of bread and set them on the little tables. The mustached man absently picked his up and went to bite off a piece. Asterope's small hand flickered out and halted him. He looked up at her, puzzled.

"No, sir," she said in a small voice. "That is not for eating. It is for the wiping of the hands."

The stranger's gaze remained puzzled. Could it be that this man did not speak the language of Mersinea? Asterope found herself at a loss.

But the light-haired man leaned over and muttered something to his companion, using a language Asterope had never heard. The first man looked at the bread in surprise.

Asterope touched him lightly and directed his gaze toward a couch where another of the guests was wiping greasy fingers on his own piece of bread.

Suddenly the stranger smiled up at her, startling her. He vigorously scrubbed his fingers on the bread until it crumbled away. "Thank you," he said. Apparently he did have a few words of Mersinean, though his accent was atrocious.

Now it was Asterope's turn to blush and lower her eyes. Had she ever been thanked for correcting a man before?

"We now present our second course of the evening," announced the steward.

At that signal, Asterope busied herself at removing the serving tables. She brought more water and again washed the rugged, calloused hands of the outlanders. They had the hands of slaves, of manual laborers, not the soft, carefully maintained hands of her master and his cronies. How strange that such ruffians reclined in this room as honored guests.

She returned to the kitchen and reset the little tables with honeyed breads, fruits, and nuts. When she carried them back out into the hall she found that still more wreaths of flowers had been passed around. The two strangers were gingerly settling masses of blue air-lilies on their extravagant hats, their expressions making it plain that they had never done such a thing before, and cared little for it now. They nibbled at the treats and sweetmeats, glancing around a little morosely. The mustached man appeared especially ill-at-ease, as he probably understood little of the fast-paced conversation going on around him.

Presently Heraminus called for the wine to be brought out, to the cheers of his cronies. Again Asterope helped remove the serving tables, returning with tiny tripods which carried various drinking vessels. Other slaves brought out great mixing bowls in which they diluted the various wines of Mersinea with large quantities of water. Their heady scents rose to fill the room.

Heraminus filled his bowl and raised it up. "My friends! Let us drink to our most honored guests, the gentlemen Stannard and Thayne from the land of Thunderbird. May the agreement we have reached enrich and enhance us all."

This was met with general approbation. The two men in question grinned and raised their cups.

Of course, so that's who and what they were! Thunderbirds. Americans!

Heraminus then raised toasts to the gods of Olympos, and to the Heroes, past and present.

Asterope watched as the Americans put cup to lip. They swallowed, but she caught their quick grimaces. Here were men of strange tastes indeed.

After the first round of drinking, Heraminus stood again and proclaimed, "And now let us begin our symposium. We must of course select a man of proper learning and erudition to act as Symposiarch. Being mortal, such judgments lie beyond our abilities, so as always we ask the Lady of Fortune, Tyche, to make our choice. Bring out the dice!"

The box of dice was passed around, with each man taking a roll. As usual, Tyche selected the obnoxious Pedemus to lead the assembly. He stood up and swept his odious leer over his audience.

"I thank you, fellow citizens and honored guests. As always, it's heartwarming to accept your acknowledgment of my intellectual merits and outstanding wit."

For that statement, which was identical to the one he used to open almost every symposium, he received the usual catcalls:

"In choosing you, Pedemus, Tyche shows herself a goddess of charity as well as chance!"

"Pedemus, we hope that by your appointment, which requires that you speak often, some of the wine may be spared for us!"

"A futile hope—it's well known that Pedemus can drink and speak at the same time."

Pedemus, his small, round head bobbing atop his long neck, assumed a look of mock hurt.

"Again, I thank you for your confidence in me," he said with exaggerated asperity. "Now let us proceed."

He poured libations and threw a few pellets of incense into the hearth in the corner of the hall. He then led the men in singing an absurd little hymn to the god of wine. The two Americans glanced around during this, trying to hide their perplexity.

"And now," said Pedemus, "Let us prove ourselves men of good breeding and advanced learning by trading in words of wisdom, before we get down to the serious business of drinking."

More laughter, quite a bit of it for such a stale remark, indicated that a fair amount of drinking had taken place already.

"Heraminus, if you may do so without compromising your professional secrets, will you reveal the bargain you have struck with our visitors from Thunderbird?" asked one of the guests.

Heraminus stood. "Certainly. My new trading partners and I have no secrets. In short, we intend a mutually profitable exchange of goods, in which each will provide those products unique to his native land." He looked around, beaming, and sat down.

Pedemus applauded politely. "Oh, Heraminus, you master orator. Your statement is the very essence of clarity."

The blond American, Thayne, stirred and pulled himself to his feet. Looking rather self-conscious, he announced in rough, clumsy Mersinean, "Stannard and I bring gifts for Heraminus, to mark our agreement. We give them now, with his friends to watch?"

"By all means," said Pedemus.

At Thayne's signal a slave brought in two packages, one small and one large. Both were wrapped in real paper which was colored red, white, and blue. Thayne walked over to join Heraminus, who stood and examined the packages as they were set before him.

"For you and your family, Heraminus."

Heraminus ran his hands over the packages and cast a quizzical smile at Thayne.

"The paper will come off," said Thayne.

"Ah." Heraminus sat down. With precise, cautious motions of his nails, he cut the drops of wax that sealed the first package, then unfolded the paper and set it carefully aside. A slave plucked it up and carried it out of the room.

Revealed were two bolts of heavy woven fabric, one deep blue, the other a barbaric pattern of red and black checks and lines, plus a parcel of soft folded leather.

"This cloth makes most of our clothing," said Thayne, indicating the blue and red fabrics. "It is woven from cotton. If you and your women like it, maybe we supply more in a future trade agreement." He tilted his head, obviously aware of his clumsy phrasing.

"Yes indeed, perhaps," said Heraminus, a trifle flatly. His attention quickly turned to the smaller package. "May I?"

"Of course. For you."

Heraminus undid the wrappings with the same care he'd used before. This time his face showed no sign of disappointment at what lay revealed.

Two large books lay on the table. They were not scrolls, but stacks of rectangular leaves bound along one edge, after the usual style of Thunderbird. The magnificent leather bindings were stamped and worked with gold. They were finer than any book or scroll in Heraminus's collection, whether of Thunderbird origin or not.

Asterope realized she was staring at the books with an unseemly avidity which she quickly replaced with a look of indifference.

"The first book is a new edition of Plato's *Republic*," said Thayne. "Plato was a famous philosopher in what we call Greece's Golden Age. We also have an English edition...but we thought you here in Mersinea would prefer original Greek. You know few books find their way over from Earth. We're lucky to have this—you can thank our gymnasium's astronomy teacher for bringing it over."

The eyes of Heraminus and his guests practically bugged out at this. Asterope could understand why. Even she had heard rumors of the famed philosophers of Greece's latter days. Yes, she had heard of them—but she, and indeed no one on their world of Colibdis, had ever had a chance to read their works. The forefathers of the Mersineans had crossed over from Earth, from Achaea, long before Plato and his contemporaries had lived. Now they could learn some of the wisdom of the Achaean peoples who had stayed behind to dwell in the land which had eventually become known as Hellas or Greece. Every literate man of Mersinea would want a copy of this new book.

Every literate *man*.

But interesting as this was, to Asterope it took second place to the revelation that someone in "barbaric" Thunderbird was studying astronomy. Her interest in these men intensified still further. Why did Thayne refer to his native language as "English" rather than American?

"The second book," continued Thayne, "is our main religious book, called the Bible. I'm afraid it's in English.

We have no demand for a translation. Maybe it will help you to learn English, if you want."

This was a matter of some interest as well. Asterope knew nothing of the religions of Thunderbird. The fact that the book was in the language of Thunderbird made it even more intriguing.

"Let the wine be mixed," said Heraminus warmly. "Let the cups be passed, in honor of Stannard and Thayne, our two most generous and honored guests."

Again Asterope was busied with the mixing and serving. As before, she paid special heed to the needs of the two Thunderbirds, though neither seemed fond of the wines set before them. They sniffed at them suspiciously and only sipped. Could they possibly suspect they were poisoned? Stannard spoke to Thayne in what must be English, producing words that sounded like blocks of wood. Thayne nodded and laughed, his blue eyes twinkling, then noticed Asterope's eyes on him. Before she could drop her gaze he smiled at her and whispered, "Tastes like pine tar."

Asterope allowed herself only the most fleeting smile in response before she resumed her duties. Resin. Yes, resin was added to all Mersinean wines. Were things otherwise in Thunderbird?

After plenty of drinking and the passing out of still more flowers, Pedemus stood up to resume his duties as Symposiarch.

"My friends, tonight the gods have favored us with the presence of the sagacious Thales of the Theological Gymnasium. In fact, it seems we are always favored by his presence. That the gods favor us with such unerring consistency can only be considered one of the many wonders which Thales studies and, we hope, understands."

"How then do we explain your own constant presence?" called out some heckler. "I would not risk a thunderbolt by calling it an act of the gods."

Thales came to his feet through the ensuing laughter. "Thank you, Pedemus. I myself take no exception to your ubiquity, since you at least have the wisdom to ask me to speak, exposing our friends here to the risk of learning something new. Tonight I would like to give my explanation of the ever-changing shape of the Greater Moon."

Asterope pricked up her ears at that. She kept an eye and an ear cocked toward Thales as she continued her labors.

"Now, we all know that the Greater Moon is an emblem and an artifact of Selene, or of Artemis, if there's any real distinction to be made between the two. And we know that these great goddesses use the changing shape of the moon as a symbol of all that is changeable and unstable in woman, as well as a convenient timer of the cycles of a woman's body. Though I'm sure we've all been vexed by trying to remember: has it been two full moonturns since our wife's last red days, or only one? It's typically feminine that each of their cycles equals two of the moon's. To do it otherwise would be too straightforward."

This produced a certain amount of half-drunken laughter.

"However, the divine purpose behind the changing shape does not require that the mechanism used to accomplish it must be beyond our comprehension. And in this case, that mechanism can be illustrated using an object dear to all our hearts."

Thales lifted his drinking cup, one of Heraminus's prized favorites, silver with a duller, darker lining of lead. He drained it off in one quick gulp and turned it so that its round bottom was presented to his audience.

"Imagine that here you see the Greater Moon in its full phase. I turn it thus:"

He rotated it about twenty degrees. "Here you see the situation the night after the full moon. As so, and so, and so..." He continued to turn the cup until it was presented to them from the side, half a circle. "Four nights later, we see the last quarter phase. The goddess continues to turn the moon..." Now the inner, darker interior of the cup came into sight, with the silver outer surface appearing as a narrowing crescent. "We arrive at the new phase, in which we see only the dark interior of the cup. The rotation continues, and we eventually return to the original condition of fullness, sixteen days after the last."

"Are you saying that the Greater Moon is nothing more than the drinking cup of Artemis?" asked one of the guests.

Thales shrugged his shoulders. "Why not? Artemis is a virginal goddess, but not one who eschews drink."

Asterope sneered to herself. This was typical thinking for the "sages" of Pantheos. Asterope had often watched the Greater Moon. She had seen that it did not rotate, for the markings on its surface always remained the same. Moreover, she had sometimes seen the darkened portions of the moon dimly aglow with a bluish light, enough to show that it always had a circular outline, not the ever-changing one implied by Thales's cup model.

But it would be beneath the dignity of Thales and those like him to go out and actually look at what he was trying to understand. This was the same man who had logically deduced that women must have a lesser number of teeth than men. He had never bothered to count them. Asterope had counted her own; the number was the same. So despite her ignorance and her lack of education, in this at least, she was wiser than Thales.

"Very good, Thales," said Pedemus. He turned his gaze toward the Thunderbirds. "My friends, what is the status of Selenitic studies in your homeland?" He could not quite keep the smugness off his face. Plainly he expected to hear that there were none.

Yet Thayne had no trouble giving an answer. "That sort of thing is all the rage in Thunderbird these days. There is a man in Two Suns City. That teacher I mentioned. The one who brought the book. He was one of the last men to cross through the Portal from Earth. You may have heard of him. His name is Leonard Ronar."

The Mersineans looked around and muttered to each other, but there was no recognition among them.

"Some call him Greylock. He played a part in the war against Namirnakh."

Certainly most of the men remembered that event. Even Asterope had heard how the fleet of Darteharn, black against the sapphire waters of Aegeos, had sailed past their harbor. Whether it was by the intervention of Zeus or simply the intention of the enemy, the fleet had never touched the Mersinean shore. Not until it was long past did the terror of the people abate. That was a good ten or fifteen turns ago, before Asterope's birth.

"I do believe I've heard of him," said Heraminus. "A helper to the Sorcerer, was he not?"

"Among other things. It turns out he was an astronomer back in Arizona. He started a school of astronomy at our gymnasium and he built huge spyglasses to study the stars. They're called telescopes."

"Tele-skopos..." muttered Thales thoughtfully. "Far seer."

"Now, I don't keep up with all their doings. It all sounds crazy to me. But I do know Ronar insists that the Silver One, the Greater Moon, is just a great big rock."

Pedemus burst out laughing. "A rock! How absurd! And what keeps this Cyclopean boulder poised in the heavens, ever circling, never crashing to the ground?"

"I don't know the answer to that," said Thayne. "But if you ever meet Ronar, I wouldn't put the question to him in that tone of voice. I've met the man. He wouldn't care for it."

By now Asterope was almost beside herself, skin tingling, eyes wide and fixed. She was so full of tension, so consumed by bliss, that she had to lock her knees to keep from sagging to the ground. A school of Astronomy! Instruments of far seeing! The study of the stars! Could this be the reason Athene had forced her back here, so she would learn of the existence of this place? If so, then surely Athene was her patron goddess, and Asterope must beg forgiveness for all her doubts. But that could wait until later.

"But surely this idea does not explain the changing form of the Greater Moon as elegantly as does my theory," complained Thales.

Asterope could never explain why she did it. Walking as boldly as a goddess, she plucked a round fruit from a bowl and strode up to Thales on his couch. She held it before his face, a flickering oil lamp lighting it from behind.

"Will you have a pomegranate, sir? It is a fine one. See how the lamp light shines upon its smooth surface." She brought it around to the side, so that it was half lit by the lamp. "You see, the light reveals scarcely a blemish on its surface." She moved it behind the flame, so that it was fully illuminated. "It appears as round and full as the Greater Moon itself, does it not?" She brought it to the other side, then, smiling, laid it before Thales on his table.

"Girl," said Thales querulously.

"Asterope..." growled Heraminus.

The voice of Pedemus suddenly piped up, "That is all very interesting, my friends," he said, looking at the Americans. "But what does this Ronar say about the Lesser Moon?"

Many gasped, slave and free alike. Everyone gaped at Pedemus, then turned to Thayne for the answer.

The American frowned at the symposiarch. "In Thunderbird, we don't talk about the Devil's Eye at parties."

Asterope cocked her head, still expecting a blow for her presumption, yet fascinated by this talk of the faint, tiny moon which was such a vexation to the eyes and a weight upon the heart. No one in Mersinea was quite sure which god lived there, but he was no bringer of joy, that much was certain.

"Nor do we here," declared Heraminus. "I say, Pedemus, direct us toward a more pleasant topic of conversation."

It took a while for the levity of the evening to return, but everyone had forgotten about Asterope. Puzzled, she looked toward Pedemus. He returned only a bright, inscrutable glance.

The symposium proceeded to degenerate along its usual course. The drinking continued and intensified, the flute and harp girls played louder, party magicians conjured colored flames and images of beasts and monsters. Asterope went about her work like an automaton, her brain whirring in its effort to assimilate all that she had learned this evening.

Her head began to spin, so drained was she by the noise, the chatter, the music, and all the strange events and dangers of the day. But she remained acute enough to sense Stannard's eyes on her, searching, questioning. She looked back at him as Thayne rose from his couch and sauntered, somewhat unsteadily, over to Heraminus, where he bent over and spoke into the ear of his host. Heraminus, looking puzzled, responded by rising up and going with him into a far corner of the room. There they conversed, Thayne speaking at some length, while Heraminus assumed a speculative look. At one point he glanced at Asterope, stimulating her to break her trance and launch into some meaningless task. Heraminus listened further to what Thayne had to say, appeared to ponder, then laughed and shook his head with a look of regret. Thayne presently returned to his couch, crestfallen. He gave Asterope a doleful glance which for some reason caused a twist in her stomach.

Later, she and the youngest slaves were dismissed from the dining hall. She was the oldest to be excused. Someday soon, she would be expected to stay.

Asterope waited in the courtyard to attend to any of the departing guests. She had glimpses of what went on inside as the curtains parted to pass some departing reveler. The flute girl now naked. Men on their knees. Men on their hands and knees. Sweaty limbs gleaming in the lamp light. Grunts and laughter. Heat and an animal odor. Chaos. Foulness. The last pretense of dignity and reason thrown aside.

Asterope, exhausted, watched with a heart now heavy as lead.

Quite early, the two Americans came through the curtain, shaking their heads, glancing back over their shoulders. They saw her, stepped over to her. Thayne looked her in the eye and said, "We don't approve of what's going on in there. It's not natural, and no one as young as you should see it."

Asterope felt Stannard's hand rest on her shoulder. She looked up at him. His eyes appeared kindly beneath his dark brows.

"We want you to know something else, young lady," continued Thayne. "We in Thunderbird don't approve of slavery, either. Our forefathers fought a war to get rid of it, and we don't like to see it today."

He patted her head awkwardly. They turned away and were escorted out of the house.

The astonished Asterope just stood there, quite helpless to know what to think or how to respond. Belatedly she looked around to see if anyone had noticed this attention, but it appeared that no one had.

Her plan must not be long in coming.

Chapter 3

Neos Asterope

"I don't know how I dare permit you to touch my hair," said Euratia as Asterope ran the comb through her long, oily locks. "Not after what you've done to your own."

"Yes, Mistress Euratia," replied Asterope in her customary impassive tone.

"What could have motivated you to mutilate yourself like that? And why were you so late in coming home last night? Don't make us regret the liberty we grant you to roam the streets."

Asterope kept her eyelids lowered. Her hands made the same mechanical gestures of combing that they had made every morning for as long as she could remember. When she did look up it was to ponder the colored shadows cast by the shrubs and furniture in the courtyard—reddish shadows cast by the fierce white sun Photos; cold ones cast by the glowering red sun that accompanied it on its course through the heavens—and occasionally devoured it.

A sudden pain in her hand interrupted her musing: a tight grip from the thin, corded hand of Euratia. The pinched face and olive-colored eyes of her mistress blazed into hers from only inches away. "You weren't trying to run away, were you girl?" she hissed.

"Yes, Mistress Euratia, I did run away," gasped Asterope, caught completely unawares. "But as you see, I did come back."

Euratia stared into her eyes for what seemed like minutes. Her eventual response was surprising; she laughed, though the sound was neither warm nor mirthful.

"Oh, Asterope, you'll say anything. But don't verge so close to disrespect. One would almost think you didn't appreciate all that we've done for you here."

"And what is that, Mistress Euratia?" asked Asterope automatically, without thinking.

Again she was subjected to that gimlet glare. Euratia's reply came soft and cold. "Well, to begin with, we saved your life and granted you a home. But more recently, as of last night in fact, we saved you from a terrible fate."

"Really?" asked Asterope, meeting her mistress's eyes with interest.

"Yes. We kept you out of the hands of the barbarians."

Something within Asterope threatened to break and wither at those words. She needed an act of will to keep her shoulders from sagging.

"Oh?" That soft syllable was all she could bring herself to say.

"Yes indeed. Those two oafs—the Americans—actually approached Heraminus and offered to buy you. Did you see those fabrics they gave us? Such coarse rubbish, such vile colors. We'll wait a few days for them to sail for their home and then pitch the rags into the harbor."

"What use do you suppose they could have had for me, Mistress Euratia?"

"I suppose that depends on just how barbarous they are. But in any event, Heraminus made his answer wisely. He recalled that you are my favorite body slave, despite your waywardness and perversity. Your hands are light and clever. And so you see…if not for our solicitude, you might be on the verge of sailing for that uncouth land."

Asterope dared say nothing. Her throat felt as if Athene's cold hand were constricting it as she might strangle a snake. But she could not stop the tears that coursed down her cheeks. Now she must surely be betrayed.

"Ah," said Euratia. "You begin to show some appreciation for our consideration. I welcome the sight of your gratitude."

"Yes, Mistress Euratia," whispered Asterope miserably.

Asterope jerked awake, flinging off the thin cloth that covered her body. The nightmare that had awakened her was already fading, yet keen enough were the images of desolation it had left behind.

In a few days, the men who might have rescued her from this imprisonment would sail away forever.

She sat up, trembling. Her anxiety was a physical presence within her, a cold smooth mass of marble pushing against her ribs. She stared into the darkness of her sleeping closet, the blank walls lit only by a slight silvery gleam filtering through the curtain-door.

Morpheus was repelled by such inner turmoil; sleep would not return tonight. Perversely, the god would probably return to shed his influence on her just as the suns were rising, when of course she'd be expected to begin the day's work.

She stood up, wrapping the cover around herself. She had to do something, not just lie there brooding and fretting until dawn. But what could she do? She paced the length of her closet, her feet whispering over the woven mat that covered the floor. She was tempted to just run away, to run down to the docks and try to hide herself aboard whatever ship the Americans would be sailing. Or to find them and beg for their mercy and protection. But one more mysterious absence would convince her masters that they were dealing with Asterope the runaway slave. Once that word was out, there'd be little chance of escaping the city.

Cautiously she poked her head past the curtain and looked into the women's courtyard. All was silence except for the gentle snoring of some of the other female slaves in their closets. Silvery moonlight slanted down into the courtyard. The hour wasn't even very late.

An act of rebellion, an impulse of curiosity—something was needed to keep her from boiling away to a vapor. She brushed past the curtain and into the courtyard.

In any other household, something as precious as books would be kept in the master bedroom, along with the other main treasures of the family. But Heraminus kept his books on display in the *andron*. He seldom read the things, but instead valued them as emblems of his supposed erudition. Asterope had had reason to be glad of that in the past, and so tonight.

She crept into the dining hall, whose only light came from the last few embers in the small hearth that smoldered in the corner. But Asterope needed scarcely a glimmer. She glided to the shelf which held the books, sure of her movements through long practice in furtiveness. She ran her fingers lightly along the bound volumes, pausing when she felt the pebbled smoothness of the two new additions. Plato's book was by far the thinner. She passed it by and lifted out the thicker of the two, carrying it out into the moonlight, holding it close against her chest.

She opened the so-called "Bible" (rather an unimaginative name for such a thing, she thought—calling a book "Book") to a random page. The leaves were extremely thin; there were a great number of them between the covers of this volume. Had anyone ever read the entire thing?

The moonlight was sufficient to reveal the script. The tiny characters were amazingly uniform and precise, so much so that they could only have been produced by the famed printing magic of Thunderbird.

Many of the letters, she realized with dismay, were strange to her. It had never occurred to her that a foreign language might not even use the same alphabet as her own.

Yet as she studied the text she found many similarities to her own language. The sentences were printed mostly in small letters, though each began with a capital letter, and some other words were capitalized as well. Only a few of the small letters looked familiar—alpha, kappa, eta, omega. But many of the capital letters looked the same as the Greek.

She flipped through the book. Near the end she found a section in which many sentences were printed in red ink, all in capital letters.

Recognizing most of these letters, and assuming they had the same sounds in both languages, she was able to guess at the pronunciations of these red-printed words, though of course she had no idea of their meaning.

She pored over the text, silently mouthing the alien words, guessing at the sounds of the letters she did not know, or ignoring them. Already, she thought, she knew far more of English than anyone else in the household.

After a while she noticed she could barely read the words. She looked up. The Greater Moon had slid across the sky, entering a bank of low-lying mists. Her studies had gone on long enough for now. Already she was lucky that no one had come out to answer nature's call.

Asterope returned to the *andron* and replaced the book. Though she could not see it, she was keenly aware of the bundle of barbarian cloth which had been thrown behind the book shelf, where it lay forgotten, or so she hoped.

Three days later she overhead Heraminus remark that the Thunderbirds would sail for home in the morning. He sounded pleased; profitable as his trading arrangements with them promised to be, he was still glad to be rid of the men and their outlandish ways and ideas.

Asterope's heart hammered at the news. All along, her greatest fear had been that they would leave without her learning of it. She certainly hadn't dared to make any inquiries about their schedules.

That night she entered her sleeping closet for what she vowed would be the final time, whatever the result of tomorrow's adventure. She lifted her sleeping mat and stared at the garments that lay flattened beneath it, along with a bronze needle and some thread, tools of her desperate handiwork of the last few nights. Her fingers were raw from the work, though they often were anyway, from embroidery and scrubbing and weaving and all the other tasks she was expected to perform. Her hands hadn't drawn any attention, but Euratia had peered closely at her hollow, dark-circled eyes and made another disparaging remark about her lack of feminine charm.

Although Asterope had barely slept these last nights, she was determined not to sleep at all on this of all nights. It would be all too easy for Morpheus to keep her eyes darkened until past the time of sailing. That was just the kind of trick beloved by the mischievous gods. Anyway, her anxiety was so keen that the idea of sleep seemed distant and illusory.

Rather than fret over the uncertainty the next day would bring, she put the time to good use, muttering the phrases she had so painstakingly decoded and memorized. There was no way she could derive much of the meaning—but the sound at least had to be as accurate as possible.

Sitting against the back wall of her closet, not daring to lie down, she mumbled to herself and watched the soft night shadows gently shift outside her curtain.

"Asterope."

The voice made her gasp and lift her head suddenly. Dazed with sleep, she looked around wildly. But no one was there.

It took her a moment to remember what was special about this night. She gasped again as she realized she had indeed fallen asleep. She scrambled forward and poked her head through the curtain.

The eastern sky showed only the first pale glow of dawn. Something had awakened her in time. She glanced at the summit of Olympos, just visible over the walls of the courtyard, wondering again at the inscrutability of the gods.

She stood, threw aside the sleeping mat, pulled her chiton off her body and flung it away. She drew on the pants, two awkwardly merged cylinders of heavy blue cloth, belted with a piece of twine. If she ever made her own pants again she would have a slightly better idea of how to proceed. The shirt came next, loose and baggy, made of the checked cloth, which was softer against her skin. She buttoned it with red wooden checkers she had stolen from a game board as she passed through the Agora on an errand. Over this ensemble she pulled a vest fashioned from the leather.

She had no way to judge her appearance — but it would have to do. Drawing a deep breath, she padded from her closet, still barefoot.

As she stole through the *andron*, she stopped long enough to dirty her fingers in the ashes of the hearth and rub some over her face. Aware of the fineness and whiteness of her skin as compared to that of a boy her age, she would disguise it if possible.

The main door creaked behind her as she closed it, a sound it had never made before, as though it were protesting her departure from the house. Once out on the street, now lit by a cold predawn glow, she straightened herself and walked toward the port with all the confidence she could muster. This time no god or goddess appeared to arrest her progress.

She arrived before all but the earliest risers were about. Walking uneasily along the waterfront, she remembered that she didn't even know which of the dozen ships at the docks was the one about to sail for Thunderbird. The round-hulled merchant tubs all looked pretty much alike.

By now the suns weren't far below the horizon. A breeze slid in off the water, slapping rigging against wooden masts. Bright-eyed harpygulls soared overhead, some clutching shellfish in their tiny hands. Activity on the docks increased rapidly. Sailors strutted by in pairs and groups, many studying her with perplexed curiosity. Some of them made lewd comments that an obvious foreigner such as herself was not expected to understand. She kept her face immobile, thought she could not prevent it from burning with embarrassment. At least she had the satisfaction of knowing that this disguise was more effective than the first one she'd tried.

Asterope looked up and down the row of ships. Many were being loaded. A few were having their mooring lines singled up in preparation for sailing. Ships usually sailed at sunrise, she knew that much. If she did not find what she was looking for soon, she never would.

A flash of color caught her eye. A bit of cloth, a banner of some kind, fluttered from the sweeping stern ornament of one of the ships. She walked toward it. None of the other ships carried any such device. Its colors were stripes of red and white, with two rectangular fields of deep starry blue: one large, and opposed to it, a much smaller one bearing a single star.

Asterope thought of the paper which had wrapped the gifts of the Americans. This was surely the correct ship. She walked up to it, trying to appear nonchalant as the sailors ran about loading it and checking its rigging. They eyed her closely. She eased away and, when no one was watching, hid herself in the midst of some bales of raw wool. She must not draw too much attention. She knew her disguise wouldn't stand too much scrutiny. She hunched down beneath the cold sky, peering out from gaps between the bales, and found that she was trembling.

The dawning of the combined suns sent level vermilion beams through the gaps in the bales. Asterope heard a commotion approaching the dock. Peeking out from her woolen fortress, she was relieved to see Stannard and Thayne stumping their way toward the ship with much laughter and exaggerated yawning. For an instant Asterope was paralyzed, then she found herself leaving her refuge and striding up to the two men with a big forced grin on her face.

They halted at her approach, regarding her with puzzlement, until all at once they recognized her, their eyes bugging out with comical amazement. Asterope did not allow them a moment to utter some disastrous remark. She opened her mouth and announced brightly, "Let he who is without sin cast the first stone!", or at any rate, something close enough so that the Americans could understand it after a moment's thought. She walked up to Thayne and grabbed a leather bag that was hanging from his shoulder, slinging it over her own. Smiling up at him, she said loudly, "Blessed are the meek, for they shall inherit the Earth!" Then, beneath her breath she said in Mersinean: "Please, may we go aboard?"

Stannard and Thayne looked at each other. Stannard grinned a little and gave a quick nod. Thayne, still a little befuddled, looked back down at Asterope, staring into her eyes.

Asterope reached over and clutched at the sleeve of his shirt. "I was naked, and you clothed me." She had no idea what she was saying, but she put as much pleading into the words, and onto her face, as she knew how.

The captain of the ship strode up to greet the men, adding a curious glance for her. "Well, gentlemen, are you ready to go aboard? We've a good breeze shaping up, and it's well to get underway at once."

Thayne withdrew his gaze from Asterope with some difficulty, and said in his rough Mersinean, "Yes, Captain, we are ready. Oh...I think I forgot to say that my—son is with me. His name is—Buck. He needs passage too. We pay his fare as soon as we sail."

The captain looked at Asterope still more narrowly, then addressed Thayne. "Yes, that will be satisfactory. Of course, your cabin will be crowded, but you must have encountered similar crowding on your voyage here, and it doesn't seem to have harmed you." He laughed a little too heartily, his gaze swiveling back to Asterope. "Is that not correct, Buck?"

Asterope was almost startled into replying. She bit back her words and said instead, in English, "Do not cast your pearls before swine."

The captain smiled, patted her roughly on the head, then bowed and turned back to the ship. The three "Americans" looked at each other in relief. They started toward the dock and the gangplank.

"Hello! You three there! A moment!" came a voice calling in urgent Mersinean.

They stopped again. Asterope turned to see a man with a balding knob of a head atop a long loose neck approaching them at top speed. Pedemus!

Asterope's heart turned to ice as the ubiquitous hanger-on waddled up to them, his himation billowing and flapping in the breeze. He took in the three of them at a glance, paying no special attention to Asterope.

"Good morning, my friends. What a fine day for sailing this is. The auspices for a sea voyage are superb on a day such as this. It must be that Poseidon and his moist cronies have been lulled into languidness and generosity by the beauty of this grand sunsrise. Ah, good morning to you, lad."

Pedemus turned quickly to Asterope. For the second time in as many minutes her head was patted.

Stannard bowed slightly toward Pedemus, a wary expression on his face. Thayne mumbled some greeting in Mersinean.

"We could not permit you to leave our land without a sendoff from those whose lives you have so brightened by your presence," enthused Pedemus. "In fact, I have just come from the house of Heraminus. You know, there is a bit of turmoil in that establishment at the present time."

Asterope felt herself getting dizzy. The world seemed to be growing pale; the voice of Pedemus was coming from far away.

"It seems that one of his slaves, that snip Asterope, has run away. Heraminus is quite angry, while Euratia conducts herself with a demeanor of frozen wrath which I would not care to bring upon myself." Pedemus shuddered and chuckled.

"They don't intend to let the girl escape, not at all. And luckily, I was able to provide them with some information that should lead to her recovery."

Asterope was dimly aware of a hard, rough grip on her left hand. She looked to the side; Thayne had taken her hand in his and was holding it with a painful strength that she nevertheless welcomed.

"You see, as I was proceeding toward Heraminus's house, I spied the little minx as she scurried along the inland trail that goes up and over the mountains, where only the lesser gods and a few shepherds are known to walk. She may eventually come down on the other side, but she'll need all the wiles of Pan to evade the pursuers I've set after her. Even with all this, Heraminus wanted to come himself to see you off. But I convinced him he was needed to oversee the recovery of his property, and that I would be happy to convey his good wishes on his behalf."

Asterope felt life beginning to return to her limbs and mind, which had begun to go gray and sparkly around the edges. Without thinking she burst forward and threw her arms around the awkward figure of Pedemus.

His hands jerked up and rested tentatively on her shoulders for a moment. "Well, lad, that's an effusive farewell you offer to such a fool as myself. Now you'd best be aboard your ship before the suns climb too high."

Asterope stepped away and stared into his eyes. The image of that ungainly face was with her for the rest of her life.

They turned and went aboard. Soon Asterope stood at the stern of the ship, looking back in awe and astonishment at a sight she had never really expected to see. The city of Pantheos, indeed the entire land of Mersinea, was already in the middle distance, and was receding, growing ever smaller in her eyes. If she had her way, never again would it grow larger in her sight.

The two Americans stood protectively on either side of her. She looked at them, turning from one to the other. Thayne at least could understand her words of thanks, and Stannard seemed to get the sense of them well enough.

Stannard pointed straight up, then made a gesture to take in the entire hemisphere above the sea. "Sky", he said clearly. "Sky."

"Sky," repeated Asterope in delight. She looked up, then broke out in laughter of sheer joy. That brought her up short — when, if ever, had she last felt such glee? She lapsed into a moment of introspective pondering before Stannard distracted her again.

He waved at the deck. "Ship."

"Sip!"

The language lesson proceeded until Stannard pointed at the straining square of fabric that propelled them forward. "Sail," he said.

"Say—"

Asterope broke off as she noticed the device that was dyed into the weave of the sail. It was an owl, a sign of Athene. This was an invitation to trouble on the waves, for Athene and Poseidon were notorious rivals. Yet the men of this ship flew the emblem confidently enough.

Asterope stared at the round-eyed bird, a vision of Athene floating in her mind's eye.

Chapter 4

The Voyage

Asterope was inclined to sleep on deck rather than share the tiny, airless cabin of her two saviors, but of course the deck was where the sailors slept too, whenever the ship's winding course did not bring it to an inhabited island by nightfall. Nevertheless, she tried it on their first night at sea, while the ship bobbed idly, anchored close to an island that was little more than a strip of sand. She awakened several times to swat away the exploring hands of sailors who had crept up on her. Finally, she gave up. It would not take them long to lay hands on something that would give away her disguise. So she pulled herself to her feet and descended into the stern of the ship to the passenger cabin. Her small knock admitted her; inside she found two sleepy men hastily pulling on red flannel underwear. The two bunks were tiny. She explained why she had come, and they offered her one of the bunks. But she was content to sleep on the deck beside them, and usually did so for the rest of the voyage. It was the first time she had slept in such close proximity to men. She was amazed by the din raised by their snoring, muttering, and farting. Were all men as smelly and uncouth as these?

She spent her days learning as many American words as they had patience to teach her. At other times she overheard them as they stood at the rail conversing in low tones, with many a glance in her direction. She knew they were discussing her disposition once they reached Thunderbird.

It did not seem to her that they were arguing over which would have the privilege of keeping her.

By day the suns swung through the sky over a glassy sea; by night the stars wheeled over whatever island they visited. Whenever the crew slept ashore, Asterope stayed on deck to watch the stars. She had never seen them shine so brightly, without the smokes and mists of Pantheos to dim them. The arms of the Whirlpool seemed to sprawl across half the sky. The profound silence of these mysterious evenings did much to quiet her apprehensions.

All in all the voyage was uneventful and blessedly peaceful.

The ship left the island of Skiros at the first hint of dawn, pulling out into calm air under the power of the oars. This was the last day of the voyage; the distance to the Thunderbird port of Homer was its longest leg.

Shortly after sunrise, Stannard and Thayne called Asterope into the cabin. They sat on the lower bunk, while Asterope perched on a stool before them.

Thayne said, "Asterope, Stannard and I have talked on where you go when we reach our home. We both are fond of you and wish you to have the best. But, I can not take you in. I have many children, and more, my wife is a good woman, but she will not accept a foreign girl of your age into our home. I know her well and say this with confidence. Therefore, Stannard will take you in. He has no wife or children, but he will be a good father to you. You know he does not speak Mersinean. You will go to a gymnasium and will soon learn to speak our language. You will do well."

Asterope nodded enthusiastically and focussed on Stannard, relieved. She'd had no right to expect that either man would take her in. They might just as well have set her ashore and bid her farewell. And, she would be sent to a gymnasium, as if she were a boy!

In Stannard's eyes she saw a mixture of pleasure, embarrassment, and worry.

The coast of Thunderbird showed on the horizon in the last light of dusk, its harbor marked by a tall beacon of flame.

Chapter 5

A New World

After a long, bumpy wagon ride into the interior, Stannard, Thayne, and Asterope arrived in Two Suns City. Although Asterope was told it was the largest settlement in Thunderbird, it was clear as they approached that it was smaller than Pantheos. Indeed, Thunderbird as a whole seemed to be a land lightly inhabited. The whole dusty, craggy distance between the port of Homer and Two Suns had contained only a few isolated dwellings and way stations.

Two Suns was situated in an area of red sandstone monoliths, a landscape unlike anything Asterope had ever seen or imagined. The indigo sky burned above it with a peculiar intensity. The light here was different, clear and direct, rather than broadened and diffused as it was in the wetter air of Pantheos. That dryness had already begun to chap her lips.

The buildings of Two Suns were variously made of wood, brick, or sandstone, depending on their function and intended degree of grandiosity. Even the wooden buildings were sometimes of two or even three stories. Houses were usually of wood, or sometimes of a dried mud called adobe, and were separated by substantial parcels of land, sometimes ornamented with small trees. People often sat on the porches that fronted their houses and watched as Asterope's party went by, sometimes waving. Her companions always waved back, even though it often seemed they did not know the people they were waving at. These houses seemed to lack interior courtyards, but had numerous exterior windows. Apparently these people preferred to look outward rather than inward, but at the same time, they appreciated a bit of space between themselves and their neighbors.

Asterope rather hoped that one of these houses would be Stannard's destination, but it was not. The structures became taller and more closely spaced as they entered the commercial center of the city. The wagon stopped at a transit station of some kind, where they disembarked. Thayne shook his partner's hand, gave Asterope a hug, and went on his way. Asterope followed Stannard through the streets of the city on foot, helping to carry his baggage.

Horses were everywhere, carrying riders or pulling a variety of carts and wagons. Their waste was also everywhere in the dusty, occasionally muddy streets. That kind of filth and clamor would never be accepted in the center of Pantheos, where men wearing long himations made their stately progress along streets paved with stone. Even the unpaved lanes of its residential areas were better kept. Luckily, wooden walkways on the edges of these streets limited Asterope's exposure to the filth. Or at least she thought herself lucky until the first splinter penetrated her heel.

Stannard lived in a room on the second floor of a boarding house. They climbed the stairs; he threw his luggage onto the bed, and they stood looking at each other, unable to communicate. After some thought on his part and some uncertainty on hers, he took her by the hand and led her back to the first floor. There they encountered a middle-aged woman wearing a long lilac-colored dress. She and

Stannard entered into a conversation of those hard-edged American words. At first the woman looked at Asterope with surprise and doubt, but Stannard's tone remained firm and steady, and eventually her glances took on a measure of understanding. Finally she nodded, and Stannard reached into his pocket for a handful of coins, dropping several into her hand.

The woman looked at her with a great show of concentration, opened her mouth, pronounced a Mersinean greeting with some effort, and named herself as Rose. Asterope smiled, bowed, and gave her own name.

Rose then led them both back up the stairs, where she unlocked the door next to Stannard's and put the key into Asterope's hands. In halting Mersinean Rose made her understand that this room was to be hers. Asterope looked around in amazement. The room looked to be the equal of Stannard's, ten times larger than her old sleeping closet. It must have doubled Stannard's rent. It contained an elaborate raised bed, a chest of drawers, a chair, and a small table with a pitcher and basin. It even had a balcony. Asterope was touched by this latest act of generosity. Luckily by now she had learned to say "Thank you." She took his hand, lifting it to her forehead.

That evening Stannard brought her downstairs to the big common dining room. There she was introduced to the other tenants of the house, mostly single men like Stannard, but also a number of youngish women with painted faces. They all nodded and smiled and slowly spoke their names while making exaggerated gestures at themselves.

Rose served dinner, proudly placing before Asterope a plate bearing an immense slab of meat in a puddle of reddish juices. Lost in the shadow of this mass of flesh were a few slices of fried onion. Asterope stared at the veins of fat and tubes of blood vessels insinuated through the thick muscle fibers, and forced a smile. The others had similar specimens before them, though perhaps not as grotesquely huge as hers.

"You eat," said Rose, in Mersinean worse than Thayne's. "Eat and you not be so thin."

Asterope thanked her and watched the others as they used unfamiliar implements to dissect their meals. She picked up her knife and fork and carved off a few pieces to nibble on. She wished instead for a loaf of good bread, some olive oil to smear on it, and a *crater* of watered wine.

That night Asterope undressed, blew out her lamp and tentatively sat on her bed, sinking so deeply into the feather mattress that she almost jumped back out in alarm. She lay back in it and felt smothered. There was a rug on the wooden floor which she knew would make a comfortable nest, but she forced herself to stay in the bed. She had eaten little of her dinner and already felt ungrateful for that. She would not also reject these strange furnishings without at least giving them a try.

She was not yet able to fall asleep in this foreign environment. After a while she levered herself out of bed and padded over to the balcony door. She turned the knob and opened it; balmy evening air flowed in. Still naked, she slipped out into the darkness, sitting in the cane chair that awaited her on the balcony. Strange noises and scents came to her from every direction. Dogs barked in the distance. The street was lit with dim widely spaced lamps. Quick-paced music played on an unfamiliar tinkling sort of instrument came from the building next door. Men came and went from it, often shouting and laughing, many staggering with drunkenness. She peered over her railing and was surprised to see Stannard sauntering through the doors of that establishment, although she had thought he was going to bed. A minute later he was followed by one of the women from dinner, except now she was wearing an elaborate red dress like some multi-petaled flower.

She sat back in her chair and lifted her gaze above the city. The stars, thank all the gods, were familiar, the same as she had always known them, though higher in the south. She did not know their names, but at least she knew their faces, and was grateful for their company. If they too had changed in this strange land, she didn't know what she would have done.

The Lesser Moon was passing overhead. She averted her eyes from it. It at least seemed less than friendly. Suddenly her nakedness felt conspicuous, although no one could possibly see her here.

Chilled, she wrapped her arms around herself. She was many times more fortunate here than she had been in Pantheos. She must remember that, no matter how lonely she might feel.

In the morning she again put on the boy's clothing she had made, having no other. She was now aware of how ridiculous it was, and hoped it would be possible to get or make something more suitable, even if she had to weave the cloth herself. Stannard snored in his room as she quietly descended the stairs.

She had meant to go out exploring, but the scent of food coming from the kitchen brought her up short. She poked her head through the door, finding Rose busily preparing breakfast over a masonry hearth or stove. Two kinds of meat sizzled in copper pans. Rose spotted her instantly, hauled her inside, and sat her at a small table, where she soon found herself facing a plate heaped with bacon, fried eggs, and a type of gritty yellow bread. She was also given a mug of some bitter hot beverage.

Although Asterope remained doubtful about these greasy foods, her stomach growled, having been subjected to a near fast last night. She gripped a brass fork and cleaned the plate with a sense of resignation, feeling rather queasy afterward.

Rose observed her wardrobe with a clear lack of approval. She left the kitchen while Asterope ate, returning from Stannard's room with a few coins in her hand. When she had served breakfast to the rest of her boarders, she again appropriated Asterope and marched her off for a shopping trip.

The clothing favored by the women of Thunderbird was absurd. It consisted of multiple hot, confining layers, most of which were never intended to be seen. The dresses and undergarments she was given to try on revealed a confused attitude toward sex. The floor-length skirts concealed her legs completely, yet the bodices were cut low in front, seeking to emphasize her budding breasts by pushing them together and squeezing them out the top. At the same time, it was anathema for her nipples to be displayed. To wear one of these dresses and then raise her arms suddenly could result in laughable embarrassment for any nearby Thunderbirds.

In the end, Asterope wished only to buy some fabric, from which she would construct chitons, cloaks, and whatever else was needed. Rose chewed her lip as Asterope made this clear, but admitted that she herself had worn clothing in the Mersinean style when she was young, as had been faddish in Thunderbird at the time. That was probably why she went along with Asterope's unconventional plan. Asterope left the shop satisfied and pleased. This way she would be able to return most of Stannard's money.

As they walked down the street, Rose suddenly announced that she had forgotten something, and asked her to wait while she returned to the shop. A few minutes later she was back with a small bundle which she did not talk about.

Rose then guided them to the main town square, where the largest civic buildings were to be found. The one that most interested Asterope was a brick structure whose entry was flanked by two large noble-looking beasts carved from white stone. People entered and exited carrying armfuls of books. "What is this?" she asked.

Rose sorted through her store of Mersinean words. "Biblio?"

Books, yes, that much was clear. Asterope thought of the change in Rose's purse. "May we buy a book here?"

At that Rose laughed. "Many places to buy in Two Suns, but not buy here," she said laboriously. "Books free in the *library*."

"The library!" repeated Asterope, entranced. "May we go in?"

They entered a solemn place where light fell from skylights onto long wooden tables. The walls were lined with shelves bearing more books than Asterope had imagined had ever been written. She darted about, flipping through volume after volume, most as beautifully made and printed as those which had been presented to Heraminus.

Here, she learned, anyone could borrow books, take them home, and read them.

Her view of the crisp type was blurred as she found herself in tears, her control dissolved by the sheer beauty of this concept of knowledge that was freely available to all, and also by her frustration that as yet she could read none of it.

Now she was convinced that fortune had brought her to the one place in the world most suited to her. As they departed the library, she paused to study the banner that rippled from a pole in the square. Thirteen stripes of red and white, and in the corner a field of dark blue with fifty stars. In the opposite corner was yet another of the small stars in a small square of blue.

And so Asterope gradually found her bearings in what was to be the happiest time of her life. She was enrolled in the public school, where, since she spoke no English, she was placed with younger children. But even here, two things worked in her favor. First, she was small, and did not appear too terribly out of place. Second, her status as a Mersinean brought her a certain respect. Although they no longer wore Mersinean clothing, the people of Thunderbird still held an undue admiration for the intellectual and cultural achievements of Mersineans and their Terrestrial forebears, whom they called the Greeks. This amused Asterope, who was often tempted to describe the pointless, foolish debates and unfounded fancies she had often heard expounded at symposia. The real achievements of the classical Greeks, she was to learn, were the work of men who had lived on Earth centuries after the people who would become the Mersineans were off the planet.

The fact that she was an escaped slave was almost never held against her. She was the ward of Carl Stannard, a respected citizen. Those who were aware of the details of her origin were simply glad that she had escaped from one of the few aspects of Mersinean culture they did not admire.

She quickly learned to read and write English and to use Arabic numerals, even the startling "zero", which had no equivalent in her native system of numbers. Learning to speak English was a different matter. Its pronunciation was maddeningly inconsistent, with certain letters giving one sound in this word, that sound in another, and none at all in a third. She had to simply guess in many cases how words should be pronounced and accented, and in many cases she guessed wrong. It was a matter of having to memorize the many, many exceptions to the slippery rules. Within half a turn she was reasonably fluent, though with an accent that never left her. The "sh" sound completely eluded her; she always pronounced it as "s".

Her reading was so copious it was described as Herculean, although of course Herakles had no reputation as a scholar. She was advanced two grades after half a turn in school, and skipped another grade half a turn after that, bringing her to parity with other students her own age.

She did her best to bring some comfort to Stannard's life, serving him as a dutiful daughter would in Mersinea, seeing to his needs as best as she could. She took to helping Rose around the kitchen, and thereby was able to arrange her own diet more to her liking, and even to change Stannard's to some extent. Imported olive oil was available, and wine, and there were a couple of decent bakers in town who knew what bread was meant to be. With these, plus salads, cheeses, and the occasional bit of meat, she satisfied herself and helped her benefactor to tighten his belly and become less florid.

She did this out of both gratitude and affection. She found Stannard to be a straightforward man, gentle to her, even cautious, as though a pat of his big brown hand might break her. He often traveled with Thayne on their trading missions, otherwise spending his days in their offices. Each time he returned home he seemed mildly surprised that he was still the de facto father of a creature as mysterious and exotic as Asterope. He never returned from any journey without bringing her some gift, usually a book, but sometimes an odd carving, a basket, or even just a flower. More often than not Thayne would have something for her as well.

She and Stannard never found much to talk about, but he was always proud of her accomplishments, and in her turn Asterope found him a comfort and a source of stability.

She had quickly learned that he was a frequent patron of the Gilded Lily, the saloon next door to their boarding house, a bright and brassy establishment whose interior she had only glimpsed, being forbidden to enter. She also knew he was a patron of the girls who worked there, some of whom also lived in their boarding house. Well, naturally he would have such cravings, being a man; at least she had no part in them.

Another prominent citizen of Thunderbird who was known to travel widely was Leonard Ronar. Word always spread around town whenever he was away on one of his mysterious, and often lengthy, missions.

The evening of her seventh birthday was warm and sweet. Seven was an auspicious age in Mersinea, being the age at which one was generally considered an adult. It meant less here in Thunderbird, where the age of majority was held to be eight. Nevertheless, Stannard, Thayne, Rose, and her friends from the boarding house had thrown her a party. It was the first time that a group of people had gathered to celebrate the fact that she existed. Although the ritual of the cake and candles seemed silly, nevertheless she dripped a tear onto the frosting as she blew out the candles. She received mostly books, though Rose hopefully presented her with a pink hair ribbon. Asterope knew she would have to wear it occasionally, but at least it was modest and not too extravagant. Her hair had long since grown out again, though its length was not excessive, as was her preference.

As always, the books were her favorite gifts. After the party, she sat on her balcony in the evening air with the new volumes piled up beside her chair. She held the famous *Noble Houses of Faerie* open on her lap, and was absorbed in the tale of that most magical of lands, when a commotion down in the street caught her attention. There were cries and halloos, hurrahs and howdys, even some isolated applause. Asterope leaned forward to see who merited this treatment.

Walking down the street was a solitary man. He was very tall, probably the tallest man Asterope had ever seen. He had a huge pack on his back, and wore filthy, weathered clothes covered with dust. A twin-barreled device made of some silvery metal thumped against his chest as he strode along.

Every T-Bird who saw him stopped to greet him, to smile, to act genuinely happy to see this shaggy-haired, unshaven wanderer. And yet he barely paid them any attention at all, giving out just a glance here and there. Mostly he kept his gaze down on the street before him, a solemn expression on his face.

So this was the famous Ronar. Asterope studied him as he drew nearer. He appeared weary, and his stride, long though it was, was slow. He bore a look of sadness, even of loneliness, despite all the jubilant people around him. His hair was a dark grey beneath the dust. His face was severe, heavy-browed, though rather fine in its way. He had an unusually long and graceful neck, she noted.

She stood up and bent over the railing as he passed. He happened to notice her, swung up his gaze, and caught her with a remote grey regard.

"Hello, Professor," she said timidly.

He did not reply, but looked aside and continued on his way.

Asterope watched him until he was out of sight, released her breath, and scurried back inside. She knocked on Stannard's door, who admitted her to his room.

"I've just seen the rudest man," she said.

"Who was that?"

"It was Leonard Ronar. He passed in front of the house just a moment ago."

Stannard jerked his head toward his window. "Ronar's back in town? Shoot. If I'd-a known, I would have gone out to say hey-howdy."

Asterope frowned. "But why is everyone so pleased to see him? He's insufferable. He didn't acknowledge a single person as he marched along. He acted as though he were the only human being within miles."

Stannard chuckled. "Yeah, well, friendliness ain't Ronar's long suit, that's for sure."

"Anyone else in this town who acted that way would soon be tossed into a horse trough."

Now Stannard laughed. "Yeah, that's true. But we cut that man a lot of slack around here. It was Ronar who arranged for Thunderbird to become a state, after all. Without him, we'd still be just a territory, not a sovereign part of the United States of America. Sure, we're separated from the rest of the USA...we can't send a Congressional delegation or anything...but just knowin' we're part of it makes us feel less alone here on Colibdis. Knowing that somewhere off in the Whirlpool are other men who think and believe as we do, it means a lot to us. We're mighty proud of that flag. Plus, Ronar saved us all from Namirnakh, and from the Despard family too. I remember all that, although I was just a boy at the time. My daddy was in the army we sent to the Bronze Portal for that final battle. So, we let Ronar get away with a lot. He ain't so bad, really. He could have taken over the state, been elected Governor, anything, but he never wanted that kind of power. He just wanted to start his astronomy department at the University. I respect that. He's like George Washington, almost."

"Hmm," said Asterope.

It was spring when this idyllic period of Asterope's life began to erode. One cold bright day, Stannard, returning from a long trading voyage he had shared with Thayne, was grey-faced and expressionless as he entered the boarding house. Asterope knew at once that something was seriously wrong.

Stannard sat heavily in a chair and gave her a bleak look.

"Thayne has vanished."

The world seemed a little less solid to Asterope after she heard these words. "What happened?" was all she could think to say.

Stannard explained that their journey had taken them west of Pantheos, to the cruder and more warlike city-states of Mersinea, a territory they little knew. Here the people did not even use the characters of the Greek alphabet, but clung to the hen-scratchings which had been brought over by their forefathers thousands of years before.

Here Stannard and Thayne had entered into trade negotiations with the king of one of the fortress cities. They were given a tour of the palace, a massive pile of stones decorated with colored floor tiles and artwork in a mannered, stilted style. The throne room contained a work of a different sort: a vividly lifelike golden statue of a woman which stood in a place of honor. The life-sized statue displayed a sad, pleading expression, and a slumped, half-swooning posture.

As soon as Thayne laid eyes on the statue he had swatted at the back of his neck as though he had been stung by a bee.

"This is my wife, the queen," the king had said gravely.

"Beautiful," Thayne had said. "You can see the pain in her eyes, the longing. This is a masterpiece. Superb."

The king and the nobles and officials accompanying him had bristled strangely at these remarks. Stannard, who understood little of what Thayne was saying, and didn't learn what was said until later, nevertheless grew uneasy at the reaction of their hosts, and at the strange avidity with which Thayne viewed the statue.

Then Thayne reached out and caressed the statue's golden flank. "I would like to buy this, if you can bear to part with her."

This would have been an offer of doubtful wisdom even if matters had been as they appeared, but both men were soon to learn that they were not. Thayne's gesture and words produced gasps of outrage from their hosts. The king was furious.

"This is my wife, I tell you! It is no statue. Turns ago, when I was young and foolish, and new to the throne, I married this good and gentle woman and had her for my queen. She sought endlessly to please me and to earn my affection. But in those days my lust was only for gold. As I strove to increase my wealth, my wife's pleas for love grew ever fainter in my ears. She pined and was lonely, but never once did she allow another man to lay hands upon her. Then one day Aphrodite, offended by my dismissal of the love which my wife craved and offered, appeared to us in a posture of wrath unusual for that goddess.

"Since gold is what you love, gold is what you shall have," she declared. "At least in this way your poor wife may know your love." And so the goddess transformed her, and so she has been ever since, though turn by turn I observe her posture to slump, and her face to grow ever more sad.

"Now you have laid hands upon her, and offered to buy her, as though she were a bale of wool or a length of flaxen rope."

Of course, at that, Thayne had turned white and apologized repeatedly, to the limits of his facility with the language. But the king ordered them out of his city, and they willingly left, or fled. That evening they camped well off the road that led to the next citadel they planned to visit. That country was rolling and rocky, with a few briar plants here and there. It was a spot typical of the countryside of Mersinea. The quiet air filled with imagined or half-heard voices. Neither man was comfortable, though Thayne was the more uneasy of the two. It did not help that they spied a faun watching them from the shadows of the twilight. Thayne remained distracted, silent, and gloomy. That night he was restless, tossing and muttering to himself until Stannard finally managed to fall asleep.

In the morning, Thayne was gone. There had been no disturbance in the night, and there were no intruding footprints nearby. Thayne was simply gone. Not daring to return to the city, Stannard had camped where he was for days, awaiting his partner's return. Finally he had been driven away by hunger, deciding to return home, asking after Thayne at every point along the way, but hearing nothing but rumors of clamor and turmoil back in the city, where a barbarian had tried to make off with the golden queen.

Asterope was mortified that the impish gods of her homeland were responsible for her benefactor's loss of his best friend and partner. She had never been demonstrative, but Stannard looked so stricken that she knelt before him, wrapped his knees in her arms, and rested her head on his lap. They remained that way for a while as Stannard spoke on about the disappearance, adding details as he thought of them. If Aphrodite was involved, thought Asterope, then Eros, with his vexatious arrows, could not be far away. No doubt one of those darts had sparked Thayne's dangerous madness. May the one god of Thunderbird spare her from the perils of romantic love, she fervently wished. Stannard gently stroked her hair.

Stannard made arrangements for the welfare of Thayne's abandoned family. Without his partner's knowledge of Mersinean and his connections in that country, Stannard's trading business suffered during the next few moonturns. Asterope tried to teach him Mersinean, but although her lessons were most lucid, Stannard was slow to pick it up. For the first time, he showed an awareness of money and its increasing lack.

Asterope did her best to support him during this period. She was more solicitous about his diet than ever, and helped him to dress well, once she understood what constituted dressing well in this milieu. When her schoolwork permitted, she visited his office and helped with the books and correspondence. She was also more affectionate, as he looked so sad much of the time. Sometimes after hugging him she caught him looking at her oddly.

Stannard took to staying out later in the evening. The gossip around the boarding house made it clear that he was not spending the time at the saloon with the girls. Asterope approved of this. Perhaps he was devoting himself still more assiduously to his work.

One afternoon, Stannard arrived home with a woman in tow. She was in early middle age, tallish, a bit thick in the body. She had strawberry-red hair piled atop her head, and pale green eyes that studied Asterope dispassionately, an impression that clashed with her freckle-cheeked smile. She wore a simple dress of light blue that emphasized her exaggerated figure.

"Asterope, this is Miss Eunice Purdue. She's been running the Sunset Ranch east of town for the last few years, and now she's becoming my new business partner."

Asterope suddenly found herself keenly interested in this woman.

"Good day, Asterope. I'm sure we shall become very good friends," said Miss Purdue in decent Mersinean. Asterope mumbled something in return.

"And, there's more," continued Stannard. "We'll soon have another kind of partnership with Eunice too. She'll be my wife, and your new mother. We'll be moving out to her ranch at the end of the month."

Asterope started and almost staggered under this unexpected news. Her natural caution kept her silent, but she knew she was doing a poor job of hiding her dismay.

Stannard led them to the dining room, where Miss Purdue joined the household for dinner. She laughed merrily, engaging the other boarders in trivial talk, thankfully ignoring Asterope as she sat staring and poking at her food like an amnesiac who had forgotten its purpose. Rose smiled uncertainly at the conversation, glancing between Asterope, Stannard, and Miss Purdue with barely concealed worry.

Well, thought Asterope, after all, she was about to lose two longtime boarders.

With her thoughts in a daze, the words of the chatter lost in a blur, Asterope was startled to the point of dropping her fork when Miss Purdue abruptly swiveled her head in her direction, fixed her with those peculiar pale eyes, and said: "Well, dear, what grade are you in at school?"

"Ah…I'm in the tenth grade, ma'am."

Miss Purdue nodded. "Oh, in high school already. You're such a slender little thing, I never would have guessed. I understand you've been helping Carl with his accounts?"

"A little bit, ma'am."

Miss Purdue laughed. "So formal. But, Carl and I won't be married for a while yet, so I shan't expect you to call me Mother before then. Will it please you to work as our bookkeeper full time, once you've graduated?"

Asterope drew herself up. "I have always intended to go to the University and study astronomy when I graduate."

"Oh dear, astronomy. Well, the University costs money, of course. We'll just have to see what's available and what's practical when the time comes."

Asterope's stare remained fixed. Stannard had never said anything about having to "see" about her education. Not even lately, with money such a concern.

The dinner ended after some interminable interval. Asterope stood in the shadows watching as Miss Purdue kissed Stannard at the door and departed. Rose gave Asterope a look of sympathy and left the foyer. Stannard and Asterope marched up the stairs.

Asterope woodenly followed Stannard into his room and stood looking at him. Stannard sighed, shrugged, and said, "Well then, child, let's hear it."

Asterope sputtered, waved her arms, then finally burst out with words. "We don't need that woman! What's this all about? We can handle things on our own. We can."

Stannard looked grave. "Now, Asterope. Eunice is a smart, canny woman. She's done a good job managing her ranch since her father died. She speaks your language and likes to travel. I can't handle the business without someone like that around. I sure can't make you my partner. You've the brains for it, but you're too young, and anyway, you've made your ambitions clear already."

"Did you hear what she had to say about my ambitions tonight?"

"Well, yes. But we've a good turn to go before we have to worry about that. We'll see how it goes."

Asterope bit her lip. "All right. You need a business partner. I can accept that. But why must you also *marry* that woman?"

"Well, you need a mother, for one thing," said Stannard with enough doubt in his voice that Asterope pounced on it.

"I need no such thing! I've never had one so far, and now I'm almost an adult. I have everything I need already."

Stannard's face began to assume a stubborn cast. Asterope hesitated a moment, then shifted tactics, though doing so meant taking unfair advantage of the poor, good-hearted, simple man. She sprang at him, wrapped her arms around him, laying her face against his chest.

"Oh please! Don't I take good care of you already? Father?" She had never felt comfortable calling him that. Her inclination was to call him "Carl", but that displeased him. "Our home here is comfortable and pleasant. What can she do for you that I can't?"

She felt like a fool the moment she spoke the words, drawing back to see what impact they'd had.

The pained expression on his face silenced and defeated her. There was indeed something that woman could do for him that Asterope could, or would, not.

Chapter 6

Professor Ronar

In school the next day Asterope spent much of her time staring out the window at the distant mesa where stood the fabled Observatory. She could just make out the little knob that was really the great dome of the sixty-inch reflector. Her distraction was so evident that Mrs. Lopez, the mathematics teacher, tried to trip her up by asking her to recite geometry proofs from memory. But Asterope had mastered that material so thoroughly that she could rattle them off without even taking her mind off her brooding.

Today the Observatory looked farther away than ever. Much less distant was the larger mesa that supported the pride of Two Suns, Thunderbird University itself. She had visited it before of course, sometimes to attend public lectures and performances, but never by herself. She considered. She needed an escape, a distraction. She could walk to the campus and back and still be home only a couple of hours later than usual. She resolved to do it.

After school she angled her way toward Main Street, her book bag slung over her shoulder, her stride as quick as she could manage. The two suns of Colibdis dropped lower on her right, their mismatched disks now close together in their orbital dance. Presently they would silhouette the Observatory. The avenue that led south to the campus had plenty of traffic, but here the land was more open and she could walk off the side of the road, keeping an eye out for chollas, rattlesnakes, and sprinterbugs. Reaching the mesa, she chose one of the switchbacked footpaths carved into its side and soon gained the summit, although she was breathing hard. Before her stood a tidy cluster of some of the most elaborate buildings in Two Suns. She had to smile at the architecture. Here again, Thunderbird's reverence for all things Mersinean had led them astray. Many of the buildings were fronted with colonnades that served no structural purpose at all. Even more absurd, the facade of the Administration Building consisted of a coarse imitation of the front of a Mersinean temple stuck into what was essentially a three-story brick box. The whole effect was so incongruous and awkward it was laughable, a misguided chimaera of a building.

She walked beside one of the classroom buildings, letting her fingers run along the bricks, musing on her cultural superiority. Of course, she was also aware of the fact that without this sometimes bumptious culture she would still be a slave girl, almost wholly ignorant of all matters save the most sordid and menial.

She also had to admit that the campus looked charming and romantic in the last rich light of day.

While admiring this she turned a corner and walked into a wall.

Except it was not a wall, but a man.

Asterope looked up and gasped. "Hello, Professor Ronar!"

Ronar, his face a good foot and a half above hers, looked down at her for a moment.

"Hello, Asterope," he said, stepping around her. "Excuse me."

Asterope turned, watching him retreat, her mouth opened foolishly. "You know my name!" she blurted.

Ronar hesitated, paused, slowly turned. He looked back at her from out of the sunsset, his figure no more than a tall silhouette.

"This town isn't so big that I wouldn't hear of a Mersinean girl coming here under such unusual circumstances."

"You know who I am," she said again, unnecessarily. She approached him, circling so that he was no longer directly in front of the suns. He turned to follow her. "I saw you once before. From my balcony. I spoke to you then, but you did not answer."

Ronar's gaze, previously so steady and forthright, began to waver a bit.

"Yes, I recall."

"But why didn't you say anything, Professor?" she probed, daring greatly.

Amusement flashed over his face for an instant, stemming from being so questioned by a barefoot girl in a boy's chiton, or so she imagined. But then he actually looked embarrassed.

"Your posture…" he muttered. "It was immodest."

Immodest? Asterope thought back. She had been leaning over the railing…she almost burst out laughing. To think that the great Leonard Ronar had been flustered by a glimpse of her small breasts! But clearly he had been, and now even the memory of it had discomfited him, for he was about to walk away again.

"Where are you going?" she asked, anxious to change the subject.

"To the observatory," he said, with an air of "Where else would I be going on a clear moonless evening?"

"May I come with you?" It was brazen, but she would not bite back her chance to take advantage of this opportunity.

Ronar's eyebrows went up a notch. "You are interested in astronomy, then?"

She nodded. "More than anything. I will someday be a student in your department, I promise you that."

Ronar stepped back a pace or two and folded his arms, studying her with renewed interest. "The entrance requirements are strict."

"I'm an excellent student. I'll graduate at or near the top of my class, even though I started late, due to my unusual circumstances, as you put it."

Ronar nodded. "And you've never seen or used a telescope?"

"You've got the only ones, don't you?"

"No. There are a few small ones in private hands around here. But I do control the largest, of course."

Asterope felt a sense of expectation. This evening might turn out to be far more interesting than she could have imagined.

"I will be completing an important observing run tonight. I'll have no time for distractions."

Or it could turn out to be a big disappointment. Her face fell.

"But, Sinanna—the Greater Moon—is new. In a few days it will be at first quarter, and there will be a few hours early in the evening when it will be too bright for deep photography. You may come then."

Yes yes yes yes yes.

"But the observatory is far from town," she said, ever mindful of practical matters.

"You have no horse?"

"No—I've never really needed one. And besides—I don't really care much for horses."

"Oh?"

"They're stupid, flighty beasts. I'm wary of any animal big and skittish enough to kill me because a feather blows past its nose."

Ronar gave her a somewhat fuller smile than she had seen so far. Why her dislike of horses should please him she did not know.

"You are an unusual girl. I will have the University send a carriage to your home on the night in question."

"Thank you sir, that is most generous."

They settled on the night. Asterope could only hope that Stannard would not object to her staying out late on a school night.

Ronar dismissed her, turned and went on his way as though he had forgotten she existed. Asterope didn't mind. On her way home she behaved with a childish glee that she had rarely displayed even when she'd been actually a child. She beamed, hopped, and skipped her way home, arriving out of breath, but happy.

She immediately found another reason to be glad she'd been late and missed dinner. Eunice Purdue was present again, seated at the dining table with Stannard, Rose and a few other boarders. The woman eyed her with a smile that probably appeared warm and tolerant to the others, but which Asterope recognized as disdainful. Both effects, Asterope suspected, were fully intentional on her part.

"Well, dear, you've been out in the dark, you're late for dinner, and you look a mess. I hope you have a good excuse for the sake of your father."

Asterope only glanced at her. Something about this woman begged to be defied, but at the moment Asterope needed Stannard's cooperation too much to risk taking her on.

"Father, guess who I met tonight?"

"Who, child?"

"Professor Ronar," she said with a sudden nonchalance, as though it had been the new hand down at the corner livery.

Stannard grinned and opened his mouth to speak, but Miss Purdue preempted him.

"Professor Ronar? A very busy man. I hope you haven't been bothering him."

Asterope cast her another glance, but this one was more lingering, and colder. With her eyes back on Stannard, she continued.

"And...he has invited me to visit the observatory on Thursday night."

Stannard's face really lit up at that. "Jumpin'..." he began, but once more, his fiancé interrupted him, laughing as though at the stories of a wayward toddler.

"Oh, Asterope. The observatory? And how do you expect to get there, young lady? It's at least eight miles out of town. Plus, that's a school night, if I'm not mistaken."

Now Asterope swiveled her head deliberately and fixed the woman with an impassive stare.

"Professor Ronar has offered to send a carriage, if you must know."

Miss Purdue's eyes widened a trifle.

"And as for it being a school night, even if I stay out so late I sleep through every class the following day, I daresay

I will learn enough from Professor Ronar to make up for missing even a week's worth of classes."

Miss Purdue's gaze lost its sheen of affability. Her paling skin emphasized her freckles, and her mouth grew tight.

"Asterope—I don't appreciate your tone of voice. I must insist on being treated with respect if I'm to act as your mother."

If my voice is sharp enough to keep you from pretending to be my mother, then let me keep it whetted and honed. But that is not what Asterope said. Instead she clamped her teeth together, silent by sheer force of will, while a wild rage whirled inside her like hot white wings. This was not the time. A confrontation now could result in her being forbidden to go.

"Yes ma'am," she said in a carefully controlled voice. "I'm sorry if I appeared rude."

"That's better," said Miss Purdue, seemingly mollified. She turned away, dismissing Asterope utterly, offering a few words of farewell and a kiss on the cheek to Stannard before she retreated to her own carriage and drove off.

Asterope glared after her, but Stannard distracted her by asking about Ronar, a topic she was happy to take up. As she described her meeting, Rose brought her some greens and a loaf of bread. Some of the other boarders who had wandered off returned at the sound of Ronar's name and joined them at the table.

"What did you think of Ronar?" asked Stannard.

Asterope chewed and swallowed some bread. "He seems mild-mannered enough. Quite polite, though distant. I don't understand where he gets his fearsome reputation."

Stannard sat back and laughed, though Asterope couldn't see why.

"Mild mannered, eh? Well, I suppose. Did you see that big red ring on his finger?"

"Yes," said Asterope, though she was unable to guess what that might have to do with anything.

"Was he handsome?" asked Ruby, one of the saloon girls, her auburn ringlets dangling over her cheeks.

"Ruby!" interrupted Rose. "Asterope's only a child. Ronar is four or five times her age."

Asterope started. "He doesn't look it."

"Well, what of it?" answered Ruby. "I only asked her if he was handsome, not if she was going to bed with him."

"Ruby..." said Stannard.

"Oh, all right."

There was a pause.

"Well, dear?" said Rose.

"Well what?" said Asterope.

"Was he handsome?"

"Oh, good grief." Asterope flung out her hands. "Yes, he was handsome. In fact, he was beautiful."

That last was not something she had intended to say. Hearing it from her own lips left her abashed.

"Beautiful?" asked Stannard with a sort of doubtful curiosity.

"Well, not like a statue of Apollo is beautiful. Ronar looks too harsh and angular for that. Beautiful in the way that Olympos is beautiful, high and remote and rugged. And his eyes are very striking. A clear grey, yet clouded with turbulence as well."

Ruby giggled. "You love him, don't you?" She flung her hand over her mouth and squealed with laughter.

Asterope felt herself go red.

"Ruby, really," said Rose.

"Oh, all right." Ruby got up and withdrew from the room, still stifling laughter.

Chapter 7

Observatory

Asterope was especially diligent at home and at school for the next few days, her anticipation of her journey growing keener each day. She was blessed by the absence of Miss Purdue, as Stannard ventured out to see her every night, which was so much nicer than having her show up at the boarding house.

At last the very day arrived. Asterope was tense, almost queasy, as though she were about to go on stage. It did not help matters one bit when she approached the boarding house after school and found Miss Purdue's horse and buggy tied up out front. She almost turned right around, but alas, the witch spied her from inside and emerged with Stannard in tow.

"Well, well. All ready for your big night, dear?"

"No, not really. If you'll excuse me, I have to go up to my room to change."

Asterope brushed past them both and trotted up the stairs. In her room she pulled out a woolen cloak, wrapped it around her shoulders, and observed herself in the mirror.

She frowned.

Thoughtfully, she removed the cloak, left her room, and walked down the corridor to another door. She knocked.

Rose answered, her face lighting up at the sight of Asterope. "Why hello, sweetheart."

"Hello, Rose."

Asterope stood there feeling pensive.

After a few moments of waiting, Rose looked puzzled. "Is there something I can do for you?" she asked kindly.

"Well…yes. May I have it?"

Rose blinked. "Have what, sweetie?"

"That dress you bought for me, turns ago at the dry goods shop. The one you never thought I'd be willing to wear."

Rose laughed. "Oh my goodness. I had almost forgotten it myself. How in the world did you know about that?"

"I didn't, not for sure. It was just an inference based on your behavior that day."

"My, if you aren't just the smartest girl I know. Why do you want it after all this time?"

"It's just for tonight. I'm not sure…it's appropriate for me to visit the Observatory dressed like this." Asterope blushed fiercely. In truth there was no good reason not to dress as she always did. Not really.

"Well, come in, and let's see if I can find it."

Rose found the dress without difficulty, tucked onto a shelf of her closet, still wrapped in brown paper. She unwrapped and unfolded the garment, holding it up for Asterope's inspection. Luckily, it was a simple dress of pale blue cotton, fabric which had perhaps come all the way from Ammon, far to the south. Asterope dropped her chiton to the floor, took the dress and pulled it on over her head. Rose buttoned up the back for her.

Again Asterope went to look in the mirror. She beheld a transformed person, definitely now a girl, her slender figure brought out by the dress.

"Oh my, I see I chose well," laughed Rose. "And I see by the dazed look on your face that maybe you think so too. It's a bit tight on you now, but maybe that's just as well."

Asterope nodded.

"You'll need a shawl as well. Otherwise you'll freeze in the dark in that dress." Rose rummaged around and found a crocheted wrap of pale rose-colored yarn, placing it over the girl's slight shoulders. "As for shoes..." Rose frowned for a moment. "Not mine. You'd step right out of them. Just a minute." She left and was back with a pair of dove-grey shoes, newer and cleaner than the two pairs Asterope possessed. "These are from Ruby, and she was happy to offer them."

They fit well enough. Asterope looked into Rose's beaming face, gave her a wordless hug, and left the room.

Downstairs, she reentered the world of Stannard and Miss Purdue. Stannard let out a whistle at the sight of her. Miss Purdue looked loftily amused.

"Asterope, you look just..."

"Just a little bedraggled," interrupted Miss Purdue, yet again. "Are you planning to do anything with your hair? You should at least—"

Stannard shot her a sharp glance. "Woman, do you mind if I speak to my daughter?"

Miss Purdue compressed her lips but said nothing.

Stannard turned back to Asterope. "Like I was saying... you look beautiful."

Asterope was absurdly pleased by the compliment, the more so since he had actually silenced Miss Purdue to deliver it. Maybe things weren't hopeless after all.

Miss Purdue remained silent, for the moment.

She joined them at dinner, of course. Asterope accepted the compliments of the other boarders with a small smile and downcast eyes. She did not feel very hungry—her stomach was fluttering. They all talked about her changed appearance and about the equal marvel of her new acquaintance with the great Leonard Ronar. She might almost have been a welcome stranger at their table, for all that they looked at her with speculative new eyes.

"I don't think you should associate with Professor Ronar," announced Miss Purdue suddenly.

Everyone stopped eating and stared at the woman. Asterope was uncertain whether she had heard correctly. "What?" she said, slightly stunned.

"By all accounts he can be a dangerous, violent man."

Asterope gave a brittle laugh. "If he threatens to kill me, you may be sure I will leave at once."

"Well, it's unseemly. He's several times your age. Everyone knows he's a bachelor and has never had a lasting affair with anyone around town. What could he want with you, I wonder? And you in your pretty blue dress."

"Professor Ronar," said Asterope slowly and distinctly, "knows of my interest in astronomy, and that I'm a good student. He has been kind enough to offer to help me develop that interest." With every word, Asterope felt a deep anger building within her, a dangerous anger.

"And that's another thing. Why would the great Professor Ronar waste his time teaching astronomy to a Mersinean slave girl not even out of high school? Surely you aren't that much of a genius."

Rose frowned and threw down her fork. Asterope could only stare in disbelief.

"Eunice..." began Stannard ominously.

"Well, as this girl's mother-to-be —"

"You are not my mother!" snapped Asterope. "I do not want you as my mother. I will not have you as my mother. You shall never be my mother."

Miss Purdue studied her for a few moments, then her expression changed, assuming a warm and indulgent smile.

"I can make things very difficult for you," she said in Mersinean.

Asterope blinked. "Oh?"

"I have my eye on you. And through me, so does my Lord."

Now Asterope was puzzled. Her lord? Did she refer to the Christian god who some Thunderbirds worshipped?

"How do you suppose my father would feel if he knew you were speaking to me this way?"

The smile grew warmer. *"I suppose he would think I was trying to get through to you in your own tongue, out of consideration for your waywardness."*

"I'll thank you both to speak English at my table," said Rose.

Asterope spoke English. "I should not be surprised, Miss Purdue, to see snakes spring from your scalp and tusks from your cheeks."

Stannard's fist crashed down on the table. "Asterope, that's enough! I demand that you apologize to Eunice."

A carriage pulled up in front of the boarding house.

"I will not."

Pain and anger infused her benefactor's face. "Then I forbid you to leave this house, or your room, tonight."

Miss Purdue did not twitch, but an obscene satisfaction entered her eyes.

Asterope looked from face to face around the table, seeing various combinations of shock and embarrassment. She bit her lip to keep it from trembling, looked at Stannard, and said the only thing she could.

"I'm sorry, Father, but I must go." She stood up. Stannard stared at her, white faced.

"I'll stop her," said Miss Purdue, rising.

Asterope ran. She reached the door before Miss Purdue was fully on her feet, dashed out, and leaped into the carriage. "Go, go, go, please!" she said to the man holding the reins.

He looked at her oddly and shook the reins. The carriage rolled down the street. No one burst out of the boarding house in pursuit.

Asterope sat there rigidly, looking neither right nor left, unbearably tense, her throat constricting. It seemed that everything inside her was surging and bubbling up uncontrollably, all at once. She flung her face to her knees, clutched herself and began to sob wildly, intensely aware even as she did so that she must seem a lunatic to the man beside her.

When the spasms finally eased she sat up, aware of the wetness she had deposited on her dress. She had no handkerchief.

A hand reached out from beside her, offering her one. "Are you all right?" asked the driver uncertainly.

Asterope took the cloth and wiped her face and nose. "Yes, I'm all right. I'm sorry, I'm sorry, I'm sorry. You must think I'm a fool. It's just…things were tense at home before I left. I'm Asterope Stannard, by the way."

"I'm Hal Holder, associate professor of astronomy at the University. Doctor Ronar asked me to stop by and pick you up on my way out to the Observatory."

He stuck out his hand. Asterope grasped it, although hers was rather clammy.

"Thank you, Professor Holder."

"You might as well call me Hal. Are you sure you're all right?"

Asterope studied him through eyes that were now clearing of tears. Hal Holder was slim and rather fine-looking, with an earnest narrow face, sandy brown hair, and greenish-grey eyes. He didn't look especially old for a professor.

"Yes, Hal, I'm fine. Thank you."

"Things a little rough at home, huh?"

Asterope pressed her lips together. This was not going well at all. Someday she might wish to study under this man. She did not want to leave him with the impression that she was an out-of-control, overly emotional little girl.

She made an effort to straighten herself up. "Not so bad, really, Hal. But thank you for your concern."

Perhaps her tone had been a little too formal, even chilly. Holder sat silently beside her, clearly ill at ease. After a while Asterope felt herself on the edge of blurting out all her troubles, just to break the awkward silence. Or maybe she was on the edge of leaping out of the carriage and running back home to her room, never to emerge again.

They rode into the sunset glow, the fat smile of the Greater Moon shining pinkish-silver in the dusk.

Suddenly a meteor knifed down toward the horizon, bright even through the afterglow, breaking up into sparks at the end of its path.

"Whoa!" cried Hal, startled. He halted the horse and sat staring at the fading trail of smoke. Asterope did the same, her heart thudding.

"I never saw anything like that in my life," she said.

"Me neither. Oh, I've seen a few meteors, but never anything that bright. Professor Ronar tells me that on Earth you might see a dozen or even a hundred meteors in a night."

Asterope was grateful to the meteor for facilitating this change of subject. They chatted about the emptiness of the Colibdian system, as opposed to the multiple planets, comets, and other denizens of the fabled, distant Solar System until they reached and mounted the spiraling ramp of a road that led to the summit of Observatory Mesa, where Hal let her off.

"Well, Asterope, it's been good meeting you. I'll be busy here all night, so someone else will be driving you home, I don't know who. I wish it was me."

Asterope was startled.

Receiving no reply, Hal continued, "Good night, now. Have a nice visit with the Professor."

"Good night, Hal. And thank you."

She watched him retreat into the late twilight for a moment, then turned to the dome of the sixty-inch telescope.

The sight, the very presence of it, drove out all thought of her situation at home, her embarrassment with Holder, everything. It was large, but not colossal, smaller than most of the temples of Pantheos, smaller even than the courthouse at Two Suns. The dome's bronze skin was clean and polished. It rested on a circular base of masonry decorated with some of those unfortunate non-functional columns which she normally sneered at. She was quite willing to overlook their frivolous presence here.

The thing about this structure that really arrested her was what it represented. Here was something built by ordinary people, at great labor and expense, not a tower raised by some magician, nor a vision offered by some god.

Its purpose was one of exploration, of rational inquiry into the nature of reality, a search devoid of the foggy mysticism that informed most other fields of human endeavor. Some might say that such a search was narrow and misdirected in a world where gods and goddesses acted at will, and where men and women willing to study magic and able to master it could dominate their surroundings. Even here in Thunderbird, where magic was not a big part of the culture, there were rumors of witches, and local ranchers might ask Indian medicine men to bring rain to their lands.

But this Observatory was a wholly different sort of affair. Here men and women devised the grandest of ideas based on the most tenuous of evidence. This much at least was no different than the beliefs of mystics. The difference, as she saw it, was that in science, old ideas could actually be overturned by newer ones which better fit the observations.

A shudder ran down her spine, brought on by the splendor, the audacity, and the mystery of the place. And the romance. She could not deny that part of it either.

She climbed the stairs and stepped through the door, which was propped open. The slit too was open, admitting the last purple twilight. A few lamps burned here and there, barely enough to pick out the shape of the huge telescope, its open truss-work tube glimmering with bronze and brass, and a whiter gleam that might have been steel.

A sharp scent filled the dome, one of metal and machine oil mixed with mellower undertones of waxed wood. It was an odor she would always associate with this place and with astronomy in general.

A tall figure moved in the shadows at the base of the telescope: Ronar. He looked up, noticed her, advanced a few paces into better light, and frowned.

"Miss, I'm busy here, and I must ask you to leave."

Asterope was taken aback. "Professor...?"

Ronar's eyebrows jumped up. "Asterope? I'm sorry, girl, I didn't recognize you, dressed as you are." He gave her a quick look up and down, then resolutely kept his eyes locked on hers.

Asterope laughed in relief. "I understand. I barely recognize myself."

"Well, I'm glad you could make it."

So am I, she thought. She looked toward the telescope. "It's magnificent."

Ronar followed her gaze and nodded. "This is your first exposure to optical instruments?"

"Except for a few lenses and prisms we play with in school, yes. May I look through it tonight?"

"No, I'm afraid not. The telescope is set up for spectroscopic observations to begin after moonset. The instruments can't be disturbed. This telescope is rarely used visually."

Asterope's disappointment must have shown.

"Don't despair. We have another option. Come with me."

He led her out into the deepening night, along a path to a wooden shed, unremarkable in every way except for the roof-high rails projecting from the back. Ronar opened the door, ducking into the dark interior. A moment later there came a screech of metal, and the roof began to roll off the shed and onto the rails.

Asterope peered through the door, then stepped in. Moonlight shone upon a much smaller telescope, though it was still considerably larger than herself.

Ronar rested his hand on the mounting with its complicated shafts, wheels, and gears. "This is one of our teaching telescopes, a twelve-and-a-half-inch Newtonian reflector. The mirrors were made at the optical shop of the University. The mechanical parts were also fabricated locally, the same as the sixty-inch and most of the other instruments in use here." He said all this with obvious satisfaction.

"Why twelve-and-a-half inches?"

"Eh?"

Asterope winced. Now it seemed a silly question, but now that she had raised it, she had to see it through. "I mean, why not twelve inches, or fifteen? It seems a rather random size."

Ronar's looming silhouette gave a shrug. "It's a traditional size. There's nothing more to it than that."

Asterope did not reply, hoping the topic would blow over quickly.

Ronar grabbed the telescope and began to swing it. "I suppose you'd like to look at Sinanna first?"

Sinanna? Oh yes, a foreign name for the Greater Moon. Did she want to look at it? "I've seen pictures of it, Professor. It's just a great barren rock, isn't it?"

"Yes."

"Well then, if you don't mind, let's look at something else. I know my time here is limited, and I'd rather use it to see something a bit more profound."

Ronar stood there looking at her in silence for long moments. Asterope suddenly felt small and foolish. Had she offended him by rejecting his offer?

"You are a girl of some discernment," he said at last. "Most first-time viewers gravitate toward the brightest and largest thing in the sky. They *oooh* and *ahhh* over the cracks and craters of a landscape so lifeless that if they were to encounter one half so bleak here on Colibdis, they would avoid it in horror. I approve of your choice."

Asterope grinned. "What shall we look at, then?"

"On Colibdis, we have two basic choices. The first is the members of the very small, poor dwarf galaxy in which we find ourselves. These stars are almost uniformly old, tired, and somewhat dull. Among them lurks the occasional planetary nebula, the best example being the eye of Glorphos. There are a few loose clusters, and many binary and multiple systems. All these are of some interest, but my main interest, if my interests matter to you, is what lies beyond them. Far beyond them."

"The galaxies?"

"Exactly." Now Ronar was moving the telescope, sighting through a smaller one mounted on the side. He did something, and the telescope mount began to tick like a clock. He stood there peering through the eyepiece, which stuck out from the side of the tube near the top. "We'll start with one of the nearest galaxies, a smallish spiral called M33. Take a look."

He stepped away from the telescope, and Asterope approached it. Her eye fell short of the eyepiece by about a foot.

"Oh," said Ronar. Asterope smiled while Ronar searched for a stool and pushed it into place. She mounted it and looked into the eyepiece, scarcely knowing what to expect.

At first she saw nothing, but then she noticed that most of the field was occupied by a large, dim oval of light, slightly brighter toward the center. It had a curious texture, crusty, as though a spot of sugar water had dried on a sheet of black paper, or as if it were about to break up into stars. The brighter clumps were arranged in a loose "S" shape.

"Yes, it looks like a much smaller version of the Whirlpool."

"It is in fact smaller, and also some thirty times more distant. Now let me target something you may be familiar with. In Mersinea it is called the Discus."

Asterope stepped down and watched as Ronar swung the telescope. Yes, there was the diffuse lens of the Discus, not far from M33. In fact, now that she knew it was there, she could see M33 itself as a tiny patch.

"You'll find that the Discus, which we here call M31, overflows the field of the telescope. It's big."

Asterope resumed her place at the eyepiece, and gasped. The core of this galaxy was very bright. The disk of it was cut by foggy lanes of blackness.

"How many stars are here?"

"Approximately five hundred billion."

Asterope had a sudden sense of the vault of the sky expanding into three full dimensions. All her life she had been used to the sight of the Whirlpool sprawling over a good part of the summer sky. Now she recognized that the sky was populated with smaller, or rather, more distant versions of it, so much more distant that the space around her now seemed to echo with its vastness.

They looked at a few more galaxies, each one smaller, fainter, and more remote, while they waited for the Whirlpool to rise over the eastern horizon. Asterope had the feeling that Ronar could show her galaxies at a rate of one per minute all night long and never visit the same one twice.

Finally, with the Greater Moon nearly set, the Whirlpool was high enough for Ronar to consider it worth viewing. He swiveled the telescope to an outer region of one of the pinwheel's spiral arms, bent to glance through the eyepiece, and stepped back. Now Asterope did not need the stool to look through it.

She saw an incredible mass of stars crowded tightly upon one another, while dark filaments drew mysterious glyphs among them. She saw more stars in this one view than there were in the entire sky of Colibdis. What a spectacle must be the sky of Earth, in the midst of that profusion!

As if following her thoughts, Ronar said, "I've pointed the telescope at the neighborhood of the Earth and Sun. The Sun itself is completely invisible at this distance, even in this instrument. But, I do see stars there that I knew as a young man, parts of ancient constellations. Giant stars: Antares, Deneb, Rigel, Betelgeuse. I often look at them to remind myself of my old home world."

Asterope found herself shivering, not only because of her awe at the knowledge that somewhere in this field was the legendary Sun of ancient man, as well as the very planet that had spawned her race. Her dress and shawl were simply not enough to ward off the chill of the desert night.

Warmth descended upon her shoulders. Ronar had noticed her plight, removed his jacket, and without comment settled it over her, heavy with his scent. She turned and studied him with warm eyes, not breaking the silence.

"Well, the moon's about to set," he said at last. "Time I was getting to work, and time for you to be getting home."

"Oh please...may I stay a while longer, to watch you at your work with the great telescope? I won't be a bother."

"Hmm. Very well, for a while. But you must stay well away from the equipment, and you mustn't expect me to entertain you very much."

"No, of course not." Asterope had to hold down an urge to skip with glee as she accompanied Ronar back to the big dome.

"Professor, what do you miss most about the skies of Earth? All those clouds of stars?"

"No—actually, I most miss the planet Mars. It was a companion of sorts for me when I was young. I knew many stories about it."

Inside the dome they found a graduate student, a rather gawky young man in Asterope's opinion, who was Ronar's assistant for the night. She stood off to the side while the two of them got the telescope aimed, conversing in terms she did not fully understand. Finally they settled down, the assistant seated himself behind a console full of dials and knobs, while Ronar peered into an eyepiece at the base of the telescope, moving only to operate buttons on a hand-held box which somehow controlled the gears that drove the instrument. Asterope had never dreamed that machines as large and yet as delicate and precise as this were possible. If anything comparable existed elsewhere on their world, she had not heard of it.

As the minutes drifted by, Asterope eased herself closer to Ronar, who did not react. Finally she was close enough to speak to him in a low tone that did not echo too loudly from the dome.

"What are you looking for here, Professor Ronar?"

"I'm searching for supernovae—exploding stars—in distant galaxies. If I can find some of the right type and distance, and measure their brightnesses and spectra precisely enough, they may reveal something critical about the way in which the universe is expanding."

"Oh. Is it a difficult search?"

"It is very difficult. Success will be mainly a matter of luck. It takes hours to photograph each galaxy, and I must search hundreds or thousands to find what I need."

"Why not build more telescopes, or even larger ones?"

"That too is very difficult. Building this one instrument strained the manufacturing technology of Thunderbird beyond its limits. It could not have been done if I hadn't introduced certain items of Earth technology. The only way I could surpass it would be to bring over still more technology, which might then get out of control and transform life in Thunderbird, or perhaps throughout Colibdis. And that I will not do. Astronomy here on Colibdis has one advantage, and one only—our vantage point, here in dust-free intergalactic space. Other than that, we are badly hampered by crude instrumentation and non-existent computational resources. Still, that single advantage is unique, and enables me to do things I could not do on Earth, no matter what telescopes were available."

"Is Earth's technology really so much more advanced than what you have here?"

Ronar snorted. "Asterope, you wouldn't believe what machines can do over there. They give Earth people powers which on Colibdis would be limited to gods and wizards, if indeed they were even imagined at all. Earth people can speak to almost anyone in the world at will, cast their vision to many far corners of the world, fly above the clouds, and command computing machines that can perform millions of mathematical operations per second. Or at least, the privileged fraction that isn't mainly engaged in grubbing for food and shelter can do all that."

Asterope's head swam at the thought of all these non-magical miracles, described in such a matter-of-fact tone of voice.

"Why would it be so wrong to bring such things to Colibdis?"

"They would eventually transform the planet beyond recognition. Probably they would result in a war between the forces of science and magic. The many distinct cultures of this world would be destroyed, or at least blurred and homogenized. Here in Thunderbird, it would mean cheap and common firearms, and that could only bring death and violence to what is now a fairly peaceful place. No, I like this planet the way it is now."

Asterope felt this answer could stand some elaboration, but she sensed that the topic made Ronar a bit impatient.

"You know, Professor, when I asked earlier what you were looking for, I didn't mean in the immediate sense of your studies tonight. I meant it more generally. What are you looking for from astronomy? What meaning does it have for you? What do you hope to find among the stars?"

Ronar said nothing for at least a minute. Only the clacking and whirring of gears broke the silence. He did not remove his eye from the guiding eyepiece.

Finally he reached up and tapped a smaller telescope mounted on the main instrument. "Look in here and tell me what you see."

Asterope bent to the eyepiece. "I see a tiny mist. A galaxy?"

"Yes. You will never see a grander thing in all of nature than that bit of mist. That glow is the combined light of suns far too distant and numerous to be seen as distinct points. You might as well try to distinguish the atoms in a wisp of fog. Yet encompassed by that dim glow is more reality, more wonder, more realms and kingdoms and empires than you or I could ever imagine. It is undoubtedly the home of beings greater than the gods of Larlaninulius, and monsters too terrible to endure. There are beings looking into skies glowing with constellations a thousand times older than those of Earth, constellations which have been observed to flow and warp with the passing of millennia. You and I are nothing to those beings. We will never be known to them, just as they will never be known to us. And that galaxy is but one among many billions in the universe, arrayed outward until they pass beyond all seeing and knowing. I look for humility among them. I look for perspective. I look for peace of mind."

That was enough to satisfy Asterope.

Presently she began to tire, conspicuously enough so that Ronar insisted she go home.

"But may I return sometime?"

The imploring look on her face must have made some impression on Ronar.

"You'll have to return sometime, if only to return my jacket. Be sure to dress more sensibly next time. Pretty dresses have no place on cold hilltops."

With that, Ronar dismissed her. He had his assistant summon someone to drive her back into town. Asterope swayed outside in the darkness, awaiting her ride. Her head seemed to ring with hugeness: huge thoughts, huge ideas, huge emotions. Only now did she have some real conception of the heavens as a three-dimensional space receding into infinity, not as a mere dome hanging above the world, speckled with lights. She felt herself under a spell, in a daze, as she stood on the steps with the stars and galaxies shining on her from above.

A buggy pulled up. Asterope climbed in, barely noticing what she was doing. She was startled by the female voice of the figure beside her.

"Howdy, I'm Amanda Sparrow, chemistry grad student and general darkroom helper up here on this knob. And you'd be the famous Asterope?"

"Famous...?" asked Asterope, bemused.

"Well, famously favored by the Grey Eminence, anyway. You don't think he provides personal tours for every schoolgirl in T-Bird, do you?" Amanda sent the buggy down the path with a slight flip of her wrists.

"I suppose not."

"You're darn tootin'." Amanda turned to eye her in the starlight. "What did he think of that outfit of your'n?"

"Oh," said Asterope ruefully, "he disapproved. He said it was impractical for observing."

"I can imagine."

Asterope's exultation now gave way to a bit of brooding. It served her right for trying to present herself as something she was not.

"He did say it was pretty, though," she concluded.

At the sound of her own words she almost jumped again. He *had* said it was pretty!

"You're jokin'!" said Amanda. "Wow, girl, I think the man has a crush on you." She gave a rather raucous laugh. "What did you two talk about?"

"Just astronomy," said Asterope, suddenly feeling defensive for no good reason. "I asked him about what interested him personally in astronomy."

"And he told you?" asked Amanda cautiously.

"Well, I expect there's more to it than what he admitted, but yes, he gave me an answer. Why wouldn't he?"

Amanda whistled. "Girl, that man just ain't big on having personal palavers with students, especially girl students. I ain't never heard of one who had the honor of hearing Ronar share his feelings about nary a thing. Yep, he likes you all right."

Asterope sat mulling over this stunning information. This night was turning out to be almost overwhelming in the revelations it contained. The more practical part of her nearly asked if Ronar were homosexual, but she did not, remembering just in time the revulsion these people felt against the practice. Besides, she found it impossible to imagine Ronar indulging in that kind of gross behavior, with either sex. Or, at any rate, she shied away from trying to imagine it.

The carriage reached the base of the mesa, where a dozen or so houses clustered together, forming a little self-contained village. Asterope looked around.

"This is where most of the full-time observatory staff people live," said Amanda. "Oh, and Ronar too. That's his place over there." She jerked her thumb to the side. Asterope peered at a Mexican-style house not much grander than any of the others.

Asterope did not continue the conversation. As they drew closer to town, she grew oppressed by the thought of the situation she was returning to. Never before had she defied Stannard so blatantly. She must mend this rift.

As they pulled up to the boarding house she saw lamps lit in the common area downstairs. She gave Amanda a hushed thanks and farewell, climbed off the buggy, and held her breath as she entered the building.

There at the table sat Stannard, hollow-eyed, looking at her with wariness and hurt. Asterope stood there to see what he would say.

"Well, girl, how was your evening?"

"It was absolutely wonderful, father."

He eyed her up and down. "Where did you get that jacket?"

"Professor Ronar lent it to me."

Stannard's eyebrow cocked up at that, and an enthusiastic glint briefly entered his eyes. But then they reverted to sad-dog eyes and locked onto hers.

"Asterope, why are you so determined to ruin my happiness with Eunice?"

Are you really happy with her? was her instinctive response, but she held it back. Instead, she walked around the table, pulled out a chair beside him, and sat down, laying her small hand over his big rough one.

"I'm not, father. Of course I want to see you happy and successful, of course I do. I also wish to lead my own life, as you have so kindly allowed me to do, and as you have helped me to do. But I don't think Miss Purdue likes to see me free and happy. She has her own notions about who I should be and how I should behave. That is the problem I have with her."

Stannard studied her for a few moments, withdrew his hand, and pressed it gently to her cheek.

"You make me very proud, Asterope. You dazzle me, bewilder me, and leave me behind. I could never have a daughter of my own to match you. I promise you, I will not let Eunice hold you back. If she keeps trying, I'll see to it that she gets reined in."

Asterope offered a smile, but he must have seen that it was tentative.

"Yes, I know, Asterope. It sometimes looks like that woman's got me buffaloed. Maybe she would, if I didn't have you to look after. But since I do, she'll soon learn that I mean business."

Asterope's smile became more genuine. "Father—I promise I will try to make peace with her the next time I see her."

"Thank you, daughter."

They sat there a little longer while Stannard listened to Asterope's recounting of her exploits with admiration.

Chapter 8

The Ranch

Miss Purdue did not appear in town for the next few days. Stannard grew oppressed by her continued absence, while Asterope herself grew anxious, concerned that she might have driven the harpy off for good, which could only be a mixed blessing.

One afternoon, while brooding about this in school, she determined to go visit the woman, talk things over, and reach an accommodation. Here at school, she was a bit closer to the Sunsset Ranch than she would be at home, so she might as well set out straight from here. It would keep her out late, but if she could return with news of peace between herself and Miss Purdue, Stannard would surely be pleased.

Thus when school adjourned she struck out for the east, the opposite of her usual direction. Her walk away from town was uneventful, though it was long, and it grew chilly as darkness settled down. Luckily, the light of the Greater Moon, now at full, defined the road in silver and shadow.

Asterope had never visited this ranch, but it was easy enough to find. The side road that led to it was marked by an arch bearing the name and the setting suns brand. Down this path she padded, the dust cool between her toes. It went on for a mile or more, ending against a tall fence of bronze spikes. The gate was locked. Beyond it, Asterope could see the dark forms of the main house and a few outbuildings. None of these structures showed a light. This was odd; it was still too early for even ranchers to be asleep. Perhaps Miss Purdue and her hands had all gone into town. If so, it must have been some time ago, for she had not passed them on the road.

Puzzled, and a little put out by this anticlimax, Asterope tried the gate, rattling the bars. It was quite secure. She looked up, but did not care to try climbing over those spikes. She turned sideways, inserted her shoulder between a pair of bars, and pushed her slight form through with little difficulty.

Now she was inside—trespassing. Her bare feet were silent as she cautiously approached the house. It loomed up; she was at the veranda. She mounted the stairs, which creaked, stepped up to the door, swallowed, and knocked.

No answer, no sound.

Asterope did not wish her long walk to achieve nothing at all. She would leave a placating note. Surely it would impress Miss Purdue that she had made such an effort to come out to her. Plus, this way Asterope was spared the necessity of actually speaking with the woman.

But she had come unprepared. She had left school with a pair of books in her satchel, and a note pad, but no pencil or pen.

She tapped her foot in impatience, then knocked again, a little more loudly. She put her hand on the cool doorknob and tried it.

The door opened. It was unlocked, which was not unusual for a home in Thunderbird. The locked gate was actually more unusual. Inside she would find something to write with. She would write by moonlight, leave her note on the door, and depart. She entered the house.

The room carried the scent of Miss Purdue, which made Asterope wrinkle her nose. The room was dark, but not quite silent. She was aware of a kind of rhythmic murmuring coming from some corner of the room. She froze, facing the vague sound, studying it while the hairs on the back of her neck tried to rise. She had not realized how keyed up she was until now.

The sound continued, unchanged. She took a few soundless steps toward its source. Moonlight shining through the windows revealed the outlines of chairs and a desk. A line of shifting red light came into view at the base of the far wall. She drew closer, recognizing a door. The scarlet glow leaked out from beneath it, shimmering and flickering. Holding her breath, she put her ear against the door.

A male voice chanted in a near monotone, speaking a language she did not recognize. At intervals the voice would pause, and a number of other men would sing some refrain, again in that strange tongue. Overall it was a dark yet passionate music, seductive yet also disturbing.

Then the men ceased their chant, so suddenly that Asterope almost panicked and bolted from the room. She was arrested by the ascent of another voice, a female voice, carrying the chant in another direction, again pausing to allow a male refrain. Asterope recognized this new singer as Eunice Purdue.

Greatly puzzled, and increasingly frightened, Asterope listened for a moment longer, then slunk with all possible stealth out of the house, through the gate, and along the road. She found it an enormous relief to be beneath the clean light of the stars again, in the peaceful night, rather than in that darkened house, one door away from whatever was going on in that red-lit room. Her passage home was considerably faster than her journey out. She was happy to climb into her bed and beneath the covers.

For the next few days she went about her business normally, all the while brooding about her adventure at the ranch. Stannard remained fretful about Miss Purdue's continued absence, yet Asterope said nothing about her experience. What, after all, had she found that was really all that terrible? So the woman and some men had been singing some spooky music. This was said to be a free country, after all.

She decided to try to see Ronar, ostensibly to return his jacket, but mainly to arrange another evening at the observatory. She walked to the campus after school, found the physical sciences building, and looked for Ronar's office, hoping he had not yet left for the observatory. Climbing three flights of wide stone stairs, she entered the lofty region where the Chairman of the department kept his offices. A woman sitting at a desk looked up as she entered, mouth opened to make some proclamation, but then she seemed to recognize Asterope, and merely smiled.

Uncertain, Asterope said, "May I go in?" and received permission.

Ronar's office was wood-paneled and high-ceilinged. The tall, narrow windows admitted light filtered by red velvet drapes. The furnishings were of wood and leather, the walls lined with books, photographs, and various strange artifacts which Asterope would normally be interested in examining. Ronar, who was evidently not expecting visitors, lay sprawled on a couch, asleep, snoring lightly.

Asterope nearly turned and left, but remained, fascinated by the unexpected vulnerability of Ronar asleep. It was amazing how his face relaxed in sleep, how innocent he appeared, and how youthful, for a man old enough to be her grandfather.

The grey eyes opened; the snoring ceased. He sat up and blinked at her for a few moments.

"Hello, Asterope."

Feeling suddenly awkward and intrusive, Asterope held up the jacket like a shield.

"Hello, Professor...I brought back your jacket."

"Thank you. Lay it on that chair, if you would. It really wasn't necessary for you to come here just to return it."

"Oh...it was nothing. I...wanted to speak to you anyway."

Ronar looked at her expectantly.

"I...was wondering when I might make a return visit to the observatory."

Ronar nodded. "Well, we're entering the dark of the moon, so it had best not be for a few days yet. I'll send you a message when I've identified a good time."

Asterope nodded meekly.

Ronar's gaze sharpened a trifle. "You look distracted or subdued, Asterope. Is everything all right?"

"Uh...yes, fine. I did have an odd experience recently, but no harm was done."

"Hmm. I've had some traffic with odd experiences in my time. Care to describe this one?"

"Well, all right. Please keep it a secret though. I don't want anyone finding out what I did." In some surprise, Asterope settled into a chair and began to relate the whole tale of Miss Purdue. Her gaze wandered to the dusk gathering outside the windows, and stayed there as she spoke. Ronar interrupted only once, early on, to make some wry comment about "evil stepmothers" and their ubiquity.

When she had finished telling of her walk to the ranch she turned back to Ronar to judge his reaction.

What she saw all but froze her blood. He was scowling, his narrowed eyes ablaze with a cold light. She shuddered and almost bolted and ran, unable to imagine what she might have said to evoke that expression.

Ronar's ring...that big garnet ring...it flickered, then spat out a spark of red. Magic! Wait, this man of science had magic? What else could that ring do?"

Finally Ronar spoke. "Asterope, this is important. This is not a time for imprecise language. When you say the light under the door was 'red', do you mean a true red, the red of an ocotillo blossom, say, or the golden yellow color of an ordinary flame?"

Asterope felt slightly offended by this. "It was, as I say, red. Not yellow, not orange. It was a strange scarlet light, quite pure, like the light passing through your drapes a little earlier. Or the light from your magic ring, just now."

Ronar's glower intensified, though by now at least Asterope did not believe it was directed at her. "And the language they spoke?"

"I didn't know it, as I said."

"The Sunset Ranch is known to employ foreign help," muttered Ronar. "Eranians, supposedly." He spoke several words in a quick, liquid tongue. "Does that sound familiar?"

"Yes! Their speech sounded something like that. But slower."

"You say you are to go live with this woman at her ranch?"

"Both my father and myself, yes."

Ronar nodded slowly. "Very well. Asterope, listen closely. You must not mention this to anyone. Speak of your visit to this ranch to no one else whatever, is that clear?"

Asterope also nodded, too riveted by his gaze to speak.

"Go home now. I'll send you a message when I wish to see you again."

She rose and departed in silence, eyes wide.

Three days later, word flashed through town that the Sunsset Ranch had burned to the ground. No survivors made themselves known, and no bodies were found.

Asterope was stunned, dazed, as though she walked in a dream. Stannard reacted with grief and dismay. He and Asterope stared at each other, oblivious to the hubbub that arose from the other boarders, scarcely aware of the efforts of Rose, Ruby, and a few others to offer sympathy to Stannard. None of them bothered to pretend it was a personal loss to Asterope.

Late that night, Asterope found herself standing in the darkness beside her bed, the bedclothes on the floor, with the echo of a scream still ringing in her mind. Had she dreamed it?

No...there came a second hoarse cry...Stannard. Asterope hastily threw on a chiton and rushed into Stannard's room, though she soon wished she hadn't.

The room was frigid, heavy with a clammy sort of cold that almost stopped her at the door. Worse were the candles, which were flaring and sputtering with the same crimson light she had seen beneath the door at the Purdue ranch.

Stannard was sitting up in bed, clutching the covers around his chin, wild eyes darting around the room, then locking onto hers.

"Father...?" said Asterope in a small voice.

Stannard stared at her. "I saw Eunice."

"W-what?"

"Her ghost appeared to me. Not more than a minute ago. She called you a witch, and said you were the one who killed her."

Asterope opened her mouth, but nothing emerged. She stood there, dumbfounded. By now the candles had subsided to normal, and the room's unnatural chill was easing. She took a few hesitant steps toward the bed. Stannard was clearly waiting for some response from her. She opened her arms.

"Father...you know I didn't kill anyone. I'm not a witch. I was right here the night the ranch burned. You know all that...don't you?"

There was a lengthy, extremely uncomfortable interval of silence.

"Her very spirit materialized here to accuse you of her murder," he said at last, sullenly.

Asterope stood writhing. She felt herself on the cusp of disaster. She knew she could not advance her case by speaking too harshly of Miss Purdue. Nor would she gain any credibility by suggesting the real culprit might be the great Leonard Ronar. She could only make herself look like a desperate liar that way.

"Father...I don't know why Miss Purdue's ghost might have thought I murdered her. You know she never cared for me very much. Perhaps it's possible for even spirits to be confused. But I swear to you, I am no witch, and I had nothing to do with whatever happened at her ranch. I didn't like her, but I am not some fiend who follows dislike with murder. You've known me since I was a little girl. You know I have always tried to be a person of reason, not of passion. Do you believe me?"

His stare continued, but it appeared to soften somewhat, or perhaps simply grow tired. "Yes, I believe you," he said heavily. "I just wish to God I knew what happened out there, and why Eunice, may her soul find rest, would think you had anything to do with it."

Asterope advanced on the bed, stifling a sob. She collapsed on it and threw her arms around him. But it was like hugging a figure of wood.

Back in her room, Asterope let loose her tears. She lay shaking with terror, unwilling to open her eyes lest she see the cold, dead face of Eunice Purdue hovering over her. Nor would she light a lamp or candle, fearing that it might flare up red.

Why should Eunice blame Asterope for her death? If she weren't simply out to destroy Asterope from sheer spite, then maybe she knew that Asterope was, at least indirectly, responsible for what had happened to her.

Or maybe the woman's wrathful shade knew it, anyway. Asterope could only hope that this apparition was Eunice's last gasp, and that she would trouble them no more.

Later that week, Asterope received a note from Ronar informing her that a carriage would arrive the next afternoon to carry her to the observatory. Stannard made no objection; in fact he scarcely reacted to her request for permission. He had been withdrawn since the day of the disaster and showed no sign of coming out of it.

For her part, Asterope wondered if she even wanted to go. Yet when the time came she wrapped herself in her warmest cloaks, acting numbly, automatically. Her driver turned out to be Hal Holder again, who valiantly tried to make conversation, but Asterope was barely aware of him, and said little.

She entered the big dome as directed, finding Ronar tinkering with the instruments mounted on the great telescope. He looked up at her entrance and regarded her blandly.

"Hello, Asterope. I thought that tonight you might be interested in learning something about the operation of astronomical telescopes. We can use the twelve-inch to make a few snapshots of Sinanna until it sets, then I must get back to work here."

Asterope studied him as he finished with whatever he was doing. She wished his face would reveal something—anything—a gleam of triumph, or pleasure at seeing her, or lust, or cruelty—anything. Anything except this unreadable mask.

Did you burn down the ranch buildings and kill everyone in them? was the question she wanted to ask. But she could not bring herself to ask whether Ronar, wizard of the stars and priest of reason, was also a murderer.

A few minutes later she accompanied him through the night in the light of the Greater Moon. They slid back the roof of the twelve-incher's shed and entered. She watched as Ronar attached a marvelously made little camera to the focuser, listening in silence as he described what he was doing. Much of the time she simply stared at him.

Finally his lecture trailed off. He swiveled on his stool, facing her, studying her with a set expression.

"Have you ever heard of the god Ahriman?" he asked in a quiet voice.

She shook her head.

"It has a different name in every country, of course. Around here it is simply called the Devil."

"You mean the god that rides the Lesser Moon?"

"Yes. I understand it has no name in Mersinea."

"And what about this god?"

"The Purdue ranch was a nest of Ahriman-worshippers."

Asterope waited for him to continue, but he seemed to deem that sufficient.

"And?"

"Eunice Purdue was an aspiring witch and acolyte of Ahriman. Her ranch hands were actually men of Darteharn, here to set up cells of Ahriman worship and to prey on the people of Thunderbird."

"Prey on them?" Asterope made no effort to disguise the doubt in her voice, or the rising anger she was feeling.

"Ahriman feeds on souls. The chief duty of its worshippers is to procure them for it."

"And so you swept in there, killed the lot of them, and burned them to ashes? Do you do that sort of thing often?" Now the anger in her voice was distinct.

Ronar nodded in the moonlight, a gesture that chilled her.

"I do it whenever necessary, to protect the people of Thunderbird, who are innocents in the ways of magic. The

Indians have strong defenses against it, but the others have never fully accepted the reality of magic on this world. They're good at commerce and tinkering, but when the subject of magic comes up, they turn away. When I learned that you and your father were to live at that ranch, I had no choice. They would have corrupted you, or delivered you to Ahriman. You would be a rare prize. With your father's business as a screen and his contacts in Mersinea, they might have tried to establish Ahriman-worship there as well, though that might not be easy, given the strength of the native pantheon there."

Asterope found herself pouring out the tale of Miss Purdue's restless ghost.

Now Ronar was grim. "If anything like that happens again, you must tell me at once. I have dealt with the spirits of Ahriman-worshippers before, and I'll do it again if I must. Now listen. It's clear to me that Ahriman is aware of you to some degree. You must never leave yourself open to it. In particular, you must never do more than glance at the Eye, the Lesser Moon. For me it is repellant that the heavens are marred by that roving point of corruption, but for you it is dangerous. Do you understand?"

Asterope nodded. She did not fully understand, but she understood enough. A tear cooled her cheek. At least now she understood that Ronar's violence had been performed in defense of her father and herself.

"May I explain all this to my father? You don't know how this has devastated him."

Ronar hesitated.

"No, I'm sorry. If it became known that another group of Ahriman-worshippers had taken root here, there could be panic and paranoia. A witch hunt. I don't want people looking for red flames flickering in their neighbor's windows."

Asterope bit her lip. "But this is so hard on him. And hard on me as well."

"I know. But would it ease his mind to know he had been about to marry a devil-worshipping witch?"

"No. But—he blames me for all this, in his heart, at least."

"That will pass. Your virtue shines through, and he cannot be blind to it forever."

Asterope looked at Ronar closely, her heart full. She belatedly noticed the gingerly way he was holding his right arm. She looked still more closely, and saw that his face was bruised.

"You're injured," she whispered.

"I walked into the yoke of the sixty-inch."

"No you didn't. You were injured—fighting the people at the ranch. Fighting for me." Her mouth hung open stupidly. She was disoriented to learn that Ronar had fought and risked his life to protect her—that it had not been a senseless murder spree, as she had cravenly believed. She was simultaneously moved and ashamed.

"Asterope—let's speak of this no more. Let's immerse ourselves in astronomy, clear our minds of the vileness of men and gods alike by admitting the clean light of the stars into our thoughts."

She nodded eagerly. For the rest of the night she nurtured a peaceful heart. When she went home she carried a sheaf of photographs of the Greater Moon, made by her own hands with the help of Leonard Ronar.

That peace did not carry over into her daily life.

Stannard's business decline accelerated into something resembling a collapse, worsened by his depression. His acting ability wasn't up to feigning confidence. Too many of his customers proved unwilling to continue a business relationship with a man who was so obviously defeated.

Nor did he warm toward Asterope. Although she did her best to be solicitous and helpful, he waved off her attempts and barely spoke to her. She offered to work the books at his office, but he refused to open them to her. Occasionally she would detect a glimmer of the old warmth in his glance, as though something were trying to break through, but always it would be concealed, as if by a layer of wax congealing over his eyes.

Asterope grew miserable, feeling unwanted and insecure. She had often found Stannard's displays of affection embarrassing, but now that they were withdrawn, she craved them more than almost anything else.

Throughout this bleak period her visits to the observatory were her main respite. Bit by bit, Ronar, and later Holder and others, introduced her to worlds of reason and learning she had barely suspected to exist. The world of her mind expanded into the universe, even as her personal world contracted into the chilly neglect she suffered from Stannard, and the glances of pity she got from Rose, the other boarders, and eventually even the teachers and students at school.

At least the ghost of Eunice Purdue had not reappeared to spread the rumor that she was a witch. There were nights when Asterope awakened to draw close the covers, a hint of an unnatural chill in the air. But no cries came from

Stannard's room, no flickers of scarlet, so she remained where she was.

On a hot day in late spring Asterope went to the campus to visit Ronar, feeling the need to see, if not a friendly male face, then at least an accepting one. But the departmental secretary greeted her with a look of pity, and Hal Holder intercepted her in the hallway. He had grown a mustache — a sandy-colored bat that looked silly spreading its hairy wings beneath his narrow nose. His eyes were mournful.

"Asterope, Professor Ronar has gone."

"Gone? Where?"

"We don't know. We only know he's gone, and we don't know when he'll be back."

Asterope felt her gut grow cold and hollow. She had heard something of Ronar's wanderings, but somehow it had never occurred to her that he might depart while she needed him, and without even telling her farewell.

Holder went on. "It happens often enough. Sometimes he has some task to perform elsewhere. Sometimes he just moseys off out of restlessness. We just wait until he wanders back. Until he does, I act in his place here at the department."

Feeling desolated, Asterope forced herself to remain for a few minutes, chatting with Holder and the others. Hal offered to let her join him for a dark run on the sixty-inch, but Asterope gave no definite answer. She was annoyed by what she felt was the mawkish solicitousness in his eyes and tone, but she concealed it. She left as soon as she could do so without appearing to flee.

When she emerged into the waning sunshine her steps faltered and halted. She couldn't bring herself to return to the gloom of the boarding house in the mood she was in.

She drifted toward the edge of the mesa, looking for solitude. The light seemed to be getting redder and dimmer by the second. She glanced at the suns; Photos was just sliding behind the tenuous outer layers of Kudu. Of course, the Gloaming. The next few days would be cool and murky. Perfect timing.

With a sigh she sat down on a projecting ledge which was sheltered and hidden by junipers. She had a fine view of the town and the sullen light that lay upon it. After a few hours the diminished light of the Gloaming would seem almost normal, but at first it was both striking and oppressive.

She saw wagons moving below, and carriages, and even individual figures, tiny as goldbugs. It seemed to her that they all moved about in serenity and calm, and she fancied she heard laughter rising up now and then. She wondered if any of them ever felt as isolated, as forlorn, as she did now.

Soon enough, the sole sun Kudu perched on the horizon, ready to depart. She sighed again, got up and shuffled her way toward home, head bowed.

A few nights later, she overheard Rose, who was something of a gossip, confessing to another boarder that Stannard had stopped paying rent on Asterope's room, on grounds of poverty.

"I don't know what he imagined would happen next. Maybe he thought I should evict the child, toss her onto the street. I'm just taking the loss. I'll be damned if I'll see that girl go homeless just because Carl Stannard seems to be under some kind of spell."

Asterope cringed away from this news. She ached inside; now she knew that Stannard had so little regard for her that he did not care if she lived or died.

After that, Asterope tried harder than ever to help Rose. She worked in the kitchen so much she might as well have been a hired laborer. She gave up even trying to ingratiate herself to Stannard. She served his food in silence, and he did not bother to meet her eyes. It was as if she had never been his "daughter". She was embittered, furious both at his stubborn foolishness and at whatever evil Eunice Purdue had worked upon him. She almost wished the hag's wretched ghost would appear to her, so that she might do whatever a living being could possibly do to a ghost. Ronar had apparently found something to do against them— perhaps she could as well.

Every night she crawled into her bed, which was once so friendly and comforting, with an uneasy feeling, as though she were a guest whose welcome was wearing out.

Weeks later, on an unusually grey and overcast day, cool with a little rain, Asterope heard something of great interest from one of the boys at school.

"I heard tell from my Paw that Perfesser Ronar showed up back in town late last night. Wonder where the heck he went this time?"

Asterope said nothing, but immediately a strange kind of fever came over her. She could not get the thought out of her mind, and was vaguely aware that she must look strange to the others as she sat staring fixedly at nothing.

Abruptly her gaze swiveled to lock onto the eyes of her teacher, who was studying her with a cocked eyebrow.

"Mister Camacho... I'm not feeling well. May I please be excused to go home?"

The teacher continued to eye her quizzically, then said, "All right, Asterope. I hope we'll see you here tomorrow, looking better."

She thanked him and fled the room. Indeed, she was not feeling well, or at any rate was not feeling normal. Nevertheless, she could not evade the fact that she had lied to her teacher. Something inside her was driving her on. She could not wait. She pattered toward the college, praying that Ronar would be there. He actually lived near the base of the Observatory, she knew, and normally didn't spend that much time on campus.

But as it turned out, he was there in his office, slouched in an armchair with his head hanging down on his chest. His hair was filthy and matted, his clothes torn and crusted. It looked as if he had spent the night on the couch right here in the office.

Later, Asterope would ask herself how she could have overlooked his evident exhaustion, how she could have ignored the look of dull despondency on his face. But her needs were so urgent she paid none of this any heed. Instead she flung herself at him, fell to her knees before him, and buried her face in his shirt. His scent flooded her mind, reminding her of better times that now seemed remote.

"Oh, Professor, I'm so glad you're back."

Ronar grunted, grabbed her shoulders and pushed her back, frowning into her face. "Eh? What's this? Asterope?"

The full tale of Asterope's woe came flooding out: all the grief, the loneliness, the abandonment of it. "Professor Ronar, I can't bear to live there anymore where I'm not wanted. Please, please. Take me in with you. I'm almost eight turns old, nearly of legal age. Let me live with you, and we'll both be happier, I promise."

Ronar stared at her, his eyes wider than she could recall ever seeing them before, and rimmed with red. Dust was caked in the wrinkles that radiated from their corners.

"Asterope..." He stopped, shook his head, apparently at a loss for words. Then he seemed to steady himself, and his eyes narrowed. "No. It can't be. I've just been away for moonturns. I traveled with Sha Totek to the other side of the world, to a country where men wear colored feathers and send human blood sluicing down flumes in the sides of great pyramids. There I met and had some difficulties with a great sorceress, who now hates me with a passion. I might easily have been killed. I might be killed the next time I undertake such an expedition. Sometimes they can't be avoided. No, Asterope. I regret that you're unhappy. But I've neither the time, the talent, nor the inclination to act as a parent." He shook his head again.

For Asterope, the world seemed to blur away into meaningless whiteness except for the central focus of Ronar's intractable face. Words seethed inside her, aching to be released: *I wasn't talking about having you as a parent, you blind fool.* She hadn't fully realized that herself until just now. Of course she could not permit those words to be heard. Ronar still thought of her as a child. She would not humiliate herself further by revealing her childish feelings.

She drew herself to her feet, a coldness, a numbness, intensifying in her core.

"I understand, Professor. I'm sorry to have troubled you." She turned and walked out the door, walked past the spectators in the hall without meeting their gazes, walked home while jagged blocks of ice formed within her, grating against each other.

It came as no surprise when Stannard vanished a few days later. When it seemed clear that he would not return, Asterope penned a letter to Ronar:

Professor Ronar:

Although Carl Stannard, my former surrogate father, has disappeared, I ask you not to hunt him down and kill him, or anyone else for that matter. There is no sign of foul play or supernatural intervention. He left taking all the cash which remained to his failing business, as well as a few personal items. I do not believe he was either himself a worshipper of Ahriman or abducted by them. He was merely an imperfect man whose character failed under the pressure of a series of reverses. Perhaps he has gone to follow his partner Thayne, or has merely gone to some other town of Thunderbird to attempt a new beginning.

Asterope

She helped Rose clear out the remaining items from Stannard's room. Among them was a packet containing her report cards, papers, tests, and even her few attempts at drawing, all carefully preserved.

A reply from Ronar arrived, printed in a bold hand on Thunderbird University stationery:

Dear Asterope,

Again, I regret the turn your life has taken. You however are an intelligent, resourceful individual. You will do well with these gifts in the future, as you have in the past.

I must instruct you to never again send a letter as foolish, rash, and indiscreet as that last. It refers to matters revealed to you in confidence. That kind of self-indulgence does not become you.

    R.

    Asterope studied this letter, her face slowly twisting into a scowl. She crumpled it and tossed it into a trash can.

    With her mouth set, she went to Rose, who regarded her mournfully.

    "Rose, we must have a talk."

    "Yes dear, we must. Your room—"

    Asterope held up her hand, cutting her off.

    "I will be vacating my room. I've noticed there's a corner in the attic that I could make habitable with a little work. With your permission, I'll move in there. I'll pay my way by continuing to help around the house until I find better employment, if that's acceptable. I realize that the pay I could expect as part-time kitchen help would not entitle me to a room as nice as the one I have now. I will also work toward paying off the unpaid rent on my room."

    Rose offered a tentative smile and a nod. "Yes dear, that's fine. I'm happy we'll be able to keep you around. What kind of employment are you planning to look for? You won't let—I mean, Ruby—"

    Asterope gave a laugh, the bitterness of which she regretted. "Heavens no, Rose. You needn't worry about me ever getting involved with anything like that."

    Rose smiled and nodded again, but it seemed to Asterope there was something a little wistful about both gestures. Asterope turned away, going to her room to pack her books and clothes. She was perversely irritated at Rose for acquiescing to her brave sacrifice so readily. She had more than half expected Rose to insist that she stay put. Tears made it hard to see what she was doing. She had so loved this room.

The employment Asterope eventually found was as a tutor in the Mersinean language, which was still fashionable enough that some families were willing to pay to provide their children with that skill. Some adults found her lessons worthwhile themselves. They enjoyed a certain prestige in being instructed by an actual Mersinean, especially one as proper and businesslike as Asterope, who even affected authentic Mersinean dress.

Although she quickly earned enough to afford the rent on her old room, she remained in the attic, preferring to save a bit of money. The attic was habitable, but scarcely pleasant. It was dark and drafty, and she had trouble keeping out black widow spiders and the blasted flipperpricks and sprinterbugs. In the winter it was chilly, and in the summer it was an oven in which she could barely sleep. She would lay naked atop the covers, sweating. The austerity of her habitat seemed to suit the state of mind she had fallen into.

She no longer visited the university or observatory. She remained diligent in school, the pride of her teachers, but made no real friends.

She attained her eighth birthday, then her ninth, and it was time to graduate from high school. She was selected as valedictorian of her class. Her speech was restrained and dispassionate. It received a muted response.

Asterope found herself pondering what to do next. Tuition to the University was no minor expense for a non-citizen, and Asterope was not a citizen. Citizenship was limited to those born within the borders of Thunderbird or the Earthly portion of the United States. Her savings would not be enough.

One day she was summoned to the front door, where Hal Holder awaited her, his silly grin half hidden beneath his mustache. Puzzled, Asterope invited him into the parlor and offered him a drink of water.

Holder held out a fancy-looking envelope sealed with wax. He cleared his throat and attempted to speak with portentous formality.

"Asterope...by order of the Chancellor of Thunderbird University, it is my pleasure to offer you a full scholarship, awarded in recognition of your many academic achievements and great merit. Congratulations."

Rose and Ruby, who had been lurking in the doorway, jumped up and down, squealing with delight.

Asterope took the envelope, which felt dense and weighty. Her lips softened into a smile.

Part Two
Asterope and Ronar

Chapter 9

The Student

Cautiously and quietly, Asterope made her way up the sandstone steps to the summit of Observatory Mesa. Her caution was necessitated by a darkness deep enough that she could barely see the stairs. On a night so Stygian the telescopes would all be in use, so of course only the dimmest of lights were permitted on the grounds. Asterope, familiar with the twists and landings of the staircase, preferred using no light at all. The stars burned brightly enough, and the rising Whirlpool provided its own soft glow, quite adequate as long as she was aware of what she was doing.

Her silence was nothing more than the deference called for by the sheer, mystical beauty of such a night. The scent of the surrounding desert was spicy and sweet, flavored by nighttime blossoms and by the rare wetness of the spring that trickled from the southern side of the mesa, invisible from here, yet giving a vivid green fragrance even now. The magic of the night added poignancy to the pride and awe she felt at being here at all, let alone at finding herself on the path to the observatory's giant sixty-inch telescope. There she would act as Prime Observer for the first time in her brief career in astronomy. She was the first foreign-born student to graduate from the Department of Physics and Astronomy and to be accepted into its graduate program.

The stairway switchbacked up the steep east side of the mesa, each bend marked and ornamented by a small landing or balcony. The road which wound up the more gradual north side was actually an easier walk, but it offered few of the charms of this far more artistic, perhaps even fanciful, footpath.

Coming around the final switchback, Asterope looked up along the remaining section of cliff face and stairway. The final landing was visible in silhouette against the stars.

Also visible there was a man in profile, a profile she had been hoping not to see. Leaning against the balustrade, there was no mistaking him: the sheer height, the long neck holding the rather shaggy head at an attitude of constant alertness, the protruding block of chin and razor of a nose.

Asterope felt a grudging gratitude to Professor Ronar for facilitating her education. Yet they had grown distant. Since their falling out turns before, they had rarely spoken, and even then only formally, out of necessity. Her anger against him had faded, but so too had her affection.

Despite that, she had once been his protégé, and she had known him as well as a girl-child could. Looking up at him now, black against the sky, she was still in awe of him. He was so remote, so forbidding. He was certainly physically intimidating, towering over her by nearly two heads. He was almost like a demigod, though she could think of no god or demigod in her ancestral pantheon who was so somber, if not Hades himself. But Hades never looked up at the stars.

As a young girl struggling to adapt to the ways and language of a foreign land, Ronar had been first a rumor to her, then a hero and obsession, and then, ultimately, a great disappointment. As an undergraduate she'd had little contact with the honored Chairman. Now elevated to the next academic plane, she must interact with Ronar more frequently.

The shadowed figure looked down at her as she ascended the last few steps.

"Hello, Professor Ronar," said Asterope diffidently.

The answer came in a deep voice, quiet, yet with an edge to it, as usual. "Hello, Asterope. You're late. Twilight ended fifteen minutes ago. That's a waste of valuable telescope time."

Asterope winced a little. "I know, sir. I'm sorry. I do appreciate being assigned to the telescope. I won't be late again." She had no excuse. She was late because she had dithered in her preparations out of nervousness.

She perceived a shadowy nod of that great head. "I'll be working with the forty-inch tonight. Come to me there if you have any problems. Good luck."

Ronar turned away and stalked silently into the darkness. Asterope thrust out her tongue at his retreating back, then turned to look out from this high vantage point, worsening her lateness through sheer perversity.

The lights of civilization were dim and scattered. The "light pollution" laws that Ronar had caused to be enacted had made the town's lamps even less of a threat to the Observatory than they had been before.

Asterope glanced over her shoulder at the domes. All were open, the telescopes barely visible within them. One was aimed east at the rising starfroth of the Whirlpool, while the others were directed at dim, star-poor patches of sky, gazing at the distant island universes which shone in such multitudes. "Galaxies", as Ronar called them, a word taken from her own language. The Whirlpool itself he called the Milky Way.

Milk! The Milky Way. What had milk to do with such vast cities of stars, near or far? If it were up to Asterope, she'd find better terms for such glorious immensities, terms more grand and descriptive. And if telescope time was so precious, why had Ronar been loitering out here, waiting to scold her instead of attending to his own observations?

Fortified by her indignation, she marched off toward the looming dome of the sixty-inch.

Swinging open the great bronze door, she paused before entering for a last look at a sky not constricted by the shutters of the dome. By now the so-called "Milky Way", which Asterope had been raised to call the Whirlpool, had fully risen over the horizon. The spiral arms swept from the central bar like the track of a finger stirring phosphorescent water. The barred hub was a bright, diffuse haze, a thick fog of starlight which could be resolved into its constituent hordes of suns only with a substantial telescope.

Somewhere in the outer arms of that great assemblage of stars lay a planet whose American name she was now expected to use. She still tended to think of it by the name it carried in her homeland. Gaia. "Earth."

Chapter 10

The Eye

Hal Holder sat at the control console, grinning at Asterope's tiny silhouette as she arranged herself at the guiding station, wrapping her woolen cloak around her shoulders and throwing off her shoes. Despite the cactus spines and scorpions which were so common, it was still impossible to keep Asterope in her shoes for any length of time.

Her first target was high in the sky, permitting her to sit beneath the telescope, safely on the floor instead of perched on an observing platform ten or twenty feet up in the dome.

"Professor Holder," said Asterope in her surprisingly slight Mersinean accent, "Thank you for acting as my night assistant tonight. It gives me more confidence that I won't break anything."

"It's no problem, Asterope. It's a tradition around here for a new observer to work with a faculty member on their first night with the sixty. Professor Ronar prefers it that way."

Asterope sniffed. "I'm sure he does. I'm surprised he even allows a silly little girl a night or two on his great instrument."

Holder held back a snicker, then frowned slightly. "Professor Ronar's cosmology program could easily absorb every dark night on the sixty-inch. He rearranged his schedule to give you enough dark time to shoot the dimmer targets on your survey list."

Holder was rewarded by the sight of Asterope twirling on her stool to face him. "Did he? I just thought he preferred the forty tonight for some reason. Perhaps he needed a wider field."

Holder chuckled. "Ronar's targets are remote. They always benefit from the aperture of the sixty. You'll just have to accept the fact that he went out of his way, again, to help you."

"Well," she said quietly, trying to think of a way to change the subject. She went back to fiddling with the guiding assembly. "It looks so faint," she said, peering into the eyepiece. "Are you sure this is the right object?"

Holder made a show of studying the readouts and controls on the main console, illuminated from behind by a red-filtered oil lamp. "Let's see here. According to the setting circles, we're at the proper coordinates for Ronar 475. An E7 elliptical galaxy. Or is it an S0? And what is that strange dust lane that appears to bisect the galaxy perpendicularly to its plane? I guess that's what you're here to find out."

"All right. Let me check the tracking for a moment." Asterope replaced her eye on the guiding ocular.

Holder listened to the whirring of the weight-driven clock drive whose mechanism was concealed in the pier of the telescope's massive bronze yoke mount. The sound was smooth and regular. That, as much as the tachometer and torque readouts on the console, told him that the drive was running well. The timer indicated they had almost four hours before he'd have to crank the weights back up for another period of tracking.

He glanced up at the dome. On either side of the slit were two dim spots of reddish light, projected by gimbaled lanterns mounted on the telescope. One of Holder's jobs was to periodically nudge the dome with its coarser drive system so that the telescope would not be obstructed as it slowly turned to follow the stars.

Holder glanced again at the coordinates of tonight's first object, and this time his frown was more pronounced. "Asterope. This galaxy is on the Road of Ahriman. Did you check the ephemeris to make sure the Eye won't be a danger?"

Asterope laughed a little nervously. "Oh, yes. But it was strange. The first time I consulted the tables I got an answer that indicated the Eye would be on the other side of the sky. But I had a strange feeling that wasn't correct. I decided to do the calculations myself for reassurance and got an entirely different result. The Eye actually isn't far from my field tonight, but it's not a danger. I just don't understand how I went so wrong in looking up its position in the first place."

"Just as long as you're sure it won't find its way into your eyepiece," said Holder uncertainly.

"It's no worry. I glanced at it before I settled onto my perch here, and it is indeed where I expected it to be."

"All right. Let's be careful you don't do more than glance at it."

"I will. Well then. The telescope is tracking correctly. The reticle is aligned on a guide star. I guess nothing remains but to begin the exposure."

"That's the way it seems to me, too," said Holder.

"Then here goes. And may Athene guide my eye and hand."

Holder heard the click-snap of Asterope removing the shutter slide from the plate holder. He set the timer at his console to the proper length of the exposure. Now the great telescope was functioning as a gigantic camera, as usual.

For a while Asterope muttered to herself as she fought with and got used to the vagaries of the drive gears and the hand paddle that controlled them. But she quieted down as she became accustomed to the rhythms of the drive's errors and began to anticipate them. After that the exposure went smoothly.

Time passed slowly. Holder had plenty of time to become reacquainted with the monotony of night assistant duty. He had little to do but tweak the dome along and generally keep an eye on things. At first he tried to engage Asterope in conversation, but she was so engrossed in keeping her guide star from jumping from its place on the cross hairs that her answers were terse. He gave up after a while, sat back, stared out through the slit, and daydreamed. Or nightdreamed. Whatever one did when one's mind wandered through the darkness without being asleep. He did not feel sorry for himself. Whatever the hardships of his task, he knew Asterope's were worse. To sit at the eyepiece for hours, scarcely daring to look away, could be an agony of tedium. Hal had often wondered why trained astronomers such as himself had to waste their time on such a mechanical task. Surely students could do that, while faculty members devoted themselves to analyzing the data and devising theories. But Ronar had gravely assured him that this was not the way things were done at his observatory.

About two hours into the exposure Asterope gave a tiny gasp. "Got a cramp?" asked Holder. Asterope did not answer. Holder shrugged and toggled the switch that activated the dome drive. It was an electrical switch, Earth technology which Ronar had introduced into critical applications at the University. To the general population of Thunderbird, Ronar's Department of Physics and Astronomy was a Jules Verne wonderland of fantastic machines.

A cold movement of air, barely perceptible, infiltrated the dome. Holder pulled up the collar of his jacket. Minutes passed slowly, even more slowly assembling themselves into hours. The two dim patches of reddish light bracketed the starry strip of the dome slit like rheumy eyes. They stared at him hypnotically, expecting nothing of him but that he keep that strip of stars centered between them. Most often the focus of his eyes relaxed on infinity, and he gazed blankly at the fragments of constellations which were visible through the slit. Ronar had told him that the sky of Earth had many more stars, more than could easily be counted. He had said that Earth's stars were often white or even bluish in color, rather than the yellowish tint which prevailed here. He knew all these facts in a theoretical sense from his study of the Milky Way. To hear them described by someone who had actually stood in their midst made the knowledge seem more real.

Holder started as the bell of the exposure timer went off. He had been so lost in reverie that the abrupt sound left his heart pounding. He sat up and looked toward Asterope, expecting her to insert the shutter slide and end the exposure. But she did nothing. Holder suddenly realized it had been a long while since she had said anything at all.

"Asterope?" he asked quietly.

He received no answer. He sat for a few moments longer, peculiarly unwilling to get up to investigate Asterope's strange silence. He could see her small figure fairly well, still seated at the guiding eyepiece, the paddle still in her hand.

He forced himself to rise, pushing his wooden chair back across the floor with an echoing scraping sound. Taking cautious steps, he approached the base of the telescope.

Once there, he was compelled by duty to look up along the tube toward the stars beyond. Hovering among them was a faint reddish-grey point which was conspicuous out of all proportion to its brightness. Somehow he'd known it would be there, exactly at the location of Asterope's target.

His mind turned cold and began to swim; his knees were ice water. He forced his gaze away from the Eye of Ahriman, an eye more avid and arresting than he'd ever seen it before. He heard his own voice calling on gods in whom he hadn't known he believed.

Chapter 11

The Insidious Moon

The sound of running feet entered the dome where Ronar sat guiding the forty-inch and its attached spectrograph. Suddenly Ronar knew his uneasiness had a cause. He stood and called to his night assistant, "Secure the telescope. That will be all for tonight." Then he stepped outside the dome and waited.

Holder ran up to him, gasping, his eyes wide and white even in the darkness. "It's—Asterope. She's got—the Eye —in the field of the sixty."

Ronar peered at him. His first impulse was to deny the possibility of that assertion, but the expression on Holder's face told him there was no point in making such a protest.

"Let's go," he said, running for the larger dome. Holder, though he was less than half Ronar's age, barely kept up.

Ronar thundered into the dome. The sight of Asterope seated motionless at the eyepiece, in the quiet of the dome, was peculiarly arresting—and sickening. He swore a smoking curse as Holder panted his way inside. "Why didn't you remove her from the eyepiece?" demanded Ronar in a voice of iron.

"It's not that easy!" cried Holder, his voice shrill with panic. "You try it!"

Ronar strode forward. He spared the merest glance for the sky above the telescope; he did not doubt that the moonlet would be there. He bent to examine Asterope. Her right eye was hard against the eyepiece. He could even see the concentrated light of the Eye of Ahriman, the color of old blood, glittering through her eyelashes. He shuddered and laid hands on her shoulders, meaning to pull her away. As he did so the world seemed to congeal into ice. Asterope appeared to recede into a smothering, nightmarish distance of space, where she sat immovable as a mountain. Ronar's very thoughts faded, as though absorbed by a mind-void of infinite capacity. He maintained enough of his volition and resolve to maintain his grip, to keep pulling, but that was all. Yet Asterope was held in place by something which was like the impossibility of movement or change.

After a time he yanked himself back with a strangled cry, breaking the contact. He stood swaying and staring at the delicate figure, her wavy hair dark gold, her skin white and flawless.

Abruptly he came back to himself and shook his head. "Hal! Rotate the dome! Close the slit! Shut down the drive! Do something to get this damn telescope off that moon!"

"That's what I've been trying to do while you stood there frozen. But the observatory—it's out of my control. It's as though it's controlled by—that devil up there."

Ronar looked sharply at Holder, who was straining against the hand wheel that should have rotated the dome even if the motor were to fail. Ronar recognized the thin tone of panic in his voice. The people of Thunderbird were less accustomed to malign magic than were others on this planet.

Ronar decided to take Hal's assessment at face value. He did not throw his weight against the telescope to try to slew it from its target. He did not leap up to the dome track to try to heave it around by main strength.

Instead he ripped the plate-holder from the back of the telescope and threw it aside. On his left hand he wore a heavy ring of garnet and gold, the stone so dark as to be almost black in the night. He clenched his fist and held it at the telescope's focus, an image of the Eye dancing over his fingers, then illuminating the garnet. Red light erupted from the ring at his urging. Caught by the telescope, gathered and focused into a parallel beam, it blazed out of the dome like a shaft of fire.

"Ahriman, do you remember me?" roared Ronar. "It's no helpless girl who faces you now! I tell you, you will not have her! You like to look at things from that rock of yours? Well, look at this!"

The red light flared into a white brilliance that burst from the telescope like a solid column of incandescence. There was a sound, like steel skittering over steel, climaxing in a further pulse of radiance and a clashing, ringing din. A great broadsword appeared in Ronar's right hand. He strode to the pier of the telescope and threw open the door in its side. Visible through it were cables which held the weights that powered the drive. Ronar thrust the blade inside, catching the cables. With a convulsive twist he severed them. The weights crashed into the basement. The drive whirred to a stop.

For whatever reason, whether Ahriman had been dazzled by Ronar's beacon, or merely because his Eye had drifted from the field of the now motionless telescope, Asterope was released. She sagged with a moan. Ronar rushed to catch her, the sword vanishing even as he reached for her. She slumped into his arms. Her body felt fragile, almost weightless. Ronar lifted her, carried her toward a bench at the periphery of the dome. "Get some lights on in here," he snapped.

Holder lit wall lamps with shaking hands. When next Ronar looked at him he was staring, slack-jawed with astonishment, not at Asterope, but at Ronar himself.

"What are you gaping at?" asked Ronar with little patience.

"I've heard about it, of course. Seen it on your finger a thousand times. But I've never seen you—use that ring—to call up that sword—before."

"Never mind that." By now people were running in from all over the mesa. Ronar raised his hand to halt them. "Someone ride into town and bring Doctor Joachim or his partner. Someone else bring blankets, hot tea, whatever we have to make Asterope comfortable. The rest of you shutter the dome and secure the observatory."

Ronar's people scattered to follow his instructions. Ronar and Holder looked at each other over Asterope's reclining form. She did not lie there peacefully, but shuddered and muttered incoherently. Her eyes were closed.

"How could this have happened?" asked Ronar quietly.

"I have no idea. She told me she'd had trouble interpreting the Eye's ephemeris. Maybe she still isn't that comfortable with our revised calendar. But she distrusted her results and did the calculation herself. Her position—"

"—was correct," interrupted Ronar. "I also did the calculation, since I was worried that the Eye might be too close to her target for comfort. But it shouldn't have come within five degrees of it."

"Then how in the world did it end up in the field of her eyepiece?" asked Holder.

"I don't know," muttered Ronar. "It's almost as if—"
He broke off.

"Almost as if what?"

"As if the uncertainty Asterope felt about its position gave the moon leave to wander off its normal path. As if its orbit became ambiguous, indeterminate, chaotic."

"But that's—that's hardly—"

"Reasonable? Rational? No, it's not. Hal, don't let the science I've taught you blind you to the filter of magic through which we on this world view the universe. Magic is the direct interaction of thought and physical reality. You've attended my quantum magic seminar. You should know all this."

"Yes—but—"

"Never mind that for now." Ronar pointed to the plate holder, a tabular brass contraption lying on the floor. "I want you to see if there's anything left of that plate. Develop any fragments. It could help us analyze the Eye's deviant path. And I want you to work with our students to derive an orbit for the Eye. Again. Do it from scratch. See if it has changed permanently. Use Tychonic instruments only—nothing optical."

"Yes sir. All right."

"And there will be new precautions. For the time being, no telescopic observations are permitted within ten degrees of the Road of Ahriman, even if the Eye itself is nowhere near. In all other cases, I want a naked-eye observer stationed at all times beside each telescope. His function will be to make sure the Eye does not again deviate from its course and place itself in another observer's field. This will be done no matter where in the sky the telescope is pointing."

"Yes. That makes sense to me, after tonight." Holder sounded a little steadier. He held Asterope's hand, stroking her wrist.

Ronar was surprised to discover that he himself was holding her other hand. It felt like cold wax.

"At least you were able to free Asterope without any great harm being done," said Holder gratefully.

Ronar wasn't so sure of that. He could feel the muscles in Asterope's hand beginning to spasm. Her eyelids were fluttering. She began to moan softly.

Suddenly her eyes snapped open.

Asterope's right eye was like a wet pearl, a nacreous blood-spattered thing from which all vision had been leached out.

She looked around wildly, and whimpered as though she had awakened in hell.

Chapter 12

Uninvited Guest

Ronar knocked on the door. He got no response, but turned the latch and entered anyway.

The room was dim, its only light filtering in through heavy red velvet drapes that covered the tall windows. The room had once been Ronar's office in the Physical Sciences building on the Thunderbird University campus just south of Two Suns City. It had been converted into a convalescent room with the addition of a bed. It retained the desk and the leather furnishings of its previous occupant. The walls were lined with beautifully bound books. A few unprepossessing-looking volumes were even from Earth.

The bed was unoccupied. Asterope, dressed only in the brief chiton which was her preferred costume, sat at the desk, her head in her hands.

"I'm glad to see you have the strength to get out of bed," said Ronar in a low voice. He approached the desk, pulled up a chair beside it, and sat down.

"I'm not ill. Not in the sense of weakness of the body," answered Asterope dully.

"That's what the doctors tell me. They even say you still have vision in that eye. Despite its appearance."

"Yes," she whispered. "May all gods be cursed for their cruelty, I do."

"Let me see."

Asterope slowly turned her pale, stricken face toward Ronar. Her right eye was covered by a patch.

"You wear that, even though the eye still has sight," said Ronar.

"It has sight of a kind I cannot abide, Professor." For a moment her expression threatened to collapse, but she managed to hold herself together. "With this corrupted eye I see only what is foul and weak and evil, in things and in places, but mostly in people. I see them as decaying sacks of corruption, seething with animal needs, their flesh ready to dissolve into the muck at any instant. I see their primal fears and lusts, their fear of darkness and their lust for it, that drives them away from me and draws them near. I see Doctor Joachim's dread of the nothingness that comes after death, and his even greater fear that there will not be nothingness, but something grey and eternal he can never hope to escape. I see Professor Holder's frustrated desire for me, his revulsion because I've been so hopelessly defiled, yet he's also drawn to me because of that, seduced by my degradation, tempted to wallow in it. He hopes I will be drawn to him, now that I've been ruined anyway. He lives in shame of these feelings, which he's never revealed to me, and never can. But I can see them. And when I look in a mirror—"

At this her control finally faltered. She covered her face in her hands and bowed her head. Her shoulders shook.

"Asterope."

"Asterope."

Slowly her face turned up to him, her expression one of ineluctable sadness and pleading. Tears flowed from her eyes. Ronar tried not to notice the color of the tears which seeped from beneath the eye patch.

"Asterope, look at me."

Her lips parted; a note of questioning added itself to her face.

"With both eyes."

Asterope gasped. Her visible eye widened with terror. "Look at *you*?" she hissed. "I don't dare."

"Do it, Asterope. Don't be afraid."

Her hand rose slowly, quivering, to her face, where it fumbled at the patch and clumsily raised it onto her forehead. Ronar steeled himself to ignore the ruined appearance of the afflicted eye. Glazed like a pink-filmed pearl, it was impossible to see how vision of any kind was possible from such an orb. The skin around the eye was bruised and purple.

Though the scrutiny of that ruined eye pierced him like a cold needle, he returned her inspection impassively. He watched as she frowned, took a series of deep, quick breaths, tried to look away, but could not. Her frown was mostly one of puzzlement. He watched it relax into a surprise into which was tinctured hope.

"Why..." She tilted her head. "Why...you're the only person I've seen who I can bear to look at. I never would have expected...not that you're perfect, mind you. Not at all. But at least you're not...I mean, at least you have..." Her voice failed. She stared at him in frank amazement.

"There's no need to list my shortcomings," said Ronar. "I'm sufficiently aware of them."

Asterope gave a start; their eye contact broke. Dismay disfigured her face. "Oh, no," she whispered. Her look of fear slowly dissolved, leaving her momentarily blank-faced, until a new expression began to emerge, one which Asterope had never worn, and which was wholly foreign to her character. Her face became a saturnine mask, her features composed, calm and cold. Now it was the normal eye that somehow appeared sightless, wandering uselessly around the room, while the corrupted eye glanced about sharply, taking in everything, ultimately coming to rest on Ronar. A small sardonic smile warped her lips.

She spoke. The voice was still that of Asterope, but it had assumed a quality of quiet malice which Asterope could not have imitated.

"Doctor Ronar. How good to see you clearly at last."

"Ahriman," said Ronar.

"And good too to see that you recognize me, despite my unusually soft and fragile guise."

Ronar shrugged. "It required no great feat of deduction. The identity of the thing that did this was scarcely in question."

"You call me a thing? Can you not at least grant me the courtesy of acknowledging me as a person?"

"In my opinion you are a thing."

Ahriman chuckled. "As you will. I would not deprive you of the shields your mind erects to defend itself from reality."

"I do not wish to chat with you, Ahriman. But since you choose to communicate with me by violating this girl, I have a message for you. Release her at once. If you do not, I will free her, and the more effort I must expend to attain that goal, the worse it will be for you."

Ahriman's eye grew wide; he threw back his head and laughed. "Those are bold words. The many enemies you have vanquished, including my own servant Namirnakh, have found good reason to respect such words of yours. But in challenging me, you challenge an entirely different order of being. I am a god. The girl is mine, and will remain mine for the indefinite period in which I foresee her usefulness."

Ronar snorted. "Is she really yours? I suspect she's less fully yours than you'd intended or hoped."

"Ah. Perhaps you believe that by dazzling me with the only magic you command, you prevented me from achieving full control over this girl? I'm afraid you overestimate your effort."

Ronar gave a grim smile. "No, I don't. I don't credit myself with your tenuous hold on this girl. I credit the nature of astronomical equipment. If that guider had had a binocular eyepiece, I daresay you would now be full owner of this girl. And I would be still angrier."

"Has it occurred to you that I have little reason to fear your anger?"

"No. It has not. Has it occurred to you that I may not wish to participate in your self-aggrandizing rantings?"

Ahriman laughed again. "When you mock me, you mock a god of mockery." The red light in the room seemed to intensify, glowing strongly in the face of the possessed girl. Her hand struck out and seized Ronar's left wrist in a grip of steel. He felt his bones bend and threaten to give way. His anger flared; so too flared the garnet ring, adding to the ruby glare that suffused the room. The ring hummed and sputtered, but the sword did not come forth. Ronar stared at his adversary through slitted eyes.

"You hold back," breathed Ahriman. "You do not wish to harm the body of this girl. You are gentle. You see, Ronar, even if I were vulnerable to your human strength, to use it against me you must first bring it to the distant moon on which I dwell. And you are unable to reach it."

"That is true," said Ronar evenly.

"Ah. Now that I have won that admission of impotence, I depart from this, my servant. Farewell, for now."

Asterope fell back into her seat, releasing Ronar. The lurid light faded to normal. Ronar quickly examined his wrist. He buttoned his cuff and sat with his elbow propped on the arm of his chair, hand up, so that the blood flowed down his forearm, unseen beneath his shirt and jacket. He watched as Asterope's own personality slowly came to animate her face once more. Once more she looked at him.

"I feel so strange. What happened?"

"Nothing worth talking about," said Ronar calmly. "I suggest you lower your eye patch."

Asterope hastily complied, and drew a breath.

"Professor Ronar. I see no good purpose in my rotting here in this room. This curse will not pass with hot soup and ephedra tea. I appreciate the kindness you and the others have shown me, but if I have any hope at all, it is at the feet of the gods who helped bring me here. I must go back to Mersinea and beg their aid, though I had hoped never to see that land again."

Ronar nodded thoughtfully. "That sounds like as good a plan as any. Perhaps one god can undo the work of another. But you must not travel alone."

Using her good eye, grey as Ronar's own, she studied him gravely. "Indeed I must go alone. I don't think I can find the strength for the journey if I must go—sickened—by the nearness of others. My own company is hard enough to bear."

"I will go with you."

"You?" she said in disbelief. "You would personally escort me? The Grey Eminence himself?"

Ronar permitted himself a wry smile. Few were the students willing to use this nickname to his face. "You are my student, Asterope. I admitted you to the program. Ahriman was able to attack you because of your work here. I will not see you destroyed by your zeal for learning."

"That zeal is gone," she whispered. "I have already learned too much, and I wish never to learn another thing."

"Do you think you will be stronger in three days than you will be tomorrow?"

"No."

"Then we will leave tomorrow."

Chapter 13

Homer

The road turned suddenly toward the pass. It had been inching that way via tortuous switchbacks for miles. The pass was little more than a notch in the great fold of rock that walled the northern side of the plateau making up the bulk of Thunderbird. They came at last over the crest, affording Ronar and Asterope their first glimpse of the sea. Ronar pulled on the reins, bringing the horses to a halt. The horses were clearly glad of the respite, for this last pull had been merely the climax of a long and strenuous journey. The whole northern part of Thunderbird was a wilderness of cracks, isolated mountain ranges, canyons, and bizarre fins and towers of red rock. To Ronar it was a land of sublime beauty, but it was never an easy traverse for a wagon, especially a wagon in a hurry. The road wasn't bad, but of necessity it climbed and dropped thousands of feet at a time, and had to circumvent many obstacles which simply could not be bridged.

Ronar sat stiffly beside the girl, looking ahead with a set jaw and impassive mien. Internally he was in turmoil. It was true that Asterope's interest in astronomy predated any involvement with him, but if he had not encouraged her, admitted her into his small circle, she would now be safe. He had known that Ahriman too had taken an interest in her. The distance that had arisen between Asterope and himself had led to his absence from her inaugural observations. If he had been present, he would have been more aware of the motions of that damned moonlet, or so he supposed.

He had failed to protect the girl.

And he had grave doubts about this plan. Why was he not taking her south, to the Tower of Sha Totek? He and the Sorcerer were not on the best of terms since their misadventure on that nightmare island on the other side of the world, but surely he would not refuse to help this girl if he could. Appealing to the notoriously capricious gods of the Mersineans was a desperate hope at best, but it was the only hope that Asterope seemed to harbor.

All Ronar knew for certain was that he could not rest until he had done his utmost for this child. If he failed, never again would he rest.

Ronar and Asterope studied the scene before and below them, Ronar alertly, Asterope with wan interest. As always, after a lengthy period spent in familiar surroundings, Ronar found the sight of some great anachronism arresting. The town of Homer was itself not remarkable, being a typical Thunderbird settlement, built in the style of the 19th Century American West, with structures of adobe, brick, and wood.

But most of the ships that rode in the little harbor were of a kind that had not been seen on Earth for thousands of years. Small round-hulled tubs, they each had a single mast and a simple square sail. Three were in port, and a fourth was approaching from the sapphire waters of the Bay of Aegeos. Ronar raised the silver-barreled binocular which hung around his neck. The ship's sail was deep crimson, decorated with a picture of a great multi-tentacled monster. The sail was barely filled, the wind having weakened with the progress of the afternoon. Even with the harbor in sight, the sailors had not unshipped the oars, but appeared content to cover the last few miles using whatever faint breezes the wind gods were ready to grant.

Ronar lowered the glass and turned to look at Asterope. She had given up her study of the town and sat slumped with her chin on her chest. Her good eye was open, but blinked frequently and appeared heavy-lidded. Ronar considered what he might say to ease her despair, as he had done often enough during their trip so far. But nothing occurred to him except the insipid, the deceitful, and the misleading. He wanted to tell her to be strong, but people either were already strong or they were not. No verbal exhortation could change that basic nature.

Asterope was strong. If she were not, she would already be dead, or lying in a gutter curled into a ball, dressed in drool-soaked rags. Or she could have given in to the seductive blandishments of Ahriman and allowed the rot in her eye to spread to her heart.

Finally Ronar settled for belaboring the obvious.

"There's the town. By morning we may be on our way to your homeland."

Asterope answered with a tiny nod. Ronar urged the horses forward, starting the wagon down the switchbacked road that threaded its way down the edge of the plateau. From time to time he glanced at Asterope. Her hair hung dank and listless, swaying to the rocking of the wagon. Her skin was sallow. It gained an artificial warmth as the suns declined, then glowed furnace red as Photos slid beneath the horizon, leaving the swollen carbon star called Kudu to shed its ruby light through an amethyst sky.

Ronar had a thought. "Asterope. Have you tried looking at the suns? With your afflicted eye, that is?"

She raised her head at that. "No. After my first few experiments with the eye, I dared look at nothing."

"Try it now."

Kudu dominated the horizon over Ronar's left shoulder, so Asterope was obliged to look past him as she hesitantly raised the eye patch. She did not flinch at her sight of him, peripheral though it was. Nor did she turn away from the blazing ball that suffused her face with such an illusion of ruddy health. Instead her head tilted slowly while the red sunlight sparkled in both eyes, both the normal grey one and the blighted pale one.

"It—it looks no different than before," she said softly. "Not evil. Not good. A star. Rather beautiful, in fact."

She replaced the eye patch and faced forward once again. For the rest of the wagon ride she was not quite so downcast.

Night had fallen by the time they rolled into Homer. The air was cool and surprisingly damp, with traces of fog diffusing the light from the occasional streetside lamp. Asterope sat huddled in her woolen cloak.

The streets were not crowded. Such people as were abroad were an incongruous mixture of cowboy-clad Thunderbirds, Mersinean sailors whose costumes were much simpler and more abbreviated, and a few women, probably prostitutes, whose costume might follow either mode.

"I wish we could simply continue by land," whispered Asterope.

"It would take too long. The overland distance around the bay is three times the distance by sea."

"But then I must be so close to the sailors. For days. It will be very difficult."

"Keep your eye patch in place. I will assure that the sailors keep their distance."

"It's not quite that simple."

"Nevertheless, we will go by sea. I'll get you a hotel room and leave you there," said Ronar. "Then I'll go to the docks and find us passage to Mersinea."

"No," said Asterope.

Ronar blinked, then turned to Asterope as though uncertain of what he'd heard.

"I must go with you," she said dully. "I know my countrymen. They must see what cargo you propose to bring aboard their ship. If you arrive there in the morning with me in tow, and they have not seen or approved me, I will make them uncomfortable, and we will never board."

"We'll see about that," said Ronar darkly.

"No," she said again. "Don't threaten them. Not unless you're prepared to buy a ship of your own and sail it single-handed. We must do things their way."

"Very well," growled Ronar through a scowl.

Asterope looked askance at Ronar and came near to a smile.

The four or five ships tied up at the docks looked like a sketchy, skeletal grove of masts and yards, barely seen against a shifting background of deep grey fog. Their hulls were out of sight, down below in the fog, the tide being low and the vessels far down by the pilings.

The only exception to this reign of silence and darkness was the ship at the end of the main pier. Muffled sounds of activity came from it as Ronar and Asterope approached.

The crimson of the furled sail showed that this was the ship they had watched putting into port just a few hours before. They stepped up to the edge of the dock and looked down. Lanterns hung from the sternpost, which flared out of the water in a sweeping curve, while behind it projected spikes which were extensions of the wales, making the stern reminiscent of the arched tail of a great spiny scorpion. The lantern light was diffused into golden aureoles by the fog. Mersinean sailors, dressed in simple rectangles of cloth wrapped casually around their bodies, grunted and chattered as they brought up amphorae from the hold and lined them up on the floating platform between the ship and the dock. The ship was a bit larger than the usual run of Mersinean merchantmen, large and elaborate enough to be completely decked over.

A man vaulted over the side, onto the platform, lifted an amphora to his shoulder, and started up the ramp that led to the pier itself. Watching his footing, he was unaware of Ronar and Asterope until he was practically on top of them.

"You there," said Ronar.

The sailor gasped and jerked back, almost dropping the big storage vase. He goggled at the shadowy figures that stood before him, the one towering practically out of sight in the fog, the other cloaked and huddled, watching him with the single eye that remained to her, the other being concealed by a patch. He shuddered in the grip of the clammy fog. "Who are you?" he hissed in decent English.

"We are looking for passage to Mersinea. Where is the master of the ship?" asked Ronar.

"He's down below, supervising the unloading."

"Call him."

The sailor set down his burden, and, still looking at Ronar, stepped to the edge of the dock and called down, "Lamarchus! A man up here is looking for passage."

Down on deck, a man separated himself from the crowd of sailors and peered up into the darkness. He was dressed no differently than his men, and looked no grander, though somewhat older than most, with hollow cheeks and a beard shot with white.

"Who's up there?" he called.

"Leonard Ronar from Two Suns City. With me is Asterope, a girl from your own land."

"Come on down, then."

They descended the steep ramp, Asterope taking care not to trip over her trailing *peplos*. The sailors paused in their work to regard them as they entered the soft yellow light shed by the lanterns. The pair approached Lamarchus and took in his level gaze for a moment.

"Welcome aboard *Dekapus*," he said agreeably enough. "What can we do for you?"

"We're looking for the quickest possible passage to Mersinea. To Pantheos, specifically."

Lamarchus nodded slowly. "I believe we can help you. Pantheos is a regular port of call. But you must not expect great luxury on a ship like this. There is only one cabin, it is mine, and it is the size of a coffin."

"I can sleep on deck. The cabin, however, must go to Asterope. I will pay you well for the inconvenience."

"Eh?" Lamarchus studied Asterope closely for the first time. "What is the trouble with this girl?" he asked with a slight frown.

"She has suffered an eye injury. I'm taking her to Pantheos to have it treated."

Lamarchus leaned closer to Asterope, squinting. "That is wise, at any rate. Certainly the physicians of Mersinea are abler, both in craft and in magic, than the quacks of Thunderbird, with their dread of tiny invisible demons and the like."

Ronar looked at the ranks of amphorae and the bolts of fabric on the deck. "Isn't it a bit unusual to unload a ship at night?"

Lamarchus smiled. "Somewhat, but it's not unusual for a crew to crave a bonus. If we unload the ship ourselves and load again in time to depart with the first morning breeze, we stand to profit by delivering live cattle for a sacrifice on the island of Thyros."

Ronar shook his head firmly. "There will be no diversions to Thyros or anywhere else. We must make directly for Pantheos."

Lamarchus looked astonished. "Directly to Pantheos? But that means cutting straight across Aegeos. We'd be out of sight of land for days."

"What of it?"

"Eh? You may be content to sleep on deck, but my men expect to shelter on shore every night, and to find a decent meal. Those are my expectations as well. It's too dangerous to strike out across open water for such a distance."

Ronar pondered this for a moment. "If you're worried about getting lost, I know the stars well enough to navigate with enough precision. After all, the Aegeos is almost a closed body of water. We can scarcely go too far astray."

Lamarchus shook his head. "There's more to it than that. There's danger in such waters for a little round tub like ours. Danger for the strongest trireme, for that matter."

Ronar again kept his silence. He was tempted to denounce the captain's fears as superstition, but he had lived on Colibdis long enough to know that in this world there was no superstition that couldn't and didn't manifest itself in reality.

The men of Thunderbird had no affinity for the sea. They were not great sailors; Ronar had personal experience of that. Their domain ended on the shore. When this ship cast off in the morning it would leave behind the relatively inconspicuous myths and magics of Thunderbird and enter the ocean realm of Mersinea. Any literate person knew the many dangers to be found in the waters of the ancient Greeks.

"I understand your concerns," said Ronar grimly. "Yet it is imperative to get Asterope home as soon as possible. If you risk the voyage, I will pay you enough to make any dangers fade from your mind."

"How much are you offering?"

By way of an answer, Ronar reached into one of the many pockets of his capacious green jacket. He extracted a leather sack and loosened the draw string, displaying its contents to the Mersinean captain. The man's eyes goggled and his lower lip trembled in his beard. Asterope leaned forward, and she too gave a small gasp. Inside was a neat cylinder of Thunderbird fifty dollar gold coins, each a gleaming wafer the size of a small cookie.

"That's more than half enough to buy the ship—and the crew," muttered Lamarchus.

"Half on departure. Half on arrival. Is this acceptable?"

Lamarchus still appeared uncertain. He looked back over his shoulder at the crew, who had heard every word. He did not see any sign of objection to the plan. The sailors craned their necks trying to get a glimpse of Ronar's leather purse.

"You've hired yourself a ship, Ronar. Be back here before the first sun comes up." That was all; Lamarchus turned away and bawled at his crew. "Continue the unloading! And someone go intercept Prodicus and tell him to return those cattle. We take on only such cargo as we can dispose of in Pantheos. The folk of Thyros must sacrifice pigeons, if they can catch them. For completing this voyage, each man will receive five times his usual wage." The sailors cheered.

Ronar turned and looked down at Asterope with a glimmer of satisfaction in his eye. "Can I convince you now to take a good night's rest in a hotel? It might be the last you can expect for a while."

"Let's go."

She took his arm and was silent as they climbed the ramp to the dock. Behind them they heard a sailor bellow, "Can you beat that? He hires the cabin for that witchy one-eyed girl, while he vows to sleep on deck. He must be perishingly fond of the little wench."

Ronar's arm tensed beneath Asterope's hand. He thrust out his chin and started to turn around. Asterope tightened her grip to halt him.

"Don't," she said softly. "I am a witchy wench, and I'd be better off if I did have only one eye."

Then they heard a thud, and Lamarchus said: "Quiet, you fool. I've heard of this Ronar; Greylock they call him. A prudent man does not offend him."

Ronar nodded, relaxed, and set out again along the pier and toward the center of town.

"I didn't realize you'd have to spend your life's savings to take me on this journey," said Asterope.

"What, the gold? That's not a major concern. One tends to come across such things in my line of work."

"My. I hadn't realized astronomy was so lucrative. Even for department heads."

"That's not the line I was referring to. I was talking about my avocation of stalking across the land and having adventures."

"You should have told them the truth," whispered Asterope.

"When didn't I?" asked Ronar, slightly aggrieved.

"Your story was a half-truth at best."

"Perhaps it was. But your true condition is no concern of theirs. You are harmless to them. If they do as they've agreed, they'll be more than adequately compensated. That's all they need to know."

"When they discover I suffer from no mundane injury, we'll find ourselves friendless in the middle of the sea."

The merest flicker of red light spat from the ring on Ronar's finger. "If that's what happens, I'll make sure they fear me more than they fear you."

Chapter 14

Departure

At first light the town of Homer was still smothered in fog. Ronar and Asterope walked down Main Street toward the waterfront. They were dressed in typical fashion: Ronar in rugged, worn clothing of dark green and grey, with a red felt shirt. Most of his garments came from Earth, made of fabrics no one here could identify or reproduce. The silver binoculars bounced against his chest as he walked. Asterope didn't understand how he could stand to wear them as if they were jewelry. They were so huge that if she wore them they'd cover her entire chest. Asterope herself wore her usual chiton, with a boy's cloak to guard against the chill that had never left her since her encounter with Ahriman. She drew a fold of it over her head to act as a hood, uncomfortable with the curious, uneasy gazes of the people they passed on the street.

Ronar had not shaved. He'd preferred snatching a few more moments of rest, for he hadn't slept well. He'd been troubled by the moans and cries that had come through the wall from Asterope's adjoining room. The girl rarely complained when in his company, but when she thought herself alone she gave vent to her distress in so heartfelt a manner that Ronar couldn't help but cringe.

They arrived at the pier to find *Dekapus* bobbing on small waves which slapped lightly at the hull. In daylight the ship looked smaller than it had the night before. Ronar had seen lifeboats fully half the size. It was broad in the beam, but no more than fifty feet long. It seemed a marginal craft for making a blue-water crossing. Possibly, Lamarchus's preference for staying within sight of land had some justification.

Ronar shrugged. He was no sailor. If Lamarchus thought the ship was capable of making the crossing, no doubt it was.

The tide was just going out, causing *Dekapus* to ride much higher than it had last night. The ramp that led to the floating dock was much less steep. Ronar and Asterope climbed down and over the side onto the deck of the ship. Lamarchus approached them, nodding agreeably to Ronar, ignoring Asterope.

"Welcome aboard. I've cleared my gear out of the cabin. I'll have someone stow your bags." He turned away. "Antiphon!" he barked. A boy ran up, studied the two newcomers for a very concentrated second or two, then gave his captain a questioning look. "Take these things into my cabin and get them squared away."

"Yes, sir." Antiphon picked up Asterope's small canvas sack and Ronar's leather satchel and hastened away. He knew the way well enough to risk a glance over his shoulder at the two of them.

"We can depart at any time, Ronar," said Lamarchus pointedly. "All that's needed is for you to give the word."

Ronar glanced at him, said nothing, and wandered away to inspect the ship. He towered over the sailors, though they were strongly built, at least according to the standards of this world, whose gravity made lesser demands on the human frame. He examined the stepping of the mast, plucked at the rigging, and kicked at the fence of woven slats of wood that stood along the sides as railings. At the bow, he leaned over the fence on the starboard side and looked down at the hull. He frowned, not seeing what he'd expected, but only a blotch of black paint, barely dry, with drip marks that led down to the water. He straightened, went to the port side, and looked down again. Painted there was an eye which gazed across the water.

Ronar pulled himself to his full height and studied the knot of men who had collected to observe his progress. Most of them wore neutral expressions, but one smirked openly at him. Ronar approached this man, who was one of the biggest. His hands and nails were still stained with black paint.

This sailor looked around with a broad, easy grin. "Where is the offense here, brothers? Our main cargo seems to be a one-eyed girl. I thought a one-eyed ship would be good enough to carry her." He made a gesture which seemed intended to solicit laughter and support for his prank, but as Ronar's inexorable approach continued, the other sailors backed away nervously.

"This ship goes nowhere until this man is removed," said Ronar in a voice of steel.

"Now, who do you think—" began the sailor. His words were cut off by the thud of the backhanded blow with which Ronar stretched him on the deck. Blood flowed freely from his mouth; apparently the man's tongue had been all but cut off.

Asterope stared in amazement. Lamarchus ran back from his own inspection of the bow. "Eunapius," he said in soft disgust. "A fair deck hand, but a strutting fool. Antiphon! Get to the starboard bow. Go over the side and scrub off that paint. I'll not have this ship putting to sea one-eyed. As for this moaning pile of carrion…"

"Permit me." Ronar bent down, seized Eunapius by the ankles, and hauled him into the air upside down. Walking to the side, he swung the man a few times and pitched him onto the dock, where he crumpled into a heap.

Ronar turned back, aware of the amazed scrutiny of every person on deck. Lamarchus stood blinking at him. It was not the first time Ronar had found reason to appreciate the advantage of his Earth-trained strength, diminished as it was after so many years on Colibdis.

Another of the sailors, an olive-skinned, handsome man with smooth, well-defined muscles, said bitterly, "I don't care to be manhandled by our passengers, no matter what their size."

"I tolerate no insult to Asterope, or to myself. Remember that, and there will be no further trouble," said Ronar.

"Keep your peace, Prodicus. The gods know you fancy yourself a scholar, but try using some common sense as well. Let us contemplate the Heraklean feat of strength we just witnessed while Antiphon makes us fit for sea once more."

"It was most impressive," admitted Prodicus. "But there are times when brains can be an answer to strength." His gaze was fixed directly on Ronar, challenging him.

Ronar merely smiled slightly in return. If Prodicus chose to think of him as a man whose strength overshadowed his intellect, so be it.

Antiphon ran up, smiling, a dirty rag clutched in his hand. "The paint is cleaned away. It wasn't fully dry."

"Good boy." Lamarchus turned back to Ronar. "And now — ?"

Ronar reached into his pocket, withdrew a stack of coins, and dropped them into Lamarchus's outstretched palm. "And now—the word is given."

Lamarchus bawled, "Cast off all lines!"

Ronar went to Asterope, who stood alone, all but forgotten. Her skin showed little more color than the fog surrounding the ship.

"I'm sorry you had to witness that, Asterope," muttered Ronar. "Let me take you to the cabin and get you settled in. The less time you spend on deck the better off you'll be."

"Yes. The more easily I can convince myself I am alone on this ship—the better."

The "cabin" turned out to be nothing more than a tiny enclosed space, scarcely larger than a closet, built into the stern, accessed through a hatch and a short ladder. It was lightless except for what filtered through a grate in the hatch. But it was dry, and contained a bunk long enough for Asterope's small frame. Ronar helped arrange her things, then brought her bread and some watered wine. He patted her hand awkwardly and climbed back up on deck.

The sailors got the ship clear of the pier by the simple expedient of pushing off with their oars. Then they went, grumbling, to their benches, where they thrust the oars out through holes in the bulwark. Five men to a side, not much even for a boat as small as *Dekapus*.

Lamarchus took the tiller of the starboard steering oar while another man took the one to port. Ronar stood between them.

"Standard speed!" cried Lamarchus. A sailor in the bow beat out a rhythm on a drum. The oars dropped into the water and began to thresh in time with the drumbeat. *Dekapus* inched away from land, struggling to gain what way it could. As they worked the oars, the ten rowers sometimes glanced at the hatch in the stern. Prodicus's glances came most often and lingered the longest.

Lamarchus sent Antiphon shinnying up the mast to keep a careful watch. Even at that modest height the boy was only half visible in the fog.

The captain himself also squinted into the fog. "It's not the best way to begin a voyage, blind as Teresias, falling back on the oars right from the start, while we wait for the winds to awaken," he said. "But I sensed you wouldn't be willing to wait for conditions to improve, Ronar."

"I don't see the need. I expect you can at least find your way out of the harbor, blind or not."

"True. But tell me, what if the fog and overcast stay with us, and we have no sight of the stars? How then do you propose to navigate across the open water?"

"That will present no difficulty," said Ronar. He reached into a pocket and drew out a liquid-filled hiking compass. He explained its use to Lamarchus, trying to distinguish its principle from magic, and, as usual, failing. Still, Lamarchus was quick to see the value of the device.

So too, perhaps, was Prodicus. At least, his eyes were locked on it keenly enough.

Chapter 15

At Sea

After three days at sea the sky grudgingly cleared enough to give a glimpse of the suns as they sank into the western horizon. The sky around them was a heavy, lurid mulberry color. The horizon was straight and sharp as a razor, black except for dancing reflections of maroon, gold, and wine. For some reason the suns looked especially remote, and cold. Perhaps it was the black clouds which scudded over their faces, making it obvious that the suns dwelt far from the realm of men, beyond the sky.

The sail popped and flapped as gusts of wind struck it from vagrant directions. In a wind so variable, *Dekapus* barely crawled through the water.

"The sea is uneasy," said Lamarchus, sharing its mood. He looked up from the steering oar. "The winds aloft seem fair enough, to judge by the dispatch with which the clouds surge by. Yet down here it fills the sail, then a moment later snaps it inside-out."

Ronar said nothing. The weather was indeed strange, chilly and unsettled, uncharacteristic of the time or the place. But he didn't wish to feed the apprehension of the men by commenting on it.

"Maybe the sea-gods do not welcome us to their domain," said Prodicus. "Ships that cross the open water are often not seen again."

"This ship seems in little danger of foundering," said Ronar sharply.

"Maybe it's not our ship's course that makes the sea so fitful, but her cargo," said Prodicus.

Ronar drew himself up to reply, but Lamarchus interrupted, hoping to avoid another confrontation between the two.

"Where would you say we are, Ronar?"

Ronar glared at Prodicus's insolent face for a moment, then unfolded a small map he'd brought along. On it he'd drawn a somewhat irregular line marked at intervals with crosses and notes. He tapped it with his pencil.

"Assuming the map is accurate, and your estimates of our speed are good, we should be about here. A little less than two hundred miles along our way."

"Assuming that little swinging needle of yours is also good and accurate," said Prodicus.

Lamarchus frowned. "Prodicus, go forward. Occupy yourself usefully. I took you aboard as a sailor, not a critic."

Prodicus sauntered to the bow, his face a disdainful mask.

Lamarchus looked after him. "Gentlemen should be forbidden to have too many sons. The last in line finds himself with few prospects, and often is forced to occupy stations he perceives as being beneath him."

Ronar made no answer. The source of Prodicus's deficiencies was of no interest to him.

Lamarchus bent down to study the chart. "There is an island about six leagues to the east. Kemenos. To my knowledge, it's free of sorcerers, witches, cyclopses, and bronze giants. In fact, it's said to be free of everything, except for a white beach where we might pull out for a night's rest, and a village of isolated fisherfolk who I'm sure would be happy to trade some fresh food for a trifling sample of our cargo."

Ronar shrugged. "Indeed. But we sail on."

"I'm sure you've heard the aphorism, 'any port in a storm'."

"There is no storm."

"But there is a storm," said Lamarchus, backing away, scanning the horizon as if looking for evidence to back up his sudden statement. "There is a storm," he repeated, more quietly. "A storm not of wind and waves, not yet, but a storm nevertheless."

"You'll frighten the men with that kind of talk," muttered Ronar.

"Then I'd best take steps to allay their fears," said Lamarchus. "Naclatus! Bring up the sacrificial wine."

When that sailor had appeared with the amphora, Lamarchus gathered the men by the port side railing, where he faced out to sea and raised the graceful earthen vessel before him. He stood there motionless for long moments, eyes closed, lips working slowly. Ronar, standing farther down the rail, could see that to Lamarchus this was a deadly serious matter.

At last the captain cried out in a clear, anxious voice, "Lord Poseidon! God of waters. Ease our passage through your domain. Accept this libation, which we offer in your honor, that you may know us for simple men of the sea, subject to your power and mercy." As he spoke he tilted the amphora, sending a crimson stream into the waves. The mixed rays of Photos and Kudu shone through it, turning it into a ripple of fire.

Ronar looked over the side. The wine stained a large patch of water, much larger than was reasonable given the quantity that had been poured. In seconds the entire sea took on a wine-red cast that faded only as the clouds closed in completely, cutting off the last solar rays. But suddenly the clouds were soft, sedate in their passage from horizon to horizon. A steady south wind sprang up, filling the sail, pushing the ship along in a quick and constant manner. The men gave out a tentative cheer.

Far off, nearly on the horizon, Ronar glimpsed a speeding mote of gold and white that might have been a chariot surging over the waves. He half wished the binocular was hanging from his neck, and was half grateful it was not.

He turned away, leaned against the railing, and stared, scowling, at the sail. The red fabric looked purple-black in the dusk. The figure dyed upon it was fully black, a stylized ten-tentacled finned sea creature of some sort, like nothing ever seen on Earth. Nor did Ronar assume it to be chimerical. On Colibdis, not even the Chimera was necessarily chimerical.

"Well, men, we are destined to spend another night at sea," said Lamarchus. "Let's eat while there's still a little light. Parsikrites! It's your turn to mix the wine. Parsikrites? What's troubling you?"

"I don't know. I don't feel well."

"No? Not seasick, I trust. Well, then, Prodicus, you're next in line. You mix the wine and prepare the food, and do it smartly."

"Very well," said Prodicus in an even tone.

The crew broke up to go about their tasks. Lamarchus walked up to Ronar and studied him quizzically. "Why are you so grim, Ronar? Our prayer worked. The gods are tranquil, and we're running before a favorable wind. What here is not to your liking?"

"How widely have you traveled, Lamarchus? Have your voyages ever taken you beyond the Aegeos?"

"Indeed they have. I've coasted all the way to Sothis, and once made the crossing to Kreteros."

"Then maybe you've seen enough to understand this. I've traveled farther than you, and everyplace I've gone I've seen a different set of gods. And I don't know if I'm seeing the same set of gods each time, but with different names and guises, or if each pantheon represents a separate collection of quasi-divine beings. Or maybe they're all nothing but manifestations of magic, created by people's expectations. I don't like to be that uncertain about the nature of things that have so much power over the world. And I hate to think that their passing whims might impact on my intentions."

"So, Ronar, the gods have mere whims, while you have intentions? Well. I'm afraid my travels haven't given me the wisdom to settle such questions. We all have our gods. All I know is that by not offending mine I've been able to survive, and even prosper after a reasonable fashion. I hope for no more."

Chapter 16

Treachery

Ronar picked his way across the icy ridge, buffeted by gusts of wind, blinded by blowing snow and by the mantle of night. Dark space yawned to either side. From somewhere below came a steady, bleating wail of terror, a sound that easily and cruelly cut through the rhythmic roar of the wind.

Ronar had heard that sound somewhere before. He found it imperative to seek it out and discover its source. Preserving his balance by the narrowest of margins, he tottered along the ridge, blown this way and that by the shifting gusts of wind. Where possible he leaned over the edge to look for the source of the cries. As he proceeded they neither strengthened nor weakened in volume.

At last, as Ronar balanced on an icy fin of rock scarcely wider than his feet, he glimpsed something on a ledge twenty feet below. The dim, shadowless light which suffused the mountain snowstorm revealed a bighorn sheep, lying in a contorted posture, eyes wide with terror. Near it crouched a black wolf, its snarls like a pitiless form of laughter.

Ronar knew with certainty that he himself was responsible for the ewe being in its predicament. There was no way to climb down the ice wall that separated him from the ledge, and no time to seek another way down before the wolf would tear out the sheep's throat.

The ewe, he could now see, had only a single sighted eye.

He leaped, intending to come down full on the wolf, oblivious to the consequences.

His eyes snapped open to confront a meaningless, incomprehensible scene. His cheek lay against a black wall which seemed to rock back and forth at intervals. He could see nothing else but dark grey blankness. The smell of salt was strong—he was still on the ship! Suddenly his inner gyroscope rotated his point of view by ninety degrees. He was lying on the deck, his cheek against its weathered planks.

One thing remained constant—the sounds, the cries of agony and fear, mixed with low-pitched snarls now shading into outrage and horror.

Asterope.

And then Ronar discovered that he could not move. He could scarcely feel his body, could not so much as blink. He might as well have been some uncorporeal mind visiting someone else's body for all the control he had over his own. Caught between dreams and wakefulness, his mind disconnected from his body, he silently struggled to regain its use while Asterope's anguish informed the hazy, dreamlike world he'd awakened into. With a desperate act of will he concentrated on doing the least little thing, even twitching the tip of his finger. He could not see his fingers, could not feel them, but could only take it on faith that they were still there.

With a sudden convulsion Ronar not only moved his fingers but broke out of his paralysis, sitting up and looking around. Scattered around the deck were dark shapes, probably the the crew of *Dekapus*. None of them moved.

Ronar shakily got to his feet. His mind still seemed muffled in cotton, and he appeared to have vision in one eye only. He reached up and rubbed at his left eye, his hand coming away black with half-dried blood. He was able to clear his eyesight, though in the darkness there was little to be seen.

He staggered over to the aft hatch, barely keeping on his feet due to the pitching of the ship. He flung off the hatch cover and peered down into the cabin.

Lit by a single candle, there on the bunk lay Asterope, naked, bruised, her afflicted eye uncovered. Standing there facing her was Prodicus, staring at her aghast, saying, "What are you, woman? What kind of demon are you?"

Asterope could not answer. She writhed on the bed, whimpering, unable to take her eyes from her attacker.

"Prodicus!" rasped Ronar.

Wide-eyed, Prodicus looked up to see him towering in the darkness. "You! What kind of foul thing have you brought aboard this ship? I should have killed you when I had the chance."

"You're right about that, but your chance has passed. Come up here and face me."

"Gladly, after I've dispatched this—this witch of the Graeae." From the waist of his chiton Prodicus drew a bronze dagger. He advanced on Asterope, whose face suddenly froze into a saturnine mask, from which issued laughter.

"No!" cried Ronar. He summoned the sword, urging it into existence with an impulse of searing will—to no result. Aghast, he stared at his ring hand, seeing no glimmer of gold or garnet, but only a circle of blood where the ring had been ripped from his finger.

No matter. He stepped over the brink of the hatch, falling onto Prodicus and knocking him down. Prodicus rolled aside, but Ronar collapsed, his knees weak as water. In the close quarters of the cabin the two men grappled. Prodicus tried to bring his dagger into play. It was a goal he accomplished all too easily, and Ronar was astounded to find himself beneath the smaller man, staring at the point of the weapon. He had only an instant to ponder the all-but-unprecedented nature of his situation before the blade plunged down. He swatted at it and managed to deflect it, but the effort was sufficient only to save his life—the blade plunged deep into his shoulder. The sudden pain swept some of the fog from his mind, enough to clear away the veil of unreality which had made this encounter hard to distinguish from a dream. The cold fire that suddenly kindled in his eyes was enough to make Prodicus flinch, despite his dominant position. Ronar's right hand whipped out and grabbed the wrist that held the dagger still embedded in his flesh. He pulled it out, then with bared teeth exerted all his strength to crush the bones of Prodicus's wrist. Prodicus shrieked and dropped the dagger. Lifting his arm, he stared horrified at his dangling hand. He was soon distracted, or rather thrown into the side of the bunk, by Ronar's fist crashing into his face.

Ronar flung himself on the semiconscious figure, who could only mumble feebly through smashed teeth while Ronar searched the pouch at his waist.

"I'll take this back, you filthy bastard," snarled Ronar, extracting the garnet ring and replacing it on his left hand. Then he stood, still unsteadily, and sat on the bunk beside Asterope. Trying to speak soothing words, he patted her trembling shoulder, tried to arrange her torn clothing, and found and replaced her eye patch. Only when the afflicted eye was covered again did she fling herself upon him, clinging to him with desperate strength.

"Professor Ronar," she gasped hoarsely, "why...why did I have to see the vileness inside this man...so horrible...and why did he have to let...*it* see..."

"Don't worry, Asterope," said Ronar, staring into her good eye from only inches away. "This man will never violate another human being. I will see to him now, and then I'll return to you. Will you be all right?"

She nodded. "Just get him out of my sight!" She released him, then fell back in the bunk while her head rolled from side to side.

Ronar looked at her for a moment, then got to his feet. He glanced down and noted the blood streaming from his shoulder, reached down and ripped away Prodicus's linen garment, using it to bandage himself. That done, he grabbed Prodicus under the arms and flung him up through the hatch, where he lay with his chest over the edge while his legs dangled down the ladder. Ignoring the pain in his shoulder, not to mention that in his head, Ronar stuffed him the rest of the way through and then climbed onto the darkness of the deck.

Ronar sensed movement on the deck. He wasn't surprised when he heard the voice of Lamarchus, a bit huskier than usual.

"Is that you, Ronar? What's happened? Antiphon! Anyone! Get a light from the brazier and let me see what in Hades is going on here."

In a few moments Antiphon appeared with a lantern. Its unsteady light revealed Lamarchus and most of his crew standing in a group, regarding Ronar and the prostrate form at his feet with dazed uncertainty.

"What's happened, Lamarchus, is that this pig drugged us all, then robbed me, and tried to rape Asterope."

"Drugged us," repeated Lamarchus. "More likely he invoked Dionysus to triple the potency of the wine. I seem to recall that last night's revelry was rather intense for a group of tired seafarers drinking watered wine. By the look of you, he decided to follow it up with a good crack to the skull."

Before Ronar could continue, Prodicus surprised him by rolling over and sitting upright. "Lamarchus!" he slurred. "We must be rid of that witch below decks. She is an abomination. That eye...the evil eye! And the things she said to me...no succubus could mouth such silky obscenities."

"No!" thundered Ronar. "Whatever you may have heard from her, they were not her words."

Lamarchus fixed him with a worried stare. "Not her words? Are you saying—that your woman is possessed?"

"Partially," admitted Ronar.

"Possessed by what?"

"Possessed by—" Ronar cast about for an answer. He remembered that he knew no Greek name for Ahriman. Their pantheon contained no real equivalent of the god of thought and magic. "—by something that has no name in your religion."

"The eye..." gasped Prodicus.

Lamarchus's mouth fell open. His eyes grew round. He staggered over to the hatch, to stare down at Asterope. "The Eye. That wandering thing that haunts the stars? The demon the Thunderbirds call Lucifer?"

"That is one of its names."

Now the whole crew fell back, muttering to one another in frightened tones. Antiphon nearly dropped his lantern.

Lamarchus turned and drew himself up. "Ronar—damn you for bringing such a creature on board my ship. No wonder the sea gods were angry—she must be put off at once, and you as well."

Ronar looked at them in astonishment. "And what of this pig at my feet? This thief and rapist?"

"What of him? True, I do not approve of my men robbing my passengers, but at least he had the sense to be suspicious of you and the witch. I count him as having done me a service, to alert me to the poison we are carrying."

"But she is harmless," insisted Ronar. "Her condition is an affliction only to herself. If only you leave her alone, we can get her to a place where she may be cured."

Lamarchus shook his head adamantly. "We will not sail another day with that creature aboard. The island of Kemenos is not far off. We will put you ashore there, to let the fishermen decide what to do with you. Or we will put you both over the side, if that is your preference."

Ronar's astonishment soared dangerously toward wrath. "You will do neither." The garnet ring flickered and flared, a red glare that overwhelmed the glow of the lantern, then blazed white with the radiance that heralded the appearance of the sword. "This is the sword of Bran," said Ronar, brandishing the great weapon before the dazzled sailors. "A steel weapon, far superior to your bronze kitchen knives."

"He is a sorcerer," quavered one of the men.

Lamarchus cocked his head and said, "No. If what I have heard is true, that is the only magic he commands."

"It's enough for the likes of us," muttered someone.

Lamarchus thrust out his beard belligerently. Cowards and fools did not become merchant captains in Mersinea. "So, Ronar, there you stand with your mighty blade. What will you do, murder us all to compel us to your will? Or will you merely intimidate us into sailing you to Pantheos? How long do you think that will work? Do you expect to sleep at all for the remainder of the voyage, or eat? No. Unless you destroy us all, we are bound to have our way in this."

Ronar glared at him while he desperately considered how to keep the situation from slipping totally out of control. Lamarchus's speech seemed to have heartened his men, who now moved forward with greater confidence, aware that Ronar's position was untenable. Prodicus stirred at his feet, casting up glances full of venom and insolence.

"Very well then," said Ronar. "Turn the ship for Kemenos."

"That is well done, Ronar," said Lamarchus. "We have no wish to harm—"

"But here is one who will not be making the voyage," said Ronar. Letting the sword lapse into oblivion, he seized Prodicus and heaved him over the side before anyone could move. Prodicus's scream ended in a coughing gurgle that soon receded into inaudibility in the waves.

"And there is more. It will not be Asterope and I who disembark at Kemenos. It will be all of you." With that pronouncement he brought back the sword, deliberately prolonging the clash of sound and blaze of light to overawe the men.

Lamarchus, his arms raised to protect his eyes, cried, "What, are you a fool? You know nothing of seamanship.

Even if it were possible to sail this ship single-handed, you don't know a clew from a brail."

"I can more easily learn to handle this ship than reach my destination without one."

Lamarchus's anger grew near to apoplexy. "But it's piracy! Theft!"

Ronar's face hardened even further. "I do not approve of robbing a man with whom I have made a bargain, it's true. But you will find your ship waiting for you at Pantheos."

"If you can make the passage," said Lamarchus bitterly.

Ronar nodded. "And if you can find a way to reach the mainland. A task which you'll find no more difficult than we would have, if you'd succeeded in stranding us."

Lamarchus made an explosive gesture of frustration. "This is nonsense! Men, we outnumber him twenty to one! He is weakened and injured. Let us swarm over him; we can wrest that blade from his grip before he can apply its edge to any one of us. Come on!"

To answer this, Ronar leaped to the stern, where he swung the sword of Bran like an ax, chopping out great chunks of wood from the scorpion-tail that curled from the sternpost. In three blows the whole structure split loose and fell into the sea. He spun and faced the sailors, sword raised high.

"That is what awaits the first man who makes a move against me. If there are any who doubt me, let him act now and lose a limb for his trouble."

Lamarchus glowered at him from beneath shaggy brows. "All right then, Ronar. We will maroon ourselves on Kemenos, and send you and your one-eyed witch off to drown like Prodicus."

This brought murmurs of relief from the crew. At this point their only wish was to escape from their deadly passengers.

"Then you'd better get your men to the steering oars," said Ronar.

"May we first consult your chart and compass, to estimate our new course?" asked Lamarchus with mock politeness.

Ronar reached into his jacket pocket. It was empty. A quick search showed that everything was gone—compass, charts, gold, jewels, even a pencil. "The compass is missing," he said, looking out over the lightless sea. "Prodicus must have stolen it. I was so intent on recovering my ring that I never thought to check what else he might have on him."

"Ah. And so your already slim chance of making the crossing is cut in half."

Ronar eyed Lamarchus in irritation. "The only navigation you need to worry about is getting us to Kemenos. Can you do that?"

"Yes. We can't have gone far from our last known position. With no hand at the steering oars through most of the night and no one at the rigging, the ship has been wallowing. And Kemenos is not so small a target."

"Fine. Give the orders."

Lamarchus turned to his men. "You heard the American! If we are to be rid of his company, we must reach Kemenos, and the sooner the better. Steering oars full to starboard! Square up the clews! We'll run directly downwind for now, and should raise the island in the morning."

The time of sunrise could only be guessed at, since their rising only brightened by insensible degrees the dome of clouds that still hid the sky. Ronar, standing a bleary-eyed guard over the after cabin hatch, scanned the horizon for the first trace of the island, as did everyone on deck who had the leisure to do so. Nearby were the sailors who manned the steering oars, while just in front of them Lamarchus kept on eye on everything, including Ronar himself.

Ronar was careful to maintain his erect posture, not daring to slump as his pain and exhaustion inclined him to do. His shoulder gave him considerable pain, and the arm depending from it was weakened. He was lucky no major nerves had been severed by the dagger's strike.

The daylight reached a dim peak about an hour after Ronar first noticed it, then, ominously, declined rapidly. The clouds took on a dull, maroon cast. *Dekapus* sailed through a smoky twilight so deep that the sail looked almost black. Ronar looked around uneasily, wondering if this gloom preceded a storm. But one of the helmsmen muttered "The Gloaming", and the other replied with something about it being ill-timed, with a surly glance over his shoulder at Ronar.

Ronar silently cursed himself for a fool. This overcast had lasted so long he'd forgotten about and lost track of the Gloaming, one of the most basic facts of life on Colibdis. For the next three days the planet would spin through a chill reddish semidarkness, as Photos, the bright, white component of the solar pair, slid behind the larger Kudu in the course of their mutual orbit.

Ill-timed indeed. Ronar could not argue with that while everyone on the ship was fearful or suspicious of almost everyone else, not while the weather was already somber and the ship's destination uncertain. Indeed, with everyone's immediate fate a matter of uncertainty, the additional oppression of the Gloaming was scarcely needed. Yet Ronar suddenly found himself working to suppress a perverse smile. The factors which had combined to create this air of apprehension were so perfect he could not help but admire them.

A sailor at the bow gave an inarticulate squawk, cleared his throat, and announced in a high voice, "Land off the starboard bow!"

Those who were free to do so crowded to that side of the ship to stare across the leaden waves. Ronar could see well enough from where he was. Kemenos made itself plain as a blunt-topped spire of rock which might almost have been a thunderhead looming over the horizon. In fact that's what Ronar had thought it was, but he assumed the seamen were better qualified to make such distinctions than he.

Lamarchus stared uneasily at the mountain. "That crag fits the descriptions I've heard of the island." He raised his voice. "Steer five points to starboard. Brace the yard; tighten the windward clew."

The ship's nose swung toward the island, though it sailed fitfully, near the limit of its ability to sail into the wind.

For the next few hours they watched the island gradually lift over the horizon. The central peak was its main feature; the rest of the island was low and flat except for a few hummocks. It was hard to make out any details in the murky illumination.

Lamarchus had to order his overwrought men to eat and drink. No one offered anything to Ronar. Neither did anyone glance at Asterope's hatch with anything less than dread and loathing. Nor would Ronar have accepted anything for either of them, not after Prodicus's trick with the wine. His best hope for their safety was to get the Mersineans off the ship as soon as possible, before exhaustion could cause his vigilance to falter. It would be too easy for his concentration to waver to the point where he suddenly realized the sword was no longer in his grip. Then an alert man might find it possible to finish what Prodicus had started.

Lamarchus looked alert enough, but his attention was reserved for the sea around his ship. The waves, Ronar suddenly noticed, were no longer smooth swells, but loomed higher and choppier.

Lamarchus stood up straight. "Get to the brails! Furl the sail and man the oars. Naclatus, take soundings. I don't trust these waters."

The men did as they were bid. A few minutes later, *Dekapus* proceeded under the impetus of slow, deliberate oar strokes.

Naclatus threw a weighted line over the side, counting the knots on the rope as it came back up. "Five fathoms!" he cried. He tossed it out again. "Five fathoms!"

Presently the island was near enough that Ronar could make out some details. A cluster of pale whitish glimmers near the beach was probably the fishing village Lamarchus had mentioned. He could even faintly hear the rhythmic roar of the breakers rushing onto the sand. Beneath that sound was a clamor like that of a large number of seabirds.

"Six fathoms!"

Lamarchus looked somewhat relieved, though still vigilant.

"Three fathoms!"

Eighteen feet of water, no great amount. Still, a vessel like *Dekapus* couldn't draw more than a few feet of water.

Suddenly the ship shuddered; the deck lifted beneath Ronar's feet like the floor of an elevator, and stopped. The ship rolled slightly to port, its bow tilted up about ten degrees. The men sent up an uproar of surprise and alarm and raised their oars.

Lamarchus ran to the side and looked over. "Sandbar," he announced in disgust. "And who knows if the tide is in or out, going up or down. Well, we can't risk that it might be going out. All hands over the side; we'll have to try pushing her off."

The crew pulled in their oars and jumped into waist-deep water. At least it was waist-deep in the troughs of the waves. When the swells rolled by the men either bobbed up with them or held their breaths. The larger waves rocked the ship a bit, but with each one that passed it seemed more firmly planted in the sand.

Lamarchus leaned over the side to address his men. "Get to the bow! Push her back! If we take her forward we'll scrape off the steering oars and the sternpost."

The distant cries of the seabirds seemed to have grown louder and more frantic. Ronar narrowed his eyes toward the island. It was hard to tell through the crash of the surf and the yelling of the sailors, but there was something strange about those cries. He almost thought he caught a word in them now and then.

"Wait for a wave to lift the ship, and then push!"

"We will if we don't drown first!" sputtered a sailor.

Ronar glanced toward Lamarchus. The captain was preoccupied with his men, who were all safely out of the way for now. He decided he could risk lowering his guard for a moment. Letting the sword lapse into oblivion, Ronar swung open the hatch and dropped into the dankness of Asterope's cabin. She was asleep, lying there stiff and tense, her face a drawn, pale mask with a sheen of sweat. Ronar rummaged through his bag and withdrew his binocular. Climbing back up onto the deck, he raised the glass toward the island.

"Ronar."

Ronar started and looked away to find Lamarchus standing beside him. There was a flare of light and shatter of thunder. He let the binocular drop on its neck strap. The sword had materialized by the time the glass completed its short fall.

Lamarchus blinked away the light and the din. "Ronar," he said again. "I only want to tell you this. No matter how far you go, no matter where you take my ship, I will someday find a way to take revenge on you."

Ronar nodded slowly at the furious face.

"I take your threat with all due seriousness, Lamarchus. But the truth is, I have worse enemies to worry about than you."

Lamarchus's glare did not abate. After a moment Ronar said, "Don't challenge me to a staring contest. Get back to your men, Captain."

Lamarchus huffed and snorted his way back to the railing.

Ronar dismissed the sword and raised the binocular again.

Now on the distant beach he made out a crowd of people facing in their direction, jumping up and down, gesturing wildly, and raising, as Ronar now realized, a distance-muted uproar of cries and shouts.

A cold zone of apprehension took shape in Ronar's mind. He left his post by the hatch and strode rapidly to the railing, where he scanned the waters surrounding the ship. A few hundred feet off the port side he spotted what appeared to be a short segment of a wave moving at right angles to the rest of the waves. Raising the binocular, it became clear that a large, barely submerged object was approaching quickly, pushing up a glassy dome of water as it came.

"Lamarchus!" he yelled. "Something is approaching from the north!"

Lamarchus ran up beside him and squinted out over the waves. "May Proteus keep us," he muttered, then spun and ran back to the bow. "Everyone out of the water!" he bawled. "Out now! NOW!"

The men began to scramble up the ropes. Ronar kept his eye on the approaching object. By now it was close enough so that the binocular was no longer needed. He discerned a sleek black shape beneath the sheath of water. His best guess was that it was a whale, though he didn't know which whale species had ever migrated to Colibdis, if any.

But it was not a whale. As the water began to shoal, the creature's back came up out of the water and it was forced to slow. It headed directly toward the bow of the ship, where most of the men were still in the water, climbing over each other to get to the ropes, cursing and wailing.

It was at least half the length of the ship, black and shiny, with a flattened body that flared into a diamond-shaped fin at the front. On the three corners of the fin were large, milky-white eyes. It mounted the sandbar, now walking on ten stubby cylindrical legs.

What could it be? Ronar quickly reviewed all he knew about Greek mythological monsters, but recalled nothing that resembled this thing. Then Lamarchus yelled, "Dekapus! Of all the damned—it's a dekapus! Watch out!"

Chagrined, Ronar thought of the design on the sail, and realized it was in fact a stylized representation of the creature which attacked them now. He'd so steeped himself in the milieu of Greek myth that he'd forgotten the dwindling, but still formidable, native fauna of Colibdis.

Suddenly Ronar's eyes gleamed fiercely. Here was an opportunity to work off some of the frustrated wrath he'd built up over the past few weeks. He dashed to the after hatch, pausing only long enough to drop the binocular onto the bunk beside Asterope as she writhed in restless sleep. Then he flung himself over the side of the ship, manifesting the sword even as his feet entered the water. By now the monster was upon them, surging toward the unarmed men who still scrambled for the ropes. It raised its flattened head, revealing a pulsing, slitlike mouth lined with rows of conical white teeth. Ronar pushed through the water toward it. It lashed out and plucked one of the sailors, Porthenetes, off the climbing rope. His torso was penetrated by dozens of inch-long teeth, causing blood to stream into the dekapus's mouth and into the water, darkening its already reddish tone. The other sailors fell over each other in their haste to escape the monster's jaws.

Ronar came within range, cocked the sword of Bran in a two-handed grip, and sent the steel blade arcing into the great shining black arch of neck, slicing it open like a waxed cheese. The dekapus gave a convulsive spasm and dropped Porthenetes, who sank from sight. Catching Ronar in two of its milk-crystal eyes, it swayed toward him. Ronar drew back for another blow, but then noticed a shadow on his right. He glanced to the side to discover a black pillar of flesh curving out of the water, tipped with a spine like a huge polished thorn. The sword was on the wrong side of his body to strike at this sting. Ronar flung himself back, barely escaping the stinger's thrust. He came up sputtering, only to find the dekapus surging away, in pursuit of easier prey. Ronar waded after it at best speed, but the monster was faster. It caught up Naclatus, tossing him around as it tried to align him with its gullet. Enraged, Ronar lifted the sword and threw it like a spear at the glistening black slope of back. It plunged in almost to the hilt, again causing the dekapus to drop its victim. Ronar let the sword lapse, summoned it again into his hand, and threw it even harder. This time the guard broke through the skin and the whole sword vanished into the monster. Again Ronar called it back to his hand. The dekapus turned now, sensing a mortal enemy it could not effectively flee. Its stinger reared up again, its stalk long enough to curve all the way over is head. It struck, and Ronar barely raised the sword in time to skewer it. The blow slammed the guard into Ronar's hands and numbed them, but he did not drop the sword. The dekapus managed to pull its stinger off the blade, but its next strike was slower, and Ronar got in a swing that sent the whole end of the stinger flying into the sea.

Now the dekapus expelled a cloud of stinking air that hissed past its lips. Ronar swung again, slicing into the forward eye and splitting the flukelike head right down to the neck. Dying, it became more dangerous than ever, thrashing around in a frenzy that threatened to crush everyone nearby beneath its bulk. Ronar backed off, then pushed his way to the monster's side, where he hacked away until the dekapus, or what was left of it, grew still. Great chunks of flesh floated in the bloody waves.

Panting, Ronar regarded the result of his work with vicious satisfaction.

He looked up to find Lamarchus and eight of his men lining the rail, all armed with spears or bows.

"Kill him!" said Lamarchus in a voice of fury.

"No."

The sailors turned, paling, gasping with a fear that even the dekapus could not inspire.

Asterope came into view, gliding slowly across the deck, her face fixed and white as a porcelain mask. Her hand came up and pulled back the patch over her defiled eye. It glimmered horribly in the wan maroon light of the Gloaming. Fascinated, Lamarchus and his men stared at her, standing still as stone.

"Harm him," said Asterope in a thin voice, "and I shall release the god who looks out at you from this eye. I will give him leave to act through me to destroy you. And when that is done, your shades shall not walk in the Elysian Fields, or even writhe in the pits of Tartarus. Rather, they will serve as food and playthings for the one whose other Eye looks down over the world from among the stars at night."

Cowering, Lamarchus choked as he tried to produce an answer. Finally he quavered, "What must we do?"

"Keep the bargain you made with Ronar. Abandon the ship, go to the island, and permit us to go on our way."

Lamarchus's hairy face worked itself into grotesque expressions as his dread of Asterope contended with his desire for revenge. Finally he turned away with an incoherent cry of rage and shouted, "All right! Lower your weapons. We're leaving. And we won't wait another minute. We'll swim ashore from here."

"Don't be a fool, Lamarchus!" cried Ronar. "It's half a mile off, at least. What if another dekapus or some other beast should come at you?"

Lamarchus leaned on the rail and glared down at him. "Then we will die cleanly, like men. Not as victims of this vile sorceress."

Ronar's concern for the safety of the Mersineans evaporated before his anger. "Go then."

Lamarchus turned away. "Antiphon! You and three others get down to the hold. Bring up supplies, and we'll lash together some wood and skins, anything that will float, to make a raft so we can carry our goods ashore." He cast another acid glance at Ronar. "You don't mind if we take some food and trade goods ashore, do you?"

"Take whatever you like. Leave us only an adequate supply of food and water for our voyage. You may take all the wine—we won't be needing it."

As the sailors got to work, Ronar swarmed up over the side of the ship, practically leaping aboard to reduce his moment of vulnerability as he went over the rail. No one paid him any attention except Asterope, who stood watching from the stern. His bad arm ached as though it might fall off. He was careful to move it as little as possible.

Swordless now, Ronar approached her slowly. Her face shifted as though she and Ahriman alternated in its possession, sometimes flickering from one persona to the other so fast they seemed to merge into a blur, an amalgam of mortal distress and inhuman malice. The afflicted eye glimmered like a white jelly. Her knees quivered; her hands shook. Ronar could barely imagine what she had seen in the terrified, hate-filled sailors, or what she might have heard from the god who watched and whose name she had invoked.

Ronar reached out and gently replaced the eye patch. "Please go below," he said in a low voice. "I'll speak with you as soon as we're alone."

Asterope nodded and complied, lowering herself down the hatch like a white worm, all but without strength.

Lamarchus and his men worked like fiends, wrapping hard biscuits in waterproof skins, tying together jars and amphorae, some empty, some filled, and throwing them into the water, where other men lashed them into larger clusters. They broke or lost half of what they handled, but were oblivious to the losses. Only Lamarchus's discipline kept them all from flinging themselves into the water and swimming for shore with only the rags on their backs.

Presently they had contrived an awkward, unwieldy pile of provisions that bobbed on the waves. They lashed their weapons atop the crude raft as well. Naclatus, his sides bleeding from a score of wounds, climbed weakly aboard it. Porthenetes, the dekapus's first victim, was nowhere to be seen.

Lamarchus was the last man to abandon the deck of his ship for the waves. He took one last look at Ronar, beard bristling.

"So, Greylock. In all likelihood your blunderings will put *Dekapus* on the bottom of the sea, if in fact you can get her free of this bar. But if by some chance you should survive your voyage, remember, you will see me again."

Ronar made a dismissive gesture. "Things did not have to be this way, Lamarchus. If not for your ignorance and treachery, you could have kept faith with me, profiting in the process, and coming to no harm. Now go begin your new career as a digger of clams."

Lamarchus scowled blackly, but Ronar, having had enough, towered over him at his full forbidding height. After a moment the captain turned and vaulted over the side.

"All right, men. Get behind the raft and push. The swim won't be long; we should be wading by the time we get half way."

With a threshing of legs the raft and its human propulsion system moved slowly away from *Dekapus*. Ronar stood at the railing, watching the surrounding waters for signs of other predators. As far as he could tell from squinting at the island, its inhabitants had quieted, and no longer appeared to be trying to warn them of anything.

After a few minutes he could no longer hear the cursing and splashing of the crew, or the exhortations of their captain. Only the top of the raft was visible in the troughs of the waves.

Ronar turned away. Whether they made it or not was no longer any concern of his.

He eyed the hatch in the after part of the deck. With nothing more to distract him for the moment, he could no longer delay the inevitable. His head drooped at an uncharacteristic angle as he stepped down the tilted deck toward the hatch. Seawater still dripped from his shaggy iron-colored hair. The blood in his torn clothing had been rinsed out, leaving brownish stains.

He raised the hatch and lowered himself stiffly into the chill dankness of the cabin. The tiny space was colder than the outside, and damper, and of course much darker. Asterope, huddled on the bunk, was barely visible in the gloomy light that leaked in from above. Her normal eye glittered at him strangely as she waited for him to speak.

"Well, Asterope, we're alone," he said in low voice. "In a few minutes I'll go into the water and work at freeing the ship. I'll throw a chest or something into the sand and use it as a fulcrum. Using an oar as a lever, I'll try to pry the ship off the sandbar. Or I could use the sword. Even if it breaks, I can always..."

Ronar could not continue this babbling. He fell to his knees before the bunk. His face fell onto the coarse linen that covered the horsehair mattress. His hands reached out in supplication, not quite touching her. His voice was only a choked, rasping shadow of its usual bold, authoritative self.

"I have failed you, Asterope. You were right—we never should have boarded this ship—never should have put your fate into the hands of these strangers. I thought I could cow them, bend them to my will, but I could not. I didn't understand how they would react to what has happened to you. And now we're trapped here. I—I ask your forgiveness, Asterope. I set myself this task of saving you, and now I don't know how I'm going to do it. Forgive me."

There was silence in the cabin for a few moments.

Asterope whispered, "You should hear how Ahriman laughs inside me. He—and I—did not think you were capable of this—this contrition. He cannot see you through me—but he can hear you. And—he's taking credit for saving your life, by giving me the power to threaten those sailors. He hopes you are—grateful."

Ronar raised his head from the mattress, and the expression on his face made Asterope gasp and draw back against the hull. His eyes blazed with a cold fire she had never seen before. The planes of his lean, ascetic face were hard and merciless as stone. She knew she was seeing a side of Ronar that was unknown in the halls of the University.

Now his voice was icy, deadly. "And that brings me to the second thing I want to say to you. Never, *never*, allow that thing inside you to manifest itself like that again. Do not open yourself to its power, or you will be forever lost. Don't do it even to save your life. Don't do it to save mine. The next time I see you giving in to Ahriman's temptations, I will kill you myself."

Asterope stared at him in terror. "You don't know what —it is offering me. You don't know—what kinds of things Ahriman is urging me to do—the vileness. Some are things I'd like to do—now—but not—not with *it* looking on."

Ronar didn't know what she was talking about, nor did he wish to. "You must resist. Ahriman is a spirit that resonates with the deepest human urges for self-gratification and self-aggrandizement. But the price it demands is utter subservience to its ambition to extend the rule of magic far beyond this small world. Utter subservience, total debasement. Dissolution into itself. You must not accept anything it offers."

"I'll do my best," said Asterope, her voice small but clear.

The muffled roar of the surf striking the ship echoed through the hull. The ship creaked and rolled slightly. The cabin seemed to sink, then rise up again, then level out. All at once the planks came alive with a gentle pitching motion. It was regular and did not subside.

"The ship was lightened with the loss of the crew and cargo," whispered Ronar. "And the tide must be coming in. We are free."

"In that case," said Asterope quietly, "I forgive you." She managed a smile that contained a trace of her old wryness.

"That's the first good luck I've had on this trip," said Ronar. Even he wasn't sure if he was referring to the freeing of the ship or to receiving Asterope's forgiveness for his errors.

He stood up and regarded Asterope with a poignant mixture of emotions. "Well. I'd better get back up on deck, and try to figure out how to keep this thing from blowing right onto Lamarchus's beach, or onto another sandbar."

He emerged into the murky daylight to find his apprehension had a sound basis in reality. Although the sail was furled, the force of the wind on the hull was enough to push the ship sideways toward the island at a substantial pace. Already it was close enough to let him pick out individual figures watching from the beach. He couldn't tell if any of Lamarchus's men were among them.

He took the tiller of the starboard steering oar, trying to turn the ship toward the left. The port steering oar merely flapped in the water. The ship's broad deck was too wide for him to handle both at once.

The ship's nose did yaw slowly away from the island, but that made little difference to her overall course. The wind merely pushed her backwards toward the surf. Ronar released the oar. The bow slowly swung back toward the island.

Ronar pondered their predicament. He did not think he'd be able to deploy the sail before *Dekapus* went aground. Even if he did, unless he also figured out how to set it properly, it would only propel them faster onto the sand. And with only one steering oar, his control would be minimal.

He looked at the rower's benches. There are times when brute strength may prevail where intelligence cannot, or so he told himself. He seated himself on one of the starboard benches, seized an oar, and plunged it into the water. His efforts immediately arrested the ship's tendency to swing nose down to the wind, and he was able to keep her pointed at a right angle to the beach. Whether he was also giving her any forward way he did not know. Whatever speed he could develop would have to be significant to get them past the head of the island before the wind could take them ashore.

Well, he told himself, if there was one thing he was good at, it was maximum, prolonged physical exertion in the face of danger. He dug the blade of his oar into the water and pulled it back hard enough to bend the shaft of the oar, and he did it again, and again.

His one-sided effort quickly began to turn the bow out from the island again. That was not satisfactory. Facing into the wind, his efforts were nullified, and soon he'd find himself merely rowing in large, useless circles.

He had to correct their course. He hauled his oar out of the water as quickly as he could, then dashed across to the opposite bench, where he deployed the oar and pulled the bow back parallel to the beach. That done, he again pulled up the oar and returned to his original seat before the bow could slew too far and point itself straight at the beach.

He looked over his shoulder as he shoved the oar back in the water. The waves were breaking only a hundred yards away. Now he could see the faces of the islanders who had waded out into the surf to assist the school of men who had just arrived, pushing before them an unwieldy floating pile of jetsam.

Ronar resumed his rowing with frantic strength. His oar snapped into a splintered shaft in his hand. Cursing vehemently, he dropped the handle and sprang onto the next bench back. He plunged the blade into the water and dug whirlpools a foot across into the foaming surface. The bow instantly swung away from the shore once more. If he was making any progress along the beach, he could not discern it.

He could not keep the ship off the beach by his own efforts. Once he'd accepted that bitter realization, he found himself glaring at the stern hatch. He must put Asterope's waning strength to the test in order to save many lives. He dropped his eyes to the deck, once more aflame with the humiliation of his failure.

Still rowing his utmost, Ronar cried out for Asterope to come on deck. A hatch crashed open, but when he glanced up he was stunned to see that the stern hatch, Asterope's hatch, remained closed. Quick footsteps came up behind him, from the direction of the bow hatch. He looked back with wide, angry eyes. A man approached—or rather, a boy.

"Antiphon!?" cried Ronar in disbelief. "What are you still doing aboard?"

"I'd like to help you, Mr. Ronar," said Antiphon, biting his lip. He looked toward the men gesticulating angrily on shore. "If it's not too late."

Now the stern hatch opened slowly, and Asterope, wan and pale as a ghost, rose up onto the deck. Antiphon, seeing her, was plainly reconsidering his decision to stay on board.

Ronar glanced back and forth between the two of them. "Antiphon! Get to the opposite bench and row your heart out! Asterope...take the starboard tiller. Try to bring us to a course parallel to the beach."

An arrow thudded into the deck between the ship's two oarsmen. "Or perhaps angling a little away from it," amended Ronar.

Dekapus crept down the beach, drifting no nearer to the breakers. Lamarchus's men, or at least those who remained, strolled along to keep pace, shouting curses and insults, and releasing arrows which occasionally found their way to the planks of the deck. Their barrage would have been worse if the wind hadn't been against them. Still, Ronar fretted over Asterope's exposed position at the tiller. Despite her frailty, she was the chief target of the hatred of the Mersinean sailors.

He looked over at Antiphon. The boy toiled with teeth clenched and brow knitted into a shield of determination. He had only a fraction of Ronar's strength, but their efforts were evened out by the wind pushing on the bow.

After an agonizing interval they drew abreast of a dike of black volcanic rock that thrust out into the water. Ronar worried that some submerged fang of it would catch the ship, but at least the obstacle hampered their pursuers, who dropped back as they tried to scramble up the sharp rock.

And then, once they were past the dike, the shore fell away from them. They continued to row, if less heroically, to put what Ronar hoped was a safe distance between them and the island. Once they were finally beyond any possible bowshot, Ronar called a halt. Antiphon collapsed onto the deck, unable even to ship his oar. Feeling shaky himself, Ronar stepped over to him and pulled the oar from the water. He bent down and gave the boy a slap on the shoulder. "Rest now, Antiphon," he said gruffly. "We'll all rest for a while. The ship's not going anywhere without us."

Antiphon nodded without even opening his eyes.

Ronar turned to Asterope, who slumped down on the deck, her back against the woven wooden lattice of the railing.

"I'll help you below," said Ronar, crouching before her.

"No," answered Asterope. "Let me stay out of that dank hole of a cabin for a while. It's better to stay in the light, now that the company on deck is—tolerable."

"As you wish."

Before Ronar could straighten up, Asterope's hand drifted out to him and traced a gentle line over his cheek. He found himself gazing into her good eye, totally at a loss for anything to say.

Later, as he prepared himself a sleeping spot on the other end of the ship, he unconsciously rubbed the stubble on his cheek.

Chapter 17

Antiphon

Ronar awoke to total darkness. He lay still, assessing his situation as best he could. He felt better. The effects of the drugged (or enchanted) wine had passed away, though his head still ached from the blow he'd taken from Prodicus. His abused shoulder ached, though the bleeding had stopped. Aside from a stiffness exacerbated by sleeping on deck with only a thin sleeping bag beneath him, he was ready to function.

The ship bobbed along under the influence of a desultory night wind. Aside from the minor creaks, pops, and slaps associated with that motion, all was silent.

After a few minutes he became aware of a figure standing against the opposite rail. He used averted vision to study the silhouette, alert for any move it might make.

A few moments later he heard a guileless sigh which relieved him of any apprehension.

He extracted himself from the sleeping bag, stood up and padded across the deck so softly that Antiphon jumped and gasped when he spoke.

"Sorry, Antiphon," said Ronar in a low voice. "I didn't mean to startle you."

"That's all right, Mr. Ronar. I was just afraid it might be —never mind. I suppose I've been standing here staring into the blackness too long."

"Can't sleep?"

"Oh, I slept, until an hour or so ago. But then I woke up. And there's very little to do in the middle of the night."

"Not when it's cloudy, anyway."

"I'll help you set the sail in the morning. I'm anxious to get this voyage over with."

"So am I."

They stood there looking into the hissing, muttering blackness of the primeval ocean. Anything could be out there, Ronar reflected. On the planet Colibdis, it could be literally anything: gods or demons, men or monsters, ten feet beyond their noses, perhaps, yet utterly invisible.

"So, Antiphon. What led you to stay aboard?"

The boy kept his silence a little longer.

"I—I was ashamed of the way Lamarchus dealt with you. He's my uncle, and I've always thought him a decent man for a merchant, but..." His voice trailed off.

And then it resumed on a brighter note. "I've heard of you too, like my uncle. I heard how you defeated that Persian, Namirnakh."

Ronar smiled quietly. He found it interesting that Antiphon thought of Namirnakh as a Persian, even though the lord of Darteharn was probably the only person of Persian derivation on the planet, and was the ruler of a decidedly non-Persian nation. As far as he knew, Colibdis had no enclave of Persian civilization. The Greeks had long memories.

"Well," he said dryly, "It's true I was involved in Namirnakh's downfall, but I can't take sole credit for defeating him."

Ronar sensed the boy's shrug. "It doesn't matter. At least you were there. I wasn't even a baby when it happened, but I've heard stories of the time when the

197

Persian's war fleet sailed past our city. On that day, the father of Lamarchus, my grandfather, pulled his ship onto the beach and hid in his house. You, on the other hand, were out there fighting. I say — you should have been given the passage you paid for, despite the — despite everything. It's only honorable."

"Thank you, Antiphon," said Ronar. "But don't be too hard on your uncle. He's a mostly honest man. I understand what he did, all of it. I simply couldn't allow it to stop me."

They resumed their silent watch into the darkness.

"There's no way to tell where we're going, is there?" asked Antiphon.

"No," admitted Ronar. "Without my compass, without a glimpse of the stars or the suns, we could be heading in any direction."

"The wind usually comes from the west," offered Antiphon hopefully.

"That may be. Unless this huge mass of clouds is some kind of cyclonic storm, in which case the winds could be coming from anywhere."

Ronar sensed Antiphon's concern and disappointment in the silence that followed.

"But we'll assume that the wind is coming generally from the west," Ronar continued. "With any luck we'll reach the coast of Mersinea somewhere along its length, or at least make a landfall somewhere on the mainland. The odds of drifting out through the mouth of Aegeos into the World Ocean itself are not great."

And yet he had raised the possibility of venturing unawares into that great ocean, into which few Mersineans were willing to go if it meant losing sight of land. Antiphon said nothing more, but the uneven sound of his breathing gave away his apprehension. Ronar stood there in an uncomfortable silence, wishing to reassure the boy, yet not willing to dilute the truth to do it.

At length Antiphon said, "I think I'll try to get back to sleep now, Mr. Ronar. Good night."

"Good night," answered Ronar.

The boy padded away, vanishing as completely as if he'd walked into another dimension.

Ronar continued his vigil at the rail, brooding, pondering. He fell into a mood as black as his surroundings. By what prodigy of stubbornness and folly had he gotten himself into this situation? Adrift in an unknown sea on a small wooden ship, his only companions an ignorant boy just past puberty, and a girl who was at least partly the possession of a disembodied intelligence whose actions exemplified malice and deceit.

And he an astronomer in his seventies. When he'd first arrived on this world he'd rashly involved himself in the struggle against this so-called "god of evil" and his minion Namirnakh, with consequences he could never escape. Perhaps his actions then had been necessary. Perhaps too it was necessary that he do his utmost to free Asterope of the curse that had befallen her while under his protection. But even as he felt the deck of *Dekapus* tilt gently beneath his feet, he was acutely aware of the railing that restricted him to a tiny, constrained area of action. How he would prefer to seek his destination on his own two legs, with the freedom to make his way as he would!

With a violent shrug and shake of the head Ronar threw off this second-guessing and self-pity. He crept back to his nest in the stern, beside the hatch below which lay the tortured, mysterious merged entity that Asterope was gradually becoming.

Wrapping himself in his sleeping bag, he lay back, wishing for a glimpse of a star to bring even a flicker of light to this darkness. Whatever wickedness prevailed on Earth or Colibdis, whatever madness distorted the lives of men and women, the stars remained ever clean.

But no star was able to pierce the veil of darkness that night.

Chapter 18

The Decline of Asterope

In the morning the clouds grudgingly took on the dim grey-maroon glow of the Gloaming. The air was chilly and dank, with a raw wind blowing fitfully from some unknown direction.

Seeing no reason to modify his plan of the night before, Ronar assumed that the wind was coming from the west. His chosen course was north, which meant keeping the wind on the port side of the ship.

Dekapus, as Antiphon explained, was capable of sailing across the wind. The two of them collaborated in deploying the sail, though it could not be easily or neatly done by only two pairs of hands. Antiphon demonstrated how to rotate the yard and tie it down, with the windward corner of the sail or "clew" pulled forward to catch the crosswind.

With the snapping, rebellious red sail finally wrestled into place, Ronar and Antiphon went astern and took the tillers, pulling the ship around to a course at right angles to the wind—to what Ronar hoped and supposed was north.

All this while Asterope lurked in the bow of the ship, looking back at them. Whenever Antiphon caught her gaze he shuddered and turned away. Ronar himself felt scarcely more comfortable beneath her scrutiny. He wished he could talk to her, so that the sound of her human voice could dispel the air of the supernatural she had acquired. But he couldn't call her back, for Antiphon could not bear her proximity for any length of time.

The wind remained fitful, but did not flag through all that long day. Although the ship made good progress, Ronar almost found himself wishing for a lull, if only to provide a rest for Antiphon, who wasn't built to wrestle a steering oar for unbroken hours on end.

Even assuming the constancy of the wind, Ronar had no way to judge the straightness of their course other than to look back at their wake and make a correction should that path of foaming green water exhibit a curve.

Sometime in the afternoon Asterope stirred from her watchful torpor and put together a meal of rock-hard bread, dates, and water. This she set out on deck and then withdrew into her cabin, taking with her whatever crumbs she had selected for herself. Antiphon kept his distance as she lowered herself down the stern hatch, watching her with a fascinated horror. Then there was no choice but to allow the ship to wallow as it would, with no hand on the steering oars, for the few minutes it took to wolf their food. Antiphon eyed that food dubiously, as it had been handled by Asterope, but ultimately devoured it.

As the sky turned dull and leaden with dusk, Ronar saw that Antiphon was spent. Though he clung to the steering oar with both hands, his arms were shaking, and he was barely able to stay on his feet.

"Antiphon," said Ronar.

The boy started and turned toward Ronar a face full of exhaustion and misery.

"Go forward and rest. I'll take over."

Without even questioning how Ronar proposed to do that, Antiphon stumbled forward and collapsed into his nest of blankets.

Ronar used his sword to hack sections from the shaft of the broken oar. These he lashed to the tillers, creating extensions which permitted him to handle both at once. Straddling the centerline of the ship, he worked these levers, prepared for a lengthy vigil at the helm.

Asterope appeared out of the twilight, having emerged from the hatch without his hearing. Her hair was loose, a disordered mass of greasy-gold clumps falling over her shoulders like snakes. Her eye peered out brightly from behind her oily locks. Her skin was like wax. She nodded toward the bow of the ship. "Antiphon. He's quite afraid of me, isn't he?" she whispered.

"He knows no better," muttered Ronar gruffly. "He's only an ignorant boy."

"He does well to fear me," said Asterope in a peculiarly avid tone. "He is not like you. He is vulnerable. More so than you."

Ronar stared at her, wondering if she intended to add to that assessment. Instead she appeared to change the subject.

"My," she said in a husky voice, "you appear quite Odyssean, standing there manhandling a ship emptied of almost all its crew."

Ronar's scrutiny lost some of its intensity. "You know the *Odyssey* in Mersinea? In its Homeric form?"

Asterope nodded. "We have always known the legend, but we only just obtained the full text of Homer from Thunderbird, no doubt thanks to you. Of course my mistress never let—of course now I've read both it and the *Iliad*.

He fixed her with a somber grey gaze. "You said, 'Of course my mistress never let me read it'?"

"That's an inexact quote," said Asterope, turning away.

"Nevertheless, I wish an answer to my question."

Her words came back to him through the wind. "It seems to me that my slip was answer enough. You once told me you knew of my 'unusual circumstances', but perhaps you never heard all the gossip. Yes, I fled to Thunderbird from a wealthy, prominent family. I fled the enforced ignorance which is expected of all females in Mersinean society. But I fled not as a child of that family, but as their slave. My parents exposed me, left me in the open to die, when I was a baby. This is common enough. Probably it was done at the instigation of a father who saw no advantage in adding another girl to his family. My owner, Heraminus, seeing a need for a girl-servant in his household, "rescued" me and raised me as a slave. When I grew old enough to realize what kind of life lay before me, I ran away, guided by the Goddess Athene herself, and aided by those two unfortunate men, Stannard and Thayne."

"Why didn't you tell me all this before?" asked Ronar.

"I can scarcely believe you were unaware of it. If so, you were the only person in Thunderbird who was."

"Of course I knew it. But, as you did not speak of it…"

"Naturally I did not boast of it to you. I thought a runaway female slave might find no welcome in such an exalted place as the University."

Ronar stared at her. "I can't speak for every man in Thunderbird, but for my part, I was most pleased to accept you, knowing what you had done, all you'd risked in reaching us."

"Out of pity for the little lost slave girl?" she asked with some bitterness.

"No. Out of respect for a fellow seeker of truth and freedom."

Asterope tilted her head toward him and blinked at him with her one sad eye.

"Professor, do you remember the good old days?"

Ronar looked at her in surprise, divined what she must mean, then nodded. "I remember them. I remember that dress you wore on your first night at the observatory. How you shivered." He chuckled. "But it was very pretty."

"Do you remember the time I spilled olive oil on the floor of the classroom building, and as I was cleaning it up you came along with your nose in a book, and you slipped, and tripped over me, and fell, and your reading glasses flew off? I laughed, and I thought Hal Holder would faint. But somehow, you did not kill me. Somehow."

They both laughed in the darkness.

Ronar realized they had few such stories to tell each other, too few, because of their mutual stubbornness. He bowed his head.

"Don't be sad, Professor. My life has been brief, but it has been much better than it would have been otherwise, largely thanks to your—your kindness."

"I was not kind enough."

"I wish we had known each other better—before it was too late."

Ronar felt something chill within his breast. "What do you mean—too late?"

"I will never be the same again," said Asterope with weary resignation. "Even if I could cast out the thing within me and return my eye to its previous state, I've already been changed forever by their influence. Even now Ahriman is within me, laughing, assuring me this is true. I have never known of a god who laughed as much as Ahriman."

"I swear—" said Ronar fervently, "—that before this is over, it shall be you and I who laugh, and Ahriman who finds no reason for mirth."

At that Asterope did laugh, bleakly, mockingly. Ronar knew he was indeed hearing the derision of Ahriman, to which Asterope was prey at every moment. Ronar burned with outrage. His hands flexed and clutched at the air. It was all he could do to refrain from stopping that laughter, tearing it from Asterope's throat, who was the only manifestation of Ahriman within his grasp.

"How touching," said Asterope in her Ahriman voice. "Truly, you are two of my favorite people in all the world."

Chapter 19

The Enormity of Ahriman

Asterope withdrew into some other part of the now-dark ship, leaving Ronar to guide their course by whatever instincts he had. Indeed he had nothing else to steer by, for the wind became erratic and blustery, snapping the sail from this direction and that. Small openings occasionally appeared in the clouds, and these Ronar eagerly scanned, but they proved nothing more than sources of tantalization. They revealed only one or two stars at a time, and closed so quickly that Ronar was unable to identify them.

After a few hours of this, Ronar had to admit he was accomplishing nothing useful. Awakening Antiphon, the two of them managed to gather up the sail, no easy task in total darkness. *Dekapus* bobbed aimlessly on the choppy waves. Antiphon stumbled sleepily back to his nest.

Ronar sat brooding on one of the rower's benches, leaning against the railing and resting his chin on his forearm. Except for the rare fugitive star, there was nothing to see in any direction—nothing but an unfathomable darkness. He now appreciated what drove Mersinean sailors to haul their ships ashore every night rather than drift blindly through such Stygian blackness.

Some of that blackness seemed to take hold of Ronar's heart. Again he contemplated his mission, doubting its chances of success. He scanned the lightless ship using senses other than vision, hearing a collection of creaks, pops, and rustles, and smelling a medley of odors: pitch, hides, salt, sweat. He couldn't even tell in what quarter of the ship Asterope lay sleeping, or stood lurking, or whatever might be her desire.

At some point his brooding was interrupted by the sound of a soft thud somewhere down by the waterline. He got to his feet, tense, wire-taut, straining his hearing into the darkness. More soft sounds came to him from over the side. He crept toward them, barely able to make out the blackness of the ship's railing against the slightly diluted ink of the sea beyond it.

A form rose into view at the railing, no more distinct than a shifting, flickering patch of blackness, but it was enough to send Ronar stepping back, a curse hissing on his lips. The hair on his nape stood up; his whole scalp seemed to contract as he stared at the form that clumsily heaved itself over the railing, landing on the deck with a wet thud. Then it came upright, swaying before him in time with the slow pitching of the deck.

Ronar needed light, and one source was literally at hand. He raised the garnet ring and urged from it a spitting flare of red light. It glistened on the wet, staring face of a figure draped in seaweed, seawater pooling at his feet as it dripped from the few rags covering its blotchy flesh.

"Lamarchus!" cried Ronar. "How did you—" He shook his head, letting the ring sputter out. "Antiphon! Bring torches on deck!"

More thuds and scrabblings came from over the side. More slow silhouettes came into view. A flicker of fire toward the bow indicated Antiphon emerging with torches. The light revealed the former crew of *Dekapus*, either standing on the deck or pulling themselves over the railing. Antiphon screamed, dropped one torch, and shrank back with the other. Without taking his eyes off the sailors, Ronar sidled over and claimed the dropped torch. A dozen forms regarded him from eyes that were filmed, or covered by weed, or in some cases absent from their sockets. Their flesh was like wax, except where chunks of it, or even whole limbs, had been torn away. There the tissue hung loosely in shreds and tatters.

These walking corpses made no aggressive move toward Ronar or the boy. Instead, to Ronar's astonishment, they shambled to the rowing benches and worked at unshipping the oars.

"It seems you'll get your money's worth from them after all, Professor," came a voice from beside him. Ronar started and stared at Asterope, who stood beside him with a satisfied smile on her face. Both eyes were uncovered, the stricken one gleaming with a horrid pale light that was beginning to be shared by the other.

"What have you done?" asked Ronar, though the answer seemed obvious enough.

"It's clear that you and Antiphon can't handle the ship alone," she answered in a light tone. "I thought you'd appreciate having some help, especially after all the trouble you took to arrange this passage for me. For us."

"Asterope," said Ronar. He paused, looked at the soulless faces of the dead men at the sweeps, and drew in a breath. "Ahriman. Whoever you are. I want you to stop this. Release these men to a clean death."

The girl laughed. "I don't think so. Like you, I want to see this farce concluded."

"Ahriman—you don't fear our arrival in Pantheos?"

The laughter resumed, this time sharper and more vindictive. "Hardly. The shadow gods of Olympos will prove no more able to remove me from this girl than you are. Especially now that she has despaired and taken me into her heart."

Ronar dumbly watched her saunter off along the deck, blending into the darkness beyond his torchlight. He heard Antiphon whimper as she approached him, and saw him scuttle down the bow hatch, carrying his torch. She merely laughed yet again, threw open the hatch, and climbed down after him.

Ronar crept to the very stern of the ship, to the narrow V-shaped space where the curving sides of the hull came together. There he sank down, head propped against the railing, facing forward. Two fish-chewed corpses, one of them that of Lamarchus, stood ten feet in front of him, handling the steering oars. The others beat out a slow but steady rhythm on the oars. No orders were given, no word spoken. Yet somehow the ship seemed to keep a straight course, in what direction Ronar could not determine.

Dawn came up like candlelight on a bar of lead, marking the third day of the Gloaming. Ronar, stiff from the dampness and his awkward posture, greeted it by tossing his torch over the side. He stared at the hellish scene on the deck, paralyzed, seeing nothing he could do, no action he could take. Visions born of exhaustion and sickness of spirit hung hazily before him: Lamarchus and his men, victims of the compulsion of the god, throwing themselves into the waves in despair, leaving the safety of the island, to the bewilderment of the fishermen and their wives. Swimming madly until their strength gave out, then even in death swimming still, if more slowly, or walking along the bottom, with crabs in their beards, nibbled at by whatever creatures they passed.

He idly noted that one of the rowing benches was unoccupied. Even as this occurred to him he heard a thumping at the side of the ship, and was not surprised when still another figure climbed out of the sea. This was Prodicus. He was in worse condition that the others, having been in the sea the longest. His lips and cheeks were gone, revealing his fine white teeth and jaws. His abdomen was a hollowed-out cave of meat and bone. There was also another difference in him. He looked at Ronar, and his gaze was not unseeing, but aware, filled with hatred of the coldest and most undying kind. Despite this, he shambled to his place, sat down, and took up his oar.

Ronar briefly considered hurling himself over the side and seeking the oblivion that had escaped these men, but in that moment he doubted whether he could die without risking his soul to Ahriman. His strength was at a low ebb indeed.

Slowly he pulled himself to his feet. If he was ever going to act, it must be now. Though no satisfactory course of action was available to him, still he must somehow act.

He walked toward the bow, between the steersmen, between the ranks of oarsmen, to the bow hatch. He looked down at it bleakly for a moment, then stamped on it. "Asterope", he called hoarsely. "Come up now." He reached down and flung off the hatch cover, peering into the darkness below. A stench rose up to engulf him, one composed of fear, vomit, and excrement. Asterope lay there with Antiphon, whose eyes, as they stared up at Ronar, were too far gone into madness. He too was lost. He gave an inhuman wail, tore free from Asterope's arms, and flung himself onto the deck. Ronar made no move to stop him as he vaulted the railing. Instead of sinking into the waves,

Antiphon somehow ran atop them, sliding into the troughs and splashing his way up the next, hollow and empty as a figure of dream. He soon vanished into the fog, though his cries reached Ronar for a while longer.

Ronar turned his attention back to the hatch. There sat Asterope, looking up at him with obscene satisfaction.

"So this is the result of all your vaunted intellect," whispered Ronar. "Ahriman, the god of subtlety and thought. When this great mind finds itself in possession of a human body, it turns at once to the grossest aspects of human life, wallowing in a filthy lust no animal could match."

He dropped to the deck, thrust a long arm into the darkness, and found Asterope's neck. He heaved the delicate form out the hatch and sent it sprawling onto the deck, where it lay gasping and choking. Before she could recover, Ronar crouched down before her, staring into that twofold gaze from only inches away.

Asterope sat up, trembling. With one hand she covered her afflicted eye; the other she rested on Ronar's arm.

"Professor," she whispered. "Don't let me go into whatever awaits me, stained with evil as I am."

Ronar stared at her. "If that should happen to you, Asterope, I will follow."

With that a small light of hope entered her visible eye. She lowered her hands and sat on the deck facing him calmly, somehow still beautiful despite all that had befallen her, somehow blessed with a weird sort of grace, a renewed innocence.

"Ahriman," he said softly. "Have you ever read the Bible?"

The figure gave a rasping laugh. "I am aware of it. But why should I waste time on a religious book whose precepts are ignored even by most of its followers?"

"Yet there is one verse which I have always respected, and by which Asterope must now live."

"And what is that?"

"If thine eye offend thee... pluck it out."

Ronar reached out and gouged thumb and forefinger into the afflicted eye socket, pulled out the eye, crushed it to a pulp, and flung the mess over the side. Asterope, shrieking, leaped up and raised her hand to her eye socket, holding in some of the blood that tried to pour out. Ronar got slowly to his feet, holding his right hand away from his body while blood and slime dripped from it.

Asterope said nothing coherent. Still screaming, she fell to her knees, knee-walked over to Ronar, and bent down, exposing her slender neck. Ronar looked down at her trembling, wasted, naked body.

"F-finish it. Please. It's...my only hope."

Ronar called the sword into being and drew back for the killing stroke. But as he held it there, his muscles tensed in preparation for the blow, something held back the blade. For a moment he stared at her, the image of her ruin and degradation burning into his brain like acid.

Then Asterope looked up with her remaining eye while an alien voice croaked out of her throat.

"It's too late for that."

She released her breath, and her body sagged to the deck. Ronar gave a cry and let go the sword, falling to his knees to take her in his arms. As he watched, the little color that remained in her flesh drained away, replaced by a greyish whiteness like the foam of the waves. Her arms came up mantis-like, and her back arched in a strange spasm. Her one eye rolled around aimlessly.

Ronar placed his hand on her chest. He could still feel a thready heartbeat beneath the clammy flesh.

He had seen this before. This was what happened to a living body when its spirit was plucked forth by Ahriman or its minions.

He stared down at her, scarcely able to think or feel a thing. After a while he laid her body on the deck and lurched upright. He clumsily sought about the ship until he found water and some cloths. He had no idea how to treat an emptied eye socket, but he forced himself to clean out some of the mess and tied a strip around her face to cover it. Fortunately she did not seem disposed to bleed very much He washed the rest of her body as well as he could, then covered her with a blanket and left her lying stiffly on the deck. It was all he could do. He turned aside to stare numbly over the waves.

Silence. Ronar heard nothing but his own ragged breath. The oar strokes had ceased. No one moved. The sailors, Prodicus included, sat or stood in their places, watching him impassively.

A powerful radiance flooded in, heating his back. He turned and beheld the red sun Kudu shining through a gap in the clouds. The white glare at its side showed that Photos, the smaller yet greater sun, was emerging. The Gloaming was over.

The fog and clouds dispersed. Ronar looked out past the bow and beheld a great jagged mass on the horizon which he knew to be Mount Olympos. A strong south wind sprang up, but Ronar made no effort to deploy the sail.

Even without it, by noon the coastline of Mersinea was in sight. The suns grew hot. The sailors began to reek of death, but still they kept their places, still animate, but without direction. Only Prodicus showed any sign of sentience, and yet Ronar could read nothing that was not ambiguous in his unblinking eyes.

At twilight the ship went aground on a cobbled beach to the west of Pantheos. Ronar threw down a gangplank and descended into the surf carrying Asterope's rigid body. It felt foreign and lifeless, so tiny and insubstantial he could hold it with one arm if need be.

Local people had seen their approach, and they came forward carrying torches. When they got a glimpse of Ronar's face and what he carried, and then saw the crew of the ship, they wanted no part of any of them, but ran off, screaming and invoking the protection of the gods. Ronar reached out and wrested a torch from one of them. Setting Asterope's body on the cold stones, he went back aboard the ship and set fire to it. The crew made no attempt to stop him or to escape, not even Prodicus. The tide went out, leaving *Dekapus* high and dry on the cobblestones. With a great flare of heat and stink it burned down to embers, watched over by Ronar, who wanted no relic of that ship or its crew to survive.

Then, standing beneath the stars, with the heat of the embers on his face, Ronar looked up and sought out the slowly moving star that was Ahriman's eye.

After some time he turned away and walked eastward down the beach, the body of Asterope in his arms.

Part Three
Ronar Alone

Chapter 20

The Temple of Athene

Ronar continued along the beach through the night. Dogs howled at his passing but did not come near. Lamps were occasionally thrust from the doors of the fishing huts he passed, but no one came forth to challenge him. A low surf muttered at his right. Sand and gravel scuffed and crunched beneath his feet. Sometimes he had to wade shallow streams and rivers as they entered the sea. The waning crescent of Sinanna rose after midnight, giving light to ease his way. Restless breezes rustled the limbs of trees just inland. Nights in Mersinea were not quiet, but alive with watchful spirits. All gave way before Ronar's relentless march.

At dawn he followed a path into a grove of trees. The warm morning light gleamed on marble beyond the branches. The grove opened up to reveal a small shrine: a statue of a god, an altar, a few benches. Ronar placed the body beside the altar, then went to study the statue, trying to identify it. It was a muscular figure with a stern gaze and an aggressive posture...Herakles, perhaps, or Ares. If it had been Asclepius, Ronar might have begged him for help for Asterope, though he doubted it could be given.

Ronar threw himself to the ground in the shadow of the altar and pushed away all thought, craving nothing but the oblivion of sleep. Although the body of Asterope lay within arm's reach, he felt completely alone. Asterope's remaining eye kept opening and wandering around in a mindless, lightless stare. He reached over and closed the lid, but it soon drifted open again. Tears began to flow from the eye…a response to being open and unblinking…or so Ronar fervently hoped.

He thought of the empty socket beneath the bandage, and an image came to mind of how he had emptied it, twisting his gut and piercing his heart.

At last he fell asleep, his mind aswirl with dark images. He did not awaken until the suns had climbed toward noon. He pulled himself to his feet, blinking.

Resting on the altar were a loaf of bread, a hunk of cheese, a *crater* of watered wine, and a pomegranate. Ronar looked around. A blue-and-bronze bird sang a few dreamy notes in a nearby tree. It had a pair of tiny arms, marking it as a species native to Colibdis. No person was in sight.

Ronar accepted the offering and ate, unsure whether it had been meant for him, or for the god, or maybe for both. He poured a small quantity of wine past Asterope's lips, but she showed no swallowing reflex at all. Eventually he turned her over to let the wine dribble out, lest it reach her lungs.

Physically refreshed, but still dark of spirit, so much so that the part of him that still craved light wondered how he would ever transcend this disaster, he set off again, the body cradled in his arms. Now the roots of Mount Olympos rose up only a few miles ahead. The walls of Pantheos were hazily visible on the horizon.

An hour later, black clouds came boiling over the passes on either side of the great mountain. A towering thunderhead enveloped the whole peak, sweeping over Ronar and the nearby city, its cool shadow bringing a scent of ozone and rain. Ronar looked up into the seething clouds, with their inverted canyons of darkness swirling and turning themselves inside-out. Lightning speared down all around, accompanied by the clean, tearing sound of thunder. The distance grew hazy and dark, and a moment later a cascade of rain blasted him from the side, wind-blown, frozen by lightning for blue flickering instants. The rain washed the brine from Ronar's ragged costume and rinsed the salt from his hair. It streamed over Asterope's colorless face, cleansing her remaining eye, soaking her filthy hair, her bandage, her rags, and her blanket.

He approached the city gate, which was open and unguarded, and entered, striding through streets running like mountain streams. People huddled in doorways, in porticos and beneath awnings, flinching at every ripping crash of thunder. They goggled at Ronar as he passed by, but he was oblivious to them, caught up in the storm's satisfying wrath as he was.

The rain was easing by the time he reached the Agora, though the paving stones still flowed with rivulets. Sunslight flared down through swift-blowing gaps in the clouds. Ronar looked north to the lowermost walls of the mountain, where great waterfalls now hung from the heights like the tails of comets.

Ronar squinted about the rain-emptied marketplace and spied a group of proud-looking men in finely-embroidered chitons and himations, standing in the shelter of a roofed colonnade. They turned to gape as he approached them, one of their number saying to the others, "I knew barbarians had strange customs, but did not know that carrying corpses through rainstorms was among them."

Another of the men laughed and cried out "Bar, bar, bar!"

Ronar halted before them, towering over the group, looking down into their faces. "This is not yet a corpse," he said in perfectly good, though accented, Greek. "And I am not a barbarian."

The first man, looking dismayed, stammered and blurted, "Your pardon, sir. You're soaked — and we have a saying here, that barbarians don't know enough to come in out of — "

"Enough!" interrupted Ronar. "I am Leonard Ronar, of Thunderbird."

Another man in this group gasped. Ronar looked at him, a pale, balding man of middle age.

"I've heard that name spoken in my own house!" he said. "I am called Heraminus."

Ronar narrowed his eyes at him, for he had heard this man's name as well.

"And I am called Pedemus," spoke up another man, a curious old figure with a small wizened head atop a spindly neck. Ronar nodded at him with a kind of recognition. Somehow he was not surprised to encounter Heraminus and his friends. Synchronicity and happenstance were enhanced by the very air of Colibdis.

Heraminus spoke on, his gaze wavering from Ronar to the ghastly grey face of Asterope. "I have heard of you, Ronar. And I've also heard that my escaped slave, Asterope, turned up in your school as a student. Ah, I know better than to hope for her return, have no fear of that. But tell me, how is the little minx? If only she knew the trouble her escape caused me with my wife..." His voice trailed off, his regard now fixed on Asterope. His face slowly twisted into a mixture of doubt and distress. "By the light of Apollo...that is Asterope you are carrying."

Pedemus suddenly swayed and sagged back, muttering something indecipherable under his breath.

"In the name of the Twelve Olympians," said Heraminus in a stricken voice, "what has happened to the poor girl?"

Ronar swept his gaze over the group of listeners. "She was possessed by an evil god, who has now snatched away her soul."

"And her eye?" rasped Pedemus.

"That was the route by which the god invaded her. I had to remove it."

Heraminus's face fell. "I am grieved to hear this. But her place in my household was secure. I accept no blame that she came to such an end."

"I offer no such blame," said Ronar. "That I reserve for myself, and for the malign entity that invaded her."

"May Zeus guard us all," muttered one of the other men.

"Why did you bring her here?" asked Pedemus.

"I have heard of the pilgrimage up Olympos, the sacred mountain. From its summit one can glimpse the true home of many gods, or so I've heard. I intend to climb that mountain, to seek the counsel of your gods. I will demand their help in recovering Asterope's spirit from the evil god and reuniting it with her body. It must happen soon. Asterope's body will not long survive in this state."

With his eyes fixed on the distance, Pedemus nodded slowly and said, "That would seem the only thing you can do for the girl at this point. Although I've never heard of such a thing being done—even Orpheus failed at a similar task, in the end. But in order to attempt this pilgrimage, one must first receive the urging, or at least the permission, of a god."

"Very well. How do I gain this permission?"

"A trip to the temples is in order."

"Who will guide me there?" asked Ronar in a voice that made it clear he expected at least one affirmative reply.

The other men hemmed and hawed, looking at each other. Heraminus, white-faced, made some excuse and bustled off after his fellows, who were scattering. This left Ronar standing in the shade with Pedemus.

"Since you're still here, I assume you're willing to guide me," said Ronar in a dry tone.

"Indeed I am," said Pedemus, meeting his eyes. "I expect my friends also feel some curiosity about the matter, but the mention of the god you left unnamed brings more practical concerns to their minds."

"But not to yours?"

Pedemus shrugged. "I have never been noted for my practicality. Shall we go?"

The two men set out through the streets, the pavement steaming wherever rainwater evaporated beneath the hot suns. They turned to face the sacred mountain and continued in that direction.

After enduring a stream of chatter from his companion, Ronar broke in. "I have heard of your role in Asterope's escape."

Pedemus nodded, a glow of nostalgia in his eyes. "Indeed. I delight in subverting my own reputation from time to time. That was a highlight of my career, to see Heraminus so discommoded by his wife's reaction to the girl's loss."

"And aside from that minor mischief, what was your interest in Asterope?"

"I admired her. I wished her well."

"She believed her escape was guided and engineered by the gods."

Pedemus shrugged again. "I serve the gods."

They made their way through residential areas until lofty red-tiled roofs began to rear up beyond the houses. They entered the temple district, where the great structures clustered around the foot of the stairs that climbed the first thousand feet of the mountain. Ronar was struck by how similar they were to Greek temples of Earth's classical period. The Mersineans had crossed over from Earth in Homeric times, long before any Greek had conceived such an elaborate architecture. There seemed to be something in the blood of their society that led inevitably to such designs.

Ronar halted, staring at the clustered temples, wondering which god to approach. The district was crowded with men in shining white himations, plus a few girls and women. They all stared at Ronar, with his grim face, his ragged garments and his unkempt beard and hair, and at the twisted form of Asterope in his arms, with her expressionless pallid face and single wandering eye. They kept their distance.

Without thinking to consult Pedemus, Ronar announced, "I'll try Hermes. He's said to be the inventor of astronomy, as I recall. He might be sympathetic to Asterope's plight."

Pedemus looked dubious, but led him toward the temple of Hermes nevertheless. Ronar climbed the stairs, passed through the first shining colonnade, letting his eyes adjust to the darkness before entering the inner sanctum. He intended to wait there a while and then emerge, claiming that the god had insisted he climb the mountain. The temple's shadowy interior surprised him. It was deserted, with neither worshippers, offerings, nor even an image of the god. Ronar stood pondering this neglect for a few minutes, and then stepped out, squinting in the sunslight.

Pedemus waited there, looking at him sympathetically. Before Ronar could make a fool of himself by claiming to have seen the god, Pedemus said, "The temple is forlorn, isn't it? Nothing has been the same since Hermes vanished. The shades of the dead go wandering, unable to find their way to Tartarus."

Ronar was brought up short. "That is interesting," he said. "What are the consequences of this for the dead?"

"It does not mean their souls are unable to make the passage to the next world, but without the guidance of Hermes, their path is less certain and more perilous."

Ronar stood in silence for several moments while he absorbed this.

"How can gods vanish? People still believe in them, still expect them to perform their functions."

"I don't know. It has never before happened in my experience. New gods rarely come into being, but I have never heard of an old one who perished altogether."

"Do you suppose that every god whose tasks include guiding the spirits of the dead is gone?"

"That I cannot say. The challenge of staying on the good side of the gods of my own land is enough for me, without worrying about foreign ones."

"I see." To Ronar, this seemed a clue to Ahriman's recent resurgence of activity and its new audacity. But he saw no reason to discuss this with Pedemus. "Well then. I still must decide which god to approach. Perhaps Urania?"

"The Muses do not have a temple. They come to those whom they favor, or they do not, and no amount of pleading can sway them one way or the other. They are most inscrutable." So too was Pedemus's smile. "If I may make a suggestion...?" He lifted a pointing finger.

Ronar followed it up the slope of the mountain, where he was arrested by the sight of a near twin to the Parthenon, set on a flat-topped spur of rock that butted up against Olympos.

"After all, it was Athene herself who set Asterope on her journey, ill-fated though it turned out to be," said Pedemus.

Ronar's eyes narrowed at this assertion, but he did not question the man's knowledge. "Very well. I will approach her." With that he turned away, leaving Pedemus to stand looking after him as Ronar's long strides took him toward Athene's citadel.

Ronar climbed flights of stairs, passing through gates and chapels devoted to various lesser aspects of Athene, before finally confronting the great temple itself. Despite the likeness of its design, it had a very different aspect than its ruined analog back on Earth. Its marble was gleaming white, but the structure was also bright with color. The friezes in the pediments were painted boldly, while the capitals of the lofty columns shone a rich blue.

This temple was busy, but worshippers and supplicants seemed to melt away as Ronar stood there studying the structure, Asterope's twisted figure in his arms.

Within the sanctuary's dim interior he confronted the statue of the goddess. It stood over thirty feet tall, magnificently armored, carrying a great shield in which was set a gorgon head more terrible than Ronar would have imagined possible. Though he could hardly tear his eyes from that, the face of the goddess was more compelling still. Its flesh was of translucent ivory, with flashing grey eyes and dark lashes. Her expression was stern and gentle at the same time, full of compassion, yet also completely unyielding. Ronar knew at once that he had found the right deity.

He stood there a few minutes beneath a grave stare that seemed aimed directly at him. He studied her glittering golden armor and the huge lifelike owl that perched on her shoulder. Then he turned and left, blinking in the brilliant sunslight outside.

There stood Pedemus, quite out of breath from the climb. "Giving up so soon?" he panted. "Sometimes the gods take longer to respond to our prayers than we might like."

Ronar replied, "I stood before the image for ten minutes and asked permission to climb Olympos. It was given."

At that Pedemus's eyes grew wide. "You saw an image of Athene?"

Ronar nodded in puzzlement and said "Yes, and a magnificent work of art it is, too."

Pedemus grew agitated. "That is no work of art, you fool! If she is still there, you had better go back in, for she must have more to say to you."

Ronar stared, then turned to reenter the temple. The goddess still glowed faintly in the shadows. And now somehow he could not mistake the fact that he was indeed facing a living goddess, her eyes locked on his own, unblinking.

Ronar had seen gods before. Certainly he had no intention of quailing before this one. Still, he had some difficulty in keeping his legs from shaking.

Finally Athene moved, walking toward him, and dwindling as she came, until by the time she stood before him they were eye to eye.

She said, "I know why you have come, but we have no power over the one who has no name on Olympos."

At first Ronar considered this some obscure oracular utterance. Then he remembered there was no god of evil in Greek mythology, no real analog for Ahriman, whether you thought of it as a devil, a god of evil, or of magic, or whatever. Therefore Ahriman must be alien to the Olympians, and perhaps beyond their influence.

Ronar said, "Then you cannot compel him to release the spirit of this innocent girl?"

"I cannot."

Ronar stared at this apparition before him. Imposing though she was, he had the sudden conviction that what he was facing was in some sense a shell, a facade, rather than a truly sentient being. He felt she was something that could act according to the fears or hopes or expectations of its worshippers, but with little capacity for independent action and conscious thought. This goddess was perhaps less of a person than anyone walking in the city below.

Ronar's scrutiny of the goddess narrowed, and Athene gave a slight nod.

"We are what we are made to be, and nothing more. As you have seen."

The grey eyes remained locked on his, calm and unblinking. Ronar sensed that this creature, this goddess of wisdom, possessed enough of that faculty to truly recognize what she was, and to be aware of her limitations. It seemed to him a pitiable state.

Athene lowered her eyes. Ronar realized she was also capable of recognizing his compassion. His hand wavered out, but how to comfort such a being?

"Do not grieve for me," whispered Athene. "I know what I am, but I also know what I am thought to be, and that is with me also. I remember bursting full-grown from my father's head. I remember the battles on the plains of Ilium. I remember the contest with Poseidon to decide which of us would be patron of Athens. So I am both less than I seem, and more."

Ronar withdrew his hand and gave one sharp nod. "I intend to fight for the soul of this girl. She is your protégé as much as mine."

Athene remained mute. Her face betrayed neither confidence nor doubt.

"But her body cannot survive for long in this condition," continued Ronar. "Can you offer it any kind of protection, until I can free her?"

The goddess did not hesitate. She stepped back a few paces and reached into her shield, grasping the head of the gorgon and withdrawing it. Ronar gasped, instinctively turning aside. His skin tingled. By his peripheral vision he saw that Athene had drawn out a large, misshapen form which dropped to the floor with a thud.

"Do not look," she said, a little belatedly.

Then the goddess stood before him. Ronar passed the body of Asterope into her waiting arm. He watched as

Athene somehow passed the body through the shield and into it. The next few seconds were difficult for Ronar to focus on and later remember. When they were over, the bright shield of Athene had a new aspect, with the calm face of Asterope embossed in its center. Ronar could not help but be a little awed.

"Here the girl's body will be safe, for as long as the gods endure," said Athene.

"Will—will you now be less formidable in combat, with Asterope there in place of Medusa?"

"This girl resisted the will of the nameless god far longer than most mortals could have done," replied Athene. "Perhaps longer than you. I suffer no diminution."

The sudden absence of Asterope's body from his arms felt strange. Suddenly he was aware of how complete his separation from her had become. He meant to save her still, though he knew not how, yet at the same time he felt he ought to mourn her.

"Well then…thanks, Athena. I don't know how long it will take to free the girl…"

"I am patient. What you mean to do could overturn the world. The Great Gods will oppose you, but I do not. Go with my blessing."

Ronar nodded again, turned on his heel, and stalked out of the temple. His eyes were burning.

Pedemus appeared stricken at the sight of his face.

"There is no point in climbing the mountain," said Ronar tightly as he marched up to the Mersinean. "Athena is protecting the body, but there's nothing more she or the other Olympians can do."

With Pedemus in his wake he started down from this acropolis. They passed a group of worshippers on their way to the temple. "You there!" called Ronar. "Don't go in there. Athena may not have removed the Gorgon's head yet." They blanched and stopped in their tracks, staring after them as they continued on.

Then he halted, so suddenly that Pedemus bounced off him. He turned to look over his shoulder, at the mountain looming there, a peak of Andean majesty, snow-clad and shining.

"I *will* climb that mountain," he said decisively. "I have come all this way. I will climb it. Pedemus, lend me your cloak, if you would."

Chapter 21

The Heights of Olympos

At the beginning of the path was a block of polished marble inscribed with the letter Alpha.

The first thousand feet of the climb up Olympos was a popular excursion, a broad marble pathway that wound up the slope with occasional flights of stairs. Frequent rest stops and overlooks provided excuses for climbers to stop to catch their breaths.

Ronar stalked past all the other hikers he encountered, though his pace was steady and moderate, his strides long and deliberate. The promenade eventually ended in a wide terrace where most of the hikers collapsed onto benches, breathless. Vendors sold dearly priced cups of wine and bits of bread and fruit, all the dearer for that they had to be carried up on their backs, for no pack animals were allowed on this path.

Some hikers looked out at the city gleaming below them, while others peered up at the shoulder of the mountain. Shreds of cloud blew into view from the heights, but from this vantage point the actual summit could not be seen.

Eighty percent of the climbers stopped here. Of those who continued on, many intended merely to stroll a bit beyond the normal limit, while only a few meant to go all the way. These true pilgrims could be distinguished by the bundles and packs they carried, and by their solemn expressions, which lacked the lightness and frivolity of the day-trippers.

Ronar did not even stop to rest. He left the chatter and laughter behind, mounting a narrower path that was more crudely paved. It was a relief to leave behind the green well-tended trees of the lower slopes, and enter rocky heights where the trees gradually shrank and grew stunted, drawn into strange shapes by almost-constant winds. This landscape better suited Ronar's mood.

Here he felt free to relax the tight control that had kept his expression impassive while he walked among the crowds. His eyes grew wild, and his mouth froze into a scowl that caused all those he approached to shy away. He barely glanced at the other pilgrims, some climbing in bare feet, some in rags, some in garments better suited to the agora. Others panted beneath burdens of food and goods, perhaps intended for sacrifice, burdens greater than Ronar himself would have wished to carry. A few climbed steadily, sedately, neither over-burdened nor foolishly under-equipped. Ronar had the feeling some of these had walked this path before.

The climbers had one thing in common: all were men. No doubt it was inconceivable in Mersinea that a woman might have business on this sacred mountain. If Asterope had been able, thought Ronar, he would have brought her to the summit, whatever the obstacles.

Daylight was waning by the time he reached the second major landing, a rough stone platform some five thousand feet above the city. From this height the city looked like a rough white blanket spread along the shore. Here a spring poured from the rock, from which even wine-loving Mersineans drank greedily. Indeed, a few filled vessels with the water and immediately set off downhill. Perhaps the waters of Olympos were a valuable commodity down below.

Ronar sat down on a ledge. Pedemus had left him with more than his cloak. He had also provided the penniless astronomer with a bundle of food. In the failing light Ronar drank cold spring water and chewed bread smeared with olive oil.

Many of the other hikers were preparing camps among the rocks surrounding the platform, or right on it. The hardier among them did not halt, but struck sparks from flint or used simple incendiary spells to light torches. A few even carried magical lumifers, with their nacreous green-white glow. It was considered an act of special piety to make the entire climb without stopping for sleep.

Ronar held no such conceit, but he had no patience for rest, nor any peace in his heart to permit it. He had no torches and was glad of it, preferring as always to walk by starlight.

Now the path was but a simple track winding among the rocks, mounting ledges and meandering over stretches of dry grass and lichens. It was plain enough even in the dark, though cairns marked it occasionally to assist the uncertain. Torches flickered far up the slope, and a few below. He'd yet to even glimpse the summit, which was still hidden behind the crags of the lower reaches.

Almost every hero of Mersinea, mused Ronar, had walked this path at one time or another. Even the mighty Hamadan, though not a Mersinean, had come this way, or so it was said.

Up the flank of the mountain, into the starry night, into air thinning and growing colder, marched Ronar. The air of

Colibdis was scanter than Earth's to begin with. Luckily, Ronar had spent his childhood living at nine thousand feet, and had grown up hiking at altitude. Pedemus's woolen cloak was enough to keep him warm as long as he kept moving.

The Whirlpool stood over the eastern horizon, a soft light that cast dim diffuse shadows behind every rock. Ronar paused to stare at the approximate position of Earth. In that winding coil of starfog he could glimpse only the very mightiest suns as distinct points. The whole starry realm of Earth, with all the constellations that had so awed and enthralled him as a boy, could be blotted out behind the tip of his extended thumb.

He passed a few hikers as they lay exhausted beside the trail, alone or in small groups. Some were wrapped in cloths and furs, having intended to camp when they could walk no further. Others sat dejected, limp with fatigue and shivering with cold, their torches or lumifers beside them.

To these Ronar said gruffly, "Better get yourself down. You're not dressed to spend the night at this altitude. You could die of it."

Even if they glanced at him it was with listless eyes. Already victims of altitude sickness or hypothermia, they were not yet halfway up the mountain. Ronar wondered how often the gods watched their supplicants falter to the point of death, and if there was any help for those who did.

He passed fewer and fewer of these as he climbed, moving beyond the stunted trees to barren heights where old snow and ice glimmered in cracks and on the northern sides of rocks. The Whirlpool now stood at the meridian, a canopy of grey-green light brightening to pale gold at the center. The night was gentle...cold, but windless, which was a mercy for those struggling far below, visible only by the wavering green or gold stars of their lights.

By the last dark hour of the night Ronar felt he'd left the realm of men behind and had entered the domain of the gods, hollow creatures though they might be. Fog moved in from the Aegeos to cover the city far below, blotting out its feeble lights. The mountain seemed to rear up from a sea of luminous milk, along with the lesser peaks which ranged to east and west.

He spied a figure collapsed by the side of the trail, its torch giving off only a few smolders and wisps of smoke. He prepared to pass it by, but a rasping voice came to him, saying, "Please, sir, help me on my way to the summit, I beg you."

Grimacing at the annoyance, Ronar halted, prepared to brush off this nuisance. Before he could speak, the figure sat up, its face a shadowy glimmer beneath a dark cowl. "I must reach the summit. I have been three days on the mountain, marching day and night, but now I'm at the end of my strength. Please help me the rest of the way, as you love the gods."

"I do not—" started Ronar, but then he bit off the words. "Why don't you rest. I'm sure the gods will acknowledge your efforts, and not begrudge you the rest you need to continue your journey."

"I dare not," came the breathless voice. "If I rest here I shall freeze."

Ronar could scarcely argue with that. Scowling, he snatched up the dying torch and whirled it through the air to coax out a little light. He held its smoking, flickering head near the frail figure, who looked up at him plaintively.

Ronar's eyes widened. The face beneath the cowl was old, and it was plainly female as well.

Ronar straightened up and blinked a little. An old woman making the ascent of Olympos, already farther up than nine tenths of those who made the attempt? He had to respect that—but at the same time, he did not wish to take her on as an added burden.

"Why must you climb the mountain?" he asked grudgingly. "What business do you have with your gods that you cannot settle in the temples below?"

The woman stood up painfully, a bent and tiny figure.

"I have lived the life of a fool. The gods granted me many gifts, but I have squandered them. I have lived in bitterness, trusting no one, seeking love from the wrong people, giving love to none, hurting those who truly loved me. I have failed those who trusted me, and offered good to few. I forgive neither those who have wronged me, nor myself for failing them. I have wandered from one meaningless thing to another, always seeking to better myself by adjusting some detail of my possessions or my surroundings. I have kept myself apart, thinking myself at once too superior and too wretched to consort with others. I have disparaged the wisdom of men and gods alike, and lived as a cynic. I have given rein to the basest of lusts, defiling myself so gradually I didn't even notice the damage until it was too late."

She halted to catch her breath, and continued.

"Now my life nears its end. I go to beg the gods for guidance, so that I may, at the last, walk a straight path, and do what is right. It is my only hope."

Ronar gazed at this now-silent figure as she stood swaying in the darkness. When he could trust himself to speak at all, he said huskily, "All right then. But first you must tell me one more thing."

"What is that?"

"Tell me you are not some god, offering me a foolish test. I've heard of such things, and I don't have the time to waste on it."

Ronar could see the head shaking beneath the cowl and hear the wry smile in the voice.

"By no means am I a god. By no means."

"Then let me gather up your things, and we'll be on our way."

The woman took a few wobbly steps up the trail. Ronar bent down and snatched up the small sack that held her possessions.

"Your name?" he asked belatedly.

She paused, looking over her shoulder at him. "Astraea." She moved forward again.

Ronar blinked, then trudged up behind her. She seemed to sense his thoughts.

"No...not *that* Astraea. Who, sir, are you? You are obviously foreign. One does not often hear of foreigners making this pilgrimage."

"I am Leonard Ronar, of Thunderbird."

She faltered a little, but made no comment. It could have been only a rock on the path.

It wasn't long before the Whirlpool, sinking toward the west, began to blend into the paling sky. Low on the opposite horizon, a band of dense, bright gold appeared over the fog, with clearer, jewel-like colors ranging into violet above that.

Ronar welcomed the forthcoming return of the suns. The woman who walked a pace or two ahead of him was shivering, obviously suffering from the cold. This was the night's coldest moment, when their metabolisms were reduced for want of sleep. Ronar knew they'd encounter worse before reaching their goal.

He pulled off the cloak that Pedemus had lent him and stepped up beside Astraea. "Here," he said gruffly, draping the wool around her thin shoulders.

"No, no,", she said, attempting to brush him off. "I have a cloak of my own. You'll need yours."

"I have a jacket," answered Ronar. "I'm not likely to get cold, as long as I keep moving."

That was true, within limits. Whether he'd encounter those limits Ronar couldn't be sure, but Astraea already had encountered hers.

She subsided and accepted the garment, wrapping it around herself.

The sky took on a brief glorious shade of magenta, reflected in the layer of fog far below. Then the suns surged over the billowing mass, throwing it into relief like a rounded range of gold-topped mountains. The skylight drained to a clear blue-black, a color of almost divine purity and remoteness.

Ronar ambled along, vexed by the snail's pace forced on him by the tottering Astraea, who nevertheless was clearly making her best effort. When the suns were high enough to offer them a little warmth, Ronar called a halt for food. Astraea immediately sank down on a rock, her breath coming in quick puffs of vapor. She was a pale, grey-eyed woman whose dry grey locks might once have been golden.

She had brought some food, and Ronar made a meal out of hers and his combined. He sat on a rock near hers and munched his bread in silence. Noting her desultory efforts at eating, he said, "If you can't eat, you must at least drink. You may not thirst, but the dry mountain air can suck the water from your body, and leave you helpless before you know it."

She looked at him, then fished out the wineskin from her bag and took a few pulls. Atypically for a Mersinean woman, she did not appear uncomfortable without the nicety of a cup. Still aware of his scrutiny, she also chewed a bit of hard bread and cheese.

Ronar did not linger here, fearing that her tired old muscles would stiffen up if given the chance. They went on, creeping along trails that grew increasingly steep and precarious as they went. They had long since left behind the amenities of the mountain's lower slopes. This was more a route than a true path, a road for travelers who were serious about making the divine pilgrimage. As far as Ronar could tell, he and Astraea had left behind all others who were attempting the mountain. He could not see anyone ahead.

As the two suns straddled the meridian, Ronar found it necessary to take Astraea by the arm, to add his strength to hers, which was plainly failing. She could not catch her breath, due to the steepening path and the thinning air. Her hair fell into her eyes, and she stumbled often on rubbery legs.

Finally, when it was clear that the old woman was about to go to her knees, Ronar could no longer delay the inevitable.

"Astraea. If you wish to reach the summit, I must carry you."

She did not look at him, but shook her head vigorously beneath her hood. "No, that is too much to ask. Perhaps I must fail in my quest, but you must not also fail as a result of my weakness."

Ronar gave a grim smile. "Neither of us will fail." He leaned forward and scooped her up as easily as he would a cat. Indeed, she seemed not to have much more flesh on her than one.

She said nothing for a hundred paces or so. But then: "Very well. But I must not sleep. I must reach the home of the gods without shutting my eyes."

"As you will."

Ronar was elated. He immediately more than doubled his speed, freed from limiting himself to the old woman's faltering pace.

"Why are you here?" asked Astraea. "A foreigner, attempting this climb?"

"I'm not sure what I hope to accomplish. Maybe it's an act of contrition for me as well. I recently took on a responsibility…a vow of protection…at which I have so far failed utterly. If there's any way to undo the damage, I must find it."

"A vow of protection…" whispered Astraea. "I also have failed to protect those in my care. I have even…once, ten turns ago, I bore a girl child. I deemed her…an impediment to the life I wished to live at that time. To avoid the inconvenience…I exposed the infant. It was a minor scandal even among those in my own circle. It was always the men who did things like exposing superfluous girl children. My husband at the time resisted the idea, but I would not be moved, not even by the cries of that tiny baby as I walked away and left her to die."

Ronar's heart was thundering. He frowned down into the face of the woman he carried, whose gaze was turned inward in bitterness and remorse. Ten turns...? Surely Astraea was too old to have carried a child so recently... and anyway, that did not fit...

Fool. He was thinking in Earth terms...a turn of Colibdis was more than two years of Earth. The altitude must be affecting his thought processes as well.

He stared down into Astraea's face, searching for any resemblance. There could be no certainty in those weathered, tear-streaked features, but Ronar could not discount the possibility that the inscrutable gods of this planet had placed into his hands the mother of Asterope.

Ronar marched ahead blindly, pondering the implications of this development. He couldn't immediately see any way in which this might affect his plans, vague as they were. But somehow it would turn out to be significant —of that he had no doubt.

"Ast—" but he cut himself off as he glanced at her face. She was sleeping, and he saw no reason to deny her that release. On he walked, trying to maintain a smooth gait.

The path led along exposed ledges. Ronar was glad his passenger was oblivious to the yawning spaces just inches from his feet. Carrying her over such narrow ledges was awkward. He would have preferred to have his hands free for clinging to the walls. As it was, he often had to inch along sideways, facing outward, judging his footing by feel. Looking down from these precipices, he could see the path winding far below, with no other figure on it, as far as he could see.

On less difficult stretches he was able to take in the view above them as well as below. A network of cirrus clouds veined the sky like cracks in ice. Ronar was weather-wise enough to realize what that implied for tomorrow.

The suns withdrew below the horizon. The mountain briefly took on a shadowless, dreamlike air of unreality in the twilight. Then the rock dimmed to black, and Ronar walked beneath familiar stars, albeit dimmed and diffused by the high cloud. The temperature dropped rapidly. Ronar had sweated through the day's long climb, but now he grew chilled. Astraea remained asleep. He resolved not to halt for rest or food until she should awaken.

That happened a few hours into the night. Her thin voice came to him saying, "I was so lost in my thoughts that I didn't even notice the coming of the night."

"Yes, climbs like this do inspire deep reveries. How are you feeling? Are you ready for food and water?"

She assented, and Ronar set her on her feet. His arms were stiff, and tended to bend upward of their own accord, but remained usable.

He and Astraea consumed a cold and cheerless meal of stale bread and icewater, Ronar still on his feet, Astraea perched on a rock. She wrapped her garments about herself as many times as the fabric would allow. Even so, he could hear the chattering of her few remaining teeth.

Nor was Ronar in much better condition. His jacket was not intended for below-freezing conditions, and the borrowed cloak had of course gone to the frail woman.

They had no reason to linger. Motion was their best defense against the invasion of the cold. Astraea insisted that her strength was renewed, that she could walk on her own again. Within half a mile she was gasping for breath, barely able to stay on her feet. Without comment, Ronar scooped her up again, pushing ahead on his long, powerful legs. Her thin body shivered against him, sheltering in Ronar's great chest and arms. His exertions produced enough heat to spare them both the worst of the cold.

Ronar began to suffer from the thinning air as he climbed through that long night. He concentrated on his breathing as he walked, pulling in deep, steady lungfuls of frigid air. He estimated they had reached fifteen thousand feet or higher. They would, he hoped, reach the summit sometime late tomorrow.

By midnight the stars had faded from view. Ronar could almost feel the layer of clouds that slid by invisibly, not very far overhead. Without starlight, the mountain was a black mass against a barely luminous background of sky. Not even Ronar could traverse this trail in total darkness, certainly not while carrying the woman.

He would resort to a trick that had saved him before, but first he must warn Astraea of his intention, not wishing to frighten her. He spoke her name, but received no answer. He could feel her breathing. She was asleep again.

Ronar called upon the ring on his left hand, not enough to evoke the sword, but just enough to bring the red, sputtering light that preceded it. Not only did it light the path in a fitful manner, but it cast enough heat to be welcome and noticeable.

Ronar did not enjoy this method of progress—the concentration needed to stimulate the ring at just the right level was taxing—but at least it enabled him to continue.

The red light illuminated shreds of cloud that blew by on a rising wind, cold and very unwelcome. The sound of Astraea's breathing was quieter, but more regular. Then Ronar noticed it had developing a wet, gurgling quality. His face hardened to a still grimmer cast. Pulmonary edema...a threat even to young and healthy climbers.

A fine sleet began to pelt his face. Astraea suddenly stiffened in his arms. She gasped, then coughed for a moment. She stared in confusion at the lurid light pouring from his fingers.

"Are you a sorcerer?" she quavered.

"No. This is the only magic I have. The ring normally calls forth a sword, but it can also be compelled to give out light. I doubt any such use of it was ever intended."

"A sword. Then you are the one I've heard of. Greylock. The Earthman."

"Yes."

"Well. Adventures of this sort aren't entirely new to you, are they?"

Ronar chuckled. "Not entirely."

She looked out into the night, squinting against the sleet. "If only adventures didn't have to be so cold."

"They can be worse than cold," said Ronar. "You're growing ill. Your lungs are filling with fluid because of the thin air. If you don't go down soon, you could worsen and die."

Astraea was silent for a moment.

"If it meant my life, would you take me down, even if it meant the delay of your own mission?"

Now Ronar took a moment of silence.

"Yes," he said tonelessly.

She nodded. "I thought as much, but I'm not asking it of you. This is my one and only effort to reach my goal... even though you're really making all the effort. You might climb down for my sake and then try again. But if I don't succeed now, I'll never have the strength to try again. Let's go on."

They went on. Astraea rested as she could while Ronar trudged upward through the raw darkness, husbanding his breath, fighting for balance against gusts of stronger wind. He could see nothing beyond the small area lit by the ring. The black spaces to either side of him were totally mysterious. Sometimes the sounds of wind and footsteps had a subtle echoing quality, and then he guessed that rocks or cliffs were nearby. When there were no echoes, but merely a vast sighing of unimpeded wind, he knew they traversed an exposed ridge or ledge. Only the rare appearance of a cairn told him they were still on the trail at all.

Concentration was getting harder to maintain. Lack of sleep and a shortage of oxygen brought a hallucinatory quality to the trek, making it harder to use good judgment. The ring flickered alarmingly, sometimes going dark, sometimes flaring with the white, clashing radiance that immediately preceded the sword. Then Astraea would hiss and tense, and Ronar would hurriedly dampen the ring before he found a broadsword appearing in a hand that was already full.

His arms began to feel as though they were pinioned with iron bars.

At the first sign of daylight he gratefully let the ring flicker into darkness. He stood for a few moments in a windy world of dark grey gloom, letting his eyes grow accustomed, then continued on. Luckily, the sleet had passed.

Astraea's breath was now a continuous gurgle from within her chest. Her mouth hung open slackly, and she coughed weakly from time to time without even waking up.

"Asterope," said Ronar, startling himself. "Astraea," he corrected himself. But she remained unconscious. By now he was desperate for rest, shaky, hungry, thirsty, and near exhaustion. But he did not put her down.

On he climbed, vision spinning, otherwise all but insensate to his surroundings. After an unknown time he felt a pressure on his lips, and looked down to discover that Astraea had awakened, and had fished a bite of food from her bag, and sought to feed him. His mouth opened stiffly and accepted the frozen bit of bread, chewing it. She kept this up for a while and then desisted when his lips no longer opened. She herself took nothing.

When he looked down she was again asleep.

"Astraea," he said softly through the cold mists that whipped around them. "It is for Asterope that I make this climb. Asterope, your own daughter, whom you abandoned. She escaped her servitude and came to me across the sea. We have both failed her, in different ways. Now we make this climb together, in search of absolution, looking for a way to undo the harm we have done to Asterope."

He blinked away the tears that threatened to freeze in his eyes and glanced down at Astraea again.

He found her gazing up at him gravely, her eyes clearer than he had seen them so far.

"My daughter," she rasped.

"Yes. It must be."

Ronar felt more than a little overwrought. He hadn't decided whether to tell Astraea of his belief, and certainly hadn't intended to blurt it out to her, sleeping or not. But now it was out.

"She was found near a temple in Pantheos, taken in as a slave by a Panthenian family. She grew into a grey-eyed beauty, a young woman of rare integrity and will. But she was not strong enough to overcome the malice of the god-thing that possessed her."

She said nothing to this, but turned her face away, looking out into the cold grey mists.

Ronar spoke on, in the grip of a wholly uncharacteristic volubility.

"Since Asterope was taken, Ahriman has fallen silent. I've been involved in other cases where Ahriman...has somehow captured the spirits of the weak or afflicted. This has now happened to Asterope. I won't relent until I've found a way to free her from Ahriman's domination. To see her spirit reunited with her body, which Athena herself carries in her shield. I don't know how to do that. But people have been climbing this mountain in search of answers for centuries. Maybe it has some for me as well."

Tears coursed down his face, the first he had shed since Asterope's loss. When spoken aloud for the ears of another, his plans sounded so inchoate, so feeble, so vague. So impossible. Yet, he knew he was right in one thing: he would not relent.

Still Astraea said nothing.

Ronar prompted, in a voice less firm than he would have liked, "I can't believe we've been brought together by accident. I'm a man who believes in rationality...but some coincidences are too vivid to be dismissed...as such. You must have some role to play in this. Here perhaps is your chance to redeem yourself for abandoning the girl. Your chance to find the peace you crave."

Her voice came to him from out of the wind. "Perhaps. I will think on it. We will see what the gods have to say."

Ronar was almost out of breath after his speech. He said no more; nor did Astraea. He continued to struggle up the mountain.

They came to a place where the trail dwindled to nothing, ending at a series of rocky slabs so steep that Ronar could not possibly mount them while carrying Astraea. Though he knew it would tax her waning strength, he set her down to totter on wobbly legs. She gazed up into his eyes inquiringly.

"Wait," said Ronar. He scrambled up the first of the rock faces. Reaching the top, he lay prone and peered down at Astraea, who seemed farther away than the short climb could explain. He shook his head to clear it and reached down toward her. "You must climb high enough to reach my hand. There is no other way."

"Can you not let down my cloak, and then pull me up by it?" she asked forlornly.

"Can you hold onto it as I haul you up?"

"No."

"Then you must climb. It's only a few feet. Climb as you saw me climb."

Ronar knew that for a woman of her age, such a thing was more easily said than done. Still, he watched as Astraea shuffled over to the rock and reached up, her quivering, bony hands grey with cold as they searched for handholds. She found a crack and clung to it, straining to lift herself a few inches. Ronar heard her feet, hidden beneath her cloak and other garments, scrabbling around. But they found no purchase, or they slipped from it, for she was jarred loose, and fell back the short distance she had climbed. It was enough to knock her off her feet. She lay there, motionless and gasping.

Ronar bit his lip, and said, "Astraea, you must try again. The success of your mission depends on this."

She lay still a moment longer, but then she stirred, bringing herself to her knees, then slowly back to her feet. Ronar was relieved that she hadn't broken any bones. He found himself bathed in a cold sweat. He was shaking, as though he were in a fever, or a nightmare. Surely this was too much like situations he had known in the past. Sometimes such situations had no good outcome.

Again Astraea leaned against the slab, and more slowly this time, began to work her way up it. Barely moving, she seemed to creep up the rock like a snail. At times Ronar couldn't imagine what was holding her there...and yet she inched her way up, face pressed into the damp stone. When she looked up at him, her grey face swam in his vision, close enough so that he could see the sparse hairs of her eyebrows, yet still too far for him to aid in her ascent. She wore the same expression he remembered seeing on Earth's moon...a sad distress, a strained concern. To his uncertain vision her face appeared no more alive, no more animated, than that lunar face of grey and white stone.

He woke up abruptly, the echoes of a cry remaining in his ears. He squinted back down the rock face. The view had changed. Two bony hands were now thrust up toward him, but they were the same hand...two identical left hands. With an effort of will he fused the images together. With binocular vision restored, he could see that the hand was within reach. He thrust his own left hand and arm over the brink, locking his fingers on the thin wrist. Astraea winced and hissed as he drew her up the rock. When she was almost level with the top he grabbed her with his other hand and nearly threw her up and over the rim, where she lay panting.

Ronar panted for a few moments as well, and then staggered to his feet.

Twenty feet away was another rock face which had to be climbed, and this one was higher.

Astraea raised her head and stared at it.

"I cannot climb that," she said.

Ronar recognized the finality of that statement. He did not even think to argue it.

"All right then. I'll carry you on my back."

He stood there swaying, trying to organize his muddled thoughts into a plan of action. It would normally have been the work of a moment's unconscious thought, but his mind was slow and jumbled. Part of it was occupied with contemplating the foolish futility of what they were doing, killing themselves to climb this mountain when their goals were so chimerical. Mother and mentor, parent and guardian, struggled against reason to redeem themselves for their separate failures at protecting Asterope.

After a while, Ronar squatted down beside Astraea.

"Can you cling to my back?" he asked.

"No."

Again he did not doubt it; it seemed all she could do to voice that single syllable.

"This may be uncomfortable then." He almost burst into laughter at the redundancy of that remark. He tore a strip from her cloak, then manhandled her around and flopped her onto his back, limp as a cape, with little help from her. He drew her arms around his neck and tied her elbows together with the rag. When that was done he tried to look back over his shoulder at her. He couldn't see much, but he could hear her breathing and feel the warmth of it on his neck.

"This will hurt. But it will only last for a few minutes. Try to hold on with your legs as well."

"Let's just get this over with."

He pulled himself to his feet, leaning forward to balance the limp figure that dangled behind him. She brought her knees up and wrapped her legs around his torso, not strongly enough to take much of the weight off her arms, but at least it got her legs out of Ronar's way as he tried to walk. He shambled over to the next rock slab, adjusted the luggage bags that also flopped down to impede him, and stood staring up at it. Ordinarily this would not be a difficult climb for him, but now, exhausted, half-asleep, freezing, with ninety pounds of extra mass hanging from his neck, things were not ordinary. He tried to think of some way to use a magic sword to scale this slab, as he'd used it to solve so many problems in the past. But it remained a sword, not a ladder.

He reached up and felt for handholds. The cold stone numbed his fingers at once. He'd left Thunderbird with gloves and many other useful items, but most of them had burned with *Dekapus*.

Magic could carry them up this mountain. Sha Totek, the great Sorcerer and Gatekeeper of Colibdis, could flit up this mountain in any of a hundred ways, assuming the gods did not resent such hubris. Ronar knew as much about magic, in his way, as did Sha Totek himself. He had even employed it himself from time to time, in extreme circumstances.

But this was not an extreme circumstance, he realized. This was a more mundane case of mind over matter, of will overcoming the weaknesses and frailties of the body. He was still on his feet. He could complete this climb on his own.

He drew in a few deep breaths and gripped the rock with all his remaining strength, pulling himself and his passenger off the ground until his toes found purchase in a crack. Then his knees straightened to push them up another foot or more, while his stiff fingers grasped a knob of rock and pulled again. After a few minutes of this he hauled himself and Astraea over the rim. He lay there panting, Astraea's weight on his back, while she moaned and muttered thanks to her gods.

He rolled over and untied her arms, then staggered to his feet to see what came next. Red sparkles obscured his vision when he stood up, but they cleared away after a moment.

They were atop a pinnacle, its flat summit no bigger than twenty feet in any direction. It dropped away into foggy nothingness in every direction except the way they had come. A few raw boulders stood scattered about, with snow and ice at their bases.

Ronar slowly approached one of them. Carved into its face was the Greek letter Omega.

So they had reached the summit. Ronar sagged down to sit on another boulder. He looked over at Astraea, who sat hunched over, barely conscious.

"Astraea," he said in as firm a voice as he could manage. "We've reached the summit. You've done it. You've climbed Olympos."

She started at that, coughed, raised her head, and looked around into the cold grey cloud that smothered them. Ronar looked around too. He did not know what he had expected to find here...but somehow he'd thought it would be something grander than this bit of snow-swept rock. Was this the only reward awaiting those pilgrims who were pious and determined enough to make the ascent?

They could not linger here...not if they planned to ever descend again.

There was a faint flash of light, and seconds later a roll of thunder. This would be a poor place to wait out a thunderstorm.

Astraea coughed again, a wet and wrenching gurgle. "Ronar—" she choked, "I cannot see anything."

He snorted. "Neither can I, in this murk."

"No." More coughing. It was at least a minute before she could speak again. "That's not what I mean. I can see nothing at all."

He shot her a look of alarm. Her head was wobbling about, her eyes blank and glassy.

"I've gone blind."

He got to his feet and walked over to her. She looked toward the sound of his approach, but her eyes did not meet his. He crouched down beside her and raised his ring, willing the red glare to blaze forth from it once more.

"Do you see this?" he prompted.

"No, but I feel the warmth. What has happened to me?"

He maintained the warming light as he considered her question. He had no idea what could have affected her this way. He had never heard of blindness as a consequence of altitude. Snow blindness, yes…but not on a dismal, murky day like this. Perhaps she'd suffered a stroke or some other malady. Or maybe her blindness was hysterical. This thought was strengthened by her next remark.

"Maybe the gods have struck me blind, to keep my eyes from their faces."

"Nonsense. I can see well enough, and your belief in these gods is greater than mine."

"But you are a great hero. A strong man. I am only a weak, selfish old woman."

Ronar winced at that. "Astraea, you are here atop this mountain. None of the other climbers we saw or passed are here. Nor have we passed any on their way down. Give yourself credit for that."

"But I will not go down from here."

Again his anxiety flared up. "And why is that?"

"I've gone beyond the limits of my strength in getting here. Now I can only await whatever message the gods may have for me, if any. And I think it must come soon."

"But what of your daughter? What of Asterope? Don't you want to help me recover her?" His words sounded plaintive, almost childishly so, to his own ears.

That brought a brief twinkle to the blind eyes. "What can an old woman do in a struggle with that nameless god? If I am to help the girl, perhaps I can do so more effectively once I am free of this body."

Ronar reached out his right hand and held hers. "I'm sure the gods will speak to you soon." He helped her, almost dragging her, into the lee of one of the boulders, and propped her up against it. Huddling next to her, he kept the ring ablaze to warm them both. He held her hand and sat looking silently into the void of blowing cloud.

After another fit of coughing, Astraea asked weakly, "What do you see, Ronar? Surely the halls of Olympos must be worth a few words, even from you."

Ronar blinked at that. Somehow it hadn't occurred to him that Astraea must be unaware of how unprepossessing a perch they occupied.

Thunder rumbled again in the seething greyness.

"Well, Astraea," he began cautiously, "the weather is bad. You can hear the thunder. Everything around us is hidden in cloud."

He looked over at her to take in her reaction. She merely looked attentive, waiting for him to continue.

"But, ah, I think now...now I see..." Ronar rolled his eyes. He did not count himself much of a storyteller.

"Now the clouds seem to be thinning ahead of us... blown clear by the wind. The light is getting stronger, and I can see...a saddle dropping down from this peak we're on...and rising up on the far side is another, higher peak..."

Ronar faltered, his words coming to a halt. He wasn't sure if what he seeing was real, or some kind of self-induced hallucination. Whichever it was, a vista was indeed opening ahead of them. The clouds *were* breaking up, aglow with a light like mixed wine and gold. Evidently they hadn't reached the true summit of Olympos, but a lesser shoulder. Indeed, there in front of them the rock sagged down to a broad saddle, which mounted in the distance to a steeper, higher peak, its top submerged in immense, ponderous clouds which scudded and twisted in the wind.

"Well?" prompted Astraea.

Ronar started. "The peak…that other peak is hidden by clouds. It must be almost sunset, because the light in them looks warm, fiery. But now those clouds are blowing though as well. I can see higher up the side of the mountain, but only in glimpses. I see flashes of white, or white lit by shifting beams from the setting suns. There appear to be columns…"

Again his words choked themselves off. Those clouds were clearing off—and in the gaps he had glimpses of vertical bars of light and shadow. He continued his description—and as he spoke, the description preceded the reality by only a few seconds.

"The clouds are almost gone—I can see patches of clear sky beyond them. There is…a city on top of that other peak. The scale of the place, the magnitude, is far beyond the human. The columns look like they were chiseled from translucent gemstones, catching and magnifying all the colors in the sky. There are great domes ablaze with gold, and vast arches encompassing huge spaces, one wonder piled atop another, reaching far into the heavens. I don't know…I can't imagine why this can't be seen from Pantheos, or from far out at sea. I see great, smokeless fires, more silver than gold, roiling in immense braziers. They flank staircases that must rise a yard at a time. I see glittering silver eagles perched on pedestals, and I think their heads are swiveling slowly, and their eyes are flashing. I see figures…"

He squinted, trying to make out the shadows that stood far back in a forest of walls and pillars. The largest of them detached itself from the others and began to stride toward them.

"A god is coming this way...I can't tell which one yet, but he's pretty imposing...he's emerging into the light now. He's a mature male, very powerful, with a high, broad forehead and flowing black hair and a plaited beard. He's reached the edge of the city, and now he's striding down the slope, covering a dozen feet at a time. I think it must be Zeus himself. Lightning is dancing around him—"

Thunder punctuated this remark.

"—and his eyes are bright blue. He'll be here in a moment...his eyes are on you, Astraea."

Ronar glanced over at her. Her eyes were shining, almost as though she could see the apparition that approached her. Her mouth was firm, perhaps with a ghost of a smile, and she seemed otherwise relaxed, in a state beyond fear.

Now somewhat diminished in stature, Zeus stood nearby, shading them like a thundercloud. Ronar studied the god's face as he leaned over Astraea, taking note of the fine, narrow nose, the dark hair lightly touched with grey, the angular face. Except for the length of his hair and the color of his eyes, Zeus was a fair likeness of Ronar's own father.

"He is bending over you, Astraea. You must feel the force of his presence...I know I can. It's a wild energy, not oppressive, but majestic, like that of a thunderstorm. His face is kind. Tender. He is looking at you...with what must be forgiveness."

Ronar wished the god would speak, but he had trouble imagining what would be proper for him to say.

Now tears coursed down Astraea's face. "If only I could see you, Lord Zeus."

"See me," rumbled Zeus, stretching out his hand to her eyes.

She gasped, and life and light sprang back into her eyes. She stared up into the windblown hair and stern face that loomed above her.

"Daughter, go from this world with my blessing, carrying with you the grace of all the gods." He straightened up and stepped away a pace or two, then looked back at her over his shoulder.

"Thank you for your blessing, Lord Zeus," she whispered. "I now leave the world, as you bid. With Hermes absent from the world, I must choose my own path into darkness. Guarded by the grace of all the gods, I put myself into the hands of the one who has no name on Olympos, the one who holds the girl Asterope. Goodbye, Ronar."

Ronar saw the world go white before his eyes. "Astraea, NO!" he roared. But already her body had gone limp. Her head flopped over, her last rattling breath released. An evil, rancorous laughter filled the air, or at least it invaded Ronar's mind, drowning out the thunder of Zeus.

Ronar found himself on his feet, glaring into the face of the king of the gods. All he got in return was a look of sorrow and regret, an almost apologetic admission of helplessness. The god dwindled still further, then faded away to nothing, taking with him the fabulous city on that more distant summit, which also vanished, along with the shining host of the gods of Mersinea.

Chapter 22

The View from Olympos

And so Ronar occupied the summit, with only the lifeless body of Astraea for company. Though stunned and emotionally numb, his survival instincts still urged him to reclaim his cloak, and to take hers as well. He sat huddled beside the boulder with the Omega carved into it, his feet dangling into space, over the edge of this, the goal of so many thousands of pilgrims. The sky had cleared completely, going from the dankest overcast to brilliant clarity in fifteen minutes or less. The suns set, bisected by a straight ocean horizon far to the west. Night came down, though Ronar was oblivious to its starry splendor.

He woke up at sunrise, though he had no memory of falling asleep. He lay wrapped in the cloaks and all his clothing, but was still stiff with cold. If he hadn't been so exhausted he doubted he could have slept through such cold. In fact he was lucky he hadn't frozen to death during the night. He had already lost toes to frostbite while traveling through Hyperborea…he would prefer to keep the rest.

Moving with difficulty, he extracted his hands from their wrappings and brought them up before his face. His fingers were blotched with yellow, but it didn't look serious. He rubbed them together absently, and was satisfied when the rising pain told him of life returning to the frozen flesh.

His tongue was thick with thirst and his lips were cracked. When his joints were limber enough he rolled painfully out from the cloaks and hauled himself to his feet. The summit of Olympos was starkly shadowed by the low beams of the rising suns. The crag was streaked with snow and ice, and bore no trace of the grand city of the Olympians.

He rummaged through the luggage, brought out the water bottles, and lay them on the east side of one of the boulders, fully in the light. If they did not warm up enough to melt, he'd have to smash one and use his ring to thaw bits of ice.

The suns soon warmed the air to an almost comfortable level, and the red clay bottles soaked up the warmth. He drank a cup of ice water and ate cold food and meat from the baggage. Then he stretched out in the sunlight and promptly fell asleep again.

He awoke in mid afternoon, ate and drank some more, and sat staring out blankly over the world. He still felt nothing. His thoughts were sluggish, a mere feeble undercurrent flowing below the level of his awareness.

He should have been exalted by his perch on this great peak, bathed in the white-gold light of those superbly disparate suns, set in a sky of the deepest violet imaginable. Yet the magnificent view did not console him. Ronar was blind to it, blind to everything but a sudden self-loathing that welled up and threatened to dissolve his soul in bitterness. He thought of Asterope and Astraea, both now possessions of Ahriman despite his "protection."

Ronar was not an unduly introspective man. His normal style was to focus so totally on the task at hand that there was little capacity left for analysis of his own character or motives. Now he turned upon himself the same cold scrutiny he usually reserved for his enemies. He was unwilling to let so total a failure as he had lately endured go by without examination.

He had failed to thwart the powerful god Ahriman from corrupting and destroying Asterope. His decision to travel by sea had been faulty, and had certainly cost the lives of the crew of *Dekapus*. Treacherous as they were, they hadn't deserved their horrid fate.

But he could not honestly say that Asterope would have been saved had they traveled by land. As for Astraea, he'd had no warning at all that she was in any danger from Ahriman. Even now, he could not for the life of him imagine what could have led her to cast herself into the hands of the god of evil.

And so, almost against his will, Ronar's cold attention turned from himself to wherever lurked that so-called god of thought, subtlety, magic, and evil.

Why did the other gods suffer the existence of one who did so much harm, one who showed no redeeming qualities? Ahriman seemed to be of a different nature than most of the other gods. With one exception, Ahriman alone appeared to be fully endowed with an independent will, with volition, with an agenda that went beyond the traditional roles assigned to the other gods. Ronar now believed that gods like Zeus were not truly sentient beings at all, but were merely projections created by the needs and expectations of the people of the planet. It certainly seemed that he himself had conjured up a vision of Olympos to comfort Astraea. If that was the case, the gods were little more than scenery, mere manifestations of the magic which so informed this planet, shaped and molded by the unconscious will of the people who inhabited it.

But then, who was shaping or molding Ahriman? Or did he indeed have an independent existence? If anyone, it must be the people of Darteharn, that dark and threatening kingdom ruled by whatever was left of the wizard Namirnakh. Ahriman's worship must have been introduced into Celtic Darteharn by Namirnakh, who was himself a Persian. Perhaps other races worshipped him under the name of their own analogous gods, those few whose pantheons contained a clear-cut god of malevolence.

The only other god whom Ronar believed to be essentially sentient was Varanu, the great god of Cosmic Order, who was also unknown to the Mersineans. Varanu had perhaps sprung and evolved from Varuna, a Hindu god worshipped by the people of Varma, the Colibdian nation populated by descendants of people from ancient India. But Varanu had other names in the other countries where he was recognized.

Ronar's own brief contact with this entity had been more than enough to convince him that Varanu was a thinking being, though on a level he could not fully comprehend. He had observed the struggle which persisted between Ahriman, with his ultimate aim of spreading magic throughout the universe, and Varanu, who sought to contain and thwart this ambition, keeping the structure of reality undisturbed beyond the bubble of Colibdian magic. And yet, without that minute bubble of potential chaos, Varanu himself could not exist. Perhaps there was a connection between that and the fact that Varanu did not destroy Ahriman, or even interfere with him unless he threatened to carry his influence beyond the confines of Colibdis.

This was a train of thought that Ronar had pursued many times in the years since his coming to this planet. He had reached no conclusions. The gods weren't free with their secrets, and no one else could offer definitive answers, not even Sha Totek himself.

By now the suns were hovering near the horizon. It seemed only minutes since Ronar had last seen them there, or years. From this perch he could see hundreds of miles into the distance. The glitter paths cast by the suns on the sea were diffuse bands, like glints on a broad shield. Somewhere along that horizon was what Sha Totek had told him was the true wonder to be seen from Olympos— Larlaninulius, the Island of the Gods, supposed home and headquarters of the master set of gods whose avatars walked the world under dozens of guises. It was from this island that Varanu himself had sprung to do battle with Ahriman, all those turns ago.

Ronar had never found or heard a solid answer to the question of why noncorporeal beings like these gods needed a home of any kind. It was this island he had climbed the mountain to see.

The temperature plunged as the suns neared the horizon, first white Photos, then the diffuse red-gold orb of Kudu. A band of low sea-haze split the disk of Kudu as it sank, making it look like a belted gas giant planet. That band was the only influence which the thin, pure atmosphere of Colibdis, most of which lay below his feet, had on his view of the sunset.

As soon as the suns were gone the sky went black. Yellowish stars appeared as fast as his eyes could accommodate themselves to the darkness.

One other light was visible, a strange glimmer just on the horizon, somewhere off to the west-southwest. Now for the first time Ronar was conscious of the loss of his binocular, that exquisite instrument he had carried for decades, now a glob of melted glass and aluminum in the ashes of *Dekapus*. He longed to apply its power to this mysterious wisp of light, the very sight of which raised the hair on his neck. But he did not have the glass, and so must observe this phenomenon as closely as his unaided eyes would allow.

He could make out no definite shape as the light flickered and seethed through the intervening expanse of air, save to suspect that it was taller than it was wide. It twinkled through pale shades of blue, white and green, which was itself interesting, since all that air should have reddened it.

Ronar dug out a scrap of paper and a pencil stub. With stiff cold fingers he noted which stars set near the mysterious light. As he made these observations he was occasionally distracted by peripheral glimpses of light and hints of piquant music off to his right. The pillars of Olympus again occupied their illusory "main peak", though in a ghostly, uncertain fashion, vanishing whenever Ronar turned to face it directly. He found this an irritation. If the gods of Olympus could do no more than tantalize him with their ineffectual half-presence, he wished they'd cut out their juvenile light show and leave him to work in peace.

A feeling of being watched alerted him to the presence of another interloper, this time above him, and to his left. He craned his neck and peered up toward the celestial equator, where the Milky Way galaxy glimmered in greenish-white transparent beauty. Its spiral arms were defined by intricate bands of curdled blackness, great lanes of opaque dust and gas, a substance absent from the tiny swarm of stars occupied by Colibdis.

The Whirlpool was not in itself an oppressive presence. Shining fitfully in the foreground was the unwelcome mote of the Eye of Ahriman, a reddish star now fainter than third magnitude.

Ronar did not fully understand its orbit. Partly that was due to the danger of observing it closely, and partly because such trivial rocks were not Ronar's concern as an astronomer. Everyone on Colibdis knew it kept itself apart from Sinanna and the suns, plying a path along the celestial equator. That circle of sky was called the Road of Evil, and most of the constellations through which it passed were of unpleasant aspect and name. The main exception was the Whirlpool itself, which straddled the equator. Here too the ecliptic had its autumnal crossing of the equator. In Colibdian mythology, the Whirlpool was not contaminated by the evil that visited it periodically. Instead it was considered to be the maelstrom where good and evil mixed into chaos, a function that maintained a balance necessary to the stability of the Universe.

Now the Eye was creeping toward the equinox point. Only when it was near this part of its path, or in the opposite celestial hemisphere near the vernal equinox, could the Eye conjoin with the suns or the larger moon. Tonight Sinanna was far from the Whirlpool, while the suns were creeping steadily toward an equinox that was still moonturns away. The Eye had the glowing field of the Whirlpool to itself. Its progress was fast enough that Ronar could discern it in only a few minutes of watching.

Though Ronar hated to see the superb Galaxy sullied by the presence of Ahriman's lair, at the moment, Ahriman was only indirectly Ronar's concern. He returned his attention to the distant cold flame that marked the Island of the Gods, pondering it, trying to penetrate its enigmatic existence.

His scrutiny was long and steady enough so that hours passed. Stars crept by the wavering light and plunged into the sea, while the Milky Way sank down from the meridian, carrying the Eye along with it.

And then Ronar sat blinking and rubbing his eyes, for the god's beacon suddenly flared to ten times its previous brightness, a hundred times, more. Even stranger, he found he was casting a shadow on the rock beneath him. He looked up, and the hackles on his neck rose again. The Eye had flared up as well, if not to the same degree as the island. For the first time Ronar had ever seen, it was no longer reddish, but had instead taken on the same coruscating cold tints as the beacon.

Ronar got to his feet. Off to his right was still another curiosity. The palaces of the Olympians now stood revealed in supernaturally perfect clarity and reality. Twelve or more towering figures stood among them, gazing out toward the flare on the horizon. All except for Athena, whose grave gaze was directed at him.

Ronar turned from this distraction back to the cold fires of the beacon and the Eye. He studied the Eye's position, noting that it had actually passed the equinox point. Evidently whatever strange alignment had produced this effect was unrelated to the crossing. He made hurried estimates of the Eye's altitude, noting the time on his wristwatch, which was about the only possession of his to survive his recent ordeal, and right now the most indispensable. Three-dimensional maps and models of orbits drew themselves in his brain. They were less than tentative, but Ronar knew with unwavering certainty that what was happening here, and his knowledge of it, would somehow change everything.

He watched as the beacon dimmed to its previous brightness, and looked up to find the Eye reduced to its usual red flickering glow. He regarded it with a predatory fierceness that would have been ludicrous just five minutes before. He turned his palms up toward the sky.

"You have just been put into my hands," he said in a hoarse whisper. His fingers slowly closed into fists.

Chapter 23

Ronar's Unflinching Gaze

The familiar buttes and mesas of Two Suns City resolved out of the horizon haze as Ronar trudged on. He expected to arrive home around sunset. The sky was laced with cirrus clouds that were steadily thickening and lowering toward stratus. The observatory would not be in use tonight. For once, that was fine with Ronar. He wasn't ready to meet with anyone just yet.

A few hours later Ronar skirted the base of Observatory Mesa and entered the hamlet at its southern foot. The little cluster of houses and dormitories was somnolent in the residual heat of evening. Only a few people were visible, relaxing on their verandas, looking up to note his return.

Ronar entered his own house, a low adobe structure with a tiled roof, dark timbers, and a central courtyard, set slightly apart from the rest.

As always, returning to this place seemed like a dream after a long and eventful absence. He looked around the house, trying to reacquaint himself with the idea that it was his, that it was his home. He could sleep in its bed without asking permission and without expectation of trouble. The place looked well-kept, but his housekeeper, Flora, was out, probably visiting her parents, having no reason to expect his return on this particular night. He walked into the kitchen, where broad shafts of fading sunlight, diffused by the clouds, poured in though the windows. He pumped himself a glass of water and looked in the pantry for something to eat, but found little except corn meal, honey, and salt. Again, there was no reason for Flora to keep a stocked larder while he was absent for weeks. Weeks that had seemed like years... He sighed.

He carried the cool water into his study and dropped into a heavy chair of wood and leather. His gaze wandered over the wall, reacquainting himself with various possessions and keepsakes that seemed like fragments of a dream. One wall was taken up by framed black-and-white photographs (there was no color photography on Colibdis as yet). The Tower of Sha Totek. Sha Totek himself, wearing a costume that looked colorful even in shades of grey, grinning into the camera. A very old portrait of his parents, showing them looking even younger than he did.

Asterope's graduating class. Asterope herself.

Ronar sat in the room's fading light and sipped his water. After a period of aimless thought he was brought to alertness by the jangle of the doorbell.

He stepped to the front door and opened it, looking down to see who had roused him. He found the smiling, natty figure of Nathaniel Deerfield, the President of Thunderbird University.

Ronar stared down at him, still too dazed by the cessation of his journey to open a conversation.

"Well, Professor Ronar," said Deerfield, "your neighbors reported your return, and I see they were correct." His smile seemed genuine.

Ronar nodded.

"You look road-weary, to say the least,"

"That I am."

Deerfield's smile changed to something more tentative. "May—may I ask if your mission was a success?"

Ronar's eyes gave the answer before his lips could form a word, to judge by Deerfield's expression of dismay. Ronar's voice was suddenly a rasp. "I failed to save Asterope. Whether any good can come of that remains to be seen."

Deerfield nodded slowly. "I am very sorry to hear that. I have no doubt that you made the greatest possible effort to save the girl from her peril. I am sorry for your—for her loss."

"She is not dead, not quite. Her body is under the protection of the goddess Athena, while her mind or spirit is a captive of Ahriman."

Deerfield's face went waxen at this news. Ronar stepped back and belatedly waved him into the foyer.

"Thank you," said the President shakily. "But I won't be staying long. I just came to remind you that this is the night scheduled by the Chancellor for the quarterly all-university colloquium and dinner."

Ronar repressed a sigh. The Chancellor of the University was Ronar himself. While this was a largely ceremonial post, the colloquium was a ceremonial function, giving the various administrators and department heads a chance to catch up with each other's wide-ranging concerns. Nevertheless, Ronar was about to decline to attend tonight's affair when the thought crossed his mind that at least there would be food.

"Very well then. I'll come along in about an hour, as soon as I've cleaned up."

"I'll have a carriage awaiting you."

Deerfield departed, subdued. Ronar set about the task of making himself presentable. Stropping one of the only steel razors in the world, he scraped off the spiny growth that covered his lips and chin. His face looked strange to him in the mirror. He thought he looked noticeably older, especially around the eyes. He was in sore need of a haircut, but he could not do that for himself, unless he wanted to look even more like a wild man.

He pumped cold well water into the brass bathtub and climbed in, indifferent to its temperature. He heard Flora run into the house as he was scrubbing off the accumulated filth of hundreds of miles of dry, dusty travel. She mumbled to herself in alarm as she charged from room to room, trying to make up for imagined deficiencies.

Stepping out of a tub of water the color of thin soup, Ronar wrapped himself in a robe and left the bathroom. He could not restrain a smile at the sight of Flora standing next to a chair in the courtyard, lamplight glinting off the scissors she held ready.

Flora was about twenty turns old, or maybe a bit less; he had never asked. She'd been quite young when she first came to work for him. Attractive if a bit plump, she had olive skin and glossy black hair.

"Hello, Flora," he said, sinking down into the chair with a certain feeling of relief and comfort. She immediately set about combing out his wet, tangled locks.

"Hello, Professor. I'm sorry I was not here to greet you. I'll go to the market first thing in the morning. I can have the pantry filled, and your breakfast cooking, by the time you wake up."

"That's all I can ask." He sat down and submitted to the flash and clack of the scissors as Flora struck off his excess hair with quick, decisive snips. She said little or nothing as she went about her work, which she'd learned was Ronar's usual preference. He was in no mood to chatter about the journey that had left him in such dire need of grooming.

It had taken him years to get used to having someone around to look after his needs. In truth, he would have preferred to care for himself as he always had before, but the University would not abide having someone as exalted as Ronar doing his own cooking and washing, especially given the meager quality of his efforts in these regards. So they had insisted, and Ronar had relented. By now he was able to appreciate the advantages of this arrangement. Flora really was an efficient and usually unobtrusive woman.

When she was satisfied with his haircut she combed the remaining iron-grey hair back from his forehead. He even suffered her to sprinkle on a few drops of the scented concoction with which the men of Thunderbird commonly anointed their hair, at least when they had the luxury of doing so.

When she was finished Ronar went to his bedroom, where he found clothing already laid out for him: his second-best suit, charcoal grey with pinstripes, which was no doubt all Flora thought the colloquium deserved. With his polished black shoes, a ruffled shirt of fine white linen, and a string tie pinned with a jewel of smoky quartz, Ronar felt and looked like an entirely different person than the man who had finished making his way back from the debacle in Mersinea just that afternoon.

Yet he was still somber as he stepped out of the house in the last glow of twilight. The carriage was there, silhouetted against the deep purple sky. The form of the driver looked familiar. Something in Ronar's stomach lurched as he recognized Hal Holder. Suddenly he was aware that of all those in Thunderbird, Holder was the man he least wanted to encounter.

There was nothing to do but slide onto the bench beside him. Holder looked over at him, the whites of his eyes luminous in the deepening night. "Hello, Professor. Glad to have you back." He snapped a ripple down the reins and sent the carriage bumping down the road towards town.

"Faculty pay not stretching quite far enough?" asked Ronar dryly.

"What?" answered Holder, looking down at the reins in his hands. "Oh. No, I asked to drive you in. I must know what happened. Have you—brought back Asterope? How is she?" Holder was not able to moderate the note of desperate hope in his voice.

"No," said Ronar. For some reason, admitting this to Holder suddenly gave Asterope's plight all the impact, the reality and immediacy, that it had somehow lacked in the moonturns since it had occurred. Ronar forced himself to go on, to state the facts as unambiguously as possible, to make any false hope or misunderstanding impossible. "Asterope is not truly dead, but she is beyond our reach. In the end she could not fight off Ahriman any longer. She never even made it to Mersinea. I lost her at sea."

Holder was silent for a long time after that, staring ahead at the dark road. Ronar sat beside him and writhed internally, feeling Holder's grief beating on him like black waves. What else must he be feeling...disappointment over Ronar's failure? Leonard Ronar, who had long walked the planet challenging its worst powers, unable in the end to save one helpless girl?

"If only...if only I'd been more alert that night, I might have..." said Holder at last, his voice hoarse and breaking.

"Yes, if only," interrupted Ronar. "If only I had forbidden her to observe anywhere near the Eye. If only it had been cloudy that night. If only. But there's no profit in dwelling on such things, Hal. We must deal with reality as we find it."

"Then that's the end of it."

"Not yet," replied Ronar, in so fierce a hiss that Holder started.

Holder drew up the reins and halted the horse. He turned on the bench and faced Ronar from inches away. His voice took on an unfamiliar intensity. "What do you mean?"

"I've seen Ahriman at work in these situations before," said Ronar. "Do you remember hearing about the Despard family? How they used to steal the souls of the weak and injured in Two Suns?"

Holder shuddered hard enough to rock the carriage. "Yes. I heard all about them. From my mother." No doubt he'd heard that it was Ronar himself who had ended their depredations, his first act upon arriving in Thunderbird.

"Well, they did not collect those souls for their own use. They were gifts for their favored god, Ahriman, Satan to them. I believe Ahriman has collected the soul of Asterope as well. What use he makes of such prizes I cannot say, though according to the Despards, they somehow go to strengthening him."

Ronar clenched his teeth. His statement brought to mind the repressed image of the essence of Asterope, and that of Astraea, at the mercy of Ahriman.

Holder stared at him wildly. The horse sensed his agitation and nickered nervously. "Then how—in what sense is this not the end?"

Ronar turned to glare straight into Holder's frightened eyes. He did not intend to go into detail prematurely, but he could see that Holder needed a bit of hope, or he might snap and be himself lost to despair. "I failed to save Asterope, but I did learn things about the Eye of Ahriman, things that hint at a vulnerability. I must do more research before I can be sure. But if what I suspect is true, I believe I can find a way to end the threat of Ahriman forever."

Holder continued to stare into that determined face, little more than a black shape in the night, yet unmistakable in its resolve. He'd heard stories about Ronar's uncanny daring, his obstinacy, and he had sometimes seen glimpses of these facets in the man himself, but this was the first time he had sat and spoken with a man who could firmly announce his intention of destroying a god.

"And how will you go about that?" he asked quietly.

Ronar fell silent for a moment.

"To start with, I'll do a complete orbital analysis of the Eye."

Holder blinked in confusion. Even in the shadows, he had the look of one who had not slept well in weeks. The corners of his mouth had a sad droop that Ronar had never seen there before.

"Don't we understand the orbit well enough already?" asked Holder in a dull voice.

Ronar shook his head firmly. "Our observations are good enough to let us produce reliable ephemerides — usually reliable. But they're purely observational, and have limited predictive power. They say less about the true three dimensional orbit of the moon than they do about its apparent path through the sky. No, I intend to do a full theoretical orbital analysis, a five-body problem involving the suns, Colibdis, Sinanna, and the Eye itself. The hardware requirements aren't great. I'll need the 6-inch astrometric refractor, the 3-inch transit instrument, and our best filar micrometer and chronographs. Maybe more—I'm not sure yet. It's been decades since I studied nineteenth century astronomy of this sort. I've never actually done much of it. I expect I'll need observations of a score of orbits of the Eye at least. Oh—and I'll be doing some work with the Cartography Department. I need to refine certain areas of the map of Colibdis."

Holder nodded absently, then rallied enough to fix Ronar with a keener gaze. "So you're going to make a long series of observations of the Eye, which is completely contrary to the strictest rule of the Observatory. Isn't that pretty dangerous?"

"I'm prepared to take my chances," said Ronar in a low voice. "And besides, the danger itself is part of the experiment. If I don't encounter any danger, then I'm barking up the wrong tree." He fell into a brief funk as he considered his remark, then made an effort to brighten his voice. "Why don't you join me at the colloquium? There's always room for faculty at these things. Then we can talk more on the way back."

"I'm—not in the mood for socializing," answered Holder.

Ronar nodded in the darkness. "I understand. To tell you the truth, I wouldn't be going either, if I had any food in the house." He turned forward. "Let's be on our way."

Remoteness settled over Ronar like a cloak. Holder, sensing his interview was at an end for now, set the horse into motion again.

Half an hour later the carriage rattled along paved paths atop the mesa which was the main site of the school. Holder brought it to a halt in front of the Administration Building, an American Greek Revival structure whose red sandstone facade was patchily lit by gas lamps. Ronar muttered a farewell to Holder, jumped down, and made his way to the main meeting hall, a high-ceilinged wood-paneled room reasonably well lit by candles and the sputtering glow of more gas lamps. The table was almost fully occupied. Some fool started clapping at the sight of him, and the rest took up the applause. Ronar scowled, which brought the accolade to a ragged halt. It might be ungracious of him, but he wasn't about to accept praise for merely surviving and then showing up again.

He took his seat at the head of the table with every eye upon him. Nathaniel Deerfield sat on his right. Ronar leaned over to him and whispered, "Conduct this meeting for me, will you? I'm no fit dispenser of amiable pomposity tonight."

Deerfield merely smiled indulgently at this, but a few others who overheard the remark looked at him askance. Ronar set his gaze on one pair of eyes after another, encouraging them to take up conversations with their neighbors. After a moment Ronar was as isolated and as ignored as he was going to be, which was the condition he sought. He leaned back in his chair, chin on fist, taking note of who was present. It was the entire upper hierarchy of the University: deans, administrators, the comptroller, and department heads, as well as any lesser faculty members who could find sponsors for seats. Several turns ago, many of these men would have been wearing the Mersinean himations then affected by the more pretentious citizens of

Thunderbird. This fashion had fallen off since Ronar's arrival. Now all the men seemed to favor the kind of dark suits Ronar wore when it was unavoidable.

Ronar's fashion preferences had not affected the few women in high positions at the school, some of whom dressed in flowing Mersinean garments, a style more comfortable and practical than the constricting dresses worn by their 19th Century American ancestors. Ronar could have done without this reminder of Mersinean women.

As the last place at the table was occupied, Deerfield dutifully stood up and cleared his throat for silence. His smile was easy and appeared unforced as he addressed the faces that turned his way.

"Ladies and gentlemen, I welcome you to the Chancellor's quarterly all-campus dinner and colloquium. Chancellor Ronar has just this afternoon returned to us after weeks of hard and dangerous travel. It was my duty to remind him of this function tonight, and frankly it was only through duty that I did so, for I doubted that even Chancellor Ronar's renowned vigor would dispose him to attending a social function so soon after such strenuous travels. But I was mistaken. Let us all welcome Professor Ronar back into our midst, and let us provide him with a peaceful and relaxing homecoming."

This time Ronar was better able to accept the applause that resulted from Deerfield's remarks. He was grateful that Deerfield had made no mention of the nature of his journey, or of its results. He had no intention of discussing such things before these people, many of whom he barely knew.

Dinner was the next item on the agenda, which suited Ronar. Wine was served, and although Ronar really didn't much care for wine, and even though it clearly came from Mersinea, he drank some, for he was still parched from his travels. He'd never had, nor desired, much tolerance for alcohol, so with his empty stomach the wine quickly sent his head swimming. Ronar hated that sensation as much as ever, and pushed away the goblet, disgusted with himself. Fortunately, the waiters soon brought in the food, heaping the table with the inevitable platters of beef. Happily there was some effort at variety beyond the endless permutations of cow, much of it based on native Colibdian species. No one could confuse a Colibdian scrub hen with a chicken because of the stumps where its delicate little arms and hands had been attached. These arms had practically no meat and were always removed. Even after all the human generations that had dwelt on Colibdis, the wizened claw-hands of a Colibdian bird were not considered an appetizing sight. Ronar ate such creatures, though it was unwise to base one's diet solely on native species. They were generally not toxic, but they seemed to be nutritionally incomplete for Earth creatures.

Ronar heaped up an imposing plate of food and set about methodically demolishing it while conversation bubbled and darted around him. He munched his salad with particular relish, having seen no fresh vegetables for weeks. When he bit down on a white disk that he'd taken for some kind of tuber, he almost spit it out. It resisted his bite like a fishy-tasting cylinder of rubber.

Clarence Harvey, a professor in the Languages department who was sitting a few places down the table, noticed Ronar's puzzled frown as he worked at this strange bit of meat.

"Well, Professor Ronar," he chuckled in his ridiculous twangy Western drawl, "looks like you've discovered one of the new 'delicacies' we're testing tonight. That's a slice of a sea critter the Mersineans call a 'dekapus'. They say one that size runs about four feet long. You ever see such a thing?"

Heedless of good table manners, Ronar plucked the ragged remains out of his mouth and stared at it. "Yes," he said in a distant tone. "I have seen a dekapus before. One too big to lay on this table."

Whether it was exhaustion, or the wine, or simply a crush of events which could not be held in any longer, some gate of volubility opened in Ronar. As he gazed into the distance he described how he had fought, maimed, and driven off a great dekapus. He did not mention the frustrated blood lust which had made the slaughter seem such an agreeable task. Somehow that tale segued into an account of how he had sailed the ship almost single-handed, and then how it had come to be manned by the rotting corpses of its drowned crew. He did not explain how their fate was due to his own arrogant miscalculation. Then he described his ascent of the legendary Olympos, carrying an old woman much of the way, to heights where the air was too thin to sustain human life for long. He did not mention how desperate a venture this had been, an attempt to redeem his failure by risking his own life, searching beyond hope for divine help for Asterope's tortured spirit. Nor did he tell how Astraea inexplicably gave herself up to the very god he meant to oppose. Finally he spoke of how, on the road home, he had routed a band of thieves who were assaulting a family of pilgrims, but not of how he had almost passed them by, for fear of what might befall those people if they were to accept his dubious help and protection.

Then his tale was done. The words stopped abruptly. Suddenly conscious of what he had done, bragging of his deeds as though he were some great hero, he fell silent. His eyes focused on the near and present again, as he scanned the faces at the table.

They all stared at him open-mouthed. The men looked stricken or awed, while tears streamed down the faces of many of the women, and of some of the men as well. They stared at him as though they had never seen him before in their lives, or ever imagined his like.

Ronar lowered his eyes in embarrassment. He noticed he was still holding the slice of dekapus tentacle and dropped it onto his plate. "Well," he said gruffly, "enough of that. Let's get on with the meal."

Somehow the affair never recovered. A few people nibbled a few more bites, then the plates and platters were unceremoniously whisked from the table. The waiters moved to bring in tea, cakes, and brandy, but President Deerfield discretely waved them away. He resumed his feet and gamely tried to steer the minds of the participants back to the colloquium, introducing Harlota Jones, the Chairman of the English Department, who tried to describe her plan to split her department into separate literature and creative writing branches. But Harlota Jones, though she was of necessity a tough and thick-skinned woman, was flushed and distracted as she spoke.

"Life on Colibdis is all most of us have ever known," she said shakily, "but our cultural memory of life on Earth is recent enough that many of us are still conscious of the extraordinary nature of our lives here. We are daily at risk from forces and influences never known on Earth. Though we have created a relatively safe and stable society here, it is an island of sanity in what is otherwise a chaotic and dangerous world. Yet even here we are sometimes stressed beyond endurance by the magical forces we try to resist or ignore. We can either plunge wholeheartedly into the currents of magic which sweep the other cultures of this planet, or we can cling to our identity as best we can. As long as we attempt the latter, it will be the task of our Creative Writing Department to encourage the literary expression of who we are and how we function in, and struggle against, this fantastic place in which we live."

With this brave effort completed, Harlota Jones sank with evident relief into her chair. President Deerfield wisely saw this as an opportunity to end the assembly, a little prematurely perhaps, but those others who had come with something to say made no complaint.

Feeling painfully self-conscious, Ronar stood up to fade back into the night. To his surprise, everyone in the room made it a point to come over to greet him, to mumble welcomes and shake his hand, all with a peculiar glistening look in their eyes.

And so, by the time he emerged onto the building's lamp-lit portico the crowd had dispersed. A carriage waited in the gloom beyond the little flicker of light, but standing beside it was a young man Ronar didn't know.

"I'm sorry, sir, but Professor Holder asked me to tell you that he wasn't up to driving you home tonight. He asked me to take over. I'll be happy to drive you."

"You're one of the Timothy boys, aren't you? That's all right, son. I'll walk back. Take your buggy back to the livery and get back to your dorm."

The boys eyes widened a bit. "Are you sure, Professor Ronar? It would be no trouble, and I was asked—"

"No, that's fine. I'd rather walk anyway. Thanks."

"All right then, sir."

Ronar turned and started down the road in the cool evening. The sky was still murky with high clouds, with only the brightest stars visible as diffuse yellow spots.

He didn't blame Holder for begging off. While Ronar had no real idea of the depth of Holder's feelings for Asterope, plainly the news had hit him hard. Ronar had nothing to say to him that couldn't wait for tomorrow.

Although he'd been hiking every day for weeks, he welcomed this chance for quiet contemplation. He had never understood how he'd managed to ingratiate himself to the people of Thunderbird. It wasn't due to his sweet personality; he had no illusions about that. He'd been given *carte blanche* to establish the Astronomy Department and equip and run it to his liking, a personal fiefdom almost beyond the influence of the University's administration. And then he'd been proclaimed Chancellor, an office that hadn't even existed before he came along, making him the titular head of the whole institution. Nathaniel Deerfield, who had been President for a Colibdian decade, had remained as affable and sunny as ever, even through this de facto demotion. Of course, Deerfield remained in effective control of the school. Though he was an ambitious man, he seemed to welcome Ronar's presence as figurehead.

Harlota Jones's speech continued to ring in his ears. He suspected it had been largely extemporaneous, and surely its subject was unusual enough. He rarely heard anyone meditate aloud on the extraordinary nature of life on this planet. His own view was that the folk of Thunderbird were largely inured to weird circumstances which, if they did not actually dominate the life of their relatively secular community, certainly lurked just outside it, with the potential to move in at any time. But perhaps these countrymen of his harbored greater fears than he realized, and were simply not disposed to discuss such anxieties in public.

Indeed, though Ronar had long ago reconciled himself to the existence of magic, it wasn't a topic he cared to dwell upon. He preferred to think of Two Suns as what it mostly was: part raucous hub of the local ranching and farming community, part quiet college town, and his base for the extension of the same kind of cosmological studies he had pursued on Earth. As if Colibdis were a mere platform for his telescopes, conveniently located outside the murk of the Galaxy. As if he were not walking on a vital, Earthlike planet in a strange orbit around an unlikely pair of suns in an ancient dwarf galaxy otherwise populated by feeble star-sparks. A planet inhabited by humans brought across the great gulf of space by a mysterious technology of unknown origin. Perhaps those technologists were also somehow responsible for the planet's strangest feature...the pliability of various aspects of quantum reality on and near it, a structure of reality uniquely amenable to modification by minds of sufficient insight, or at least discipline. In other words, magic.

But despite its pandemic availability, magic was not a tool or a weapon in the hands of every man and woman on Colibdis. True, wizards, sorcerers, and witches of every level of competence contended with each other everywhere on the planet. Two Suns itself was only a few day's journey from — was practically in the shadow of — the greatest focus of human magic in the world, the Tower of Sha Totek. And yet the common people did not use magic in any important way. Magic was unlike technology in that in order to be used in any safe and consistent way, it had to be understood. Understanding took dedication, with long study of the spells and ritual actions though which the inherent chaos of magic was refined, constrained, and controlled. And so not every inhabitant of Colibdis was a magician, any more than every Earthman was a physicist.

One aspect of magic in which every human mind played a part was the existence of gods and other supernatural beings, brought into being from nothingness at the urging of the needs, traditions, fears, and expectations of people of many cultures. Some of them had physical bodies made through the same means, while others did not. The latter were the most dangerous. These creatures could not be opposed by steel or bronze. They could not be walled out by stone. They could not be fled. These incorporeal beings, whether called demons or gods, could prey on mortals more or less at will.

Ronar took a moment to absorb the sensations of his walk: the dry, faintly resinous scent of desert plants; the luminescent whiteness of night-blooming Sacred Datura flowers; a hundred whirs and clicks and whistles of nocturnal creatures; the dusty impact of his shoes on the road; the sense of a planet turning, moving smoothly through space, at peace with itself and with the universe.

The only thing which did not belong here was a sibilant undercurrent of voices and whispers which could be heard by those who were open to it. Ronar now chose to lend it an ear, his face a bleak mask. This was the subliminal magical life of the planet, always present, even when not clearly manifest.

Ronar sacrificed much to take up the observing program he had outlined to Holder. He gave up all claim to the sixty-inch, setting his cosmological studies aside. He gave up time he would have used to wander among the mesas and arroyos of the area, explore the riparian woods in the canyons, or visit Indian villages. He turned the administrative work of the astronomy department over to Holder, signing the documents put before him with barely a glance.

He could not sacrifice his peace of mind to the cause, because he had none to begin with. He spent his nights in the roll-off shelter which housed the six-inch refractor, an instrument with an Alvan Clark lens he had brought from Earth.

There it was his unpleasant task to make the most exacting measurements ever made of the position of the Eye of Ahriman.

The tick of the chronometer on the desk, its face lit by a dim candle lantern, blended with the whir of the telescope's driving mechanism. Ronar had to steel himself every time he looked into the eyepiece to see glimmering there the malign flicker of the Eye, a mocking light that seemed to insinuate whispers into his mind, whispers that grew nightly until he knew they soon would grow into voices.

The work would be long and painstaking, but one thing he learned quickly enough. On every orbit of the Eye, each time it reached a certain geocentric (or Colibdocentric) position in its path, it briefly flared up with a cold bluish light. The effect was not as strong as it had been from

Olympos, perhaps because of some quirk of the viewing geometry there. Still, it was plain enough. He had never heard of such a thing before, yet he doubted this was something that had begun just recently. Perhaps it was not so odd that it had been missed...after all, the Eye was a thing to avoid, not to study closely enough to notice a minute's extra brightness.

Every morning, after submitting to a few hours of sleep while haunted by the voices and faces of the dead, he sat at his desk reducing his observations, beginning the calculations that would gradually refine the elements of the moonlet's path. This was onerous work indeed, with nothing to supplement paper and pencils but printed tables of logarithms.

He soon found that observations of the Eye were not in themselves sufficient. He would also need refined observations of Sinanna, and also of the two suns on their tumbling path about each other. He quickly realized that with all these interacting bodies the calculations would become a nightmare for one man whose mathematical gifts had never been great to begin with. No doubt men on Earth possessed computers capable of making such work trivial, but he had no such luxury here. On this world, computers walked on two legs and liked to get three meals per day.

Given a need for such demanding observations, which now had to be conducted in darkness and daylight alike, Ronar lacked the time for desk work as well. He began to consider who he could enlist to assist him with the computations. Holder was out; Ronar would not take him from the maintenance of the Department, though he would no doubt have wished to help Ronar in his efforts. This was astronomical dirt work, an inglorious slogging effort in support of someone else's research—perfect for a graduate student. He mentally reviewed the corps of graduate students, a small enough group to be sure. When he applied the criteria of stolidity, unimaginativeness, and apparent indifference to boredom, he settled upon Daniel Durgala, who had recently transferred in from the mathematics department. Durgala was engaged in a tedious, and so far almost unrewarded, search for other planetary bodies in the Colibdian system. He had competently calculated orbits for the two small asteroids he had discovered so far, objects which were probably captured wanderers from beyond the Colibdian system.

And so, on one bleary-eyed morning Ronar summoned Durgala into his office. The stocky, bland-faced youth faced him with a certain heavy-lidded equanimity. A crease of doubt appeared between his eyes when Ronar suggested he drop his work to concentrate on the orbit of the Eye, but he agreed readily enough when Ronar informed him he would consider the work sufficient to complete his master's degree.

Ronar sat reflecting as Durgala shambled out of the office, taking with him Ronar's observations to date. Durgala's would be only the fifteenth master's degree ever conferred by the Department. Of those, eight had also gone on to receive PhDs. Ronar was gratified that anyone was attracted to the program, as being an astronomer was of little practical value on Colibdis, where the very concept of science was deemed both foreign and useless by almost everyone. Many undergraduate students studied astronomy as part of their general academic load, but the prospects for someone with an advanced degree were limited. One of his PhDs had gone off to work at the Skye Island "observatory" in far-off Eranior. Four of the others were on the faculty here. Of the remaining three, one had disappeared, one had married and gone into business, and the other was said to be prospecting for iron somewhere to the south. Ronar doubted that the Department could absorb any more additions to the faculty. He was aware that only his own personal glamour attracted most people to the field at all. Of course there were clear exceptions…those who were drawn to the mysteries of the heavens as clearly and honestly as he was…people such as Asterope.

A man such as Durgala was opaque to Ronar. He showed no passion for his work, and was not overawed by Ronar himself. He was considered something of a colorless cypher by the other members of the department, a silent figure who kept to himself. When offered the chance to name the asteroids he had discovered, he had called them One and Two.

The moment he had been expecting happened one night about four weeks into the program. Even as the words bloomed in his mind he congratulated himself for holding them off so long, despite so many nights spent gazing into the Eye.

Ronar…it's good to have this insight into your remarkable mind once again.

Ronar straightened up from his seat at the eyepiece, held himself very still, and was intensely aware of the quietness around him, undisturbed by the words which had formed in his mind.

Practically the first thing Ronar had done on his advent on Colibdis was to study the Eye through his binocular. That unsettling experience had left his mind more open to

Ahriman for some time. Just as seeing the Eye through the sixty-inch's guider had opened Asterope's mind to immediate invasion, Ronar's observations had finally offered the god another pathway into his.

Your interest in my abode and its path is flattering, but I must warn you, it may lead to a greater intimacy with me than you presently desire.

"I have that already," muttered Ronar with a grimace. "But don't get too comfortable in my head. It's not a hospitable place for you."

He heard an indulgent chuckle. *Indeed, we do find you uniquely resistant to our attempts to renew our acquaintance. But I find you somewhat chastened, compared to the man who first challenged and threatened me from his blanket on the Red Plain all those turns ago. You have learned something of the difficulty of opposing me.*

"'We' find me uniquely resistant?" questioned Ronar.

An affectation. I sometimes grant myself the distinction of the divine or royal we.

"Nevertheless...don't delude yourself that you can possess and corrupt me as you did Asterope. Unlike her, I can always return to Earth if necessary, a place where you cannot follow."

That may truly be your only recourse, someday. But tell me, what did you mean by saying I corrupted Asterope?

Ronar growled before he could craft a coherent answer. "Don't play coy games with me, you vile shadow. I saw the filthy acts you drove her to, at the end. She was depraved."

You think I caused that behavior? The tone of the invading thoughts was surprised, yet amused. *What would I have to gain from spurring her to such acts of gross carnality? I am not even a material being. Lust is not what I seek from human minds and spirits. When Asterope found herself under my influence, she took it as a license to indulge in acts which she had always craved, but had always suppressed as beneath her.*

Ronar's sudden rage threatened to reduce him to impotent raving against such lies. It took a great effort of will to direct his anger toward a more useful response.

"It's because of your immateriality—your unreality— that you crave and provoke such acts. You do this out of your envy of real bodies, real spirits, real minds."

Your chagrin at the revelation of Asterope's weakness hinders your logic. You have seen lesser gods assume human form. I could do so easily. But I am a god of the intellect, and as such I work and exist most freely when I flow through the substance of magic itself, not contained in some limited physical vessel like your body.

"Shadows. Phantoms. Those are the forms gods take. You cannot assume a real living body, except by invading and possessing them. But even if I were to stare you in the face for eternity, you will never possess me."

And I had thought you were at least somewhat humbled. Why do you suppose you could resist, if I were to choose to do what you suggest?

Ronar slammed his fist down on the desk hard enough to send the chronometer bouncing up. "Because I am *real!*" he cried to the heavens. "I am a real mind, a real being, a real soul! Not some simulacrum of magic, and you are only that!"

Now the answer came low and silky.

Indeed. And what was Astraea, for example? What were all the others who have joined themselves to me, some willingly, some not? Are you somehow different from all of them?

Ronar's eyes glittered, half mad. "*Yes*. I am different. I will never yield to you. I do not yield. That is my difference, and it always has been."

He heard an answer like the massed chuckling of a theater full of people reacting to some dry jest in a play.

Very good, Ronar. Hold yourself above the rabble. Above Asterope. We'll continue our chat soon. For now, I'll leave you to your work.

But Ronar did not immediately resume his work. He sat breathing heavily, grimacing, staring upward, awaiting the next alien thought to bloom in his mind. His heart raced, and cold sweat chilled and sickened him.

But the voice was silent for now. Gradually he regained his self-possession and brought his attention back to the task at hand.

He looked at the chronometer, standing askew on the desk. The jar he had given it had probably thrown it off enough to compromise any further observations. It would have to be calibrated and re-synchronized with the master chronometer. His work was over for tonight.

Though he might have used the time to catch up on his sleep, he remained seated, brooding in the starlight until the Eye finally set. Only with it absent from the sky did he feel some relief from the oppression that had suddenly made his inner being so dark a place.

Even that relief was an illusion. For he knew that from now on, Ahriman need not have a line of sight to him to access to his mind.

Ronar had hated Ahriman since the first moment he became aware of its existence as a corrupted mind defiling the heavens. The contents and nature of the starry universe were great mysteries to Ronar. His knowledge of astronomy contained only the broadest outlines of cosmic geography, and nothing at all about the details. For those details he had only two points of reference: Earth and Colibdis, both populated through some strange means by humans who had originated on only one of those worlds. Of what might lie beyond these two human colonies he knew nothing. Perhaps other worlds were hives of the same lust, greed, and foolishness which prevailed among his own species. Or perhaps, hidden among the star clouds of the myriad galaxies, was something better. As long as the stars held out the promise of some kind of redemption for the pain of human existence, he would not suffer a construct formed from the worst parts of the human spirit to spread and taint what was clean and pure in the night.

And so began a nightly contest between Ronar and Ahriman. As long as Ronar stayed out of the observatory, the voices in his mind remained silent. But as soon as he swung an instrument toward the Eye, or eventually toward Sinanna or the suns as well, there commenced a running commentary from Ahriman: a wheedling, sly, corrosive monologue which Ronar did his best to ignore, but which nevertheless took its toll. Night after night he forced his eye to the ocular of the astrometric refractor to note the Eye's position among the stars. While that reddish point of light flickered behind the reticle the voice was clearer still, until it seemed that the god was sharing the very volume of his skull.

And then came a day when the voice did not fall silent when he left the observatory. After that it spoke to him at any time, in any place: while he ate, while he tried to speak with others, while he lay in bed, or even in his dreams. And new voices were added, or perhaps the voice of Ahriman became more finely resolved, so that Ronar could hear the voices of the spirits who had been made a part of him, willingly or not. These voices variously cried or giggled or chanted or cajoled, sometimes in concert with Ahriman's words, or sometimes as an inescapable background to Ronar's own consciousness. He could not yet hear these voices well enough to make out their words, or to recognize any of them, for which he was grateful, though he knew this remaining grace was only temporary. There were so many of them.

Doggedly he collected his data, handing it over to Daniel Durgala.

Eventually Durgala announced he had a preliminary orbit determination which was probably ninety percent as good as he could ever achieve. Ronar met with him and Hal Holder in Ronar's office. There the two senior men pored over the orbital elements and plotted future positions on star charts, while Durgala looked on with his usual heavy-lidded impassiveness.

Ronar required the utmost concentration to make any sense of the charts and numbers. Ahriman chuckled at him, pointing out oddities in the results which Ronar doubted the god could have noticed or understood if not for its increasing access to Ronar's own thoughts and knowledge. Ronar tried to ignore these comments, as well as Holder's frequent worried glances. Ronar knew he looked unwell... he could see it reflected in the eyes of everyone he passed. He was pale and sallow, with sunken cheeks and eyes rimmed by dull purple. His gait was no longer the great flowing stride that had carried him across the planet, but was now shaky, unbalanced, uncertain. He was no longer as erect as he once had been. He felt every year of his age, and more.

At last he could withhold his judgment no longer.

"This is not what I expected," he muttered.

Holder looked at him with that annoying wide-eyed concern mixed with puzzlement. "This looks pretty much like the orbit we always thought it had. I don't see any surprises. What were you expecting?"

"Something other than this."

"Uh...can you be more specific?"

Ronar ignored the question. He turned his attention to the diffident young man sitting quietly in a straight-backed chair. "Durgala—this is truly the best orbit you can determine with the data I've provided? You didn't fudge anything to make the results look more plausible, did you? I want only honest, accurate results, no matter how strange they may seem."

The slightest trace of annoyance flickered over Durgala's brow. "Well, Professor, as I said, I will continue to refine the orbit. But this is a close approximation of the final result, and I have confidence in it. I see no chance of anything 'strange', as you put it, arising."

Ronar let his gaze linger on Durgala's heavy, unblinking face. Of all those under him in the department, only this man showed no sign of being overly impressed by him. Ronar saw it as proof of his own decline that he could no longer intimidate a trudging nonentity like Daniel Durgala.

So, my friend. All that effort, only to see your elaborate theories on the motions of my moon fall to dust. And at such a toll to you, too. You are no longer quite the imposing figure you once were.

Ronar's lethargy burned away in a flash of action. His fist slammed down on his desk. "Shut up, damn you!"

Durgala finally blinked. Holder flinched back in his seat, paling.

Ronar sagged over the desk, shaking his head.

"No, I wasn't talking to either of you."

Holder's eyes only grew wider at that, then a wave of horrified comprehension passed over his face. Durgala's expression remained inscrutable, though perhaps his eyelids drooped a little lower.

"I'm not going to stop here, Hal," muttered Ronar. "I'm going to gather more data and refine this orbit. Somewhere in these numbers is the answer to everything I seek."

That is pleasant news. I do so enjoy our conversations beneath the stars.

It occurred to Ronar that he need not answer aloud and so further alarm Holder. Here at least was one advantage of Ahriman's access to his thoughts.

You have barely begun to learn how entertaining I can be, Ahriman, thought Ronar, putting into the thought all the defiant vehemence he could muster.

Chapter 24

Night Visitors

Oddly, Ahriman fell silent for the rest of the day. Even that night, as Ronar sat at the astrometric telescope, forcing his eye to the eyepiece while the Eye swam in the field like an outpost of death, the god said nothing to add to his misery. The moonlet seemed to flare and swell in his vision, alternately burning a dire red and then puffing up into a pale, whitish, seething glow like some weird ectoplasm. He was obliged to consider his every action carefully and in advance: setting the telescope so that the Eye lay directly on the reticle; getting up and reading the big graduated circles, interpolating from the verniers by the glow of a lamp held aloft by a shaking hand; noting the exact time from the chronometer, recording the observation, then starting the process over again. It was simple, repetitive work, but in his present state it required all the concentration he could bring to bear, and all his will each time he must again peer at that point of light, which was like a lighted optical nerve linked to his mind, bringing it ever closer to the mind and thoughts of Ahriman. Several times an hour he picked up a small mirror and stared into it, dreading to see that his observing eye had taken on the blight that had been the ruin of Asterope. So far both retained their natural storm-grey color, though their glitter was dulled, and the whites were bloodshot.

Yet the god's silence did nothing to increase his serenity. Even as he inched his way through this meticulous work, Ronar kept his senses alert for the interruption he knew must come, though in what form he didn't know. Thus when he glimpsed a flicker of red light on the wall of the observing hut he immediately turned from the telescope, knowing with a strange sense of calm that Ahriman was no longer content to try to thwart him with words.

The deep red light washed briefly over the wall again, streaming in from over the top of the opposite wall. Ronar went to that wall and stretched up to look out into the night. Approaching on the path were half a dozen hooded, black-robed figures, each carrying a staff topped with a seething nimbus of a peculiar red flame.

Ronar had seen robes like these before, in places of the worship of Ahriman. The red fire was also a distinctive and well-remembered tool and emblem of the god.

Ronar stood blinking as he considered how to react to this incursion. He could bolt the door of the hut, crank the roof into place, and try to hold out until someone noticed what was happening and brought members of the town militia. But the wooden structure was little protection against any group of determined men, let alone men armed with magic fire.

Once he would have hurled himself at this group, sword in hand, and routed them. Now Ronar knew his remaining strength was only enough for a single effort, and that it wouldn't last long once invoked. With a shrug he opened the door and stepped out onto the path, letting himself be silhouetted against the lantern inside the hut. The figures faltered slightly, but then resumed their steady approach.

"Stop where you are," he commanded.

They straggled to a halt.

"I thought I had cleansed Thunderbird of the likes of you," said Ronar with contempt. "Yet here you slink, with your craven faces hidden from sight."

The answer came muffled from beneath a black hood. "We suffer religious persecution here in Thunderbird. Freedom of religion does not seem to extend to us."

"I think the intent is that you should worship gods, not devils. What do you fools want here?"

"Our lord Lucifer, the Lightbringer, or Ahriman as you know him, wishes you to cease your probings into his secrets and ways. These are matters outside the domain of any mortal being, let alone a scornful unbeliever such as yourself."

"Unbeliever? Don't confuse my hatred for lack of belief. I bear disrespect for your god, not disbelief in its existence."

Ronar felt an unfocused and, he suspected, unwarranted sense of triumph. If Ahriman was reduced to so feeble an effort at persuasion as this, it was proof that Ronar's course was the right one.

"At any rate, why doesn't Ahriman convey this message to me itself?" he continued. "It has no difficulty in making its thoughts known to me." Ronar knew from experience how it irritated the followers of Ahriman to hear their god referred to as "it".

"We cannot answer your question about our lord's intent in sending us instead of dealing with you himself, but Lucifer has many ways of earning your respect," said their spokesman (whichever one that might be) with a deceptive mildness. "Perhaps by sending his devoted servants, who are also countrymen of yours, he seeks to return you to the neutrality which you have shown toward him for many turns."

Ronar eyed this group with narrowed eyes. All were male, he guessed, though that was uncertain in the shapeless robes. One man standing off to the side had a certain lumpen stolidity to his posture that seemed familiar.

"I have never been neutral toward Ahriman. I have always loathed and despised it. I have merely been weak and foolish enough to permit it to go unmolested. Ahriman forever sacrificed any apparent neutrality on my part the instant it dared to violate the sanctity of this observatory by harming Asterope!"

Ronar charged them without warning. Without being aware of it he gave out a battle cry. At just the right distance to produce the maximum effect he invoked the sword: first the red light, a clearer, keener radiance than Ahriman's fire; then the white blaze, which showed his harshly-lit face pale with rage, teeth clenched, eyes bulging with mad wrath. The sword appeared with a hard clash of sound. Still running, he drew it back two-handed, about to hew with a single blow half the members of the party, who stood transfixed.

"Will you murder us then?" This challenge rang out shaky but bold from one member of the group who had more presence of mind than the rest.

Ronar gave a strangled grunt of frustration, arresting the stroke of the sword with the greatest difficulty. Holding it still cocked and tense, he grated out, "Who are you to complain of murder?"

"Who has been murdered, and by whom?" came the answer. "Who has died who would not have died, if not for your interference?"

Ronar let the sword lapse into nothingness. Taking a long step forward, he seized the collar of the nearest worshipper of Ahriman, pulling those wide, hooded eyes into close proximity with his own in an extremity of stress and wrath.

"*Asterope!* She started dying from the first moment of your god's corrupting touch! Do you think your god's gentle failure to kill her outright was a kindness to her? Not all people are so degraded that they can thrive under his domination, the way you worms do!"

"We are neither degraded nor corrupted," said Ronar's victim with some asperity. "We are respected citizens of this city. It is your conceit to characterize the Lightbringer as a 'god of evil'. Whatever brought about Asterope's downfall came from within herself."

Ronar made an incoherent sound of disgust and cast this man away, where he collapsed in a heap against some of the others, his flame-tipped staff clattering on the pavement.

Through some decision of his subconscious, Ronar's long right arm licked out and snatched away the hood of the short, stocky man who had seemed familiar. Revealed there was the heavy-lidded glare of Daniel Durgala.

"Durgala," growled Ronar. "You're a *scientist*. What's here for you among these degenerates?"

"What's here for me at this absurd place?" he said wildly, waving his arm around to take in the observatory. "What does this astronomy of yours reveal, except a cold, sterile universe which is indifferent to our very existence? What purpose do you serve, with your futile struggle to extract meaning from a mute, inaccessible void dusted with a few pinpricks of lifeless matter? Ahriman is a *mind*. He is like us, a conscious being, and his goal is to remake the universe as a place that serves the other minds that inhabit it."

Ronar's voice was freezing with scorn. "I'm sorry the universe doesn't exist to coddle you, Durgala. You worship a golden calf. Ahriman is like all the so-called gods, a creation of men, given substance by the magic of this planet. Without the belief of men, it would wither and die."

Durgala's eyes glittered. "Even if that were true, what of it?" he hissed. "If the universe does not provide the means for our ascent into mastery, then let us devise one for ourselves."

"And what is the goal of this mastery you seek?" demanded Ronar. "Power over those who haven't sought it? Knowledge of a reality you hold in contempt? Or is it merely the gratification of your whims, no matter how debased they may be?"

"No. The goal is to grant some purpose and dignity to life, both of which it now sorely lacks, as you must surely realize when you see some worthy person dying in misery, reduced by time's brutality to a frail, withered husk before being wiped out. Do you really see some virtue in decay, diminishment, and death? Even your friend the Sorcerer sees the injustice in that, though he is willing to exempt only himself from this fate, and perhaps you."

Ronar held them with the power of his gaze while his thoughts churned. He could feel his strength collapsing. He had squandered the moment of adrenal energy he had summoned to kill them. Now it was all he could do to maintain his erect posture. When he spoke again his voice was lower, carefully controlled to prevent any quaver of weakness.

"Tell your master he will never drive me from this planet."

Durgala spoke on. "If our lord chooses to send you from his sight, you will indeed go. But though he prefers subtlety to overt action, we have been instructed in how to deal with your obduracy. Since you will not yield, you must be punished."

And with that he raised his flaming staff. The original spokesman got to his feet, and all six of them held forth their staffs, the scarlet fires roaring up, casting forward a withering heat. Ronar called forth the sword once more, but his fingers would hardly clutch the handle, which seemed to have the weight of a mountain. His head suddenly rang with the mocking laughter of Ahriman.

A new voice came from out of the night. "Okay, boys. Reach for the zenith."

Hal Holder stepped into the circle of seething scarlet light. In his hands was a huge rifle of bronze and wood, one of the weapons made for the war against Namirnakh many turns before. Ronar wondered how he had gotten it, since all firearms were controlled and regulated by the state militia.

The black-clad six drew back, more intimidated by Holder than by the faltering Ronar.

"Get back," said Holder in a steady voice. "Get off this mesa and away from this city. Daniel, needless to say, your position at the university is terminated. As is your citizenship in Thunderbird, I'd say."

They lowered their staffs and backed away. As they retreated, Ronar cried out, "Remember! I will not leave this planet!"

Durgala's voice came back high and wild. "You are fools! This is nothing compared to what Ahriman will do to you now! To you, to this city, to this country!"

As the red flames dwindled into the distance Ronar saw no further need to remain on his feet. He crumpled to the pavement, the sword vanishing once again. Holder knelt down beside him, still looking into the darkness on every side, though Ronar was certain the danger was over for now.

Ronar found himself looking at Holder in a different light.

"That was a very timely arrival, Hal. I thought I was supposed to be the man of action around here," he said quietly.

Holder turned to him with a crooked grin. "Well, Professor, I couldn't risk any harm coming to you. Not just because I was your first student and whatever—I can't permit your administrative duties to fall on me permanently."

"Where in hell did you get that gun?"

"Oh…" Holder brandished the weapon, which gleamed dully in the lamplight coming from the telescope hut. "It's not even functional. Ha! It's just a replica I grabbed from Porter's office. Haven't you ever noticed it?"

"That was a good one, Hal." Ronar's eyes remained shut, but a grin brought a semblance of life to his face.

"You know…I think it's a safe bet that ol' Daniel didn't do his best work on that orbit."

"Yes…that seems obvious. I'll recalculate it myself… and I'll gather as much data as I need…despite all interference to the contrary."

"No, Professor."

Ronar forced his eyes open to stare in amazement at his suddenly rebellious and firm-voiced subordinate.

"I'm sure you've already got all the data you need. I want you away from that eyepiece. I don't want you staring at that damned rock up there for another minute. I'll take over the calculations too. I can get other students to pitch in. I can solve a differential equation or two if I have to."

"But what about the business of the department?"

"We'll let Marjorie look after it. You know departmental secretaries know more about what's going on than their chairmen do anyway."

Ronar tried to summon the will to make an objection, but all he could bring himself to feel was relief.

"All right, Hal. That sounds good to me."

And yet even as he spoke, Ronar felt his mouth flooding with bitterness. He was defeated. Ahriman had cowed him, had rendered him all but helpless. Now he must retreat while others carried on his fight. He looked into the future and saw himself cowering at home, cared for like an invalid by Flora with her stricken face, while he labored to fend off the ignoble thoughts Ahriman planted in his mind like so many filthy spores.

It was too much to bear.

"No," said Ronar.

Holder jerked to a halt, turned back and looked at him. "What was that, Professor?" he asked uncertainly.

"No, Hal," repeated Ronar, his voice a little stronger. "I can't sit back and let others act for me. I will make the calculations. I will make any further observations that are needed. I will do these things...and if the thing that shares my skull doesn't like it, it can turn me into a pile of ashes, if it has the power. But as long as I can stand, and walk, and act, I will do what must be done."

Holder stared at him in silence for a few moments, his mouth tight. Then he shrugged, shook his head a trifle, and said, "All right, Professor. If that's the way it has to be."

If that's the way it has to be, echoed the quiet voice in Ronar's mind.

"It is," Ronar assured them both.

And so Ronar began the difficult process of hauling himself to his feet. Holder hovered nearby, eager to help, but knowing better than to push his assistance on his stricken superior. Ronar got to his knees, pausing a moment to look at the stars that had been his anchor throughout his life. They looked the same as ever... remote and impassive, blessedly beyond the influence of Ahriman, beyond even the taint which the god's influence was putting on his view of the smaller world under his feet... and its inhabitants.

Ronar stood erect and threw back his head. An odd, febrile exultation surged somewhere below the sickness that had been imposed upon his mind. The cold observer's portion of his mind took a moment to note that this was a strange juxtaposition indeed.

He fixed Holder with his gaze and said in a husky voice, "Come look into my eyes, Hal."

"What?"

"See if you can detect the kind of blight that afflicted Asterope's eye."

Holder approached him hesitantly, a look of uncertainty on his face. He peered up at Ronar, squinting in the poor light.

"No—no. I see no change. Your eyes are just as clear as they ever were, Professor."

I leave you now, my friend. Do as you must.

Ronar gasped and staggered back. This was the last thing he had expected, but the feeling of a shroud tearing away from his mind erased his doubts, if not his confusion.

"Professor, what's wrong?" demanded Holder.

The voice came again, but this time it came from outside of Ronar. The words were quiet, but Ronar felt the air quiver as each was formed, flowing out over the land.

"But I have one warning for you."

Holder's eyes bugged out. Ronar spun around, making a gesture of negation at the unseen source of these words.

"Spare me your threats! Either act on them, or shut the hell up!"

Ahriman continued as though it hadn't heard.

"The real gods of this world do not favor those who pry into their secrets."

Ronar's mind spun and seethed. He had an inkling that somehow Ahriman had lost control, that if it were not actually defeated, it was at least stymied for now.

Yet at the same time Ronar had a sense of immense danger. He found himself opening his mouth to do something he had never foreseen — offer a compromise.

"Ahriman! You want me to keep my nose out of your secrets? Very well then. I'll leave you to your business — if, and when, you free Asterope and return her to her body, whole, clean, and unharmed."

There was a silence…a normal, natural silence that made it seem as if Ronar had made a foolish offer to the empty night air.

But the reply finally came.

"I cannot do that."

The voice of Ahriman fell silent.

The regret in those words seemed to echo over the world.

The two men stood there, gazing up into the sky, awaiting the night's next prodigy, wondering what had just happened.

Ronar was in a daze. But one thing was unmistakable... a sense of blessed relief and release.

He walked slowly back into the six-inch shelter, sat in a chair, rested his head against the back, and fell asleep.

Ronar went about his business with renewed vigor. With Holder's help, he tripled his efforts at making sense of the orbit of the Eye. Ahriman remained silent during all this, even when Ronar boldly made a few final observations of the Eye.

Yet Ronar's emotions remained mixed. A wiser part of him scoffed at his feeling of triumph over Ahriman. Whenever he walked over the desert at night he felt he was walking on eggshells. Peace reigned over both land and sky, but it was a watchful, uneasy peace, taut with a sense of imminence.

Chapter 25

Decision

Ronar walked into the conference room carrying a sheaf of handwritten papers and diagrams, some of which were a little smudged as a result of being stacked before the ink was dry. He was the last to arrive. The three people whom he'd summoned were rendered in smoky shades of copper by the sunlight filtering through the drapes. The hot gloom of the room might, thought Ronar, be responsible for the sweat which dampened the faces that turned to him. Or it might be something else.

He walked around the table and deposited a single scribbled sheet of figures before each person. They seemed to flinch as the sheets fluttered to rest.

Ronar took his place at the head of the table. He glanced down at the more substantial pile of manuscript before him, then swept his eyes over the grave figures seated around the table with him.

He broke the silence with a quiet word. "So. Here then is the result of the labors we have undertaken on behalf of Asterope. Much of this is your own work, and you all know the gist of the results. But let me make this initial statement to be sure we're all agreed. The orbit of the Eye of Ahriman is unnatural."

Hal Holder cleared his throat and stirred in his chair. "The conclusion is unavoidable. The Eye could not possibly remain in its present orbit if gravitation were the only thing acting on it."

"That's right," asserted Dr. Porfilio, a chunky woman with glossy black hair. "For one thing, the influence of the Greater Moon should quickly pull the Eye off the plane of the equator. I've always thought there was something odd about that, but I knew study of the Eye was frowned upon, and so never pursued it," she said with a glance at Ronar.

Ronar nodded and looked back down at the papers. "So the moonlet is somehow being constrained to remain in the plane of the equator of Colibdis. The other main anomaly is its orbital speed. At its current altitude—which varies not at all; its orbital eccentricity is too small to measure—the moon's orbital motion should be slightly faster. Put another way, in order to orbit at its slow pace, the Eye should be at a higher altitude. So some agency—presumably Ahriman—is either retarding the moon's speed, pulling it lower, or both, if there's any distinction to be made between the two."

Professor Ramos, a nervous-looking man with a high brow and short mousy hair, jabbed out his hand and handled his sheet as if it were aflame. "But what's accomplished by doing that?" he asked.

Ronar pushed back his chair and went to the large globe of Colibdis that stood in a corner. Details of the planet's geography were increasingly vague as one went farther from Thunderbird, but it was still the best available, better probably than any other map in the world. He frowned at the murky light that fell upon it, then stepped aside and threw back the curtains, allowing a shaft of brilliant sunslight to fire the globe's bright colors. The others drew back from the brightness, then flinched from Ronar's face as he studied them.

"We will not hide here," he said. "We work in the light of day, and we do not fear the consequences."

"Oh, don't we now?" muttered Ramos.

Ronar silenced him with a quick glare, then returned to the globe and ran his finger along the equator west of the main Colibdian continent.

"I can't yet answer your question, Ramos. The one thing I know is that this artificial orbit makes possible the phenomenon I observed from the summit of Mount Olympos. Once in every orbit of the Eye it reaches some kind of an alignment with a particular point on the planet's surface. That point is Larlaninulius, the island of the gods."

Professor Porfilio gasped, her hand going to her mouth. It sank slowly back to her lap as Ronar stared at her.

He continued.

"During that alignment, some kind of influence is exchanged between the two. I can't even be certain which way this influence travels. whether from the moon to the island or the other way around. It may have something to do with the moonlet's orbit, or it may have a broader purpose. At this point I can say no more."

Holder spoke up uneasily. "How is it that we've never noticed this exchange before, Professor?"

"For one thing, it happens only for a minute or two once every four days. And by some trick of geometry, the phenomenon looks much brighter from the summit of Olympos than it does from here."

Ronar looked around. No one met his eyes.

"Now—unless there are any more questions—we'll adjourn until we have more answers."

Ramos and Porfilio pushed back their chairs and shuffled out of the room, their faces tense and distracted. Holder remained seated, studying Ronar closely.

Ronar made as if to get up, then made a quick gesture of frustration and sank down again. "Hal. Why is everyone so ill-at-ease?"

Holder's silent study continued for a few moments. Finally he pursed his lips and answered. "You're picking into the secrets of the gods. That may be old business with you, but for us, it's different. The stars and galaxies don't object when we poke around in their affairs. Half the town heard it that night when Ahriman tried to warn you off. That's not a voice that folks can hear, then shrug off and go back to their chores."

Ronar nodded stiffly. "I see." It wasn't enough that he sought to relieve the world of the centuries of torment it had suffered under Ahriman. He also had to deal with the petty fears of people who weren't even involved in the struggle.

The two parted company with little warmth. Ronar stalked through empty corridors to the office of the departmental secretary. There on a wooden pedestal sat an elaborate contraption of brass, lead, and even a bit of steel. It was a typewriter, handmade in the shops of one of Thunderbird's largest printing firms, according to Ronar's descriptions. It was one of five in the world, all but one located here at the University.

Ronar lit a lamp against the onset of night and sat down at the typewriter. He rolled a piece of paper into position and typed:

The Secrets of the Gods

He sat back in thought for a few minutes, then resumed his two-fingered typing.

What I know:

Magic on Colibdis makes it easier for minds to influence reality by facilitating direct conscious interaction with underlying quantum phenomena. The rituals and instrumentality of magic serve to make this interaction more consistent and controllable. There is a pervasive myth that the source of magic is a mysterious island, called Etheros by the Mersineans.

The two major gods I know of are:

Varanu
God of truth and cosmic order. Cosmic order is defined as natural law minus the influence of consciousness. There is an unavoidable aspect of chaos in this "order" due to the inherent randomness of the underlying quantum nature of reality.

Ahriman
God of magic, thought, subtlety, and evil. Has an interest in remaking the laws of nature to better suit and serve his own needs and desires. Ahriman adds to his power and knowledge by capturing and somehow incorporating the essences or "souls" of human beings. He can't take anyone against their will unless they are extremely weakened. His main goal is to expand the magic

of Colibdis throughout the universe, thereby extending his influence. Once he is universal he will become a ubiquitous influence, reordering reality to suit himself. Varanu opposes him in this.

Irony: in a real sense, Varanu is a god of chaos (due to the uncertainties of quantum phenomena) while Ahriman is a god of order, given his desire to make all creation tractable and manageable by conscious minds.

He went on to record his scanty store of facts, followed by a page or two of speculation, guesses, and hypotheses, little of it strongly supported by facts, as yet.

Speculation:
The Eye is near the outer limit of the influence of Colibdian magic. Its orbit is modified to keep it within this area, probably to preserve some alignment which is somehow vital to the gods.

Ronar halted and sat scowling at the sheet again, his mouth a hard curve. Then he leaned forward to type a final sentence.

If the gods could be forced, or tricked, or distracted, into discontinuing the modification of the eye's orbit, it should soon leave the zone of magic.

Ronar sat back and studied this paragraph. The room was very silent. He could hear his heart beating slowly.

He pulled the sheet from the typewriter, folded it carefully, and put it in his breast pocket. He pushed back and pulled himself to his feet. The office fell into total darkness when he blew out the lamp. This startled him; he hadn't realized he'd been sitting there that long. He shrugged and picked his way into the corridor, dimly lit by widely spaced lamps. The halls were deserted. Ronar's footsteps echoed as he marched toward the exit.

He pushed open the door, stepped out onto the portico, looked up, and halted abruptly.

The sky had taken on a curious aspect. A milky white light stretched over it, not obscuring the stars, but giving the sky a pearly or filmy look. Ronar stepped away from the building and surveyed the horizon. Twilight was over; no glow lingered in the west. No special brightness played in the north, so this was not a rare auroral display. It didn't look like one anyway. It was a featureless, static, yet faintly sinister glow.

Ronar observed that others thought so as well. He looked around the campus and found knots of people standing and fidgeting here and there, pointing, muttering, staring up at the sky, sometimes glancing uneasily in his direction.

Ronar was thoughtful and subdued as he descended the mesa and ambled towards his house with an uncharacteristically indecisive gait. He kept trying to convince himself that this odd sky phenomenon had nothing to do with him. Surely not every anomaly on this insane planet was directly related to his activities! But he was not very successful.

Reaching his house, he entered and proceeded to the courtyard without lighting a lamp. He flopped down into a wicker garden chair and stared up at the milky, luminous sky with its peppering of stars. The phenomenon incited in him only a watchful, passive calm. The outrage he usually felt at such magical manipulation of the heavens was absent, but that did not mean he felt this effect to be harmless or benign. For some reason he wanted only to ignore it, though for now he couldn't bring himself to let this cold fire burn without his seeing.

Presently he found himself in his bedroom, undressing for bed with automatic movements. With scarcely a thought in his head beyond a vague sense of foreboding, he crawled beneath the covers and was asleep almost at once.

His slumber was of that uneasy sort in which one cannot distinguish between reality and dream. He knew his room was dark, yet it seemed to him that the ceiling glimmered with that pale wash of light that had spread across the stars. He heard cries of dismay and anguish, and faint strains of sinister music.

Someone was in the room with him. The glow revealed a tallish, brown-skinned man with straight black hair pulled back and bound at the neck. His flashing black eyes were wide and locked on Ronar's. His costume was brief yet gaudy, a bit of red and purple silk held together with golden chains, plus a mantle of iridescent feathers.

"Hello, Sha Totek," said Ronar.

"What in the Sam Hill are you up to this time, Ronar?" cried Sha Totek in a strained voice.

Ronar winced. He'd always found it grating that this ancient Egyptian sorcerer affected a cowboy accent stronger than that of most of the people of Thunderbird.

"I'm trying to rid this world of the oppression of Ahriman."

Sha Totek shook his head violently. "Hey there, pardner. The people of this planet have lived with

Ahriman's oppression for centuries, and it just ain't been all that bad. Yeah, he gets out of hand once in a while and has to be slapped back into place, but not by the likes of us. And he picks on the odd poor, vulnerable soul now and then. But he's got his eye mostly turned outward, not towards us. You'd better leave it that way, unless you want to open the gates of Hell to satisfy whatever vendetta you're throwing yourself into. I've never seen the gods so riled up."

Ronar had heard enough. His anger was surging at the description of Asterope as an "odd, poor, vulnerable soul", and he sat up to say so.

He found himself facing an empty, silent room. He looked around in confusion. There was no sign of the sorcerer.

A dream. He might have known it. Sha Totek rarely left his Tower long enough to visit him here.

Although Ronar was now awake, he still heard faint sounds of alarm filtering in from outside. Soft footsteps came running towards his room. In burst Flora, so distraught that she took no notice of the fact she was half naked.

"Oh Professor, please come out and tell us what is happening to the sky. I can't bear it; we're all going mad, and you lie here snoring. You can deal with such things; we cannot."

Ronar stared at her, curiously reluctant to get up and face whatever was going on outside.

"Very well, Flora," he muttered at last. He threw off the covers and stood up in the shadowy room. Again, Flora took no notice of his nudity, which was unlike her. He threw on yesterday's pants and padded barefoot after her.

She headed toward the courtyard, but Ronar turned her aside. He wanted to see not only whatever was happening in the sky, but also its effect on the people. He stepped out the front door. Flora hung back, at last aware of her own nakedness.

The sky was still filmed over with milky light, but the glow was no longer uniform. It was condensing here and there into areas of stronger light. These bright patches began to bulge downward, as though pulled by their own weight. They drooped into pendulous sacs, which eventually pulled free, dropping silently to the ground, disappearing behind house, tree, or hill. It was like watching drops of water condense on a ceiling, then fall.

Flora came out wearing a robe tied at her waist. "What is it, Professor?" she whispered.

"I don't know, Flora."

Groups of people, some fully dressed, others half-dressed or in their night clothes, stood around crying to each other in dread and uncertainty. One of them darted a finger straight up. "Look there!"

Ronar looked overhead. The light there was condensing into a circular glow. He could sense it growing full, bulging, preparing to drop. It separated and fell like a great dim hazy moon. His neighbors cried out and ran from the area where it seemed likely to impact, which was the square that fronted Ronar's house. There it quivered for a moment before condensing into a twitching, pulsating thing like some mixture of a flailing spider, a tumbleweed, and a shambling, spastic human figure. Its indeterminate geometry glowed with the same soft white light from which it had formed.

It darted and rolled back and forth over the square, silently, following no pattern Ronar could discern. It was hard to judge its size, but it seemed to pulsate between ten and thirty feet across.

Most of the locals had the sense to run from this apparition, but one woman approached it with wavering steps, apparently fascinated by it. Ronar strode forward and yelled, "Get away from that thing, you fool!" His admonition came too late. The chinese-puzzle ghostlight darted at her, immersed her for a fraction of a second, and then rolled away again, quivering. The woman appeared physically unharmed, but she had not escaped without trauma. She staggered about, staring madly, crying and gibbering. When her husband, who was one of the observatory's maintenance workers, rushed up and shook her, she remained oblivious to him, to her surroundings, to everything except whatever shambles the apparition had made of her mind.

"What the hell is that thing?" muttered Ronar.

"It's a nexus of divine intellect," said another voice. "It roams about, and whoever gets in its path finds that all barriers of time and space are shattered."

Ronar looked aside. A hooded, cloaked figure was approaching, its face obscured by the brim of its cowl. It drifted up to him with an odd floating gait and tossed back the hood. There gleamed the manic face of Sha Totek the Sorcerer, heavy earrings dangling, a massive jeweled pendant around his neck. Ronar took note of the shimmering air of unreality about him.

"Another dream?" he asked.

Sha Totek stepped in quickly and shoved Ronar with both hands, staggering him. "Yes, I'm a dream. Or an image. But an unusually substantial one."

"I don't suppose there's any point in asking if you can do anything about what's happening here."

"You're right, there's not. This is the act of a god, one which is dang near unprecedented."

Ronar gave an incoherent snort of anger. "Ahriman, that wretched bastard. It would do anything to stop me. But what I don't understand is this. Why does Varanu permit this? Is Ahriman free to to commit any outrage it pleases against the people of this planet?"

Sha Totek goggled at him, cutting off a laugh. "Ahriman? Ronar, you blind, mule-stubborn son of a bitch. Does this look like the work of Ahriman to you? It's Varanu who's doing this!"

At that, Ronar lost all pretense of control or understanding. He wobbled, gaping, taking in sharp breaths.

This time Sha Totek did laugh, a quick crazed bray. "Haw! It's almost worth all this trouble just to see you so hornswoggled. Would be worth it too, except for all the people who are being hurt. And this is only the beginning."

"But — why?"

"I reckon Varanu doesn't like whatever you're doing to Ahriman," said Sha Totek dryly.

"Varanu doesn't like it..." Ronar turned away, staring into the night. Occasional shrieks and demented yammerings marked the dissolution of another's sanity in the depths of one of the pale glows. New ones were still dropping from the sky. "Varanu doesn't like it that I'm opposing Ahriman, and getting somewhere. Why would that be? What's the connection between them? Why doesn't Varanu simply destroy me, instead of torturing all these people?"

Sha Totek shrugged irritably. "Who knows? Why don't you mosey over to one of those quivery things and find out? You've been in communion with Varanu before. As I recall, the experience seemed to clear your mind, or fog it in a peculiarly useful way. That's the kind of *hombre* you are. But these folks ain't ready to have their perceptions of reality stripped away. They're not up to having the barriers that separate now from forever break down, or the barrier between here and everywhere. It's taking a terrible toll on them, Ronar. And you're the only one who can stop it."

With this Ronar turned his grey gaze on Sha Totek's magical effigy. "How?"

"Stop. Whatever it is you're doing, stop. Destroy whatever knowledge you've gained. Make a truce with Ahriman and leave the business of the gods to themselves."

"No!" Ronar's reply was thunderous. "I will not cease until I've pulled Ahriman from the heavens and ended his threat forever."

Sha Totek cast a narrow, fearless look into Ronar's wrathful face. "There's something here that goes beyond your old hatred of Ahriman. Something personal. I don't expect you to tell me what it is; that would make too much sense. But whatever it is, you must move beyond it, for the sake of everyone in the world. This is not going to stop. It will get bigger, and meaner, and spread out from here, until you stop."

Ronar shut his eyes, drew in a ragged breath, fought to control himself. "I ask you again. Is there anything you can do to end this?"

"Yes, there is," answered Sha Totek in a low, dangerous voice. "If need be, I can cast you off this planet."

Ronar's glared at him defiantly.

Sha Totek returned only a brittle chuckle. "Don't think I can't do it, pardner. Oh, I know what kind of a man you are, better than anyone else. I've seen you do things that no other man would have attempted. I've watched as you've crushed obstacles that might have daunted Hamadan himself. I've even known you to work a strange kind of magic at times of great need. But I have been gaining strength for five thousand years of Earth. I am this world's greatest power, excepting only the gods. You must give up your vendetta against Ahriman. If you will not put aside your vengeance and act responsibly for the good of everyone on this planet, then you must leave it. If you will not leave it, I must put you off it. And I will."

Sha Totek loomed there, glowering at Ronar with a force exceeding his own, though different in character. Instead of Ronar's grey wintry fierceness, Sha Totek's was darker, though it was a darkness through which glimmered colors as rich as the tapestry of all human history.

Still Ronar stood there grimly, unyielding.

Sha Totek made a savage gesture that took in the increasing bedlam around them. "Look around you! Look at what you are doing to your countrymen! These are people like you, who have tried to keep magic at bay, to live by the works of their hands and minds, as their ancestors did. Partly they do that to try to please you, their great hero! Now look at the chaos you've called down upon them! They cannot deal with it! But while they are being driven mad, you stand there with your eyes glittering! Your noble jaw juts out in defiance! Will you go, or must I drag you?" The sorcerer's eyes were wide. Ronar had never seen him so enraged.

Ronar had trouble forcing his throat to produce coherent sounds.

"I—will—go."

Sha Totek's voice broke. "You will go! Marvelous! When?"

"I will ride immediately."

Sha Totek's eyes blazed. "Good for you, Ronar. Good for you. Thank you for making this wise decision. Now be silent for a moment."

The sorcerer's image grew still. His eyelids fluttered, his hands drifted up, his breathing grew slow and deep. Faint sounds escaped his lips, but they were no more than drawn-out whispered syllables, like a distant surf.

Ronar looked around. The light-things twisted and shook themselves into nothingness. The milky glaze over the sky faded away. Peace palpably descended over the world. Even those who had been taken into the light grew silent.

Sha Totek opened his eyes. "Varanu knew your decision as soon as you made it, but I made sure of it. He pledges peace, as long as you keep your word. To tell you the truth, I'm not sure it would have been enough for you merely to stop what you were doing. I believe Varanu wants you gone."

"As does Ahriman," said Ronar, in as tightly controlled a voice as he could muster.

"That is not so clear. Go now. I know you have few possessions to slow you down. Come to the Portal as quickly as you can. Stop by the Tower before you go through, so I can say goodbye." Sha Totek's expression was pained as his image faded away. Ronar thought that was curious for someone whose will had just been done.

Flora crouched nearby, gaping at him with so dazed an expression that Ronar feared she was one of the victims of the light. But finally she whispered "Professor!" and ran into the house.

A group of men rode up to him, the trio nominally in charge of Thunderbird: the mayor of Two Suns; the Governor; President Deerfield. "Professor Ronar!" huffed the Governor as he tried to catch his breath. "The town's a shambles. We've got dozens of crazy folk on our hands. What happened? Are you responsible for ending it?"

"It was an attack from the gods. And yes, I'm responsible for ending it, just as I was responsible for bringing it down on us."

The governor blinked. "Will it happen again?"

Ronar shook his head. "No. Gentlemen, the only way I can guarantee your safety is by leaving Colibdis at once. I —I don't know if I can ever return."

Their reaction to this proved they were not beyond shock, even after the night's events.

"President Deerfield. I wish to appoint Professor Holder as—acting Chairman of the Department of Physics and Astronomy—in my absence. I'll leave it up to you—to determine when my absence has become a permanent one, to make the appointment official and final.

Deerfield nodded slowly. "Very well, Professor Ronar," he said in a subdued voice.

"Professor, do you suppose the people who were driven crazy by those lights will ever recover?" asked the Mayor.

"I don't know. The stronger ones will, I hope. When they do, you may find they've gained a different perspective on things, and I'd appreciate it if you'd treat any eccentricities they may exhibit with patience and kindness."

"Yes, I guess I will," said the Mayor thickly. "I do still love my own wife and son, even if they do come up with some strange ideas in the future. It would be better than their current state of mind."

The Governor drew himself up and began, "Professor— despite this night's disaster, I'm sure I speak for all of us when I say…"

Ronar cut him off with a tired gesture. "Please. I must be on my way. I'm sure we'll all miss each other, but I don't have time for speeches. I don't own a horse. I'd be thankful if one of you could lend me one for the trip to the Portal."

"You're still a departmental chairman at the University, and the Chancellor," said Deerfield. "Transportation will be provided for you, as always."

"Thank you."

Ronar returned to his darkened house for the last time. He couldn't find Flora, though her scent was still present. It was the work of ten minutes to throw together the equipment and supplies he'd need for the three-day ride to the Portal. He reserved one large knapsack for souvenirs of his years on Colibdis. He gave most of it over to books.

Among them he stashed the notes and papers he had assembled concerning the Eye of Ahriman and its peculiar orbit.

When he came out he found a black mare saddled and tied to the post in front of his porch. He loaded the animal, mounted, and rode off into what little remained of the night.

Chapter 26

Leavetaking

As was his habit, well-ingrained through a hundred thousand repetitions and more, Sha Totek the Sorcerer stood at a western window of his lofty sanctum, looking out at the evening that was engulfing the world. The two suns had recently set, and the sky had deepened to the richest possible shade of amethyst, with paler smears of dusty lilac and milky rose along the horizon. The first yellow stars were just glimmering into view. The Greater Moon was absent tonight, making this one of those dark nights which were of such interest to Ronar and the disciples he had gathered around him at the University. At least they interested Ronar whenever he was actually in residence at the University, which was rarely enough, and soon to happen no more.

Sha Totek breathed deeply of the evening air that stole through the windows of his Tower. Left to itself, that air would carry only the faintly spicy scent of the red desert that surrounded the Tower in all directions. As it was, the garden within his walled enclosure did more than delight him when he walked its pathways. It perfumed many a breeze as well, even at this great height.

Small sounds of nature also found their way up here, so still was the evening, so peaceful. The *chir* of night insects. The keening of nighthawks. The concerted yapping of coyotes. Tonight even the call of a barcha, a peevish demand that someone should appear and offer himself to be eaten. Sha Totek discouraged these beasts from hanging around the Tower, as they could be a serious danger to any stranger coming through the Portal. The Sorcerer put a high value on anyone willing to make that crossing and provide him with a little news of Earth, or simply with a break in his routine. The last man to come through had been Ronar. All the gods knew how Ronar had added novelty to Sha Totek's life on more than one occasion, sometimes even in excess of what the sorcerer desired.

If the barcha survived the night, Sha Totek would send it on its way in the morning.

Twilight was fleeting, a brief exhalation of beauty as a day died to give way to night. Sha Totek leaned out from his window to look upon the stars, shining now in their full numbers, not so many as to bewilder the eye, but not so few as to seem sparse or niggardly. A good and moderate number of stars.

Plus one. Sha Totek sighed. Ronar had assured him that the Eye of Ahriman had no more than one chance in two of being visible at any given time. He had even drawn a rat's nest of lines, circles, and ellipses to prove his assertion. Still it seemed to Sha Totek than any time he looked at the night sky he was very likely to find the Eye looking back at him in its dim, flickering malignity, all the more often since Ronar's advent in the world, it seemed. Perhaps now that Ronar was leaving, the Eye would grow sleepier.

Sha Totek withdrew into his sanctum, unwilling to bear the gaze of Ahriman unnecessarily. Suddenly the evening had a different character. The quiet was still there, but now it was not the quiet of peace, but of watchfulness. The Eye was turned this way; there was no doubt. Sha Totek knew this brittle silence, a breathlessness that kept men looking over their shoulders and made beasts unwilling to reveal themselves in the night.

All except that barcha. Its cry came again, and this time it had a more urgent note. A distant rhythmic pounding came to Sha Totek's ears, who went idly to a window to look out. He could not see the barcha, but its heavy running gait sounded like a drumbeat. It squalled again, this time with a childish triumph.

Far out in the desert came a brief flare of white light, followed a few seconds later by a quick, hard ringing sound. The barcha howled again, this time in dismay. Sha Totek could actually hear the blows, chopping, hacking, like an ax biting into a tree. The barcha erupted into incessant wailing, increasingly frantic, more and more desperate. If Sha Totek had not known the true nature of the barcha he would have been moved to pity.

The cries came to a sudden halt. Silence returned to the Red Plain. The insects took a moment to resume their chorus.

Sha Totek smiled mirthlessly. He drew back, bending his thoughts and words to conjuring refreshments.

His small smile was still in place a short time later when Sha Totek sensed the expected presence at his back. He turned.

"Welcome, Ronar. Be seated. The sapphire carafe on the table beside you contains an exquisite wine made from grapes which grow beside phosphorescent fungi in faerie-woods which never see the suns. The glass pitcher contains that sour fruit excrescence you sometimes crave after hard travels—lemonade. It is even iced."

Ronar snorted, sank down upon a divan with ornately embroidered silk cushions, and poured himself a tinkling goblet of lemonade. He even thought to fill another goblet with musky faerie-wine and push it toward Sha Totek as he sat at the opposite side of the table.

"Thank you. And so we part, after many a reckless escapade. I drink to you, Leonard Ronar. I salute your deeds, and in the end, your wisdom."

Sha Totek raised his goblet and regarded Ronar over its brim. Ronar seemed capable of only two seated postures: one so achingly erect that his back might be used to gauge the straightness of the Tower, and another, as now, where he flung himself back in such a slouch that he could barely sip from his cup without spilling it. His eyes glowered over the cup, shifting restlessly about the chamber and beyond.

"Oh—let me thank you for keeping my environs free of pests."

"I wish you hadn't done that," said Ronar. "I didn't enjoy slaughtering that beast. Plus, my damn horse almost threw me. The next time you're expecting me, if there ever is another time, please clear out any such animals yourself. I don't have access to the same gentle means of persuasion you do."

"I'm sorry. I was tired, and lazy, and I hoped you wouldn't encounter the monster. But I should have known better. You seem to draw monsters of all sorts to yourself."

"I've come to pass through the Portal. There are fewer monsters on the other side. Just the odd chupacabra that sneaks through now and then to confound the natives and attack their goats."

Though Sha Totek had of course known Ronar's intention, he was still relieved to hear it again. "I know you have felt—the recent activity of Ahriman, his restlessness."

"Of course. In fact I suspect I have felt it far more keenly than you."

That caught the Sorcerer's full attention and promptly quenched his sense of relief. "Well, if Ahriman has offended you, I would expect you to devise some mad scheme against him, as apparently you did. Instead you are about to withdraw, to remove yourself from Ahriman's influence, to spare the world from the wrath of the Great Gods. I hope this is the beginning of a new, more prudent phase in the life of Leonard Ronar."

"I don't know about that. I have no way of reaching Ahriman on his distant moon, and therefore I cannot chastise him as I would wish."

"Ah. I see. If only you could reach him, you would wield your magic sword and give the god of evil the sound thwacking he so richly deserves." Despite his better wisdom, Sha Totek found relief trying to steal back into his heart. At least Ronar wasn't demanding that he attempt to use his magic to transport him to the Eye. He might therefore live another turn or two.

"A good plan, but impractical," answered Ronar, with what degree of irony Sha Totek could not guess.

Sha Totek sighed, replacing his half-full goblet on the table. "You've been chafing against Ahriman for as long as I've known you, and yet up to now you've been content to establish your astronomical kingdom, and to wander the planet at times, pitting yourself against foes you have at least some chance of overcoming. I ask you now—on this, our final evening together—what happened to set you on a course that nearly led to such a disaster?"

Ronar's eyes glittered in the shadowed twilight of the sanctum. Somehow, without Sha Totek's noticing, Ronar had raised himself to that arrow-straight posture.

"I will tell you.

"A few turns ago a young girl named Asterope arrived in Two Suns in the tow of a pair of Thunderbird traders named Stannard and Thayne. She had been the slave of a well-to-do citizen of Mersinea, a child who had been exposed by her natural parents, left in the open to die because her mother had no use for a daughter..."

Ronar went on to relate the whole story of Asterope, speaking in some detail, revealing thoughts and observations he hadn't even realized he had had or made. Striving to remain calm and objective, he found this an increasing challenge as he neared the end of the tale.

"...Asterope told me how her world had changed, how she had become prematurely a strengthless shade, wandering in a dreary world populated by vile, hopeless, deceitful monsters, herself not the best among them. I knew the influence of Ahriman must be driven out of her, before she could be corrupted forever."

"Ronar," said Sha Totek quietly. "Why didn't you bring her to me?"

Ronar looked at Sha Totek levelly. "You've told me often enough that you prefer not to openly cross Ahriman."

Sha Totek returned the gaze. Before the truth of Ronar's answer he could make no reply.

A heaviness welled out of Ronar, a bleakness that surpassed any that Sha Totek had ever felt from him before. Ronar sketched out the tale of Asterope's doomed voyage and his role in it.

"And so here I sit. My failure to help Asterope was disastrous and complete. Not only was I forced to mutilate her, but many men whom I involved in my scheme are dead. And now great harm has come to the people of Thunderbird. I have no way to carry my fight to Ahriman. It's just as well that I leave the planet. Let it be."

Ronar stood up decisively and took a moment to work the gold-and-garnet ring off his finger. He stepped up to the sorcerer and dropped it into his palm. "Keep this for me. It doesn't belong on Earth."

Sha Totek nodded. "I guess the royal halls of Eranior will now go undisturbed by the din and flash of the sword of Bran leaping into your hand."

Ronar caught Sha Totek with a probing look.

"I can't swear to you that I will never show my face on this planet again."

The sorcerer nodded again, thoughtfully. "I know. I would not expect it of you. I don't know what the consequences of some future return might be. If you ever do return, make sure you know your purpose, beyond doubt...and come only if you are in a position of strength."

"If I cannot do both—I will indeed never return."

Ronar grabbed Sha Totek's hand, bringing the sorcerer to the brink of a wince.

"Goodbye then, Sha Totek. I will never have a better friend than you."

"Awww, shucks." Sha Totek felt abashed out of all proportion to what Ronar had said. "That's true. Same to you, pardner."

And so Ronar turned and stalked toward the spiral staircase that led to the base of the Tower. As Sha Totek watched that wild grey head bob down the shaft his heart filled with more words he wished he could say. But in truth, his throat tightened like a wet leather sleeve around a stick of wood, and he was quite unable to make a sound.

Soon afterwards Ronar stood beside the shadowed, angular form of the Bronze Portal. It didn't matter which of its openings he entered; they all led to the same place. It was utterly dark within, but Ronar didn't trouble to strike a light. There were few obstacles within the Bronze Portal, and it was impossible to go astray once you entered it, as long as you kept moving.

Ronar stared into a starry sky that had grown more familiar to him than the dimly-remembered white stars of Earth. Among them, waiting to see him off as he knew it would be, was the hateful flicker of the Eye of Ahriman. Ronar studied it impassively, considering with an odd detachment the growing urge he felt to blast his hatred and defiance at the moonlet and its occupant.

But in this last moment on Colibdis, another need rose up and overpowered even his need for revenge. He forgot the Eye, taking in instead the great expanse of the heavens, in which the Eye was nothing but an inconspicuous mote.

"Asterope," he said aloud, "soon I'll be two hundred thousand light years from the scene of your life and death. I feel I am abandoning you. I ask you to forgive me for leaving, and for the follies that put you in this plight in the first place. I will not forget you. Someday I will find a way to save you, to restore you to the body that still rests within the shield of Athena. Don't despair. Be strong. I will never forget."

Ronar turned and walked steadfastly into the darkness of the Portal, that echoing, dusty darkness. He walked until the floor grew too steep to keep his footing, and then he fell, seemingly back the way he'd come, yet in truth through some incomprehensible void that somehow spanned the distance between galaxies. The passage took only minutes, but as the wind rushed past his ears he felt the widening gulf between himself and the world that had come to be his home...the world that contained everything he loved and hated.

Finally he slid to a halt on a different floor. He adjusted his pack and got his knees under him. It wasn't easy. He had forgotten the crush of Earth's gravity. He swallowed hard to clear his ears. The air seemed thick as soup.

And it was quiet. The night on Sha Totek's Red Plain had been almost as quiet, but this was a different kind of silence. Here there was no whisper, no susurration, no vibrating undercurrent of magic in the air. This was just—a place, where everything worked as he had been told it should work when he was a boy. Now he was truly cut off from Ahriman, from Varanu—and from every other god and spirit that walked the Colibdian night.

He walked toward a brilliant square of light that soon stung his eyes to watering. It appeared to be daytime in Arizona.

Part Four
Ronar on Earth

Chapter 27

Kitt Peak

Ronar stepped out of the Portal, squinted in the brilliant light, and gasped. He had forgotten the hugeness of the Earth. The horizon, so distant, the farthest mountains made misty by the thickness of air. The sky itself, a fathomless milky blue bowl, semi-opaque compared to the transparent indigo dome of Colibdis. And the sun—the grand solitary sun—less intense than Photos, but apparently larger and far brighter. Far smaller than Kudu, yet hotter, brighter. That smallish nearby sun offered Earth the same amount of light that the combined but more distant suns of Colibdis granted their planet.

He drew the thick, hot air into his lungs and felt the desert gravel pressing firmly into his heels. Very firmly. It was as if the pack on his back weighed nearly as much as he.

He turned toward the north, squinting at Kitt Peak, the observatory mountain from which he'd first glimpsed the Portal all those years ago. It was studded with twice as many domes as he recalled. Just how long had it been since last he'd stood here? He'd first made the crossing in 1959, when he was forty years old. The last time he'd visited Earth, NASA was preparing to fly its Space Shuttle. Now he was over seventy years old—Earth years. Yet thanks to the spell of immortality which Sha Totek had placed upon him during his first visit, he had aged only a few years. Of course, now that he was beyond the reach of magic, he supposed he'd find that reprieve from aging at an end.

He had better be prepared to face other changes as well. As far as Earth was concerned, he was essentially a man of the fifties. The pace of change here, driven by technological advancement, was far greater than it was on Colibdis, where the prevalence of magic slowed or discouraged technological and cultural change. The gleam of light off those new domes was enough to remind him that he should take nothing here for granted.

He looked around for signs that the Portal might have been discovered, but found nothing. He could even still see traces left by the pack horses he had used to carry parts and equipment for the Thunderbird observatory, years before.

He started along the half-remembered track that lead to Kitt Peak, paying close attention to his steps in the heavy gravity. He slid down a short steep pitch onto a broad shoulder.

There, a hundred feet from the Portal, were the remains of a recent campfire. He kicked at the ashes and found some rubbish...thin-walled cans, probably aluminum... beer cans. He turned and looked up the pitch. The Portal was hidden. That was the only thing that had kept it from being discovered by some group of hikers, herdsmen, or migrants. Anyone finding the Portal and actually entering it would find themselves making the acquaintance of Sha Totek, who would prevent them from ever returning to Earth. They were not the problem. The Sorcerer could do nothing to stop a discoverer intent on mere vandalism. The Portal's aged bronze could be flattened by one man wielding a large rock. Its destruction would separate Ronar from Colibdis with a finality he shied away from considering. Worse, if the Portal were ever discovered by the so-called "authorities," Sha Totek could face the incursion of armed, arrogant Americans that he and Ronar had always sought to prevent.

At first he'd wondered how this Portal, which was so isolated and lonely, had ever managed to populate Thunderbird in the relatively brief span of its existence. During his many years on Colibdis he had learned the answer from the local Indians, a few of whom had made the crossing themselves in their younger days.

The Earth-side Indians had once known of the Portal, considering it a gateway to the Underworld. It had become a part of their tradition, and a rite of passage. Young people of both sexes were required to go through it upon entering puberty. Sometimes they would penetrate only a short distance, become paralyzed with fright, stop moving, and die. Most completed the passage, as anyone must who kept moving at all. Sometimes they would reach the other side, peer out through the opening, see they were in another place, and return to Earth in triumph. Others would leave the Portal, sealing their fates as new permanent residents of Colibdis.

Sometimes the Indians had conflicts with white people. If white captives were taken, they were forced to enter the Portal on pain of death. These invariably were never again seen on Earth. Sometimes other whites, upon learning their fate, followed them deliberately, out of the hope that something other than death awaited them.

Ronar trudged along the trail, discovering more signs of human presence in the first mile than he'd ever previously seen along its whole fifteen mile length. Cans, bottles, orange peels, trash of all sorts, even the tracks of motor vehicles and bicycles! He must do something to protect the Portal as soon as possible.

Two hours later he was hiking in the shadow of the strange rocky tower of Baboquivari. From here, Kitt Peak looked scarcely any closer, yet his trembling legs and aching shoulders told him he'd been hiking through a day and a night at least. He never should have stayed away so long, letting his strength and endurance diminish to nearly the level that was typical of native-born Colibdians, who were subject only to that planet's gentler pull. Now his pack felt like a man of his own weight perched on his shoulders, while his feet were like lead bricks. Yet unless he were content to languish here without food or shelter, he must walk on, at least as far as the observatory. What he would do upon arriving there was an open question.

After another few hours he halted long enough to unplug his canteen and pour some of its contents down his dusty throat. He'd filled it at the fountain in Sha Totek's garden. There the water had been scented and subtly flavored; here it was merely water. He dared not sit while he drank for fear that his overtaxed body would find it hard to rise up again. A few more swigs and he trudged on once again.

Night came on long before he reached the peak. The Moon rose at sunset. He'd never been more grateful to see a full Moon. It lit his way, large and dazzling. Despite its light, the deep blue sky was filled with almost as many stars as he'd ever seen in the darkest nights on Colibdis. They were arranged in patterns so classic and yet so far in his past that it was like looking at illustrations in a well-loved children's book. Straight ahead was the Big Dipper, and near it, somewhere near the bowl of the Little Dipper, lurked the vanishingly dim patch of the dwarf galaxy that contained Colibdis and its suns. He had to trust his knowledge that this was so, rather than his senses, for this phantom galaxy was so faint that a large telescope was needed to see it at all. He was walking almost directly toward the planet from which he'd been recently ejected.

The position of the two famous star-pictures told him it was September on Earth. The night air was gentle and sweet. It was a beautiful evening which Ronar might have enjoyed had he not been hungry, exhausted, and weighed down by the memory of what he had left behind and what he had left undone.

After some unknown time he found himself sprawled out on the trail looking up at the sky. So be it, he thought, shrugging out of his pack, wrapping his jacket around himself, and dropping at once into sleep.

He awoke and lay there a few moments while his brain retrieved the memories it needed to make sense of the strangely pale blue sky which stretched out before his eyes. His confusion finally resolved into a picture of where he was and how he had gotten there. He attempted to rise.

And immediately fell back. He was extremely, excruciatingly stiff and sore. Walking was going to be quite a trial today, even a challenge.

With his head pounding, he slowly propped himself up on wobbly hands and knees before making the painful effort of unfolding himself from the ground to an upright posture. Once he'd achieved that, he cursed at the sight of his pack still down on the ground. He bent down with difficulty, grabbed it and pulled it on, moving as little as possible. The straps dug strips of soreness into his shoulders.

Like a fool, he had brought nothing to eat. He must have thought he'd be able to make quick work of the hike, as he'd always done before. At least he had water, though not as much as he would wish. He sucked some of it down. It did take up space in his stomach and quiet his hunger a bit.

Kitt Peak was now close enough so that the domes were visible in detail. Even at the ant-like pace that was all he could manage, he'd arrive in a few hours.

And so he did, still sore and weak, but at least loose enough to let him move his limbs without wincing.

He felt conspicuous on the Peak. The summit was now almost full of domes, offices, and other structures, so crowded that he barely recognized the place. The old 84-inch dome looked about the same, but not much else did. Tourists, many of them carrying tiny television cameras, wandered everywhere, gawking at this and that. He himself attracted a fair bit of attention. He was still wearing the same clothes he'd had on when he left Two Suns four nights before, Thunderbird clothes of nineteenth century styling.

He didn't intend to remain here for long. He wouldn't have come this way at all, but this was the quickest way to reach a main road. He needed information, to catch up on the world and orient himself to its changes. He glanced up at the sky, which was crisscrossed by three jet contrails. They must be an annoying impediment to astronomy.

And then there came a hurtling white speck, a wingless dot which flashed by just over the Peak, noiseless except for the rush of air. For an instant he could see its curved, hourglass-waisted shape and the orange light that flared from a lens at the rear. He stared after it as it dwindled to nothingness as quickly as it came.

The tourists around him were chattering, also staring after it, wide-eyed.

"What was that? Was it a Vigil flyer, or one of Perturbare's?"

"I think it was one of Doc Possum's. The Vigil flyers are darker, and boxier."

Ronar studied these people more closely, then looked again toward the point in the east where the "flyer" had disappeared.

It looked like things on Earth had changed more than he would have guessed.

Chapter 28

Tucson

During his previous visits, Ronar had learned how to maintain a sketchy identity on Earth. He still had bank accounts in Tucson, his old home town, though after an absence of about nine years he had to argue with a bank officer and produce his carefully preserved records and papers to convince the woman he was really the same person.

He rented a cheap motel room, bought some clothes and other necessities, considered renting an apartment, but hoped he wouldn't be around long enough to make that worth the effort.

He spent his days at the libraries of the University, trying to work out the current situation on Earth. No one on campus recognized him after an absence of thirty years or more.

He read about the so-called Para-Men, a mysterious group of space aliens, based in Antarctica, who had promised to protect Mankind from its own folly.

He read about the Vigil, a motley assortment of other aliens and peculiar beings, based in Boston, who were pledged to maintaining human autonomy, for better or for worse.

One of the few human members of this organization was Ronar's own younger cousin, Ben Raintree, a noted physicist. That was certainly interesting.

Mostly he was intrigued by the mystery man, Dr. Possum Perturbare, as he called himself. No one knew who he really was, where he came from, or where he went. He seemed to be a general purpose super scientist and inventor, but his goal in life was evidently to make mischief, plague authority, expose corruption, and assault complacency.

He sounded like a potentially useful fellow.

If anyone knew more about him than that, it would be the Vigil, he reasoned. They had a public, listed phone number. Ronar called it from a pay phone, waiting a long time for an answer, feeding change into the annoying machine. At last he was answered. He identified himself as Leonard Ronar and asked to speak to Ben Raintree.

After more minutes a tentative voice came on the line. "Hello?"

"Hello, Ben? It's Leonard, your cousin."

A significant silence ensued.

"Like hell you are."

"No, Ben, it's really me. I realize it's been a while."

"Thirty years, give or take. I was a kid when he disappeared."

"Well, I'm back."

"Prove it."

"Your favorite comic book character was Mysta of the Moon. When she ceased publication, you tried to draw your own, unsuccessfully."

Another silence.

"Where are you?"

"In Tucson, on the university campus."

"I'll be there in forty five minutes. Meet me...outside the planetarium."

"How can you—" But the call was ended.

Ronar hung up and set out for that fancy new planetarium, which was not far off. He had not received the hero's welcome he had hoped for, but he supposed he didn't deserve it.

It was late afternoon. Lurking near the entrance of the planetarium, he tried to appear inconspicuous.

After a few minutes he noticed a very old man approaching that entrance with the aid of a cane. He looked familiar; could it be?

"Stanley? Stanley Cohen?" he called.

The old man, once his colleague on the faculty of this very school, and the last man he had spoken to before his first crossing to Colibdis, halted and jerked his head in Ronar's direction.

"Do I know you, sir?"

Ronar stepped closer. "It's Leonard Ronar. Surely you remember."

Cohen looked first befuddled, then wary. "Ronar—? Good lord, it does look like you. I don't believe it, what's it been, thirty years? Where the hell have you been?"

"I've been…living on another planet, most of the time."

"Oh, really? Which one? Mars, I'll bet."

"No, you wouldn't have heard of it. It's in the Ursa Minor dwarf galaxy."

Cohen laughed, coughed a bit, then looked around, uneasily, and Ronar knew he feared he was confronted by a madman.

"Professor Cohen…"

"Emeritus," he snapped. "How is it that you look the same?"

"Long story." Ronar tried to steer the conversation to shop talk. "What were you working on before your retirement?"

"Galactic morphology," said Cohen shortly.

"I'm a little behind the times here, but did you know the Milky Way is a barred spiral?"

"Oh? And how would you know that?"

"I've seen it. From the outside."

"Of course you have. Ursa Minor dwarf, and all that."

"There's more. For example, you might be interested to know that the hub of the Milky Way contains, in addition to its own nucleus, two smaller, distorted nuclei which I take to be evidence of past galactic cannibalism. My study of their dynamics suggests they will merge with the Galaxy's own nucleus in a few million years, probably turning the Milky Way into a Seyfert-type active object and emitting nuclear jets as significant numbers of stars fall into the central black hole."

Cohen stared at him. "I hope you haven't come hoping to resume your post here at the University. Your disappearance caused quite a scandal back then."

"No, no, I have no such intention. I'm here——"

Two women and a man left the planetarium and approached them. "Professor Cohen? It's almost time for your presentation. Is this man bothering you?"

Cohen hesitated. "No, he's someone I used to know, apparently. Come on, let's get inside. I'm done here."

They surrounded Cohen and led him inside, with dubious glances at Ronar over their shoulders.

Hail the conquering hero! Ronar, feeling chagrined and unwelcome, moved farther from the planetarium.

At the appointed time an astonishing thing appeared in the sky. It looked like a van in black and silver, but without wheels. It hovered a few feet above the ground, silently, apparently supported by nothing but some small orange lamps mounted on the bottom. Its big port was directed at him, but Ronar could not see inside. After a few moments it settled into the grass.

On every side was the red "V" emblem of the Vigil.

A door swung open and a man hopped out. Tall and gangly, he had a long, homely face, and unkempt hair that had been white since he was a child.

"Hello, Ben."

Someone called, "Look! It's Ben Raintree!" A chattering circle of students and others formed around them, keeping a respectful distance.

Raintree walked up slowly, staring and frowning.

"So that's how it is," he said after a while. "After all these years, you just appear out of nowhere, and there you are."

"Yep."

"And you look—you look barely older than the last time I saw you. Which was when I was about—nine years old? How do you explain that?"

"It's magic, Ben."

Raintree looked at Ronar with incredulity. "Magic. I don't think I've ever heard you use that word before. So, where have you been?"

There was no help for it, he'd have to try this story again. "I've been living on another planet, Ben."

Raintree stared at his cousin, waiting for him to add something. Finally, Raintree was forced to put the question. "Um—which one?"

"You'll not have heard of it. It's called Colibdis. Located in the Ursa Minor dwarf galaxy."

"Never heard of that planet? I've never even heard of that galaxy."

"It's not conspicuous."

"And what are you doing back here? Now?"

"Back on that planet…I bit off more than I could chew. I took on something there—someone, rather—and found I couldn't finish what I'd started. Things started to get out of control—and I was forced to leave. I disappointed a lot of people. Failed them, in fact." Somehow, speaking of these matters here, so very far from their scene, they felt and sounded remote and unlikely, even to his own ears.

"Colibdis is a strange, turbulent place. The forces in operation there are foreign, bizarre, even compared to the recent changes here on Earth.

"I'd like to study the new technology that's so rampant here. I've seen propulsion beam flyers, like yours. I've tried to study propulsion beams and the like in the scientific literature, but I find only the vaguest descriptions, fuzzy speculation about new subatomic particles. It seems that the Vigil and this Possum Perturbare character keep their secrets close to their vests."

"That's true", said Raintree. "We have no incentive to share such technology. Our goal isn't to remake human society, after all, but to preserve it. Why do you want to study it?"

"That technology represents options I hadn't expected to find. I want to learn all I can, to see if it can help me."

"What about this planet of yours? How do you reach it? That must take some extremely advanced technology… beyond anything we, or even Perturbare, could offer you."

"Not really. It's about as simple as falling into a hole. But I think it's best to limit your knowledge of Colibdis for now."

Raintree frowned. "Why is that?"

"I've read what I can about your Vigil. I don't want to involve them in my affairs. They have their own agenda, and I have mine. I won't have them rushing through the gateway to Colibdis in search of whatever they think might help them in their struggle with those Antarctic aliens. I'm not asking the Vigil for help."

Raintree regarded his cousin with a certain thoughtful discomfort. Ronar's attitude awakened boyhood memories which were usually overshadowed by more pleasant ones. There had always been more than one side to Leonard Ronar. In addition to the adventuresome guide and mentor, there was also the saturnine, self-centered Ronar whose will must be considered law.

"This needn't go any farther than me, Leonard," said Raintree cautiously. "I can help you on my own. I do have full access to Vigil technology."

Ronar shook his head decisively. "No, Ben. I'm not asking for your help in this either. It would require too great a commitment of your time, and too much danger. I know the importance of your mission against the Para-men. I won't allow you to jeopardize it, or to divide your loyalties by helping me."

Ronar walked a few steps, stopped, gazed around the campus. "And there's more. I hope you'll forgive me for saying this, but you're not the right man for the job. You don't know the kind of insanity that prevails on Colibdis. It's all I can deal with myself, if not more. It was enough to break me, or very nearly. You've always been sensitive. I won't risk you on a task like this. I won't see you broken too."

Raintree's frown returned and deepened. So—he was too delicate, too weak, to help the mighty Ronar with his mysterious task? So be it.

"I see," he said with some asperity. "Exactly what can I do for you, then?"

"You can direct me to a better candidate. An independent man with access to advanced technology."

"I have just the man for you. Doctor Possum Perturbare."

Ronar nodded slowly. "That's just who I was thinking of. What do you know about him?"

"Probably not much more than you. He's independent, all right. Seems to have plenty of time on his hands. No obvious loyalties. Very elusive. When he does turn up, he divides his time between thefts, pranks, subversion, outing hypocrites and crooks, and practical jokes. His technology beats ours. He has a sentient computer—"

"Yes. Brainchild. I've heard mention of that. I agree; he seems a perfect choice. Where can he be found?"

Raintree blinked. "I'm surprised your research didn't make it clear that no one has any idea where Perturbare can be found. He just appears. Then he disappears. We think he might be based in the southern hemisphere, but that's just an inference derived from his patterns of appearances and disappearances."

"I see. I thought perhaps your organization had additional information on the matter."

"Not at all. He's the most evanescent man in the world, except maybe for you. You'll have quite a time finding him. And a worse time convincing him to sign up for your cause."

Ronar nodded again. "Yes, I can see that. Ben, I appreciate your help. You have no idea how important this is to me. Someday, when Colibdis is a safer, saner place to visit, I hope to bring you over and give you the grand tour."

Raintree's ire softened a little at that. It was just like Ronar to throw out a pebble of consideration, just enough to trip up and misdirect the full anger of whoever he might have offended.

"Are you interested in hearing anything about our family?"

"Yes. Of course."

Raintree spent a few minutes conveying news about Ronar's various cousins, aunts, and uncles. Ronar's own parents had vanished decades before, so there was nothing to be said about them.

"All right, Ben. Thank you. It's been good to see you. You know, you could really be a miserable whiny brat when you were a young boy, but you've shaped up into someone interesting. I'd like to hear more about that process someday. For now, I'd better be moving along."

Ben nodded. "I stand dismissed." He turned, re-entered his miraculous flier, and flew away.

Their audience looked at Ronar quizzically, then broke up. Ronar walked away quickly, feeling like an outsider and a man without a home.

Chapter 29

Patagonia

The weather was typically leaden, dreary, and cold, slightly warmer than it had been recently, but showing little sign of the approach of spring. Gomez Elizondo disliked leaving his apartment in this chilly morning fog, but there would be no sun today. Besides, today he had a job prospect, something rare enough of late. He couldn't afford to ignore a little work, much as he'd like to.

Gomez's broad-brimmed felt hat dripped with moisture as he strutted along the main street of Punta Arenas. He crossed the plaza, where the cathedral's spires vanished upwards in the fog. A few blocks more and he turned onto a side street that led toward the waterfront. The American was not staying in one of the grander hotels that catered to the few tourists who found their way here to southernmost Patagonia. The establishment he approached was used mainly by Chilenos visiting on business, military men, and locals of less than opulent means. It was a slightly decrepit stone structure of three stories. Still, Gomez had done business of various kinds here in the past.

Punta Arenas had few enough hotels; he knew them all. He also knew who he might expect to find behind the desk at this hour, which lent some spring to his stride. He swept off his hat and crossed the lobby with a grin on his face.

"Good day, Consuelo my dove. Where is the tourist? Is he rich? After I have fleeced him, I will have the money to buy you the luxuries you deserve."

Consuelo gave him a slightly pitying look. She raised a finger, on which gleamed a prominent wedding ring. "He's sitting right over there in the lobby, listening to every word you say."

"Oh." Gomez swung around, trying to recast his face into the guise of one who makes a joke. He almost started when he saw the man he had come to meet—how could he possibly have missed him on the way in? Though he sat in a threadbare armchair with a posture as rigidly upright as a mortician's, his legs sprawled out across half the room, or so it seemed. Further scrutiny dampened Gomez's hopes of quick riches. The man was unkempt, his craggy face covered with grey bristles, his grey hair sloppily cut and wild. He wore a battered green canvas jacket and leather boots that looked as if they'd walked the entire length of the Andes.

Gomez studied the man more closely. He seemed to be making an effort to appear stern and impassive, but Gomez had the feeling he was actually more unhappy, and probably arrogant. Probably this was a man who would be a pain in the ass to deal with.

Gomez considered turning around and walking out. But the man had already caught his eye. Gomez decided he must at least speak with him.

He approached the man with an uneasy smile. The American stood up in an unhurried manner. Gomez found himself looking into a face almost a foot above his own.

"Señor Ronar? I am Gomez Elizondo. I am told you are in need of a guide."

"Not a guide. An interpreter. I do not speak much Spanish. For example, I did not understand all of what you said to Consuelo."

Gomez was careful to keep his expression from revealing any guilt or uncertainty. Ronar himself revealed nothing, but remained perfectly impassive.

After a moment Gomez decided that Ronar's comprehension had included nothing at which he might take offense.

"Ah, very good. And where will you be wishing to go?"

"To the south. Into Tierra del Fuego."

Gomez chuckled. "Señor, this *is* Tierra del Fuego, or practically so. It is certainly the southernmost point where you will find many people for me to translate."

Ronar nodded. "And yet the stories I seek are to be found farther south. Surely we will find someone there to talk to."

"Yes, a few. The odd Indian, shepherd, fisherman. The guanacos are more numerous, but sadly, they do not speak." Gomez laughed at his own joke. The only response he received was a minor quirking of the corner of Ronar's mouth, and that might have been half a sneer.

"Eh—what kind of stories are you looking for?"

"Stories of strange sights. Mysteries. Lights in the sky."

"Ah—you will not be disappointed. Tierra del Fuego is full of mysteries. It is the strangest place in South America, and one of the wildest."

Was this Ronar some manner of fanatic? A UFO enthusiast? His eyes were bright as those of a prophet, and his demeanor was as wild as a woodsman's. The light in his eyes might well be the light of madness.

"Very well, then. Shall I summon a taxi to take us to the airport?"

"No need. I'll provide the transportation."

Ronar lifted a duffel bag that seemed to contain all his possessions. Without looking back he proceeded to the door. Gomez was compelled to follow. Once outside, Ronar led the way to a large, nearly new four-wheel drive vehicle parked nearby. Startled, Gomez glanced at it, then at Ronar's shabby apparel, at the cheap hotel, and back again. Ronar took note of this and finally gave up a smile, albeit a hard and ungenerous one.

"I am rich enough to pay for what I need. I prefer to spend money on things that matter."

Gomez blinked at him, once again uncertain as to his exact status with this man. He meekly got into the truck beside Ronar.

Only then did he think of his own pocket, an omission out of character for him. He turned in his seat and said hesitantly, "Señor Ronar, we have not discussed the matter of my payment..."

"I have little money," said Ronar.

Now Gomez was thoroughly confused. "But—you just said—" He struggled for a way to phrase his remark without giving offense.

Ronar fished in one of the pockets of his jacket. "I have these." He held out his hand. In it was a number of rough sapphires and rubies.

Again Gomez was careful to conceal his reaction, though he could not lift his eyes from the stones. He knew what Ronar held there, and had some idea of their worth. But perhaps the American did not—?

"Bits of colored glass, Señor?" he asked with feigned contempt.

Ronar snorted, snapped shut his hand, and looked away. "Get out," he said. Without the gems to distract him, Gomez was free to take note of those hands. They were large and powerful. Veins and tendons stood out from them like cords.

Gomez's heart hammered in his chest. "No, no, Señor, it is only a joke. I recognize the jewels for what they are."

Ronar slowly turned to silence him with his gaze. "Don't insult my intelligence again. The terms of our arrangement are these. At the end of a period of service not to exceed one month, you may select any two of these stones, assuming your service has been satisfactory. Is that acceptable?"

Gomez hesitated. "So, depending on whether you believe I have done well for you, I may get two of these excellent gems, or I may get nothing?"

"That's right."

"I must rely on your honesty in judging whether I have performed well?"

"Exactly."

"Well, Señor, I see no problem with that. Shall we go now?"

"Yes." Ronar dropped the jewels back into his pocket, where they tinkled like a handful of fairy bells in Gomez's ears. Ronar turned away and started the engine. Gomez looked at him, at his cruel face chiseled out of a cinder block. Why was he, Gomez, not at this moment on his way back to his apartment, instead of sitting here, dependent on this stranger's integrity to determine his income for the next month?

Chapter 30

The Mysterious Island

Ronar and Gomez huddled before the fireplace of the shepherd and his wife. The fire was smoky and rank, fueled by something Gomez did not wish to have named. Its meager heat was better than the cold that seeped into the hut from the howling night outside. Its fitful light cast weird shadows on the walls, the biggest and weirdest being that of Ronar, of course.

Gomez dutifully translated Ronar's questions and the shepherd's answers. They were the same questions he always asked, but this time the answers were even more nonsensical than usual.

"That island is always shrouded in fog, always. It has been years since I have seen its shores. But sometimes this fog is lit by fire. These are not ordinary fires, such as the Indians sometimes light on these remote islands. They move through the air. Sometimes they draw fiery golden lines through the air."

The shepherd raised his hand to draw a line. Gomez opened his mouth to speak, but this time he received a jolt of pain in his jaw. Again he was reminded of Ronar's cruelty, as he was a hundred times a day. A week ago Ronar had caught him trying to extract a few of the gems from the pocket of his jacket. Ronar had caught him, searched him and found the stones he'd already filched, and then had clouted him. Gomez had gamely tried to fight back, but Ronar's superior size and reach meant only another blow, one that laid Gomez out on the ground, where he looked up at Ronar with fear and resentment.

And then Ronar had helped him to his feet. "Don't do that again, you fool," he had growled.

For some inexplicable reason, Ronar had been willing to keep him on. Even more incredibly, Gomez had agreed to remain. Nor was it solely through greed for the stones, and certainly not through some futile desire for revenge. Gomez knew his limits. From what he'd already seen of Ronar, he knew what the result of any attempt at retribution would be.

Ronar was muttering a question. "Have you or anyone you know ever visited this island?"

Gomez translated it.

"No, Señor. I am not comfortable even living so close to this island. But this is the land given to me by my father, and poor as it is, I have no other place to go."

The shepherd looked about nervously, his hands twitching as if they meant to do something, but were restrained. His wife knew no such limitation. Her weathered hands flew through the sign of the cross. Her husband quickly followed her example.

Gomez looked to Ronar for the next question, but the American only regarded the peasants with that disconcertingly steady gaze of his. After a moment he stood up, filling most of the tiny room.

"Thank you for your information. It is useful." He fished around in the left pocket of his jacket and produced a lambent ruby. He dropped the gem into the shepherd's hand. "This is for your trouble." The shepherd looked at him in astonishment.

Gomez observed this exchange with extreme interest. They'd interviewed dozens of people, but this was the first time Ronar had rewarded any of them so lavishly.

"Let's go, Gomez."

Gomez followed Ronar out the door into blowing icy rain and utter blackness. Ronar walked into that darkness as if he were strolling down a sidewalk in Santiago, leaving Gomez no choice but to follow, stumbling along the rocky path as best he could, trying to keep Ronar's broad back in sight.

The deep voice came back to him against the wind.

"I think it's too dark and rough to take out our boat, Gomez. We'd better wait out the night tied up where she is."

"Si, Señor Ronar," Gomez agreed fervently. That was a relief. Another night spent in the boat's cramped, damp cabin was not to his liking, but it was better than trying to survive the open channels in the little craft. Ronar's decision was a little surprising, given the horrid weather he had already braved in a variety of fragile vehicles.

Yet as he staggered along, Gomez grew more fretful as he thought about the two they had left behind. Over and over he prepared to speak, but stopped himself at the thought of what it would mean.

At last he could not keep silent. Another few paces and he would never bring it up. "Señor Ronar. I am sorry, but there is something we must discuss."

Ronar halted, swung around, studied him.

"The shepherd and his wife—they are simple people, lacking in sophistication. They will not know what to do with that ruby you gave them. They will not know where to sell it. If they find a buyer, they will be cheated, they will not know how much to expect, they will be told it is worthless. They will have nothing to show for it. We must go back and explain these things."

After a moment Ronar nodded. "Very well. We go back." He started back the way they had come. The return trip seemed twice as long. Once Gomez tripped over a wet rock and fell hard on his left side, barely avoiding landing on his injured arm. Ronar did not even slow down. By the time Gomez found his feet he was alone. Only the faint glow of firelight now visible from the hut guided him the rest of the way.

Ronar awaited him at the door. They went in. The couple looked at them with dread, as if convinced that the strangers had reconsidered their gift and had come to reclaim it. Gomez soon reassured them. He told them where to go, how to bargain, how much money to expect for the gem. When he was finished they thanked him with grateful smiles.

Again Gomez found himself out in the cold and wet. This time Ronar did not immediately stride off into the darkness. He produced something from a pocket.

"Gomez, would you find this helpful?" It was a flashlight.

"Si, Si, gracias." Gomez took the light and thumbed it on. It projected a cone of light into the rain.

Ronar was already well along the trail. Gomez followed at his own pace, moving much more easily now.

At last he came to the tiny dock where their boat was moored. He climbed up onto the deck. Ronar was already inside the cabin, lighting a kerosene heater by the glow of a tiny wall lamp.

Without turning, he said, "That was an admirable thing you did back there, Gomez."

"Si, thank you, Señor." Yes, it had been generous. It was good of Ronar to notice. Even more noticeable to Gomez was the ever-present fishy odor of the old wooden boat. He peeled off his rain-soaked jacket.

Ronar continued. "I now have all the information I need. Our association is at an end. Tomorrow I'll take you to the nearest airstrip and send you on your way."

That riveted Gomez's attention. He scarcely dared to ask, but of course it had to be done.

"Then, Señor—has the time now come to settle our account?"

Ronar could not stand completely erect in the cramped cabin. He turned to Gomez.

"Yes. The time has come to settle our accounts."

Gomez watched, mesmerized, as Ronar's hand moved, not to the left jacket pocket where he kept the gems, but inside his jacket. Gomez's eyes bulged. He could see Ronar's fingers flexing and seeking something beneath the fabric of the jacket. He heard a click. The hand withdrew and extended toward Gomez.

The hand opened. Lying on Ronar's palm were three great flawless emeralds, each the size of a grape. Gomez goggled at them.

"Remember, only two."

Chapter 31

Possum Perturbare

The sea kayak had been bright blue before Ronar splashed it with a murky greyish paint he'd mixed up from mostly-used cans of red, green, and white. The paint didn't adhere to the plastic very well, but at least now the boat was less conspicuous than it had been.

The sea was also a murky grey, as was the air, which was opaque with a chilling fog. Ronar hunched down as he paddled the tiny craft, trying to present a minimal profile to radar or whatever other sensors might be monitoring these cold, heaving waters. It was hard to believe that any technology more advanced than the boat existed within a hundred miles of these desolate islands. Only the shepherd's tale led him to suspect otherwise...that, and his evaluation of this area as a place he himself might choose to conceal superior technology from an inquiring and hostile world.

Ronar eyed the compass mounted at the front of the cockpit. With his vision limited to less than twenty feet by the fog, it and his hearing were his only guides through these swells. A straight course should bring him to the island he believed to be the lair of Dr. Possum Perturbare. The compass should guarantee a straight course. His ears must reveal the nearness of surf which might either sweep him gently onto a cobbled beach or dash him against a wall of rock. At the moment he heard only the hissing of the waves along the hull and an occasional breaker somewhere just out of sight.

The water was turbid, cold. Ronar glanced at its silky grey surface, a boundary beneath which nothing human could live for long. Beneath that dimly-lit surface was a realm of unknown darkness. The warmer waters of Aegeos hadn't seemed quite so threatening. But then, while aboard *Dekapus* Ronar's face hadn't been just three feet above the waves, either.

Asterope.

He forgot the ocean for a moment as his eye returned to the compass. The needle was spinning. A moment before it had been pointing with good consistency, but now the needle had gone wholly adrift.

He stared at the dial, considering explanations, already convinced that this anomaly was a sign he was right about the island.

A blackness looming to the left registered in Ronar's peripheral vision. He just had time enough to snap his head around and behold a green-black hill of a wave about to crash down on his head. It did so with a roar, leaving Ronar head down in the water without even remembering being flipped. For a startled instant he looked into the green-grey gloom, seeing nothing in the few feet through which the light could filter. The water was frigid and he needed air. Remembering what he'd read in the manual he'd bought with the kayak, he wrenched himself to the side. He had to do it three times before finally righting himself. Once back in the air he gasped and coughed and roared with shock and relief.

The paddle was still in his hands. He dug the blade into the water, dragging his craft through the waves even as he realized he no longer had any way to judge his course. The compass needle still wandered. All he could do was steer to keep the waves coming in from his left, since that was the way they'd been before the compass lost its way.

He paddled on for another hour, straining his senses for any hint of change or clue to his proper course. His hair and clothes could not even begin to dry for all the spray that was blown onto them. He was cold, spared from hypothermia only by the exertion of the paddling. Even so, his thoughts grew fuzzy as his arms began to ache.

Something strange was off to the right. He squinted into the fog, trying to make out the source of the oddness that had drawn his attention. Unless he was hallucinating, it looked as if the waves were marching into some grey wall and vanishing. It was a boundary much more abrupt than the gradual concealment of the fog, though the fog made its reality more doubtful to the eye. Ronar veered a little toward it, trying to understand what he was seeing. He stopped paddling, bobbing about as he stared. His neck hairs stood up in the same way they had when he'd first sighted that other great anomaly, the Bronze Portal. The waves did not splash off this featureless grey wall, but merely passed through as if it were nothing. He made a few cautious strokes to bring himself nearer, then extended the paddle until the blade touched the greyness and entered it. When he withdrew it, it dripped water as placidly as if it had passed no boundary at all.

Ronar listened intently. He could just make out the regular beat of distant surf. Somewhere out there, land was halting the march of these waves, and he would be surprised if it were not the land he sought.

And so he turned the bow of his little boat toward that grey wall and stroked his way through it with two pulls on the paddle. There was no resistance, no sensation at all except for a momentary blurring of vision.

Things seemed no different on the far side of the boundary. Ronar shrugged in bafflement and again bent to the paddle, this time more decisively. The boom of surf grew louder, and the shriller cries of sea birds began to penetrate it. He still couldn't see more than ten feet ahead, but at least he was confident he was approaching his destination. The swells that outraced him were rearing up, beginning to peak, about to topple into foam. They began to break, sweeping him along. After a few swift seconds he was washed up on the cobbled beach he had expected. With some difficulty he pulled his stiffened legs from the kayak and dragged the little boat away from the surf.

Penguins gave grating cries that belied their comical appearance. They scuttled out of Ronar's path with obvious annoyance as he wandered over the island. Other sea birds were plentiful too, but he was not ornithologist enough to recognize any of them. Most were nesting, trying to defend the few square feet of territory they had chosen as their own.

Except for these birds the island was a barren place, cold and windswept, its vegetation limited to dry grasses and stunted shrubby growths. Ronar found no structure or sign of habitation, though with this fog he might pass thirty feet from an office tower without seeing it.

He came to an outcropping of grey lichen-stained rock and sank down on it, staring around him, wondering if all his searching had merely brought him to an empty, useless, forgotten corner of the world.

Well...only if such places were commonly surrounded by walls of inexplicable grey nothingness...or had that been nothing more than a dense patch of fog, seen through eyes addled with cold and exhaustion?

The outcropping had a niche that made a reasonable chair. Ronar pushed back into it and sat in its shelter as he looked out at the limited landscape open to his gaze. Vague shapes of fog drifted by like indistinct figures. At least here on Earth he could be sure they weren't actually ghosts. Their stately passing was hypnotic. The warmth of his little cubbyhole in the rock tempted him to sleep.

His head jerked up in sudden wakefulness. Indeed, the rock was warmer than seemed reasonable, now that he thought about it. He ran his hands over its rough surface. The stone felt as if it had been soaking up sunlight an hour before, but surely it had not. He pried up a loose flake and examined it. Tiny grains of quartz and mica glittered within it. It did appear to be real rock, at any rate.

Ronar rested his head against the stone as though he were still intent on sleeping. With his ear pressed against it, he heard a faint buzzing whine, and below that, a rhythmic thumping.

The island changed completely in Ronar's perception. The sense of being alone on a remote speck of wilderness vanished. Suddenly he felt watched.

Might as well take that nap, he thought. Now that he was convinced he had reached his goal, his tension was leaking away, replaced by weariness. Perhaps seeing him fall asleep would convince the mysterious Perturbare that Ronar did not know the truth about where he was...

Ronar awoke in a field spiky with grain stubble. It was a cool breezy day with a pale blue sky. An eddy of air sent up a little whirlwind of chaff.

Ronar sat up to find himself under the quizzical gaze of a burly man wearing denim overalls, a flannel shirt, and a baseball cap. He carried a shotgun, though he was not aiming it at Ronar, but rather holding the end of the barrels casually in one hand while the stock dug into the earth.

Ronar cleared his throat, swallowed, and said *"Buenas dias. Donde esta aqui, por favor?"*

The man answered, "I don't speak no Spanish".

Ronar stared at him fuzzily.

The man continued. "That boat you got there won't do you much good. There's no water bigger than a cow pond for fifty kilometers."

Ronar glanced to the side. There lay the sea kayak, plus his pack and other goods. He turned back and said in a subdued voice, "Where am I?"

"This'd be about ten kilometers west of Bickleigh."

"Which is where?"

"Saskatchewan. How'd you come to be on my land?"

"It seems I was kidnapped by Doctor Possum Perturbare and dropped off here," muttered Ronar.

"Yeah, well, I hear that happens. I'll be thanking you to clear out now.

"Fine then." Ronar pulled himself to his feet and picked up his pack and whatever else he had that was of any use. He raised his hand to his jacket and felt the hard cluster of lumps that was his little store of gemstones. "You can keep the kayak. Which way to the road?"

The farmer pointed.

"Good afternoon to you then." Ronar tramped off through the field, feeling the farmer's eyes on his back for some distance.

The road was narrow and deserted, lined with barbed wire on either side. Ronar didn't know which way to go, so he picked a direction at random and started walking.

"It won't be that easy, Doctor Perturbare," he vowed.

The airport was little more than a runway, a few hangars of corrugated steel, and a weathered office topped by a shack that passed for a tower. After a very long day the sun was finally approaching the horizon. At these latitudes, November nights were brief indeed. The day had been warm, but warm nights were not the rule in these parts, even now in late spring.

Ronar entered the office, letting the screen door slam behind him. A mustached man sitting behind a counter looked up from his magazine at Ronar's approach. Ronar dropped his bundle beside the counter.

"Si, Señor? Yes? How may I help you?"

"I wish to purchase an airplane," said Ronar carefully, glad to speak English.

The man's eyebrows rose. "Purchase one? I am Julio Clemente, owner of the air charter service. Here we sometimes rent out our planes for sightseeing flights. Isn't this what you mean?"

"No, I want to buy a plane."

Clemente nodded slowly and thoughtfully. "I see. You are an American? Do you know how to fly a plane? Do you have a pilot's license, either American or Chilean?"

"Of course I know how to fly a plane," said Ronar irritably. "Am I fool enough to propose to fly a plane without knowing what I'm doing?"

"No, no, of course not. Er, planes are expensive, even used airplanes in Chile."

Ronar bent down to his bundle and produced a thick sheaf of American dollars. "This is a fair price for any of the aircraft I saw out on the apron." He flipped through the stack of bills, riveting Clemente's attention.

"You may well be right, Señor. You know, you could save most of that sum by simply renting the plane. I feel obliged to point that out."

Ronar shook his head decisively. "That won't be possible. Shall we go examine the merchandise?"

"Si."

Ronar took up his bundle and preceded Clemente to the three airplanes parked just outside the charter office. "Which of these has the greatest range?"

"The Piper."

This was a twin-engine plane with underslung wings. Ronar eyed them critically and said "That won't do. How about this one?" He indicated a green single-engine Cessna.

"That plane has a cruising range of four hundred kilometers."

"That should be enough. I'll take it."

"The price is twelve thousand dollars," said Clemente firmly, yet with some evident trepidation.

Ronar nodded. "Fair enough. I'd like it fueled and serviced for immediate departure."

"Certainly." Clemente waved over a man from one of the hangars and put him to work. "If you'll return to the office, we'll complete the transaction." Back inside, he said, "I'll need some information to complete the receipt and transfer the title of ownership. Could I see your license and identification please?"

"How much did you say your price was?" asked Ronar. "Fourteen thousand?" He held Clemente with a steady gaze.

Clemente paused and returned the look. "On second thought," he said slowly after a while, "maybe it will be best if my name is not associated with whatever business you may have. Let us keep this exchange on an informal basis."

"Very well. Fourteen it is." Ronar gave over the money. "Now, if you think the plane is ready to go, could you come out and start it up while I stand nearby? I want to see how the engine sounds."

Clemente shrugged; they returned to the apron. Clemente climbed inside and started the engine without difficulty. He looked expectantly at Ronar, who walked over and boomed out "Leave it running. I'll be leaving at once."

"Bueno." Clemente climbed out and shook Ronar's hand. He bent down and unchocked the wheels, then set off for his office without looking back.

Ronar tossed his bundle onto the second seat, climbed into the tiny cockpit and squeezed into his seat. He wrestled the harness into place, then unzipped a pocket on the side of his duffel bag and pulled out a slim pamphlet. This he opened to a diagram of the instrument panel of a typical light plane, sliding it partly beneath the duffel so it would stay open.

He compared the diagram with the instruments and controls before him, checking them off in his mind. The layout was not identical, but close enough, and thankfully he could ignore the radio and navigational instruments for this mission.

He dared not linger too long or Clemente might come out wondering what was wrong. Taking a deep breath, Ronar put his hands on the yoke and his feet on the rudder pedals. He released the brake, causing the flimsy plane to lurch. Then he very gingerly pulled out the throttle, listening as the engine's growling stutter grew louder. The plane began to move. So far so good.

He spied the windsock, standing out stiffly along the runway. "Take off into the wind," he muttered. He reached the narrow taxi way and heeled the plane over. It didn't turn quite as readily as he'd expected, and he veered out briefly into the runway. He overcompensated trying to bring it back on course, and wobbled back and forth until at last he was moving beside the runway in the correct direction. A cold sweat ran beneath his jacket. His heart was thudding. He pressed his lips together and stared out through the windshield.

Reaching the end of the runway, he closed the throttle and inched out, trying to line up with the strip, which now seemed about as long and wide as a grade school ruler. An unsettling feeling of unreality was coming over him.

"Flaps, flaps," he said, looking around for the crank and lowering them. He stared down the runway. The sun was setting a bit to its right. There were no more excuses for delay.

Asterope.

He opened the throttle with one long pull and immediately came close to veering off the runway as the plane surged ahead. He checked that and turned back, overcompensating again. By now the plane was rolling so fast he didn't dare make any more wild corrections for fear of flipping the plane. Having no other choice, he kept it straight, clenching his teeth as the plane ran off the runway and onto the grass beside it. These planes were built to fly off unprepared fields...or so he kept telling himself. At least he was past the hangars and all other large obstacles. As he rattled and jounced along he kept a blurred eye on the airspeed indicator. When it showed sufficient speed, and he spied a cluster of six-foot termite nests not too far ahead, he pulled back on the yoke. The plane instantly left the ground. "Not too steep! Don't stall!" yelled Ronar to himself. He pushed forward a notch, half convinced that the move would send him into a nosedive. But the plane continued to climb, and the airspeed did not fall into the danger zone.

He was flying an airplane.

First he struggled to maintain a level altitude, using trial-and-error and a novice's understanding of balancing throttle and elevators against each other. He cranked up the flaps, which introduced more instability, sending him rising and plunging all over again. The trim tabs had something to do with this, he knew, but he hadn't troubled to learn about them in detail.

Once the altitude was under control he gingerly banked to the left, trying to line up on the course he had plotted. He kept the yoke turned until the plane's roll and rate of turn struck him as excessive, then returned it to its neutral position. He watched the compass dial swing around as the plane approaching the desired heading. Having reached it, the plane of course kept right on yawing around for a considerable distance. Cursing, he banked right, this time anticipating his course and reversing the controls just before reaching it, trying to level the wings on the right heading. He overshot again, but not so seriously this time. Like a pendulum slowly coming to halt he gradually closed in on his course and finally settled on it.

His hands gripped the yoke so tightly that they ached. His jaw was tense and his shirt soaked with sweat. Landing, he knew, was considerably more difficult than taking off. Luckily, that was a challenge he need not face on this trip.

Once he quit wrestling with the controls, he found that the plane tended to fly straight and level almost of its own accord, which was a blessing. He was free to look out at the wild patchwork of islands and channels below him, painted in shades of purple and steel blue by the twilight. He'd lingered here for weeks waiting for such a fine day. In no season of the year was the Land of Fire habitually sunny and mild.

The luminaries of the far southern sky began to appear in the deep purple sky. These were stars he had studied well in the last few weeks. Crux and Alpha and Beta Centauri were almost dead ahead, the Southern Cross pointing like an arrowhead at the south celestial pole. Orion hovered upside down in the east, while Sagittarius did its somersaults on the western horizon. Ronar nodded with satisfaction.

His airspeed was 150 knots. He had about a three hour flight ahead of him. The sky would grow no darker. At this time of year this latitude knew no true night.

He saw no lights below...nothing but treeless islands set in an intricate network of glinting waters.

His instruments went awry two hours into the flight. The compass spun as before, while even the altimeter and climb indicators began to behave erratically. He kept his nerve and was not misled into making wild corrections for a condition that didn't exist.

The stars, of course, remained where they were supposed to be, quite enough to guide him on his way.

A few minutes later Ronar spied something on the horizon that made his spine tingle. Rising up just a bit west of the plane's course was a low, soft shield of luminosity colored by the residual sunset glow that marched along the southern horizon. As he approached it resolved into a fog bank, shedding shreds and streamers of itself for miles downwind. This isolated mass of fog was the only one visible in all the miles he surveyed. Ronar nodded again. It was a little off his course, just north and west of another island of similar size, but his erratic takeoff and shaky steering might easily have resulted in a few miles of error by now. Later he would thank Perturbare for marking his island so unmistakably. He turned the plane a few degrees, now confident enough to do it without going greatly astray.

A push on the throttle reduced engine power enough to put him into a shallow descent. Nothing rose up out of the fog to stop him. He released the controls, undid his harness, and pulled the parachute out of his duffle, shrugging into it with difficulty in the cramped cabin, cautious for fear of bumping the controls. He snapped the buckles just as the edge of the fog bank passed beneath him. With no time for doubts or even thought, he flung open the door and tossed himself blindly into the wind. He yanked the ripcord so fast that the parachute almost fouled the plane as it opened. The parachute opened and Ronar watched as the plane continued on its way, pilotless, door blown shut again. So much for his brief career as a pilot and an aircraft owner.

With a peculiar clarity of vision, Ronar scanned his surroundings as he descended toward the fog. He recognized the shore from which he had once set out in his kayak. The island nearest the fog looked familiar. He turned back to the plane just in time to see it plow into the waves. The drone of its engine fell silent a few seconds later. It was a sad waste, but a necessary one.

The fog was now just below. Only as he entered it did Ronar realize he wouldn't be able to see the ground until the last second, too late to prepare for a safe landing. The island could rear up and swat him with just an instant's notice.

Only then did he recall having seen the pond set in the angle of a V-shaped ridge on that nearby island. He'd seen it, and indeed sat beside it, as he explored Perturbare's island. He'd been tricked.

A grey shifting surface appeared below him. He tensed, and an instant later plunged into icy grey seawater. He had not taken a breath. The parachute settled over the water above him. Its lines drifted down, entangling him as he struggled to free himself. He kicked to the surface, but the parachute clung to the waves and to his face, preventing him from taking a breath. He was forced under again, dragged down by the lines, his diaphragm locked by main force of will, lest he cough and drown at once.

The lines and canopy of the parachute were a mare's nest. Ronar managed to tear himself out of the harness. Given a minute's use of his hands he might have freed himself completely, but now a minute seemed as vast a barrier as the thousands of light-years between himself and his adopted home world. His vision went dim, grey, then red, then orange.

Orange?

Something bumped him in the back. The bump became a steady pressure, pushing him forward, then up when he was clear of the parachute. His head broke the water; he convulsed with gasping and coughing. A shape slid along his side. Ronar grabbed it with the heedless desperation of all drowning victims. It was smooth, rubbery, and very warm, which was welcome because this water was frigid enough to stiffen his limbs in minutes. It surged forward, carrying Ronar along with it. It was a dolphin. Or rather, it was something dolphin-like, for its flukes did not move as it slipped along. Was that a faint orange glow trailing in the water?

The most inarguable sign that his rescuer was some sort of device was the cloying little ditty it kept singing, something about Flipper, King of the Sea.

Gritting his teeth, Ronar allowed himself to be swept along by the mock cetacean. He looked it in the eye. It looked back. Someone, he knew, was looking at him through that glossy orb.

"Perturbare. Quit playing games with me. I must speak with you. You are needed for a greater purpose than these juvenile stunts."

There was no answer. Ronar's jaw ached with the effort of keeping his teeth from chattering. Finally he just let them chatter. He concentrated on staying conscious in the icy sea rather than chatting with this dolphin-shaped torpedo.

Ronar eventually felt a pebbly bottom rise up and brush his belly. He tried to get to his feet, but his legs were numb. The dolphin lifted smoothly out of the water, hovering. It closed its conical teeth on his belt and dragged him out of the water, lifting him, flying as serenely as a tiny blimp.

When they were beyond the reach of the surf the dolphin gently lowered Ronar to the beach and then settled down beside him. It had a small cask slung around its neck like a cartoon St. Bernard. Ronar grabbed it, opened the little stopcock and sucked down a hot liquid that might have been mildly alcoholic but mostly seemed to consist of heat and sugar. The dolphin itself grew quite warm, radiating so much heat that for Ronar it was like huddling near a fireplace. He studied its glassy eye in silence, trying to read its silly, permanent smile.

"Please," he muttered. "Don't keep me alive just to torture me. For mercy's sake, turn off that music."

The rescue dolphin fell silent, but its gaze retained a merry twinkle. Ronar raised his hand and moved it back and forth near the eye. Reflections shifted within it as it focused to follow the movement.

"Doctor Perturbare," said Ronar in a steady, measured voice. "Brainchild. Whoever is listening. Please don't repel me again. I am Leonard Ronar. I have something to discuss with you, something which is potentially vital to you and to the Earth as a whole."

The robot made no reply. Ronar waited, considered, and then added, "I'm related to Ben Raintree. Ask him if I'm someone who should be ignored." He hated to bring Ben into this, but he could think of no other way to augment his credibility.

Still the dolphin was silent, giving not even a squeak or a whistle. Ronar did not trouble to cajole it anymore. After a while his clothes were dry and his limbs thawed out. The dolphin lifted off, floated out over the sea, submerged, and was gone.

Ronar stood up and looked out over the waves. Perturbare's island was fully revealed. This rare visibility of the forbidden island seemed like mockery.

He looked out that way for awhile, then turned and walked inland.

Ronar had grown so familiar with Punta Arenas that he had a favorite restaurant. It was a modest, slightly shabby place, more so even than most restaurants in what was truly a modest city. It was poorly lighted, filled with the clatter of dishes and the smell of greasy food. It was a hangout for odd, disreputable-looking characters, which was why Ronar felt comfortable there.

He took a table in a corner beside a tall window streaked with grease and dust, where he sat staring moodily out at the waterfront. The waiter, a grinning black-haired man wearing an eye patch, came to take his order. Ronar carefully pronounced a few Spanish words from the menu and resumed his thoughts as the waiter retreated, nodding and chuckling. The man's eye patch reminded Ronar of Asterope, further blackening his mood.

Ronar had exhausted his ideas for reaching the island. He had been repelled by sea and by air. He wasn't up to walking on water. He had no submarine, no underground burrower, no robot dolphins, no teleporter, nothing that might evade Perturbare's watch over his island. Where did that leave him?

The waiter returned carrying a tray. He set down a plate of fish, then contrived to spill a bowl of seasoned rice in Ronar's lap.

Ronar glanced up sharply at the man, who grinned even wider, revealing gleaming white teeth beneath a black mustache. His one black eye twinkled. "Oh, sorry, Señor, I have been clumsy all day, let me clean you up, I'm sure the rice is hot," he rattled. He started fussing around Ronar's lap with a napkin, succeeding in doing little except pushing clumps of rice into Ronar's pockets. Ronar sprang up and snatched away the napkin, causing the waiter to jump back like a cat. He brushed the rice onto the floor and pointed to another table.

"That table. Bring more rice."

"Si, Señor." Ronar stood aside while the waiter transferred the fish and set down the remaining dishes. At last he was left in peace.

The island. He was forced to admit defeat. He had found Perturbare's hideout, and even paced its shoreline, but he'd found no access to Perturbare himself. If he were ever to speak with the man, he must somehow give him a reason to want to speak with him.

A day-old newspaper lay on the next chair. Ronar picked it up and guessed at the headlines on the front page. One of them referred to Possum Perturbare. From what he could make of the story, it seemed the prankster had bent his extraordinary technology to seeding American grocery stores with turkeys modified to get up and walk around when placed on Thanksgiving tables. Ronar snorted. What was the man's purpose in life? Americans were outraged, as they usually were by Perturbare's deeds. Ronar could not restrain a grudging grin as he glanced through a recap of earlier incidents. The article did not indicate that anyone in Punta Arenas thought of Perturbare as a local phenomenon.

The waiter returned with a fresh bowl of rice. Ronar flinched away, but the man set it down successfully. He glanced at Ronar's paper and said, "Ah, that Doctor Perturbare. He is a real *cut off,* isn't he?"

"That's *cut up,*" growled Ronar. He forked up some of the rice, chewed it. It took some seconds for the full impact of its searing spicy heat to register on his senses. He strangled, choked. For a tenth of a second he debated reaching for a napkin, but that would take too long. He spit the rice all over the table and sluiced his throat with icewater. Once again he had to stare down the other patrons who had watched his performance.

"Too hot for you, Señor?" asked the waiter genially. His one black eye glittered.

"Waiter, what is your name?"

"Roberto, Señor."

"Well, Roberto," said Ronar slowly, patiently. "You will please bring me something that a living man may safely eat."

Roberto nodded agreeably. "Very good, I will bring you rice that could be fed to an infant."

Ronar stared blackly ahead, oblivious to his surroundings until a third bowl of rice landed in front of him. He looked up, but the man who had set it there was not Roberto, but a different waiter who apologized to him in embarrassment.

The rice proved edible, and Ronar was finally able to eat his meal in peace. His train of thought about how to speak with Perturbare was demolished.

When he finished his dinner he stalked out of the restaurant and wandered morosely along the waterfront, where fishing boats were beginning to straggle in for the night.

"Hola, Señor."

Ronar turned to the source of this cheerful voice. There sauntered Roberto the waiter, no longer dressed in a waiter's whites, but wearing crisp black slacks and a pearl-grey jacket.

"You seem like a man who could use a guide. What is it that you seek?"

Ronar stared at this man, a head shorter than himself, pale of skin, his thick black hair brushed back stiffly.

A conviction appeared from some intuitive corner of Ronar's mind, coming to the forefront plain and insistent.

"I'm looking for you, I think," he said.

Roberto nodded, smiling. "And here I am," said Perturbare. He folded his arms over his chest and held Ronar with an amiable, if challenging, gaze.

"So," said Ronar. "You...work as a waiter?"

"Only when it suits me. It's easy to arrange, since I own the restaurant. My base is pretty isolated. I like to get out sometimes and mingle. I've driven a cab. I own a campground in Pennsylvania, and sometimes I go there to hobnob with the hobbits who show up there. Things like that."

"I am—"

"Yes, Leonard Ronar, we know. Born in Colorado, November 17, 1918. Discovered a minor comet at age twelve. Winner of the gold medal in cross country skiing at the 1936 Winter Olympics, bronze medal in archery in the summer games of that year. Visited Nazi Germany during the war under strange circumstances. PhD in astronomy from Cal Tech, 1952. Joined the faculty of the University of

Arizona in 1954. Disappeared in 1959, few reliable sightings since then. Remarkably well-preserved for your age. You seem to operate a private observatory somewhere, but even we don't know where. Well, not really."

Ronar stood blinking. "We?"

"Oh yes. There's a third party in this conversation; let me introduce you. But let's walk. I don't want to attract too much attention."

Ronar paced at Perturbare's side as he was led away from the water into little-traveled side streets. As they went, Perturbare reached up and peeled off his eye patch, revealing a perfectly good blue eye. Somehow both eyes were now the same bright shade.

"Why the eye patch?" asked Ronar.

"Oh," said Perturbare, studying it. "There's sort of a tradition that gods who wander among mortals must wear eye patches." He appeared to be completely serious about this. "Also, there's a camera in it. See this little sequin?" He held it up for Ronar's inspection. "That's a lens. Anyway..." he stuffed the eye patch into a pocket and withdrew a small white box, smaller than a paperback book. It had a bulging fisheye lens and a tiny screen. "I'd like you to meet Brainchild One."

A bright, youthful voice emerged from the box. "Hello, Dr. Ronar, I'm pleased to meet you."

Ronar goggled at the tiny device. "That's your computer? Your sentient computer?"

Perturbare laughed and shook his head. "Oh, no, no. Brainchild is compact, but not this tiny. Not yet. This box is just a wireless communicator. I carry one all the time. Someday everyone will have something like this in their pockets, only they won't be as smart as mine." He clipped it to his jacket, where it could, Ronar presumed, keep an eye on things.

"I see." Ronar gazed at the box, but did not think to return the computer's greeting. "And how is it that you know so much about me? Did you ask Ben about me?"

Perturbare laughed. "Your cousin? No…I don't have much inclination to chat with him, or with anyone in that club of his. I suppose knowing you were related to him might have led me to take you more seriously." He shrugged. "We watched your admirably sneaky, he-man attempts to storm my island. Brainchild analyzed your steely brow, your brick-like chin, and your smiling face popped up in some old records. Plus a few recent ones. Brainchild has access to every networked computer in the world. He practically owns them. The FBI has an old file on you, did you know that? It's not active anymore though."

"After your repeated rebuffs of my efforts," said Ronar grudgingly, "what inspired you to approach me now? And why those damn tricks in the restaurant?"

Perturbare guffawed. "Oh, you didn't like the service? I wanted to test you, to see how such a stern-eyed rascal would react to provocation from an average shmoe like Roberto. You did all right, though I did feel my eyebrows crinkling from your frosty stare. As to why I'm here…" Another shrug. "Curiosity. Your story is unusual, even among the many who are trying to track me down. Respect for your tenacity. The stirring sight of your scowling face as you tried to keep that poor little plane on course to my fog patch." At that his eyes wandered away from Ronar's face. He broke out into laughter, then composed himself again.

"Sorry. By the way, how did you figure out where to look for me?"

It was Ronar's turn to shrug. "I asked myself...where in this hemisphere would I go if I wished to stay hidden, in solitude? I guessed right."

Perturbare nodded. "Hmm. Intuition, brawn, and rugged good looks all in one package. You are indeed blessed. So what do you want with me?"

Ronar said firmly, "You may find this hard to believe. For the past thirty—"

"-odd years you've been living on a distant planet in the Ursa Minor Dwarf Galaxy, and all that," finished Perturbare.

Ronar's jaw dropped. "How do you know that?"

Perturbare snorted. "Your friend Stanley Cohen talked about it in range of a computer with a microphone."

"I see." Ronar felt relief. For a moment it had seemed as if Perturbare were some kind of omniscient watcher over his affairs, almost as if he too had access to Colibdis. Could he? There was something oddly familiar about the man. "And do you credit any of that story?"

"Well, hmm," said Perturbare. "You don't strike us as the kind of man who goes around ranting about his delusions. You're more the type who keeps his delusions to himself. Considering some of the events on Earth of the past few years, I don't dismiss your story out of hand. But I do require some evidence, if for some reason you want me to be convinced. How do you get to this planet of yours?"

Now Ronar was on the verge of a commitment that would be difficult to revoke. To do what he had set out to do, he must reveal his most precious secret to this mischievous renegade, whom he had met just half an hour before. Normally he would never have done so, but here he was a supplicant, with no leverage over this man, no way to hope for his cooperation other than through his good will.

"I've never revealed this to anyone before," he said soberly. "In southern Arizona is a portal, a gateway, between this world and that. I don't know how it works or who built it, but I believe it's some kind of a topological anomaly, a multi-dimensional object of some sort."

"Hmm. Are you prepared to show me this thing?"

Ronar hesitated again.

"Yes. If need be."

"All rightey then. We'll leave it at that for now. But tell me, why should I care? Your story is all fine and dandy, but what has it got to do with me? My concerns are here on good old Earth."

And what concerns are those? Ronar almost asked. Instead he said, "Colibdis is distant, but that doesn't mean events there cannot affect those here on Earth. Even without the connection of the Portal, they are connected by being in the same universe."

"And...?"

Ronar stared into that bright, quizzical gaze. This was the moment he had most dreaded. Possum Perturbare might be an odd sort of rascal, but he was clearly a man of science and rationality. Now he must hear the fundamental fact about Colibdis—that it was infused and informed by magic. Ronar remembered the extreme discomfort he had felt at his own immersion in that chaotic force, his own reluctance to accept it and fit it into his view of the universe. He had integrated the knowledge over the years, but it had been a painful process. How would it sound to this consummate technologist?

He felt his mouth twist as he forced himself to say the words. "I will make some assertions and then I will explain them as best I can. Colibdis is dominated by something which is effectively magic, and is called that by its inhabitants. It also has many gods, like those of ancient myth. One of them, called Ahriman, is a dangerous mind who plans to extend his influence throughout the universe. He must be stopped."

"My goodness!" said Perturbare, wide-eyed. "Well, that does sound serious."

"Don't patronize me," growled Ronar in discomfort.

"I'm not. Not yet. Is this magic magic-magic, or is there some explanation for it?"

"I believe there is an explanation, or at least a description. I believe Colibdis is surrounded by a zone of space which has been somehow altered in a fundamental way. In that space, minds are more firmly and directly connected to the underlying quantum structure of reality. Using formalized systems of symbols and spells, which serve to define and limit the effects they achieve, magicians there are able to influence that reality. I know this sounds absurd to you—"

"Nope," said Perturbare flatly.

Again Ronar was quelled by his interruption. "No?"

"No, not at all. You may not have studied physics since the fifties, but things have changed. I have a different view of such things than anyone could have had back then. Half my inventions wouldn't work if it weren't for the manipulation of quantum effects. No, your story is oddly plausible, but that doesn't mean I believe it. Tell me more."

Ronar described the notions that had first come into his mind while he was chained to a wall in a torture chamber in the city of Nartar. He did not describe the setting that had forced these thoughts into his mind.

When he had finished, Perturbare nodded thoughtfully. "That's very interesting indeed. You've obviously given this a lot of thought. Assuming all this is true, what's the danger again?"

"The so-called god Ahriman. It has always sought to expand that sphere of magic to encompass the universe. There are other gods who oppose this, but Ahriman is always striving to overcome or circumvent those restrictions. And this is the cleverest god of them all. It is a non-corporeal mind, a spirit or presence that is somehow coded into space itself. If it succeeds in its aim, magic will be everywhere. The universe will be ruled by a kind of chaos which will permit any sufficiently disciplined and ordered being to do pretty much whatever it wishes. Any unordered mind, any tinkerer or dilettante in magic, will destroy himself or do worse mischief. Ahriman itself would be imminent in the very shape of space, everywhere, all-seeing as it only wishes to be now."

Perturbare pursed his lips wryly. "Very dramatic."

"Yes, I know," snapped Ronar. "Believe me, I'm not disposed to hyperbole. If I didn't know this thing so very well, I wouldn't be here now."

Perturbare held up his hands. "Okay, settle down, big fella. And why *are* you here at all? Why aren't you back there on that planet, plotting your campaign against this god? What do you want with me?"

Ronar glanced around at the two-story houses on the narrow street, their windows dark. "The whole story is a long one. I'd rather not give it standing on this street corner."

"Fair enough. Come with me."

They marched up the street, toward the bleak hills just west of town. The houses began to thin out, but still Perturbare paced on up the slope.

"Do you mind if I ask you a question?" asked Ronar as they walked.

"Spill it."

"You—seem pretty amiable for a man who goes to such lengths to preserve his privacy. You went to unusual lengths to keep me off your island. Tell me, once it was clear I knew your secret, why did you treat me so gently, when I might have revealed your location to the world?"

"Well, I had intended to lobotomize you and wipe the memory centers of your brain, of course. But Brainchild convinced me you were a minor risk at worst. Let's let him explain. He does it so much more succinctly than I."

The box clipped to Perturbare's jacket piped up. "Dr. Ronar, my study of you has led me to believe you would not reveal a secret which gives you an advantage over others. Assuming your story of Colibdis to be true, you have zealously guarded your knowledge of it for many years. You declined to reveal much information even to your own cousin. You mentioned the planet to your old colleague, but you did not reveal your means of access to it, nor did you really expect to be believed. You show a pattern of extreme self-reliance. Therefore I too am curious about your motivation for coming to us now."

Perturbare smiled easily. Ronar looked at the box, considered a response, but found none worth making.

They reached the crest of the ridge, stepped over it, and saw no work of man for miles ahead except for some fences and a distant road.

"Brainchild, bring down the flyer," said Perturbare.

"It's on its way."

Perturbare looked up, and Ronar followed his gaze. Seconds later a gleaming shape plummeted into view, slowed dramatically, and settled to a silent hover just in front of them. Ronar marveled at it. It was unlike any machine he had ever seen. Its gleaming white surface was flawless, unmarked. In overall shape it was like a fluid hourglass, wasp-waisted, with smoothly-sculpted lobes or pods fore and aft. The forward pod's lines were broken only by a tinted bubble canopy mounted on a bright metal bezel. At the back of the aft pod was a great faceted lens, barely aglow with an orange light.

"What a wondrous thing this is," said Ronar without thinking.

Perturbare beamed, evidently proud. "Oh, you like this better than your little airplane? It does have a bit of style, doesn't it?"

Ronar put out his hand and touched the rear lens. The glassy, knobby surface was barely warm. "This looks like nothing more than a huge brake light. How does it produce any thrust?"

Perturbare chuckled. "Well, that's one secret I'll keep under my hat until I've heard some more of yours. Open her up, Brainchild."

The canopy rotated into the forward pod. Perturbare hopped over the lip and took one of the two seats behind the console. Ronar swung his long legs in and sat down beside him. The seat whirred faintly as it reconfigured itself to accommodate his size. The console before him glowed with precision, control, and information. The canopy closed again, encasing them in silence and a faint complex scent he couldn't identify. To Ronar it was the smell of technology. For the first time in his life, Ronar found himself envying another man's possessions.

"Take us straight up to 200,000 feet and hover," said Perturbare casually.

Ronar immediately felt himself pressed down into his seat as the ground dropped away. He might as well be falling up. The main propulsion beam could contribute nothing to this level ascent, Ronar realized. This was the work of whatever smaller thrusters were hidden in the fuselage.

When the acceleration ceased, Ronar found he could see the whole southern tail of South America, plus the hazy whiteness of the Antarctic ice shelf to the south. The edge of night was a diffuse blackness just to the east, creeping closer as he watched. The sky was black. The sun's glare, filtered by the canopy, prevented any glimpse of the stars, but presently the sun would be gone from sight.

The flyer hovered effortlessly at the edge of space. Not that mere immersion in the atmosphere of a planet actually removed one from "space," reflected Ronar...

He came back to himself at Perturbare's prompting. "I'm glad you appreciate the view. Now...you were saying?"

Ronar took a deep breath, marshaled his thoughts, and commenced a concise account of the nature of Colibdis, the conflict of the gods, Ahriman's mysterious residency on the errant lesser moon, Ronar's campaign against him, Varanu's apparent treachery, Ronar's expulsion from the planet, and almost everything else of potential relevance to his mission on Earth.

When he had finished, Perturbare looked at him mildly and said, "And you, of all men, are such a threat to these gods that they would trample the planet to force you to leave?"

Ronar felt his ears burning with embarrassment. "I've told you what happened, and nothing more," he said stiffly.

Perturbare nodded. "And you want me to come to this world, supply you with technology, and assist you in bringing your war against this god, to his moon."

"Exactly."

Perturbare's expression, which had been benign and neutral, suddenly sharpened, though his posture remained casual. "This is a really good story you've spun here. As far as I can tell it's internally self-consistent, with lots of good details. But—even if I saw any reason why I should involve myself in this—any reason why I should walk away from my affairs here, exposing myself to all these dangers—the fact remains that I don't believe a word you've said."

Ronar's jaw dropped in incredulity. His thoughts seemed enveloped in a white haze. He could not recall another time when anyone had ever doubted his word. It was almost beyond his imagination that anyone might think him a liar. "How can you say that?" he asked a little hoarsely.

Perturbare made an impatient gesture. "Because the whole story is just so perfect for you, just so flattering. A lonely, alienated astronomer finds a magic doorway to a world where everyone's so overwhelmed by his good qualities that, after many stirring adventures, he practically takes the place over. So formidable is our hero that even the gods quail before him. Only he can save the world from their threat! And so he is cast out, reappearing on Earth after a long absence, now a shiftless wanderer."

Perturbare's eyes blazed at him challengingly. "Maybe it's more plausible that you've *been* a shiftless wanderer all these years, ever since you had your breakdown and wandered off from your job on Kitt Peak. Maybe you really believe these delusions, really do think of yourself as this sword-and-sorcery astronomer. Anyone might believe it to look at you. You certainly have a prophetic fire in your eye. But I've met delusional megalomaniacs before. I'm at least the latter myself, so I recognize the breed. They often concoct glamorous back stories to explain their present poor circumstances. And stop clenching those meathooks of yours, buddy boy. Do you see these little lenses here and there?" He flipped a finger about, indicating small glassy protuberances scattered throughout the cockpit. "They contain zappers that will slice you into geometric shapes if you get belligerent with me, and that would really stink up the cockpit and ruin the upholstery."

Ronar shut out his words, forcing himself to relax. The futility of his outrage was manifest; he must choke it down. Eyes closed, head back, he spoke, each word toneless and carefully enunciated.

"In the first place...as you admitted, I was born in 1918. Do I look my age to you?"

"No, more like forty-five, or maybe fifty. You're very well-preserved, as I said. You don't seriously think that means I believe you have a magical anti-aging spell, do you?"

Ronar swallowed.

"In the second place...I carry a small sack of valuable gems in my pocket. Is that something a wandering lunatic would be carrying?"

"It happens more often than you might think that wandering lunatics carry money or goods that they don't use. They often don't trust currency and prefer gold or jewels. I happen to know you have another cousin, one who collects and deals in gems. Your little hoard could be a sign of his affection for you."

Brainchild spoke up then. "Doctor, recall that when I analyzed the gems I found they have unusual isotopic compositions."

Ronar found himself appreciating the computer more and more.

Perturbare waved this off. "Yes, yes. Extraordinary claims require extraordinary proof, blah blah blah. It's not enough." He fixed Ronar with his bright blue eyes again. "Do you have any proof? An indisputably alien artifact, or any knowledge to prove your claims?"

Ronar's thoughts raced. He had by now discarded and replaced most of what he'd brought over from Colibdis, which had been little enough. Short of offering samples of his own flesh for isotopic analysis, he could think of nothing.

"No."

Perturbare shrugged and turned away.

"Yes."

Perturbare turned back, curious.

"Do you know anything about the Ursa Minor Dwarf Galaxy?" asked Ronar.

"Hell no."

Ronar irrelevantly noted a touch of a New York City accent in this statement. "Then let me tell you something about it. I'm sure Brainchild can correct me if I say anything wrong. The galaxy is barely worthy of the name. It's a thin, ancient scattering of a few thousand tired old suns, mostly red and white dwarfs and red giants. There should be no young suns there. But Photos, one of the stars of the Colibdian binary, is an F-type main sequence star, a bit brighter and hotter than our sun. At two hundred thousand light years away, no telescope on Earth should be able to detect it. But maybe you can. Maybe with your technology you can locate the pair, and know I must be speaking the truth."

Perturbare drummed his fingers on the armrest of his seat. "I'm no astronomer. Brainchild? What do you think?"

"I find no flaw in Dr. Ronar's reasoning. We have no dedicated astronomical instruments, but we could use one of our spy satellites to search for the pair. Dr. Ronar, what is the maximum separation of the two stars?"

"About fourteen million miles."

"That is an angular separation of only .002 arc seconds at this distance. We will not be able to resolve the binary."

Ronar thought furiously. "But you can separate the spectrum of an F-type star from that of a carbon star? I can tell you about where to look in the galaxy for the binary. Can you distinguish them like that?"

"Yes, our instruments can be adapted to that purpose."

"Very good." Ronar turned to the very slightly smiling Perturbare. "Let's fly over to one of your satellites and take a look."

The smile quirked up into perplexity. "Fly over...? Oh, you don't understand. There's no eyepiece on these things.

It'll collect the data under Brainchild's direction and send it to us."

"Oh. Of course." Ronar was too excited about the prospect of making some progress to be embarrassed by his mistake. He defined the area that Brainchild must search and estimated how bright a star to expect. "Brainchild, how long do you suppose it will take?"

"Once I identify likely candidate stars, it will take several minutes to integrate enough light from each one to make an analysis. I have acquired the galaxy."

"Let's see it," said Perturbare lazily.

By now the sun had sunk beneath the curving rim of the world, darkening the cockpit. Ronar was too preoccupied to take note of the clouds of stars that shone beyond the canopy. His eyes were instead locked on the console's main display screen. A faint bit of mist appeared there, with only a few pallid star points marking it as anything of substance. Ronar stared at it avidly. He could not turn his head and look at the spot where that galaxy lay in the real sky, for the bulk of the Earth was in the way, but he could look at this small screen and see an image of the galaxy itself. The display zoomed in to a smaller, central area of the feeble glow. As he watched, more and more stars popped into view. Every one of them must be a familiar part of the constellations that adorned the skies of his distant adopted home. One of them, indeed, warmed that home itself. It was his first view of home in over a year, though given the distance, it was also a view as it had been two hundred millennia in the past. Ronar was grateful for the darkness of the cockpit, for if a tear escaped to trickle down his cheek, Perturbare was not likely to notice it.

A cursor flickered over the screen, settled on one of the medium-bright stars for a few minutes, then flicked on to the next. Ronar watched in fascination.

Some time later a discordant buzzing sound came to his ears. He twisted his stiff neck to look at Perturbare, who lay back in his chair, snoring, his mouth agape. Ronar dismissed him and turned back to the screen.

Over an hour later, the view on the screen drew back to show more of the galaxy. The cursor rested on stars near the edge of the frame. Ronar frowned at this, but he did not break the silence.

An hour later still, the cursor began to pick out fainter stars. Ronar's frown deepened. This could not be right. Yet again he was unwilling to speak, lest the computer give up the effort.

Ronar's tension mounted. Perturbare eventually yawned and stretched, bending to peer blearily into the display.

At that moment Brainchild spoke.

"I have found no binary system to correspond to Dr. Ronar's description."

Reality seemed to veer and waver around Ronar. No such system? "That is imposs—" he began roughly.

"However, I have located a single F-type star. Its spectrum indicates a very high radial velocity relative to the other stars of the galaxy. It appears likely to encounter a carbon star, which lies along nearly the same line of sight, about a hundred and fifty thousand years from now. At that time the two stars may enter into a mutual orbit. Of course all this is as seen from Earth; these events are in reality all deep in the past."

Ronar's jaw dropped open.

The display zoomed in to feature two widely separated points, one ruddy and one white. Ronar peered at them avidly.

"Well, well," said Perturbare softly. "I must say, that is pretty cool. But Brainchild, what are the chances that this encounter could result in a nearly circular orbit for the planet Colibdis, which presumably first orbited one of these stars? Could it enter into a stable, circular orbit around both?"

"If the encounter is by chance, the chances of such a stable outcome are remote," said the computer.

"Then it is not a chance encounter," said Ronar. "And it will happen. It did happen." Ronar's voice sounded decisive even in his own ears, but his head still spun. He had known that the Photos-Kudu star system was unusual, even anomalous, but he had never considered that the entire thing might have been engineered.

Perturbare seemed to guess his thoughts. "The work of those gods of yours?" he asked wryly.

"I don't know."

"The F-star exhibits the highest radial velocity of any main-sequence star ever recorded," said Brainchild. "It may indeed have been flung out of our galaxy by some unknown agency. The carbon star is also unusual. Its low luminosity indicates a diameter of only six to seven million miles, much less than that of any other known star of a similar spectral type. Doctor Ronar, is it variable?"

"Yes, it varies about twenty percent in brightness with a complex light curve, " said Ronar absently. He might well have sat there with his eyes glazed over in contemplation for a considerable time, but the thought of his mission reasserted itself. He gathered himself and flung a keener gaze at Perturbare. "Well then, Perturbare. Are you prepared to believe me now?"

"Yeeeaaahhhh…" he drawled. "I think so. Brainchild, is there any way our friend here could have known of these stars without having, er, visited them?"

"That is a broad question, but I would say he could not have learned of them using any conventional astronomical instrument. These stars are well beyond the grasp of any existing ground-based telescope."

"There are still more astronomical anomalies in the Colibdis system. I have data. I could show them to Brainchild." Ronar said this calmly, but the possibilities suddenly revealed to him excited him greatly.

"Hmmm." Perturbare studied Ronar for a few moments. Ronar worked to keep his face neutral.

"Well, O Great Stone Face," continued Perturbare, "how about a little visit to that island of mine? You'll be the first person ever to be both an invited and an uninvited guest."

Ronar contented himself with a nod. He had won his argument…and he hadn't needed to do it with a sword, which was always satisfying.

A mischievous grin spread over Perturbare's features. "Free fall?"

Free fall? Ronar shrugged. "Why not?"

"Brainchild, you heard the man."

And the flyer dropped. Ronar lifted out of his seat, held in by the straps alone, all sense of weight gone. The craft wasn't stable in its fall, and soon began to tumble, while Perturbare laughed and snorted and chuckled. Ronar stared at the horizon, swiveling his head madly to follow it, just to inform his inner ear that there was a reason for its disorientation.

After a few minutes of this plunge the flyer righted itself. Ronar sank back down in his seat, and then felt weight on his back as the craft surged ahead. He swiveled his seat, though his head resented this latest gyration, and looked back through the canopy. A dim beam of orange light trailed them. There was no rush of jets or roar of rockets. The vehicle skimmed along with that glow as the only sign of its passage.

He faced forward again, slumping down in that accommodating chair. He looked at Perturbare, whose hand rested lightly on a sculpted black joystick, humming happily and tunelessly, ignoring Ronar as he guided the craft, its course shown by graphical displays which even Ronar understood at once. No doubt Brainchild could fly it as well or better, but a man liked to keep his hand on the controls now and then. Ronar nodded to himself.

Apparently the trip was over already, for the flyer abruptly slowed. Ronar looked over the side, toward the dark water far below, but saw no light or shape of any kind. The flyer descended. The stars disappeared abruptly; Ronar couldn't tell if they'd entered a fog bank or penetrated a cloud deck. He turned long enough to glance at Perturbare and found him studying the displays with a relaxed air, their shifting colors tinting and shadowing his face in the darkness.

Light suddenly blazed into the cockpit. Squinting, Ronar found they were sinking into a huge cylindrical pit. He stared upward where the view was unobstructed. The top of the great shaft was already closing and already distant. Brightly-lit platforms, struts and ducts receded into the distance upward. They continued downward for at least a hundred levels. It occurred to Ronar that this was the exact opposite of Sha Totek's black tower of magic: this was a white-lit shaft of technology, extending into the earth even farther than Sha Totek's tower reached into the sky.

Their descent slowed and halted. The flyer slid in toward the wall, over and onto a projecting landing platform, and settled down. The canopy slid open, admitting cool, sharp-smelling air and a pervasive rumble and hum of unknown processes. They climbed out of the flyer. Ronar wandered over to a railing, leaning on it as he stared up and down.

Perturbare joined him there, cleared his throat, and said portentously, "Would you like to see some more of the, er, Krell wonders?"

Ronar smiled slightly. "All right, Morbius."

"A man of taste and erudition."

Perturbare waved toward a sliding door. Ronar followed him toward it.

"Rather a big place just for you, isn't it?" said Ronar dryly.

"What makes you think I live here alone?" asked Perturbare without looking back.

"Hmm. I don't know; I just assumed...all right, who lives here with you?"

"Oh, no one, it's just me."

Ronar rolled his eyes.

They stepped into an anteroom, then a ready room full of various equipment, and through other compartments until they entered a shining white laboratory full of gleaming equipment of which Ronar recognized almost nothing. He wondered how many such places there must be in this vast honeycomb.

Perturbare sat on the corner of a desk—that much at least Ronar could identify. "You said you had some data on the Colibdis system...?"

Ronar reached into his jacket and produced an envelope from an inner pocket. From it he extracted a sheaf of papers which he unfolded and carefully smoothed before handing it to Perturbare.

Perturbare flipped through the sheets, eyeing the columns of figures with interest. "Handwritten, very quaint. We'll see what Brainchild can make of this." He walked over to a slot in the wall and inserted the pages.

Whatever mechanism was within the slot whirred briefly, and Brainchild said, "The orbit of the moonlet called the Eye of Ahriman is being actively modified. Whenever the moonlet is over a certain planetary location, it receives an impulse of some kind which slows it slightly, resulting in a reduced orbital altitude. Without that intervention, tidal friction would cause the moonlet to slowly but steadily gain orbital altitude, while the influence of the larger moon would draw it away from the plane of the equator. I can provide exact figures and models if needed."

Ronar felt a blaze of triumph. So easily had Brainchild dealt with the data that had been such a strain to the astronomers of Thunderbird University. So beautifully did its analysis confirm what Ronar had believed to be the truth.

"What are the coordinates of this planetary location?" asked Ronar in a husky tone.

Brainchild read off the figures. Ronar envisioned the map of Colibdis. Only one thing was plotted near the place the computer had just specified.

"The Island of the Gods," hissed Ronar.

"Furthermore, the orbit of the moon is perfectly circular, which is itself an anomaly. Nor does it orbit the barycenter of the Colibdis/Eye system. The orbit is instead centered on another point on the planet's surface. This situation is clearly artificial."

Ronar blinked at this revelation. This was unexpected, and was even stranger than he had expected.

"What are the coordinates of the center of the moon's orbit?"

Brainchild stated them. As far as Ronar knew, this was an empty expanse of the great world ocean of Colibdis.

"Well, then, this is great," said Perturbare cheerfully. "I'm glad we could help you out, do your math for you, and solve all your mysteries. I guess now it's up to you to get back there and straighten everything out."

Ronar focused his vision on Perturbare. It must have been a bright gaze, for Perturbare wilted beneath it a little. "What are you talking about? Knowing this still doesn't empower me to do anything about it. If I return to Colibdis, the gods will likely attack me at once, or attack innocent people for my sake. And I still have no way to reach the Eye."

Perturbare waved his arms and gave an exasperated frown. "So get your sorcerer buddy to help you out! For all the *sturm und drang* of your story, you still haven't told me why I should care about something happening in your remote little clump of stars. I have important work to occupy me here."

"And what is that work?" Ronar demanded hotly. "As far as I can tell, all you do with this fantastic technology of yours is perform ridiculous pranks and thefts!"

Now it was Perturbare's turn to offer up a bright gaze. "I serve an important role! Far too many people here are complacent, fat, and lacking in imagination. Their lives proceed from birth to grave along channels dug deep in stone, by television and other media which insist that the current order is not only right, it's inevitable, and the only reasonable way to do things. I show them otherwise. I reveal the false assumptions beneath the way they live, rub their noses in their fragility and their foolishness. I introduce a much-needed element of chaos into the world. Not only to average hicks and rubes, but also to rich people who devour the world as if it were their right. Warlords, tyrants, oppressors, I put bees in all their bonnets. I am needed here. And it's all so damn much fun, too."

Ronar found himself in sympathy with this position, but brushed it off with one decisive gesture. Some other time he would be ready to listen; now he had more urgent goals. "Listen to me. There's a thing out there...a bodiless mind sitting in a bubble of twisted space the way a spider sits in its web. At any second that web might suddenly expand to encompass the universe. Then that thing could turn its vision anywhere, including right into this pit of science of yours, right into your soul. The Earth would change. Unicorns might frolic and pixies flitter in the twilight. Demons would terrify some and dragons wither others. Wizards and sorcerers would set up shop, surpassing scientists who need machines, materials, and tools, using only their minds and their hands. Anything that man has ever feared could and eventually would come true.

Churches would fall, and in their place would arise black temples lit by red flames. Worship would turn to the one god clearly manifest in the world. Self-indulgence and evil would become divinely sanctioned parts of society."

Perturbare's eyes were wide. "Even more than they are now? You almost make it sound like fun."

Ronar growled in annoyance. "Are you telling me that dealing with this threat is less important than your goal of exposing public figures who say stupid and venal things to television viewers?"

Perturbare's gaze grew sharper, more penetrating. "It's quite a scenario you create. You have an unexpected flair for language. But you still haven't told me everything, have you? You've known about this god and his evil plans from the first day you set foot on that planet of yours. That was, what, forty years ago now, nearly? In all that time you've been content to leave him alone, to trust in the other gods to keep a lid on his ambitions. It doesn't sound like anything he's done recently is really very different than anything he's tried or done before. Yet now you're absolutely set on destroying him. Why now? What has changed? What is this really all about?"

Ronar returned the gaze. He could feel his face twisting into what he knew must be an alarming scowl. He had hoped to keep what was deepest in his heart away from this inquisitive scoundrel, but now he saw that if he did, he must leave here with nothing of any real value. He opened his mouth, closed it. Finally he took a grip on himself, opened his mouth again, and forced out the words.

"There—there was a girl…"

"AH HA!" cried Perturbare. Finally we're getting to something I can relate to. Go on!"

"Her name was—is—Asterope. She was a student of mine…"

Ronar went on to tell it all: Asterope's history, her affliction, their journey, his ultimate failure to save her. As he told the tale the words came easier. He almost forgot he was speaking to another person; it was as if he were telling the story to himself for the first time. Many of the details surprised him, and as he laid out the narrative, parts of it made sense to him for the first time. By the time he got to Asterope's body being taken into the shield of Athena, and went on to tell of his ascent of Olympos, the tale was reeling out as though he were a bard, his voice deep and sonorous.

When he finished he stared into Perturbare's face.

Perturbare's eyes were bright and glistening. "And you loved her. You loved her more than you ever imagined you could love any human being."

Ronar's fist crashed down onto the desktop. His voice rang. "Yes, I loved her, and I will never rest until I have…" His words faltered. He gazed off into space, amazed at what he had just said.

Perturbare sprang up from his perch and bounced towards Ronar. He slapped Ronar on the shoulder, laughed and whooped. "True love! Rescue the damsel! Down with the tyrant! Yes! Ronar, buddy…" His blue eyes took on a fire, with nothing of ice in it. "… We're going to that planet of yours, and we're going to kick us some non-corporeal divine ass."

Ronar stared at him, his emotions too much a welter to sort out gratitude from all the rest.

Part Five
Return of Ronar

Chapter 32

Through the Portal

The flight to Arizona was slow. Ronar had insisted on keeping a low profile, which meant a winged stealth flyer, a low-powered subsonic vehicle with small propulsion lanterns mounted within to hide their telltale orange fire. It looked like a curvy black manta, with the wings also acting as radiators for the waste heat of the hidden lamps. Ronar was unwilling to risk compromising the location of the Portal with a more conspicuous vehicle.

Perturbare showed signs of restlessness during the long flight, fidgeting, asking unnecessary questions of Brainchild and looking at the displays. At last he reclined his seat and began to snore, the flyer secure under Brainchild's control as it skimmed just over the waves of the dark Pacific.

Ronar used the time to compose his mind. When he'd been ousted from Colibdis he'd had no real plan to return. He'd expected to make a new life for himself on Earth, maybe writing a book about his experiences, no doubt casting it as fiction. And yet he'd never gotten around to that. He'd persisted in behaving like someone with no other intention than to return. Now he again approached that seminal site where his life had truly begun, nearly forty years before. In the year of his exile he'd done all he could to prepare for his return. He'd made an alliance with the one man on Earth best suited to helping him.

He had no illusions. The test he was about to face might be the harshest of his long and strenuous life.

Now that the test was upon him at last, his spirit gave him the gift of a peaceful mind, at least for now. He drew that peace around himself, lay back, and fell asleep.

They came up through Mexico, settling down just at dawn, as planned, in the midst of the upright stones that stood near the Bronze Portal. The canopy slid back, admitting the air of a cool winter morning. Both men hopped out to study the anomaly of the Portal.

Ronar regarded it with his usual sobriety, but Perturbare seemed delighted with it, dancing around it, staring into all four faces, each apparently an endless tunnel, somehow coexisting in this one smallish cube with no sign of any mutual interference.

"I'd say this is a multi-dimensional object, all right," he said excitedly. "A simple tesseract, maybe. What do you think, Brainchild?"

The computer's voice came from the box clipped to Perturbare's natty white tunic, and also from the duplicate box attached to Ronar's belt. "As far as I can see, that appears to be the case."

"Ronar, I guess you're right about not taking a flyer in. Thing's barely big enough."

"It would be rash to try flying through the Portal," said Ronar, not for the first time. "It seems to be designed for creatures on foot. If we tried flying through I honestly don't know what would happen, or where we'd end up. We might punch through the wall of the thing and wind up in who knows what corner of nowhere..."

"Okay, okay, that's already decided. We walk."

Ignoring the Portal, Ronar investigated its surroundings. In the shadow of its west side he found the remains of a campfire, plus some camp garbage: foil, cans, and so forth.

"Pigs," he muttered. In all likelihood, Colibdis now had a few more Terrestrial immigrants. It had to happen sooner or later.

Perturbare was busy hauling equipment out of compartments in the flyer's wings. He extracted a small pod of lenses and vanes that looked like a 6-D camera and shook it, causing a slender tripod to fall into position. This he set down a short distance from the Portal. "Can you see and hear through this all right?" he asked it.

"I can, Doctor." This time the computer's voice came through the little watcher-pod.

Perturbare next produced a spindly antenna mounted on a broad-based tripod. This he planted just inside one of the Portal's entrances. He glanced at Ronar, who by now had wandered over to watch and to help if needed. "Well, that's all we need to do here. Let's load up and get going."

The flyer yielded up hard backpacks made of the same glossy white stuff that was so ubiquitous in Perturbare's equipment. Ronar shouldered one, a heavy, awkward load even for him, fastened the straps and buckles, and peered at the glowing button on the main buckle. He looked at Perturbare, who stood grinning at him, his own pack in place and apparently not a burden.

"Go ahead, don't be shy, press it."

Ronar pressed it. The weight of the pack abruptly all but disappeared.

Perturbare's grin persisted. "The pack's equipped with my new propulsion diodes to negate the weight. You may have arranged this to be a hiking trip, but that doesn't mean it has to be a low-tech one."

"I have no objection. Shall we go?"

"By all means."

And so they entered the Portal. Ronar trudged purposefully ahead, while Perturbare danced and turned, studying the old bronze walls while there was still light to see them. In minutes the entrance was nothing more than a blazing star in a void of blackness. Ronar heard Perturbare halt; he did as well.

"Uh…shouldn't we have brought some lights?" asked Perturbare. His voice betrayed a hint of unease.

"I never thought of it."

"Never—can't we get lost in here? Trip over something at least?"

"There's not much in here to trip over. No, I don't think it's possible to get lost. As long as you don't give up, and keep moving, you'll find your way to the other side. That's just the way the thing is built. Anyway, a light wouldn't reveal much. After the walls fall away, there's just an unlimited plane of bronze."

"Brainchild, are you still reading us clearly?"

"Yes, Doctor."

"Let us know at the first sign of any signal loss. Ronar…can we use the tether?"

Perturbare sounded so small and lost that Ronar almost laughed, but he did not. "All right. If it will make you feel better." He pulled a length of line from his pocket, clipped one end to his belt, and the other end to Perturbare's.

"Thanks. I'm going to make some lights before I try coming back this way again. Let's go, wherever the hell we're going."

They trod on. The entrance presently dropped from sight. The odor was of old dust. The only sounds were their breathing and the echoless beat of their footsteps on the bronze floor.

Perturbare stopped again. Ronar rolled his eyes and stopped too.

"I had no idea this place would be so spooky," whispered Perturbare. "It seems haunted."

"I don't know why it would be. Few people have died in here, as far as I can tell." And yet Ronar spoke in the same hushed voice.

"You're climbing." Brainchild's voice made Perturbare jump. "The air pressure is decreasing as you proceed."

"I can't even tell yet," muttered Ronar.

"Thanks, Brainchild," said Perturbare shakily. "Next time you hear us whispering, do the same yourself though, okay?"

"Of course, Doctor."

They went on, and soon the slope of the floor became unmistakable.

"Er—soon after this point, things start to become a little unnerving," said Ronar apologetically.

"They *start*...? What have they been up till now?"

Ronar did not reply. They walked on, and soon the floor was so steep that their footing became doubtful.

"Ah—this is the nasty part. We have to keep going until we eventually fall. There's no other way."

"Shit!" said Perturbare with conviction. "Well, if that's how it is, let's not pussyfoot around. Let's get it over with."

Ronar heard a breathless laugh, a few rapid footsteps, and the tether attached to his waist fell loose beside him. Perturbare ran off, his reckless laughter receding and then changing into a wail of fear that swiftly faded into silence.

Ronar stood in the now solitary darkness.

"You'd think the man was riding a roller coaster," he muttered.

"The doctor did seem rather ebullient for someone showing such clear signs of fear and stress."

This time Ronar jumped. "Yes. Are you still in contact with him?"

"I am."

"What's his status?"

"He's in free fall, tumbling wildly."

"He should have stayed with me. Let me talk to him."

Brainchild relayed Ronar's voice. Ronar guided Perturbare through his long fall, warned him to expect the reappearance of the wall/floor, told him how to skid and slide to a halt. When he was finished, Ronar heard Perturbare breathing heavily out of excitement.

"All right. Just wait there. I'll be along presently."

With greater deliberation than Perturbare had shown, yet no less decisiveness, Ronar pulled himself upwards with his long legs until the slope was too great to walk on. He crawled briefly, then let himself slip down this impossible shape which was steeper in every direction. The fall through the darkness seemed as interminable as ever. He could still hear Perturbare breathing and humming through their radio link, which lent an additional aspect of absurdity to the drop.

And then, as usual, the wall was back, slowly tilting toward the horizontal as he fell, becoming a steep slide, and gradually a floor. Eventually he came to a halt, stood up and brushed himself off.

"Perturbare...?" he whispered.

"What's that stink?" came the hissed reply.

Ronar's senses came to full alertness. This was an element new to the Portal crossing, one which immediately raised his hackles. It was a smell of rotting flesh.

"I don't know. Let's find our way out of here."

They proceeded nervously. The stench did not abate; to the contrary, it intensified until it gagged them. They heard the buzzing of a mass of flies.

"Brainchild, can you see anything?" choked Perturbare.

"No. There is a weak infrared signature three meters in front of you, but I cannot identify it."

"Now I wish I did have a light," said Ronar. "Brainchild, can you light up the screen on my box? That would be something."

"Certainly."

The screen lit up white. With their acute dark adaptation it was as good as uncovering a window on an overcast day.

The scene revealed by the glow was not pleasant. Two ragged, incomplete shapes sprawled on the bronze. Though mostly skeletal, enough flesh was left on them to feed a seething mass of maggots. Their clothes revealed them to be hikers, male and female. They lay atop spread-out sleeping bags which were soaked with the liquids of corruption. Empty food bags and water containers lay around them.

A piece of paper lay beside the female corpse. Ronar approached unwillingly, holding his breath, and plucked up the sheet. The eyeless face of the woman in its nest of red hair stared up at him.

He and Perturbare retreated from the stench and read the note by the light of the tiny screens.

I am Kay Whitley. Beside me is my fiancé Ron Blaine. We found the way out, but now it is blocked. We don't know what to do. We need water but there isn't any. We didn't tell anyone where we were going. If anyone finds this, please contact our families. Tell them we love them, that we think about them as we lay in this dark place. Tell them we love each other and are not too afraid. Goodbye and God bless you.

Ronar swallowed hard, handing the note to Perturbare. "Will you honor her request?" His voice was rough.

"I will. I guess they thought they'd found the same doorway they'd used to enter in the first place, only now it was blocked. They didn't know this thing is a two-way street."

"This is wrong. There's no reason for the exit to be sealed. Let's go find it."

"Something I need to do first," said Perturbare with unusual sobriety. "I should have thought of this before. Step away from them, and don't look directly at the light."

Ronar heard a few clicks, then an intense yellow laser beam leaped from the gun in Perturbare's hand. Flames leaped up from the bodies wherever it touched them. He drew lines of fire over them until they and their gear were a bonfire.

Ronar stared into the merciful flames. "Good idea. I wonder where those damn flies came from."

"Where don't flies go?" asked Perturbare bleakly.

The blaze lit up the interior of the Portal. Walls and a smoke-shrouded ceiling were now in sight. The entrance could not be far off. They skirted the fire, walking along what was becoming a corridor, their long shadows leaping before them.

In the lesser gravity the backpack was now trying to pull Ronar off his feet. He turned off the lift system. It looked like Perturbare already had.

"Do you feel it?" asked Ronar.

"Feel what?"

"Magic. A whisper in the air. A confusion."

There was a silence from Perturbare.

"I don't know. I feel something—but I'm not sure it's not plain old nausea."

"I wonder if the gods know I'm back already."

A faint grey glow appeared ahead, something like the afterglow of a television set which has been turned off in a darkened room. The dull clang of their footsteps on the bronze suddenly changed to the muffled crunch of dust and gravel. They were out of the Portal, on the surface of Colibdis, yet they were not free. The Portal was encased by a globe of material which transmitted very little light. They stepped up to it, gingerly touching its smooth surface. Ronar held up his Brainchild box. The sphere gave back a perfect magnified image of it.

"This looks like a mirror field," said Perturbare. "A forcefield of a type I've seen before. Very formidable. My ERASER pistol would be useless against it."

"I've known Sha Totek to seal off the Portal with such things before," said Ronar.

"Do you think your sorcerer friend has sealed it now?"

"He may have sealed it against me." Anger began to darken Ronar's words. "Or it may be the gods who have done it."

"Does your plan include a way to get us out of here?"

"No. What about your bag of tricks?"

Perturbare was visible only as a silhouette in the dimness filtering through the barrier. "I don't have anything capable of dealing with a mirror field, not even a magical one. We have a small nanoconstructor, but making things with it will take time, and it has only so much capacity. I was planning to start by making a larger constructor."

"I don't think we should stay here that long," said Ronar tightly. He knelt and scratched at the dirt at the base of the field. The field extended down into the soil. There'd be no digging their way out. "Can you make anything capable of cracking us out of here?"

"Mirror fields are pretty fundamental. I've never needed to try to get past one, and I've been pleased by that. What do you think, Brainchild?"

"I'm aware of no elegant way to defeat a mirror field. Any brute force attempt would probably destroy the fragile Portal."

"Maybe we should head back to Earth while we look for a solution," said Perturbare uneasily. "We don't want to end up like those poor—"

"No," said Ronar flatly.

"Why not?"

"Something is wrong here. There's little time. We're needed." Ronar looked around at the dimness, fretting over these vague convictions, yet unable to shake them. "I can feel it."

"Hmm."

"Get your equipment set up. Get that larger constructor underway."

"Well, okay. But if my tongue starts swelling up with thirst, I'm heading for home, whether you like it or not."

They shrugged out of their backpacks. Perturbare rooted around in them. The first thing he did was set up a communications relay like the one on the Earth side of the Portal. Ronar then watched as Perturbare snapped together a device that looked like a bread box with a hopper on top and a bin underneath.

Perturbare knelt to turn it on. It hummed, and a few lights glowed. He scooped up handfuls of sand and gravel, dropping them into the hopper. "Get busy, Brainchild. Let me know if you don't find the elements you need. Not that there's a huge variety of raw materials here."

Perturbare stood up. "That's begun. Once we have a few good-sized constructors we can start making whatever we need. Building stuff atom-by-atom is slow, but with a few more tools to work with, things will speed up."

After that there was nothing for Ronar to do but wait. Perturbare kept feeding the hopper. After a while a few finished parts dropped into the bin. A small pile of powder accumulated behind the machine, unneeded waste elements.

"How useful is this stuff, Brainchild?" asked Perturbare as he piled in more dirt.

"It is rich in iron oxide. It contains traces of iridium and other platinum metals. Silicon and carbon are insufficient. We will need to supplement the soil with another material when I begin making electro-optical components."

"All right. We'll throw in our clothes if we have to."

Ronar barely listened to this conversation. He was standing against the mirror field, his palm laid flat upon it. Within the barrier was peace and quiet. Outside...

"Do you...hear something?" he asked hesitantly.

Perturbare twisted to look at him. "Hear something?"

"From outside. Some kind of cry, or howling, or wailing."

Perturbare got up and came to stand beside him.

"I think I do hear that," he said in a small voice.

"I think I can even feel vibrations."

Perturbare put his hand on the mirror bubble. "I feel them too."

They stood there, silently taking this in for a few minutes.

"You know, now that I think of it, it's odd that the mirror field is transmitting any light at all. I've always understood them to be absolute barriers against any form of energy," said Perturbare.

"The field's light transmission is slowly increasing," chimed in Brainchild.

"Oh," said Perturbare in a neutral tone. "Maybe we won't have to worry about breaking through the field. Maybe something outside is breaking it for us."

Ronar was less complacent than Perturbare pretended to be. A chill gripped his spine.

"Make weapons," he said suddenly.

"What?"

"Make weapons. Big as you can. Right now. You're right, this field isn't going away on its own. Something is wearing it away. Something outside."

Perturbare stared at him open-mouthed for a moment—Ronar could now see his features a little—then turned away.

"Brainchild, abort the constructor. Make a tripod-mounted ERASER cannon. Light on the tripod, heavy on the cannon."

Suddenly both men were consumed by a sense of urgency.

"Here, take these parts." Perturbare fed the new constructor parts right back into the hopper.

"We'll need additional refined materials," said the computer.

"Dammit," said Perturbare anxiously. "What can we spare? Here, take this relay. Maybe we'll get a chance to make another one later." He yanked the antenna head off the squat tripod, tossed it into the hopper. It sank down slowly as it was dismantled. "What else?" he fretted.

"Back there," said Ronar. "In the Portal."

"What? Oh, of course, poor Kay Whitney's camping gear. Ugh. All right, damn it." Off he ran.

By now the muzzle of a large ERASER weapon was protruding from the bin.

Ronar stood stiff and tense as Perturbare returned and fiddled with his machines. Something was going on outside, Ronar was sure of it. Whatever it was, it was breaking down this magical barrier. When that barrier fell, he and Perturbare would be plunged into a situation he could not predict. Until then, there was nothing he could do. His anger smoldered.

"Um...Ronar? What's that red light?"

"Red light?" Ronar turned and looked around.

"Back here in the Portal a bit. I think there's smoke, too."

Ronar stepped inside. There, tucked away against the wall, was a tiny, inconspicuous wicker basket, with a pure red glow shining through its woven openings. It looked and smelled as though it were about to ignite. Ronar kicked it over, knocking off its lid. Out tumbled a massive gold ring set with a blazing red stone.

A surge of exultation filled Ronar as he looked at that ring lying on the bronze. Silently he thanked Sha Totek for his foresight. He bent to lift the ring, brushing off the dust.

It was warm but not scorching. He stood, his face lit by the lurid glow, to strange effect, to judge by the slack-jawed look on Perturbare's face. Ronar slipped the ring onto its accustomed finger. With a long-unused but familiar act of will he called forth the ring's full magic.

There was a flash of intense white light, then a vengeful clash of metal that merged with Perturbare's startled yip. Ronar felt the weight of the Sword of Bran in his hand, savoring it. He had never dreamed he could feel such satisfaction at holding this terrible weapon. It was a dreadful, savage thing, but now he felt it was an ally he badly needed.

"Holy—look at that thing!" cried Perturbare. "That was magic! That was fantastic!"

"Doctor Perturbare. Doctor Ronar," interjected Brainchild calmly. "Please observe the increasing translucency of the mirror field. I believe it is about to fail."

"Oh, crap!" blurted Perturbare, wide-eyed. "How's that cannon coming?"

"It's nearly ready. I'm adapting it to fit the tripod of the radio relay."

"Perturbare," said Ronar, "you realize you may have to use that weapon to kill."

Perturbare turned to him with a troubled brow. "Not anything cute, I hope?"

Ronar snorted and turned away.

The mirror field rang like a bell at some great impact. Vibrations blurred the reflected images.

It's about to fall," said Ronar. "Step away from the Portal; it won't protect us from whatever's out there."

"What if whatever's out there kills us instantly?"

"Then we'll discuss that later. But it won't," answered Ronar, gripping the sword in both hands.

"You have a lot of confidence in that thing."

"It's hard to stop."

Perturbare turned away and spoke rapidly. "Brainchild, if we should lose contact, I'll try to reopen the Portal in exactly two days. Be ready with everything you can get together."

"Understood. The cannon is ready."

Perturbare yanked the weapon out of the bin and cradled it in his arms. He dragged it one-handed for the moment it took to grab the tripod and drop it into the hopper. "See what you can do with that. I don't think we'll be staying put long enough for me to use it as it is."

"Perturbare!" hollered Ronar.

Perturbare trotted out of the Portal to stand beside Ronar. By now they could see vague shapes moving outside the bubble, becoming less vague by the instant...

...and then the bubble was gone.

Chapter 33

Maelstrom

Sounds boomed in: whirs, whines, and drones of all pitches, deep and shrill, rising and falling over each other in an endlessly-changing chord. It was almost music, yet it was too alien, too insistent to bear the name.

The odor was of hot metal, electricity, chlorine, a thin, bitter mixture that made Ronar want not to breathe, impractical as that was. He forced himself to fill his lungs despite the alarm bells in his brain.

His sense of balance was subtly disoriented, as though the horizon, what he could see of it, were slowly tipping before him.

The scene was one of greyness: a grey, pocked surface dotted with pools of some silvery liquid. Immense planes of reflective greyness swooped and orbited through the air, moaning or humming stridently as they swept by, or rotating, passing through the landscape and each other without resistance. One of them approached the two, an infinite wall. Ronar saw his staring form and Perturbare's reflected in it as it hummed and boomed upon them, passing through the Portal and then through the Earthmen themselves, leaving a sensation of abrupt heat and nausea. The passage seemed to have no lasting effect, except that the grey muddy landscape looked slightly rearranged, and the sword had vanished from Ronar's hand. Ronar turned to look at Perturbare, whose face was as grey as the weird environment around them.

"Is this what you were expecting?" cried Perturbare in a wavering voice.

Ronar shook his head, pitching his voice to rise above the strident humming. "This is not Colibdis."

"What is it then? What can we do?"

"We won't retreat. Step away from the Portal."

They left whatever shelter the Portal might have provided and stepped fully into that alien landscape. A plane moved down from above, passing through them, sickening them again and leaving everything slightly changed.

"Look," cried Perturbare, gesturing.

Ronar looked back. The mirror bubble had reappeared, blocking off the Portal.

Ronar turned away. As he did, a black mass appeared in front of him, not quite fully hiding the scene beyond it. It branched and bloomed silently, throwing out curving stalks in various dark colors, each composed of nodes consisting of great numbers of thin parallel spines. They did not quite grow, but rather faded suddenly into view like projections. The whole chaotic mass grew until it took up most of Ronar's field of vision, then faded wholly away, leaving nothing changed except a weirdly lingering afterimage in his eye.

"What do you suppose that was?" muttered Ronar, with no hope of an answer.

"I don't know," said Perturbare dutifully. "Some crazy fractal thing." He looked at Ronar like a child seeking reassurance after a bad dream. "You know, I don't think this is exactly our universe."

Ronar nodded. He turned away and scanned the horizon as best he could. At any given moment it was mostly blocked by the various sweeping planes. In a gap he saw a towering silver cylinder, or perhaps a cable, rising straight up, so tall its upper reaches vanished through perspective. He put his hand on Perturbare's arm to rouse him from the wide-eyed paralysis that seemed to grip him. "That cylinder stands at the site of Sha Totek's tower, relative to the Portal. I don't know what it is now, or if it has any relation at all to what I remember, but it's the only reference point we've got. That's where we go."

"So is this Colibdis, or not?"

Ronar shrugged. "I don't know."

Perturbare nodded, though Ronar saw the doubt in his eyes as they stumbled off in that direction. It was understandable. The miles to the Tower had never seemed longer. They moved beneath a grey sky that swirled with colorless vortices, whether of gas or energy or space and time, Ronar could not discern. Nor did the silvery pools look inviting.

"The surface of that pool is bulging," said Perturbare.

"What?" said Ronar. He turned to find Perturbare pointing at one of the metallic puddles. Its surface was indeed convex. "It looks like it's trying to fall up."

"It's not quite heavy enough to do that," said Perturbare, a wide-eyed look of revelation on his face.

"Why do you say that?" asked Ronar, frowning.

"I don't know. It just came to me. Holy crap, I'm scared. Is this the kind of bullshit you deal with all the time on this nutty planet?"

"Well, this is new."

They looked at the pool for another moment, then hurried on, their confusion and disorientation only growing.

Ronar began to breathe heavily. A thin pain stung his lungs.

"I don't know how long we can breathe this crap," gasped Perturbare.

"I know. Are we still in touch with Brainchild?"

Perturbare glanced at his box. "No."

Ronar in turn raised his ring. It failed to react to his mental command with so much as a flicker.

A plane caught them from behind, passing though them, leaving them a bit more debilitated and disoriented.

"Miserable thing," muttered Perturbare, raising the ERASER cannon he was still lugging, although the act almost toppled him. He triggered it, sending a fierce, narrow beam of blue light into the receding plane, which swallowed it. Half a second later a much wider, more diffuse blue beam shot out from another plane and caught Ronar full on. It felt like an intense ray of sunshine when so diffused.

"Yow!" yipped Perturbare. "Oops." He snapped off his weapon. "Sorry."

"Perhaps you'd better save that thing for a situation we understand a little better," said Ronar with forced mildness.

Perturbare only nodded contritely.

They turned back toward the distant silver cable, visible only in glimpses permitted by the passing of the humming, throbbing planes. "How tall do you—suppose that thing is?" gasped Perturbare as he stumbled along.

"As high as the limit of the magic around this planet," guessed Ronar.

"So you do believe this is Colibdis, despite appearances?"

Ronar shrugged. "I can either believe that, or admit I know nothing."

And then all at once the planes faded away. A silence fell over the land, which lost its look of grey-silvery greasiness. They now stood on a red plain of clean dust and rock, broken here and there with scrubby stands of desert plants in muted shades of green. The sky thinned and clarified into a dome of pure deep indigo, in which burned the oddly paired suns Photos and Kudu, white and red. Sweet-smelling desert air swept in to displace whatever remnants of sour grey air might remain.

The Portal and Tower remained encased in silver, inside dome and cylinder, respectively.

Ronar and Perturbare looked at each other.

"Changeable weather you've got here," remarked Perturbare. "Not that I'm complaining."

Ronar did not reply. He looked around, studying their surroundings carefully. They were now familiar, except for the mirrors that still sheathed the structures. Yet he felt no sense of relief or deliverance. He glanced down at his ring. The garnet smoldered. Magic was present again; so too must be the gods. Now he stood naked before them, they who had forced him off the planet half a Colibdian turn ago. He glanced at the mirrored cylinder and hemisphere. Who had created them—Sha Totek or the gods? And for what purpose—to protect the Portal and Tower, or to prevent the Portal's use and the Tower's interference?

A stillness settled over the landscape, surpassing even the silence that had prevailed before. Somewhere beneath that stillness was a ringing sense of imminence that Ronar had felt once before, in the frigid fastness of the polar continent of Hyperborea. Then that imminence had been a wonder and a joy, a promise of relief. Now it was different.

"Something is happening here," said Perturbare edgily.

Ronar studied Perturbare, whose eyes were darting around in search of whatever had disturbed him. It did Perturbare credit that he showed this sensitivity to the ineffable.

A zone of clarity was forming ahead of them, an ovoid area neither light nor dark, suffused and informed with an infinity of pale motes that flickered and danced. They appeared chaotic, but sometimes a kind of order suggested itself when Ronar wasn't thinking about it, only to vanish when he became aware of it.

"What *is* that?" demanded Perturbare. His jaw was slack with awe.

"That is Varanu. Perturbare, listen. Take your weapon and hurry to the Tower. Sha Totek will probably admit you, but try to dig or blast your way through his shield if he doesn't or can't. I will stay to hold this thing off. I'll follow you when I can. If I do not follow, then continue with our plan. You can do it without me. You're a highly capable man. I know you can do it."

Perturbare gave him a sidelong look of narrow appraisal. "You'll hold off this weird quantum god of 'order' all by yourself, huh?"

Ronar's answer was terse. "I must deal with it here and now. There is no escaping it. Its problem seems to be with me alone. It will probably ignore you. Go."

"All right. You keep this god at bay and I'll scoot on over to visit your buddy. I'll see you later." Perturbare stepped up and punched Ronar in the shoulder, then strolled off, whistling, but Ronar had seen how pale he was. He saw how carefully he skirted the pale shimmer that was Varanu.

Ronar turned to regard Varanu. The god had never been known to speak. Perhaps an entity that was so much a part of the innermost nature of reality had no use or comprehension for anything as imperfect as symbols.

Nevertheless, Ronar would attempt to communicate with it.

"Varanu, why are you persecuting me? Why do you protect Ahriman from me? After all, you yourself keep Ahriman under control. You keep it from overrunning the universe, perverting the natural order you represent. Why do you then interfere so blatantly with my efforts to confront your enemy? I've communed with you in the past. Let me do so now. Show me what's in your mind."

With his eyes locked on the colorless glitter that was Varanu, Ronar stepped forward, conscious of every step, every foot that brought him closer to this inscrutable god.

At the same time Varanu moved toward him.

Ronar expected that at any moment his perceptions would expand to the godlike level of awareness he had experienced during his first encounter with Varanu. He remembered little of what he had learned on that occasion; it was difficult for a human mind to retain knowledge derived from senses it did not possess.

He recalled that Varanu had no ability to directly influence other minds. The fact that consciousness was beyond the control of the god of Cosmic Order was an enigma always in the back of Ronar's mind, but the knowledge made him confident that at least Varanu could not tamper with his thoughts.

This time the enhanced perceptions did not come. He stepped into the field of whirling lights and felt nothing but a vague numbness. The visual effect spun and flickered around him, no more profound than a chilly fog.

It was quite an anticlimax for Ronar. He looked around, his hands opening and closing as he strove to make sense of anything that had happened since his return to Colibdis. He had expected answers of one kind or another from Varanu, but instead the god offered nothing but confusion.

Ronar's great anger, long tamped down, now blazed up like a white furnace. "All right then, you hovering pile of pixie dust. Say nothing, do nothing, mean nothing. But do not interfere with me anymore." He radiated wrath at the god as an almost palpable force.

Varanu's pale dazzle folded in on itself, vanished, and reappeared in the middle distance. It then unveiled itself in some way, its appearance remaining the same, but the impact of its presence expanding a thousand fold, ringing silently in the space around Ronar, shaking his mind, nearly bringing him to his knees. Filmy shapes rose up from the sand, pearly diaphanous things that darted at him with limbs or extensions too complex and shifting to define or avoid. Ronar brought out the sword, the din of its arrival a hard welcome reality compared to the silent cosmic shout that came from Varanu. He swung it at one of the emanations, and its blade was caught within it, shuddering and twisting in an impossible manner as if it were being yanked through more than three dimensions of space. Ronar released it with a cry, watching as the blade began to shiver and dissolve in the grip of that construct of flickering shifting geometry. He let the sword lapse and then called it again, but this time its din was lower in tone and slower in coming. Again he tried to defend himself with the renewed blade, but again it was caught, torn from his hand, and the edges of the blade were eaten into nothingness by some unseen force. Once more he let the weapon disappear. When he summoned it again the clash of its coming was prolonged. It shuddered, wailed. The sword did not come. The sound was not the triumphant ringing it had always been, but a keening of fear and distress. Finally the blade shivered into being in his hand. Ronar stared at it; it was whole. Nothing before had ever interfered with its magic. Whatever he was facing now was greater than that spell.

He let the sword pass away. It could do nothing for him now. Varanu's constructs hemmed him in. Though his mind might be safe from the god's tampering, the atoms of his body were definitely within its domain.

"Sha Totek," muttered Ronar, "if you're watching, this would be a good time for you to help. This is beyond me. I cannot defeat this."

Just like that, Ronar found himself plucked up and carried aloft by a great unseen hand. Varanu's constructs rose to follow, but a curved surface of altered space took shape beneath him, a thing so dire he could barely stand to look at it, blocking them. Ronar threw back his head, savoring the relief of this unexpected rescue, ignoring the fact that he was being drawn high into the air, already higher than the summits of the distant Red Hills.

A peevish voice sounded in his mind.

I dislike taking gross physical actions such as this.

It was the voice of Ahriman.

Chapter 34

The Eye of Ahriman

"Ahriman!" shouted Ronar. Most of the emotions in the human spectrum of feeling tried to take possession of him at once. Neutralized, his eventual response was a rather lame "What are you doing?"

Saving you, came the remote, distracted reply.

"I don't want you saving me!"

I am the only one who can. Your sorcerer friend can't do it. He's now the greatest magician inside that shining tube he's made, and nothing at all outside it. That man you brought over from Earth also seems to lack the means to hamper Varanu. Therefore, I am left to act.

Ronar's thoughts were a welter. He watched as the cylinder enclosing the Tower slid off into the distance, dwindling to a silver hair connecting the plain far below with a still unplumbed depth of sky even farther above. He was being drawn to the east as well as up.

"Where are you taking me? Put me down."

You wouldn't be safe anywhere on the planet. I'm taking you to the one place where Varanu will not interfere. To my Eye.

A white veil seem to pass over Ronar's sight at these words. His ears rang. "But I don't understand. Why do you want to save me? Don't you know I've come back to destroy you?" he blurted.

He heard a dry chuckle. *I don't think you'll succeed at that.*

"Don't be too sure."

Again the chuckle. *Your confidence is one of your greatest charms.*

Ronar's heartbeat thudded in his ears. The wind snapped at his hair, but it was growing weaker. His ears popped several times. The air was thinning and growing frosty. The color of the sky thinned from its usual deep indigo to a shade of black suffused with a violet glow.

"If you plan to get me there alive, I'll need a little air and heat."

Yes. I am familiar with the details of being human.

The wind died away. Ronar's ears popped again as air pressure increased around him. He continued his ascent enclosed in an unseen bubble of air. Now the suns blazed unrivaled in a black sky, their glare more than he could endure. He turned away from them and looked down at the receding planet below.

Ronar's plan had always included a trip to the Eye, but one facilitated by Perturbare's technology. In fact, that was the essence of his plan. To be scooped up and swept there by Ahriman itself was unexpected at best. He had not been able to confer with Sha Totek, while Perturbare was alone down there, a stranger in a mad world, cut off from help or retreat.

One way or another, at long last, Ronar was on his way to do what he must. There would be no more compromise, no more retreat. Either Ahriman or Ronar must perish.

Asterope.

With his course set at last, and nothing to be done about it, Ronar was able to do what he had not truly done since the very night of Asterope's affliction: compose his mind, set down his anger, and view his situation with a quiet heart. Ignoring even the fact that he was under the direct control of Ahriman, he looked down to see Colibdis spreading out beneath him as he'd never seen it before. The lands, whether veiled beneath silver-pearl layers of cloud or glowing in full sunlight, extended far beyond anything he knew through his own travels, or the maps he'd seen or helped to make himself.

The regions surrounding Thunderbird looked as he expected, as they were well shown by the maps made by the Cartography Shop at Thunderbird University. The Red Plain was now well toward the western curve of the globe from where he floated. It was clearly revealed as a great impact crater, its collapsed southwestern wall serving as an imperfect dike against the sea. Thunderbird itself was a cracked, ruddy land northeast of the crater, its northern boundary being the Bay of Aegeos which separated it from the pale multicolored peninsula of Mersinea. South and east of the crater sprawled the golden savanna called Eandaland, beyond which lay a great desert, the ancient country of Ammon, with the river Tal running north from southern highlands like a loose cord of brown silk. Along its banks, and in the green delta of the river Suul farther south, stood the oldest civilization on Colibdis, a culture still living the ageless, dreamy existence of ancient Egypt, worshipping a plethora of gods who truly walked its fertile valleys and sometimes hunted with its Pharaohs. South and east of this country were green lands which Ronar had never visited or heard much tell of. They stretched on until they were blue-grey with distance, ending suddenly in a long tropical coastline.

Directly below him was a mighty chain of mountains running east and west, a barrier that bisected the whole great continent. To the south was a projecting tongue of land he knew must be the mysterious kingdom of Varma, which he had never visited. Far to the northwest sprawled Tíuheimr, where wild seafaring Norsemen had curiously been confined to a rugged landlocked country, their sailing exploits limited to the freshwater seas which snaked around the roots of the mountains. Immediately south and west of that was a shimmering bluish land whose borders were not easy to cross unless you were one of those so steeped in magic that you became partly a creature of magic, in which case that kingdom of Faerie was the only home you would crave.

Still farther west was the great kingdom of Eranior, the Celtic land that had long stood guard against its western neighbor of Darteharn, seat of the wizard Namirnakh who had been humbled long ago. And that was as far west as Ronar could see. The polar continent of Hyperborea was merely a glimmer of white on the northern horizon. He turned toward the east, where lands wholly unknown to him stretched out toward a distant purple haze of dusk. Below and before him were deserts, wild plains, and mountains. Somewhere in that region must lie the kingdom of Assuria with its famous lion gates.

A hazy blue-green jungle lay along a southern coast, pierced by a smoking volcano so huge he could see it rearing up even from this height and distance. Far to the north and east stretched a vast subarctic plain. Due east, in dim clouds and dusk, he thought he glimpsed another shore, and islands which he supposed might be the seats of the mysterious Eastern Kingdoms, which he knew only through the tales of Sha Totek.

He drew near to that dusk, still rising ever higher, until all of Colibdis was laid out below him, half black, half clear dazzling sapphire finely etched with clouds, whose details were inscribed layer upon layer until they blended into a mist at the limits of his vision. The lands he knew were now drawn against the curving western flank of the planet, golden in the sunlight. He could still barely discern the shining line of the cylinder surrounding the Tower. Like an arrow it pointed down to the country he knew best and loved most. There lay the Portal, and the home of his friend, and the gateway to Thunderbird, his chosen home. Somewhere north of that slender thread of silver was the town whose modest brick and wooden structures he was always pleased to see at the end of his wanderings, his own adobe house, and the observatory he had built with such labor.

This dazzling view went suddenly blurry. Ronar realized tears were accumulating in his eyes. Ever the keen observer of rare phenomena, Ronar delved within himself to seek out their source. It was not difficult to find. For the first time in many months, he was getting a clear view of the beauty of the world, a view not filtered through a dreary fog of grief, or loss, or self-absorption, or even obsession. His thoughts were clear. His mind was easy.

And now as Colibdis dwindled beneath him to a shining crescent, he turned his eyes upward to behold a much smaller body, one that was now swelling into a visible disk. In all the turns of Ronar's life on Colibdis it had appeared as nothing more than a dim yet evil star. Now it bulked larger, a more palpable presence. Asterope was the only person he knew who had ever seen it in any detail, and she had not spoken of the sight. Ronar had tried to photograph it through various telescopes, but the plates and films had never revealed anything more than a smeared trail of light. Now as he turned his gaze toward it he was inclined to squint, to shield his eyes, knowing its influence and power, remembering all the warnings he had issued against just such study. But for now at least, the malicious gaze of the moon seemed veiled. Ronar had half expected it to appear as a literal Eye, but all he saw was a reddish-grey rock, only approximately spherical, and heavily cratered. Indeed, one huge, fresh-looking crater in the center of the disk dominated the entire moon, giving it, in the end, a faintly eye-like appearance. It seemed to be nothing more than a natural moonlet or asteroid. He discerned no artificial structures, no temples or palaces, nothing to indicate that this hunk of rock was the home of a god, and a peculiarly self-indulgent one at that. Ronar regarded it with a calm, cold sense of antipathy. Harmless it might appear, but here, he knew, lurked his oldest enemy. And he knew what Ahriman must intend.

"Why are you so determined to incorporate me into yourself, Ahriman? So determined that you thwart Varanu to save me? So determined that you even leave me capable of fighting you?"

Among my many reasons, I need your knowledge of astronomical matters. As you've surmised, I'm in charge of steering this moonlet on its course. I wish to learn how to bend its path more to my advantage.

Ronar frowned. Something was odd about that statement, but Ahriman interrupted before he could pursue the thought.

As for you ability to fight me, I thought that had already been dismissed.

Ronar warmed to that provocation at once. It might have been wiser to leave Ahriman's smug sense of invincibility intact, but Ronar could not suffer it to go unchallenged. "By no means. You are a mind; I am a mind. You prefer to fight your battles on that plane; that is clear. Therefore we are equals, and on that basis, I can defeat you. And I will."

Ahriman fell silent. Ronar felt a peculiar stillness, as though the formless intellect surrounding him had suspended time to consider his remarks.

No. Formidable you are indeed, and unusual. Yet you are still human. I have taken thousands of human spirits into myself, each one adding to my strength and knowledge. You are only one man. You know I cannot take you against your will, not while you resist and are strong. But I will leave you on my moon to dwell in hopelessness for as long as it takes. Perhaps you will finally welcome the prospect of joining with me, and cease your resistance.

"But you don't understand," said Ronar, his tone low and deadly. "I don't intend to resist you. I'll fight you from within, and destroy you."

Again the silence. This time it contained an element of surprise and doubt.

We shall see.

Now the moon loomed up in all its bland, pockmarked lifelessness. Ahriman had carried Ronar across tens of thousands of miles of space in only a few minutes, yet he had never felt any acceleration. It was as if he had hung motionless in space while worlds were rearranged around him. Now he descended into the moonlet's great central crater, a depression about two miles across, almost half the diameter of the moonlet itself. The crater rim cast a deep shadow into the bowl. The shadow fell just short of the crater's center, where a black dot was just coming into view. As Ronar plunged downward he saw it was an opening, a pit of some sort. Ronar fell into it and was brought to a halt in a space poorly lit by sunlight glancing off the lip of the opening. He looked around its shadowy interior, which was of no great size. He thought he could make out the openings of other caves or tunnels leading off from this entryway.

Then that faint light began to fade. Ronar turned toward the opening. It was rapidly being blocked, its lip closing up like a wound being healed. As it narrowed the light vanished entirely. Ronar felt himself released by the invisible hand that had drawn him between the worlds. The chamber was filled with chilly, gunpowder-smelling air. He drifted downward in the moonlet's weak gravity, bringing him to the bottom of the chamber, where he half-stood, half-floated, swaying, peering about uselessly in total darkness.

There was a great silence, a stillness, as though even Ahriman were absent, or was studying him from a vast distance. The air here had a feeling of Eternity, as though in this tomb he would dwell in sightless loneliness while galaxies rotated and stars guttered into ashes. Ronar felt his heart falter. In the absence of vision, the reality of his position rang in his mind: locked inside an airless rock thirty thousand miles from Colibdis, his life sustained only at the whim of Ahriman. In the darkness he touched one finger to another, aware of his body, aware that he would soon be taken from it, that he might never again know life as a man with a physical form, or perhaps indeed life of any kind. The touch of his own hand was suddenly vivid. The realization that these might be his final moments as a living man made the sensations of his body seem all the more wondrous after he had all but ignored them for so long. Now that the moment was upon him, he realized he had never really understood or visualized what it would be like to be disembodied, or to be somehow merged with another consciousness. In this cold darkness he suddenly doubted whether in that condition he'd be able to pursue his goals as relentlessly as he had as a living man.

At the same moment, Ronar realized that this delay was calculated by Ahriman to induce just such doubts and fears. It was working all too well.

Ronar remembered the side tunnels that led off from this chamber. Rather than be unmanned by his last-minute fears he decided to explore them. With a dreamlike, slow-motion, half-swimming gait he moved toward the side of the chamber, groping in the darkness. Belatedly he remembered his ring and its light-giving properties...

Without warning, Ahriman sprang upon him, seizing his mind. Ronar gasped and instinctively began to fight off that grasp, which he could certainly have done. But that was not his purpose. He forced himself to relax, to offer no resistance. He felt a moment of sheer terror, with a second vertiginous glimpse of Eternity. Something parted inside him and he was pulled out of himself into a realm of being he had never guessed at.

The first thing he noticed was that he was still himself. The second was an intense internal pressure, an urge to let his being explode, letting everything he was spew out into the great psychic void around him. It was as though he existed in some spiritual vacuum, a nothingness which was avid to draw out his essence and disperse it, in an effort to fill itself. For a fraction of a second Ronar almost gave in to this impulse, the next step in a process he was committed to following through. But...he sensed dissolution there, an ultimate loss of self, and held back. His true mission, he reminded himself, was not to join with Ahriman, not even to destroy it, but to fight it, through any and all possible means, for as long as he possibly could. That was all. It was a simple goal, one he could focus on despite the disorientation of no longer being a living man.

And yet...

Ronar's plan was to fight Ahriman from the inside, as part of the god itself. In his current rigidly-held encapsulated state he couldn't even sense Ahriman's presence, let alone engage it. He sensed only emptiness, nothingness...but perhaps whatever senses he possessed in this state, if any, were directed inward, leaving him oblivious to what might be a greater spiritual realm thronged with all the spirits of the dead.

He must not cower here, defeated in the end by a need to preserve his individuality at all costs. To achieve his goal he must make this one last leap of faith.

He gave up the ghost...

He expanded into nothingness...

He was still himself, yet at the same time he was something more. Suddenly it was *his* eye looking down upon Colibdis, seeing it with a completeness and detail he could not have imagined, and more: seeing every human mind on the planet, as well as the minds of every other intelligent being, of which there were far more than he had ever supposed. This new vision was confined to the eccentric bubble of magic surrounding Colibdis. Beyond it was only a vague impression of the greater universe.

Ronar/Ahriman concentrated his gaze on the Red Plain. The silvery thread encasing the Tower remained opaque. Whatever was within it was beyond his sight and influence. But to the surprise of the Ronar part of Ahriman, he found that he could dimly see through the Portal all the way to Earth, gaining, through an effort of will, misty impressions of what went on there.

The Eye was indeed a nexus for Ahriman, who was a potent presence throughout the realm of Colibdian magic. Even with the addition of Ronar, Ahriman could not study the entire planet at once with his most intense scrutiny. But this new vantage point was still a revelation for Ronar. Seeing through the eye of the god made many things clear at last. With these divine senses, space itself gained a texture he could feel, and a structure he could plainly see. The modification which made magic possible was slight. Normal space was constantly trembling on the verge of this subtle transformation. It would be easy to extend the change, to send that little fold rippling outward until the Universe was remade. It was easy...he had already done it...Ahriman had stretched out his hand and re-wrought great expanses of space less than a score of turns before. Only the mindless intervention of Varanu had prevented him from completing his work. Now, with Ronar's help, Varanu would be at Ahriman's mercy at last. The moon would be moved, and the cold, implacable forces that Varanu embodied would be without their defender.

Ahriman's resentment of Varanu was very emotional. Ronar could not help but share it; had not Varanu attempted to thwart and destroy him too?

Ahriman sent his perspective out from the moon, and Ronar's point of view followed perforce. Ronar could now see into the moon, riddled with a network of tunnels and caverns. At its heart burned a core of crimson fire. The moon orbited barely within the limits of the sphere of magic. Barely indeed...in fact, the boundary passed through the very center of the moon. The sphere was not concentric with the center of Colibdis, but was centered on the island of Etheros, a place of which even Ahriman knew little. Therefore the Eye too must orbit eccentrically to keep its station just at the limit of magic. Its heart of fire, maintained there by the mind of Ahriman, swept along the interface between magic and non-magic. There it generated a force of combined magic and nature, a hybrid power, useless to the God of Magic, but life itself to Varanu, Lord of Cosmic Order, maintainer of the chaotic natural order, who nevertheless clung to an incomplete semblance of sentience. Whenever the moon passed over Varanu's Mirror, which was the Island of the Gods, Ahriman released this power, strengthening Varanu, informing it with an all-encompassing understanding which Ahriman envied but could not share, making Varanu a power which none on Colibdis could defeat.

Yet even Varanu had limitations. It could not or would not deflect the Eye from its natural orbit: that would be contrary to its purpose and nature. Only the mind of Ahriman could bend the path of the moon to keep it within its narrowly prescribed bounds. Only the god of Consciousness could create the red flame of being, which, through its interaction with the realms of magic and nature, could generate the hybrid force that exalted Varanu into a class of its own. Only for these reasons was Ahriman suffered to exist. And for these reasons, Ahriman was protected by Varanu as well. But Ahriman would never be permitted to expand beyond this little bubble of possibility, which floated isolated in a Universe teeming with minds.

So that was it! Far from being the great nemesis of Varanu, Ahriman was a mere servant of the god, a tool, a slave who made occasional, doomed escape attempts!

At last you begin to understand.

The solution to Ahriman's problem, Ronar saw, was laughably simple. He need only center the Eye's orbit around the natural center of gravity of the Eye/Colibidis system, thus putting the Eye entirely outside the eccentric magic field half the time. As easily as that, Varanu would be deprived of infusions of cosmic force and must then fade. True, Ahriman would have to be careful not to be in residence at the Eye when it passed beyond the reach of magic, or he would be snuffed out. But that was a minor inconvenience, if it meant the diminution of Varanu.

How had Ahriman come to be in servitude to Varanu like this? Ronar now had access to Ahriman's memories; they were his own memories as well. He looked into the past as Ahriman settled back to his resting place within the Eye. Hundreds of turns ago, Ahriman had been—nothing. There had been various minor gods of evil or magic, but no great independent mind such as Ahriman. Then the Persian wizard Namirnakh had come to Colibdis through the British Portal. He quickly recognized the true nature of the gods, seeing that they were little more than shadows, brought into being by the beliefs and expectations of their worshippers. Still, they wielded power, and could do much to bolster the ambitions of a wizard who sought to conquer and to rule. So Namirnakh had decided to create a god of his own. He took the name of Ahriman, the dark god of his Persian religion, and set it before his followers as that of a great and potent deity. Ahriman came into being at once, gaining strength as Namirnakh caused more people to worship and fear him. At first Ahriman was only clay for Namirnakh, shaped and guided by the wizard's statements of Ahriman's goals and desires, which were then made real by the belief of his followers. Thus did Namirnakh make himself the only magician on Colibdis who had a god for a servant. So might things have remained indefinitely, for at that stage Ahriman's mind was as unformed and illusive as that of any other lesser god.

But then Namirnakh made a mistake which put Ahriman outside his control. Eager to build up the cult of the god, he sought those who were willing to give themselves up to it. The first such willing sacrifice was, to Namirnakh's surprise and displeasure, Protartes, one of his chief priests and fellow magicians, and a rival. Namirnakh could not refuse this offer without suffering embarrassment, as it had been made in a very public setting. So Namirnakh had watched nervously as this man Protartes opened his own veins, setting his spirit free to join with the god, whom he knew to be merely a shell. The entry of that spirit into the god awakened it to true sentience for the first time. Namirnakh became aware of this and feared for his life, but he need not have. Ahriman's goals, as they developed, were similar to Namirnakh's, though on a larger scale. Namirnakh sought Earth; Ahriman the Universe. There was no real competition between them. They could coexist; indeed, they would even continue to cooperate from time to time.

Ahriman's true conflict was with Varanu. Varanu had seemingly existed in some nebulous form from the instant magic first came to Colibdis, whenever that had been. As far as Ahriman could tell, the interaction between the Universe's natural order, that complex and subtle mix of large-scale predictability and small-scale chaos, and the magic field of Colibdis, which brought that flickering subatomic chaos closer to the macroscopic level, had produced in that bubble of the cosmos a kind of self-awareness. Varanu was the only god who had no need of believers or worshippers. In fact, it seemed almost oblivious to thinking creatures, as though consciousness itself were foreign to it and the order it represented. Certainly it had not hesitated to react when Ahriman first moved to extend the sway of magic throughout the Universe. Varanu was apparently content that whatever sentience it possessed be confined to the environs of Colibdis. It would not permit the self-regulating flow of events in the rest of space to be brought under the direct control of any mind, even its own.

That first battle between them had been epic. The war of Consciousness and Desire versus Being and Silence was then a far more equal thing. In the end it was Varanu who proved to control the more fundamental forces. Then Varanu might have dissolved Ahriman, but chose instead to enslave him. Varanu set Ahriman to driving the Eye across the heavens, generating that hybrid force which made Varanu even greater, and delivering it to the Mirror which Varanu constructed to receive it. From then on Varanu saw more clearly, its mind broadened. Curiously for a being so unsympathetic to the goals of thinking beings, it did not itself wish to lose its expanded awareness. Thus Varanu suffered Ahriman to exist, and tolerated much mischief from him, but did not allow him to realize his chief ambition of extending magic throughout the stars.

Now at last, Ahriman had the knowledge he needed to escape this servitude and turn this trap against Varanu. Thanks to Ronar's knowledge of astronomy, he knew precisely how to change the orbit of the moon so as to deprive Varanu of the greater part of its strength.

This prospect filled Ronar with a burning satisfaction. He had never before allowed himself to consider the advantages of spreading magic throughout the Universe. Once that was done, his mind would be free to flow into any part of space with little effort. Instead of painfully ferreting out the secrets of creation with the clumsy instruments his hands could devise, he could simply know whatever it pleased him to know. For that matter, if he found matters not to his liking, he could change them. Certainly there was much that needed changing, on Colibdis, and most especially on Earth.

It was only through the incorporation of Leonard Ronar that Ahriman could hope to do all these things. After all, only he, an astronomer...

A stunning white flare briefly rocked that part of Ahriman which still thought of itself as Ronar. Why had he been necessary to this scheme? One of Ahriman's most ardent followers was Daniel Durgala, a man who knew at least as much about orbital mechanics as Ronar himself. Even if Durgala could not be persuaded to give up his spirit for his god, surely he would have been happy simply to explain to him what to do.

And for that matter, what about...

The white flare returned, leaving Ronar, and to a lesser extent, Ahriman as a whole, reeling.

Asterope.

Asterope had already been incorporated into Ahriman. Her knowledge was more than sufficient for Ahriman's purposes.

Ahriman was aware of these doubts, of course.

Your integrity is truly remarkable, Ronar. Any other person would already have dissolved fully into me, and I would not be having this conversation with a part of myself which still stands to some degree apart. Yes, Durgala could have told me what I needed to know. But in you, I also gain something else that I needed to succeed. I gain the will and the courage to carry this plan forward. This is embarrassing to admit, but soon enough I shall have no more cause for embarrassment.

But that did not answer the question about Asterope. Ronar now turned his full scrutiny upon the whole of Ahriman, peering deeply into his manifold mind until it began to resolve into the merged parts that made it up. He found there fragments of thousands of once-living minds. There was Protartes, the core personality, the basis, great and proud, priest and magician, a cunning man who had achieved greater power than Namirnakh ever had. There was Sephet, a young girl of Ammon, who, dying of a fever, had been taken from her home and sacrificed to Ahriman in his Egyptian guise. There was Kurkiatl, a farmer of the Maya, who had sold his spirit to Ahriman in exchange for the power to strike down the king who oppressed his village. But Ronar had no time to examine all these remnants. He found no sense of Asterope. Asterope was not here. She had never been absorbed into Ahriman!

Your Asterope rejected me. I was not free to release her as you once bid, because she was never part of me in the first place. You may be pleased at that.

447

Ronar's spirit blazed up with a poignant fire that stunned and shook the whole of Ahriman. There was something here, something tucked away in the back of Ahriman's mind, inconspicuous, half-forgotten. He perceived it as a smooth black ovoid embedded in Ahriman's thoughts. Ronar touched it, and knew that here was Asterope, that she had held herself apart from Ahriman, whole and unsullied. Just as Ronar had at first kept himself apart, blind to anything outside his own being, so too had she, and not for mere moments, but for many moonturns. She must have existed here in her own little cosmos of total, bodiless isolation ever since her body fell onto the deck of *Dekapus*.

Ronar tried to send a thought past the walls she had erected around her being. He did not know if it was possible to pierce such a barrier, or if all the strength of his spirit would be enough to do it.

Her response, when it came, was not gentle, but came as a torrent of wrath that shook him to his depths.

How could you?

"Asterope? What do you mean?"

Look at yourself! You gave in to Ahriman. You allowed yourself to be drawn in, and now with every passing instant you lose yourself more completely within him. He will have won, and you will help him win with a smile on your disembodied face, until the last shred of your individuality is burned away. You arrogant fool, you aren't fighting Ahriman, you're becoming *him!*

He could not argue; it was obvious once so baldly stated. For a moment he felt like laughing at his own folly. The rest of Ahriman did laugh, but only briefly.

Asterope had said the right words. Ronar's thoughts burned with cold fire. Disparate parts of his being which had spalled off from the whole and wandered away fell back into their old pattern. Pieces he hadn't even known were missing returned to brace him like armor.

"That has now changed, Asterope. This is the end of Ahriman."

Ahriman's laughter came again, still echoing from within Ronar's own mind.

Once again I compliment you for your extraordinary sense of integrity. Never before has a part of my own being reared up and threatened to smite the whole. I admit it is not entirely pleasant. But I warn you…I have what I need from you now. If you insist—

"*Enough!*" Ronar was tired of listening to threats and speeches. With all his strength of will he reached out, enfolding as much of Ahriman as came within his mind's grasp, and tore at it, seeking it to rend and break it, to cause this aberrant spacial structure to collapse back into the gentle noise of quantum fluctuations.

Ahriman found himself assailed with unprecedented agony. That great prideful mind was under attack by its own strongest, most implacable component, a thing new to its experience. This pain was not a pain of the body, but rather a fearful agony of dissolution, a conscious sighting of the void of nothingness which threatened to swallow it. Nor was Ronar spared this experience, but oblivion was far better than assimilation into this self-serving mind.

Ronar now knew in intimate detail the kind of universe Ahriman would create, a charnel pit of the most loathsome aspects of human self-indulgence. Ahriman's seeming fascination with the squalid and the degraded had been no illusion. An Ahriman free to reshape reality would perceive no more challenges, no more potential for growth. It would see only license, the freedom to pursue any pleasure, however horrid and perverse.

Perhaps Ahriman's nature need not have been so vile. Shaped as it had been, fed mainly with spirits weak and vain, it could not now be made any nobler, unless it should absorb Asterope and a thousand like her.

Degenerate Ahriman might be, but it was not also weak. Those massed minds lashed out at Ronar, gripping him, flaying his personality, leaving it stretched naked to Ahriman's scrutiny and to Ronar's own. Ronar saw his every motivation, his every hidden desire, presented as forthrightly as the organs of a dissected body, and he could not turn his mind's eye away. Much of this he already knew or suspected about himself, but he never would have chosen to put it all on such obscene display for Ahriman, of all the creatures in the cosmos. Some of it was new to him, and unpleasant. He had set himself above humanity and sought his answers in the stars. He disdained all weakness and lacked real compassion. He feared to open himself to love and was cold at heart. When thwarted or enraged he took pleasure in the savage butchery of his enemies. There was more, and worse. Self-doubt gnawed rat-like at Ronar's resolve. Was he fit to carry on this battle? Was he worthy of victory?

He suspected he was being prevented from seeing the better, nobler aspects of his personality. Surely he could not be so wholly wretched as he was being made to appear. Ahriman would not fear or respect such a person.

A vision came into his mind: Asterope and himself, writhing naked together, their eyes glazed and fevered with lust.

Why didn't the two of you give in to your natures? The desire was there. Why did you hold yourselves apart from the natural course of your humanity?

This vision expanded before Ronar, grew richer, took on sensory aspects he thought he had left behind: scent, hearing, touch. He fell into the image of his own former body, and he was the one thrusting his urgent flesh into Asterope's sweaty body, her face only inches from his own.

Even now it's not too late. Tempt Asterope out from her shell. Merge with her into me. The most genuine parts of the two of you can mingle in me forever.

Ronar found himself staring into the eyes of this vision of Asterope—two human, unafflicted eyes. But they wavered, and did not meet his own. They contained no thought. They had no depth greater than the animal sensations of her body.

It was Ronar's turn to laugh. "Fool. Asterope had many concerns beyond the urges of her ape-body. She had those urges as well, no doubt, but she chose to transcend them. She would not be dominated by the glandular imperatives of a body no longer quite fit to contain a mind that saw both deeper and higher. You pathetic thing: lacking a body as you do, you fixate on what little you miss, though all the resources of mind are yours if you choose to explore them. 'God of subtlety and thought' indeed. Voyeur god. God of the gutter is more to the point."

Ahriman was angered, and Ronar's wrath waxed strong again. Again they grappled. The combat between them stretched on interminably. Eventually Ronar felt that he was braced beneath a mountain of red-hot boulders, and that he must not move or shift, lest they crush him. The weight of Ahriman's malice increased with every hour that passed, or with every year—by now Ronar had lost any reckoning of time. Whatever Ahriman's deficiencies might be, its centuries of existence had not left it without patience. Ronar began to consider whether this stalemate might not persist into eternity, or at least as long as his still-finite mind could endure.

At some point Ronar began to be distracted by a strange sound, a silly tinkling run of a few musical notes. It certainly had no place in this formless arena of psychic combat. Pondering it with what fraction of his attention he could spare, Ronar found himself slipping into a vision. In the midst of blackness he saw a dim, ill-defined shape, hard to interpret, until he recognized his own body lying on the floor of the cavern in the Eye. It was puzzling that he could see at all in that total darkness. But then he noticed the small white box, totally forgotten, clipped to the belt of the inert figure. Its tiny screen glowed blue. From its speaker came the cheerful little march of notes.

This gave Ronar new hope and new strength. Ahriman of course was aware of both, though Ronar sensed it was puzzled by their exact cause. Still, Ahriman felt the need to double its efforts to crush Ronar, and did. Ronar felt himself buckling, the abyss of nothingness looming before him again.

Asterope!

There was no answer to that call, but suddenly another name came to Ronar's mind.

Astraea.

Ahriman shuddered, and Ronar with it. Ronar waited, having a sense that something new was happening to Ahriman.

Ahriman shuddered again, then quaked. Then screamed, a soundless cry of agony, a cry in which Ronar may have joined, for he was not spared the ripping pain and confusion of what was happening to the god. A small part of Ahriman tore free, fluttered away, swelled up, and began to burn with a blue-white wrath that made the whole great tapestry of Ahriman seem pale and thin. It flung itself in fury against the formless being of the god, its cry like the scream of an eagle. Ahriman recoiled, lost its grip on Ronar, and fell back to fend off this incredible attack by that which had been fully a part of itself.

Awestruck, Ronar recognized the presence of Astraea. No frail old woman was she now, but a flame of vengeance, a spirit of steel. She tore at the god, her anger terrible to behold. Gradually Ahriman overcame its pain and shock and reasserted itself, looming over that striking, smiting blaze of fury, threatening to envelop it in a blackness tinged with scarlet flames. At last Ronar shook off his amazement and sprang back to the attack himself, combining his icy will to victory with Astraea's fire. Her thoughts came into his mind, answering questions he'd not yet asked.

"I was never the girl's mother...the details of your story made that clear. But having witnessed your kindness to me, and your determination to save your Asterope, I saw a chance to seek redemption for my failure with my own child, and for all my other sins. And so I slept as part of Ahriman, until you called me awake. I know him well. Now let us take this monster with us to oblivion!"

And so Ahriman suffered the attack of two terrible enemies, and yet he was still great with the strength of centuries and of thousands of men and women.

And then yet a third spirit rose up against him, for Asterope chose that moment to end her seclusion. Her attack was like neither the icy wrath of Ronar nor the scorching fury of Astraea, but had a cooler, more self-possessed quality, a steady, unrelenting scrutiny. Her unseen eye was locked on Ahriman's, and it did not flinch. Her words came to them all, calm and resolute.

"Ahriman's rule of the heavens is ended. He is in our hands. Yet we are also in his. The world may never know what we do here, but over centuries to come the name of Ahriman will also be forgotten."

But Ronar now felt still another presence building in their midst. This was not the darksome fire of Ahriman, nor the outraged spirits of any of its victims. This was a presence he had known before, a colorless clarity of thought and being. Varanu was coming. His fellow warriors felt this onset too, and were stilled by wonder. But Ronar knew only bitter despair.

Ahriman laughed.

Enjoy the irony before you are dissolved, my children three. Varanu feels threatened and comes to protect his servant. I will yet live.

Or perhaps not.

Farewell.

And then against all expectation Ronar found himself back in his body, back in the dark chamber within the moonlet. His heart was beating, and a wind was rushing out through the entrance, which was no longer blocked. Ronar was swept out among the stars. His eyes burned; he could not draw breath. Bits of soft light seemed to be dispersing into space in all directions. Already the edges of his vision were fading to grey, but he did not care. He would have laughed if he'd had air in his lungs. Ahriman was gone. So was Varanu. That was unintended…but it seemed to Ronar that Colibdis had had a little too much of Varanu's kind of order. He did not know the fate of Asterope or Astraea, but at least they were free. To die now in view of the stars was a better end than any he had hoped for.

A smooth-surfaced white object moved into his field of view. A glistening bubble withdrew into its graceful fuselage. The flyer moved toward him. Ronar tried to grasp the seat or console, but he could not control his limbs. The flyer insistently pushed against him until he was inside the cockpit, laying awkwardly across the seat. The canopy slid closed, and air rushed into the compartment.

Ronar gasped his lungs full of air. The flyer's acceleration ceased, leaving him to float in the cockpit. He was alone, which was just as well. His body stank. His eyes ached, and his lungs felt as if they were lined with icy needles. His head pounded. He tried to speak, but his throat closed up. He suffered a fit of coughing.

"Congratulations, Dr. Ronar," came Brainchild's sunny voice.

The flyer rolled. The former Eye of Ahriman came into view through the canopy. Half of it was ablaze with pinpoints of golden light. The flyer swept closer to its surface, which was studded with thousands of white cylinders, each tipped with a flaring orange lens. Beams of orange light flashed over the cockpit as the flyer did a slow pass over the surface of the moon.

"Your conflict with Ahriman occupied and distracted it for two days until Sha Totek deemed it safe to drop the shields around his Tower and the Portal. It continued for the three further days necessary for Dr. Perturbare to put into place enough propulsors to move the moonlet in a decisive manner. It is now wholly beyond the influence of Colibdian magic, and still climbing."

"Five—days?" croaked Ronar.

"Yes. Perhaps you would like some water." A squeeze bulb emerged from someplace behind Ronar and drifted by. He grabbed it, broke the seal, and sucked at it eagerly.

"Doctor Ronar, if you will now take your seat, we will descend to the Tower."

"No," rasped Ronar.

"No?"

"Take me to M—Mersinea."

"To Mersinea? Dr. Ronar, you would benefit from medical attention. Perhaps you would delay your—"

"No, I must go now. Take me there. Tell Perturbare that it cannot wait. Sha Totek will understand."

The computer paused before its reply. "Very well, I have been instructed to obey you. I have seen Sha Totek's maps and am familiar with this world's geography and political arrangement. Do you wish to go to Pantheos?"

"Yes."

Ronar arranged himself in the seat and fastened the harness. Brainchild pitched the nose down until Ronar was looking straight ahead at Mersinea itself. It was, he estimated, nearly time, or just past time, for Ahriman's regular transmission of energy to Varanu's Mirror. He smiled. It wouldn't be happening today, or ever again.

Brainchild applied power, pushing Ronar back into his seat. An hour later the great tawny land mass loomed near at hand, the dark bay of Aegeos separating Thunderbird from Mersinea to the north. Mount Olympos reared up directly below. Brainchild spun the flyer and braked with the main lamp until the blackness outside lightened slightly to violet. Then it reoriented the flyer for atmospheric flight. Ronar leaned against the canopy and stared downward. The snowy summit of Olympos knifed by just below. Interlopers such as himself and Bellerophon were traditionally struck down for having the audacity to fly to that sacred place, but at the moment it was only a mountain, with no sign of the palaces of the gods.

The flyer dropped rapidly. Ronar directed Brainchild to land in the plaza just in front of the lofty temple of Athene. Crowds of supplicants scattered as the strange vehicle settled among them, silent as a leaf. Ronar watched without emotion as they fled. The canopy rolled back. Ronar emerged unsteadily onto the marble pavement. He heard marching footsteps and clattering metal. Up the stairs came a squad of armored temple guards, armed with spears and shields, advancing on him, to their credit, despite their evident trepidation. Ronar raised his palm to them and they halted. When he turned away it became clear that they had not halted at his bidding.

There on the steps of her temple stood Athene herself, tall and shining. Ronar approached her, his eyes locked on the face of Asterope which gleamed from the great shield. Athene descended the stairs to meet him on the plaza.

Ronar reached her and said thickly but firmly, "Athene. Release Asterope's body from your shield."

The goddess silently reached into the shield and drew out the body of Asterope. She dropped it loosely to the pavement, where it flopped down, the head coming to rest at an odd angle.

"Take greater care with her, goddess!" roared Ronar. His heart ached to see how wasted that small body was, how its empty eye socket gaped. He knelt before it, choking, tears rolling down his cheeks. He caressed Asterope's hair, and her face, which was cold and grey. She did not stir. She showed no trace of life.

"That body is ruined," murmured Athena. "It will not live again."

Ronar stood, aware that he was about to become unmanned, thinking only of returning to the flyer before his grief and despair could injure or dismay those who watched.

Before he turned away he glanced into Athene's eyes and was arrested by them.

He studied the goddess, aware of a quality of life which her eyes had not possessed before. They were grey, like his own, but paler, sparkling and gleaming with a peculiar vividness as he regarded them. Her hair was dark gold. Her face...

He tried to speak. His breath caught, and he had to try again.

"Asterope...?"

"Yes. Asterope. And Athene as well."

Ronar's thoughts and vision spun. He opened his mouth again, not sure of what was about to emerge. "Why—why do you not return to your body? It has been kept for you—"

The goddess Asterope nudged the forlorn corpse with her foot, her greaves gleaming in the sunslight.

"Professor Ronar—I cannot return to this. Too much has happened to me. I have known Ahriman too well. I would always be injured, lessened, by what happened to me as a human being. I could have let my spirit pass on to the Just Path, as Astraea has now done with her own. But in getting to know Ahriman, I learned the knack of joining my spirit with that of a god. I had felt Athene's lack, her desire to live more fully, to be truly and completely a thinking, sentient being. And now she is."

Athene/Asterope drew herself up, towering, eyes flashing. Her spear seemed to loom up into the heavens. Ronar could only gaze at her, open-mouthed, but he did not falter before her.

"Now the world has a new god of Consciousness," she said in a ringing voice. "But unlike Ahriman, she is also a goddess of Wisdom. And also, I am determined, a goddess of Mercy and Charity. These weapons of mine shall never be used in any unjust cause."

Ronar heard her words. He felt her conviction. He saw and knew the rightness of it all.

He had never been one to plead his own case, or to wish to sway others from their decisions. Yet on this one occasion he could not help but say: "But Asterope. If you reclaimed your body...you could...we could...you could be healed. I would care for you—" He could say no more. He only stared at her mutely, begging her to see what was in his heart.

The face of the goddess softened, grew tender. The light in her eyes warmed him. She smiled. "Yes...Professor...we could. It could have happened. Perhaps it should have. Sometimes we are both too intent on remaining high, aloof, and pure. But now we must let that thought pass. It would be...uncharacteristic of Athene Parthenos. And I am now her, as much as she is me. It would be uncharacteristic of you as well, and even of Asterope the mortal girl, for all of that. We are not people for whom such things come easily. But do not think..."

She stepped forward suddenly. The spear and shield fell to the pavement with a ringing clash. Her arms went around him, living arms of warm human flesh for all he could tell. He embraced her, clinging to her with all his mortal strength, her face buried in his shoulder.

"Do not think," she continued, "that I will forget you. You are to me all that a hero could ever hope to be. I will love you and hold you up as an exemplar of mankind as I seek to serve it, for however long I choose to remain in this role. You now have a patron goddess, Leonard Ronar."

She broke the embrace and stepped back. Her gaze sank to the tiny body sprawled on the pavement. She frowned slightly, and a mist moved over the body. When it had cleared, the body was restored to cleanliness. Its eyelids were closed, but now neither socket was empty.

"Now take the body of your Asterope. Take her home, and bury her somewhere near to you. Do not forget her." Then she frowned at him as well, and a sweet, clean scent enveloped him. Suddenly he felt well and strong. Instead of filthy rags, he found he was dressed in garments of shining white, a color he had never dared choose for himself.

The goddess stepped forward again, and kissed his forehead. His eyes closed, and when at last he opened them, she was gone.

He bent and lifted the body of Asterope, weightless as a figure of mist and light. Tenderly he carried her to the flyer, gently he laid her on the deck behind the seat. Then he stood leaning against the bezel while tears blinded him to the astonished gazes of the crowd that had assembled in the plaza.

"You have done well," said a familiar voice.

Ronar turned, wiping his tears like a little boy. "Pedemus."

"You have both done very well."

Ronar had no reply to make.

"A wise man of Earth has said, 'Whomever fights monsters should see to it that in the process he does not become a monster. When you look long into an abyss, the abyss also looks into you.' The abyss that was Ahriman looked deeply into both you and Asterope. In the end, what he saw there did very little to comfort him."

Ronar bowed his head, reached out and placed his hand on the shoulder of Pedemus. Then he climbed into the flyer and had Brainchild bear him away.

Chapter 35

Epilog

The flyer set down in the garden of the Tower of Sha Totek. As it descended, Ronar was amazed to see in the near distance the sprawling industrial facility which Perturbare had thrown up beside the Portal.

Ronar climbed out of the cockpit and stood looking down at the peaceful figure lying behind the seat.

"Brainchild," he said quietly. "I won't be staying here long. I'll want to bring Asterope to my home in Thunderbird, and there put her body to rest. Can you protect her until I'm ready to leave?"

"It will be my honor to do so, but I believe some kind of protection is already in effect. I detect no change in the condition of the body."

Nevertheless, the canopy swung shut and a mist of cold air appeared on its inner surface.

The scientist and the sorcerer sauntered toward him with great grins splitting their faces. Goggling at his radiant garb, they led him into the Tower, where they proceeded to its topmost level, Sha Totek's very Sanctum. There, as they ate and drank among its opulent furnishings, Ronar told all that had happened since Ahriman snatched him up. Then it was a contest between them as to which could muster the more outrageous expression of astonishment.

"So then, Sha Totek," concluded Ronar. "Are Ahriman and Varanu truly gone forever?"

"Near as I can tell," said the sorcerer thoughtfully. "Though it was mighty lucky that Varanu visited the Eye just as it was finally nudged out beyond the magic. But I don't think either of them is truly destroyed. Varanu at least had an existence independent of any function of the Eye, though without it, and caught outside as he was, I doubt he can ever again be more than a glimmer of what he was. As for Ahriman…there's probably even less left of him than that. He should grow weaker still as it becomes clear that his influence is gone, and his worshippers drop away."

"When Perturbare and I first came through the Portal—we encountered a hellish mess—an alternate space of some kind. Was that Varanu's doing, or yours?"

"Mine! Almost as soon as you left Colibdis, Varanu started trying to destroy the Portal, he was that afraid of your return. Well, I've been watching those Portals for thousands of turns. Nobody ever told me to do it, but nobody ever told me to let some god destroy them either, not even Varanu. The only way I could protect it was to put it outside the reach of Varanu's power, which means outside our Universe. So I overwrote the local laws with those of another place I know about. It was quite a siege, let me tell you."

"It was well done," said Ronar.

"Ronar," said Perturbare, "let me ask you something. This story of yours is fantastic. You've carried on like some epic hero. To be honest, I can't even find anything to joke about here. Why aren't you a king or something on this world?"

Ronar raised his eyebrow. "King? Kingships tend to be hereditary. They aren't handed out for good deeds, as a general rule. Not that I want to be a king anyway. There's nothing kingly about me."

Sha Totek smiled. "I wonder."

"Perturbare...I thank you for your help. You are as responsible as I am for the downfall of Ahriman."

The scientist beamed. "True. Good of you to notice."

"But now I'm asking you to remove that factory of yours. I don't want Colibdis contaminated by advanced technology. It would be the end of the place, as it stands now."

Perturbare pursed his lips and nodded slowly. "I agree. I have no more fish to fry here anyway. I've done my job, seen the sights, had a great time, and now it's time to go home. I'll have Brainchild disassemble the facility to its component elements and restore things as they were. And hey, if you ever show up on Earth again, be sure to stop by my place and we'll have a few laughs."

"Thank you."

"And another thing I'll do... just in case our activities have made the Earth Portal a little too conspicuous...I'll keep watch over it."

Ronar nodded. "That's an excellent idea. Let the Portal have its guardians on both sides." He looked at the two of them as they sat grinning side by side on a plush velvet divan. Sha Totek wore a kilt of shimmering green and an extravagant collection of gold and jewels. Perturbare wore his usual natty white tunic and black slacks. Both men were black haired. Sha Totek was taller, and much darker of skin, with diamond black eyes and a beakish nose. Perturbare was pale, with blue eyes and a straight nose. But something about their grins...and their eyes...

Ronar started. "You two look exactly alike!" he exclaimed.

They looked at each other. "What are you talking about?"

Ronar appeared at the Observatory at dusk, glimmering in the twilight like a ghost, carrying in his arms the pale body of Asterope. All who saw him were awestruck, and fell back, unable to approach him as long as he had that peculiar look in his eyes. He laid her down, and with his own hands began to dig her grave in the dust and gravel near the entrance to the 60-inch dome.

After a while he looked up from his work at a sky that was now dense with stars. The former Eye of Ahriman—it would need a new name—was prominent among them, ablaze with an unnatural orange fire, still being driven into a higher orbit.

No, she would not rest here, at the site of her downfall.

He took up Asterope's body again and carried it down off the mesa, into the little astronomy village at its base. His house was as he'd left it. The door still bore his nameplate. A lamp glimmered inside. He recognized the silhouette of Flora as she sat beside it.

He laid the body in the garden, went to the tool shed, and brought back a shovel. Beside the little flower bed which Flora carefully kept and watered he began again to dig a grave. Figures appeared and stood quietly watching: Flora, Hal, others. Ronar placed Asterope's body in the grave, climbed out, and covered her up. There would be no marker or monument save the flowers, for Asterope yet lived, though in a form neither of them could have predicted.

That night, as he lay in his own bed, he dreamed of her, tall and splendid, smiling into his soul with grey eyes that missed nothing.

And that is how the escape of a slave girl led to the downfall of the Great Gods of Colibdis.

THE END

Appendix

How Asterope Came to Be

I had always known and intended that after helping to defeat Namirnakh, Leonard Ronar would eventually pit himself against a far more dangerous enemy, the dark god Ahriman.

The thing I didn't know, until well after I began writing the actual novel, is why he would do it.

My first outline of *The Astronomer Who Hated a God* begins with Ronar already on Earth, making a prankish presentation before an assembly of astronomers, meeting with his cousin Ben Raintree, and hunting for Possum Perturbare. He has finally decided to go after Ahriman, and he realizes he needs help.

Why was he doing it? Long, long ago, in the 1970s when I was first plotting primitive versions of these stories, Ronar's war against Ahriman amounted to little more than a real estate grab. My notion was that Ronar coveted the Eye of Ahriman as the ideal location for a huge telescope located outside the atmosphere of Colibdis. Ronar was to conquer and evict Ahriman, and then, with the help of Possum Perturbare's technology, he would build an immense instrument, like a steerable radio telescope operating in optical wavelengths. This orbiting base would also become Ronar's new home and headquarters for his further adventures.

Eventually I decided this was all too grandiose for the increasingly human character Ronar was becoming. But, I still wanted him to battle Ahriman, and thus in 1994 I began to write *The Astronomer Who Hated a God* (then called *Return of Ronar*).

In the first draft, Ronar essentially wakes up one day, says "Well, I guess it's time I got around to kicking Ahriman's ass," and then gets up to do it. He announces to Hal Holder that he's off to Earth to drum up support, then checks in with Sha Totek before using the Portal.

At some point it occurred to me that this was all pretty inadequate storytelling. A hero who goes against a foe merely because he doesn't like him isn't exactly a great source of drama or character development.

I reasoned that if Ahriman were to pick on someone who was important to Ronar, it would provide all the motivation the big guy would require. Making it a female someone would allow me to explore and elaborate on Ronar's perpetually lousy relations with members of the opposite sex.

Thus I added a section in which Ronar explains to Sha Totek that his campaign against Ahriman is due to the fate of one of his students, a Mersinean girl named Asterope. He narrates a changed, simplified version of her story beginning with her fateful night at the eyepiece of the sixty-inch telescope. In this version, Asterope is either the daughter of a rich Mersinean or at least passing herself off as one. Asterope probably wouldn't have appeared onstage at all in this version, as she was nothing but a crude device to get Ronar moving.

I was dissatisfied with this long stretch of Ronar's first person narration, giving up on it as Ronar was preparing to accompany Asterope up the slopes of Olympos. Ronar is not the best character for first person narration because of his naturally laconic style. Any account he might provide would be a spare one, unless he were experiencing an unusual outburst of emotion. I rewrote the whole thing in the third person, fleshing it out greatly and adding many important incidents such as the voyage of the *Dekapus* and Ronar's dealings with Astraea. In this version, the novel opens with a nervous Asterope thinking how much she dislikes Professor Ronar while she prepares for her inauspicious observing session.

So, I finally had a character whose degradation and fall might plausibly goad Ronar to an extremity of wrath. But as I went along I thought, "Why will any reader care about Asterope? They won't know her. They won't see her as she really is for more than a few paragraphs. Who is Asterope? Why is she important to Ronar? Why aren't they getting along very well? Why is Ahriman interested in her?"

I therefore devised a prologue consisting of Asterope's slavery and her escape from Mersinea. A good start, but there was still quite a gap between the little girl sailing away from Pantheos and the young woman who turned up years later as Ronar's graduate student. Eventually I went back and filled in the blanks, writing the whole long story of Asterope's girlhood in Two Suns, her relationship with Ronar, and the complication of Eunice Purdue, which served to bring Asterope to the attention of Ahriman.

With the novel in its final form at last, the only remaining gap is the story of Asterope's undergraduate career, which I expect was fairly uneventful. *The Astronomer Who Hated a God* is now as much Asterope's novel as Ronar's, which would have surprised me greatly if it had been foretold when I first began to write it. The first draft was completed in 1997.

I came to like Asterope so much that I'm now unhappy with the length of time she spends offstage. I also disliked torturing her as much as I did, but I tried to make it up to her by giving her the best outcome I could salvage out of so much misery and disaster.

Joe Bergeron

March 2023

www.ingramcontent.com/pod-product-compliance
Lightning Source LLC
Chambersburg PA
CBHW071632260626
47170CB00001B/66